d. l. dickson

While the World Waits

An Epic World War II Novel

Dedicated to:

All the men and women who fought and fight
for freedom
 - Especially during the dark years of WWII

— In remembrance of my fathers
     Veterans of WWI and WWII

High Flight

Oh! I have slipped the surly bonds of Earth
And danced the skies on laughter-silvered wings;
Sunward I've climbed, and joined the tumbling mirth
of sun-split clouds,—and done a hundred things
You have not dreamed of—wheeled and soared and swung
High in the sunlit silence. Hov'ring there,
I've chased the shouting wind along, and flung
My eager craft through footless halls of air. . . .

Up, up the long, delirious, burning blue
I've topped the wind-swept heights with easy grace
Where never lark nor ever eagle flew—
And, while with silent lifting mind I've trod
The high untrespassed sanctity of space,
Put out my hand, and touched the face of God.

John Gillespie Magee Jr.
No 412 Squadron RCAF
Poem written September 3, 1941
Died December 11, 1941

WHILE THE WORLD WAITS

Chapter I -April – Russia, 1940

The End of That Day

Again, he had that sense of 'imbalance', so sharp was it that he almost turned back from the dark Katyn Forest. But instead, Christian looked ahead and saw an intense light. On this morning of his fourteenth year he did not want to disappoint his father.

Mesmerized, he let the light pull him in, even though everything inside told him to run and never look back. He did not realize his dog, Dame, had stopped, nor did he hear her low unearthly growl. He walked into the light. A profound pain plunged him to the ground. The Boxer, whimpering, crawled to his side and began licking his face and fists. Never had the 'feeling' been so intense - or lasted so long.

Christian thrust his clenched fists into his shut eyes to stop the daggers which shot through his temples and lodged themselves in the sockets behind each eye. The dream would pass - he told himself - like it always had all of his young life, but this time he could see the faces vividly, appearing out from behind the fog. The blond young men with blue hollow eyes too old for their young faces came one after another. Most were missing teeth as they vacantly looked past one another with mouth agape and drool at the corners of their mouths.

This time it was no dream. He was awake. They passed in single file in front of him. He could see the entire human parade -. If a man occasionally stumbled and fell, the one behind just stepped on him. No man in the line had the awareness or strength to step over the fallen ones. The faces of the men he had sketched for years in his journals walked in vivid color in front of him.

In those minutes, Christian could see through the line of shadows to the great earthen mounds which seemed to reach halfway up the pine trees. None of the men looked to the sky. He shook his head; the pain was gone, but the men kept coming. Now, the sound made sense to him. The sound that he had heard all his life - through the years - the slow push and stumble of leaden feet through pine needles which couldn't muffle so many footsteps. For the first time he looked down to their feet- swollen purple, pus filled, bleeding and lined with streaks of gray; the feet sloshed through the mist - methodically leading each man in the parade of the almost dead.

Christian could no longer look at their wounded feet or empty faces. Instead, he focused on the blur of uniforms in front of him. Tattered, dirty, and thread bare, they must have held glory at one time, for he could discern an occasional mark where a bar or epaulette should have been. The uniforms hung from the frames of these once muscular beautiful young men. A ripped off sleeve or shredded shirt revealed sharp protruding shoulder blades, and ribs thinner than any child's. Then he saw the eagle insignia and heard a hoarse whisper in Polish.

"Please... mama ... help."

The boy fell forward and Christian could clearly see his face when it hit the soft pine needles. The blond boy was no older than he. His face was bruised and one eye was swollen shut. His blond hair lay dirty and matted to his cheek.

"Get up my son." The older man behind him said in Polish. He hesitated but bent down to pull him up. "Remember the other soldier... for the love of God, get up!"

The boy was on all fours, and as he raised his head, his eyes looked straight into Christian's.

"Have mercy," he cried.

Christian buried his head in Dame's fur. He understood

every word of Polish - and understood he could not answer. With his ear pressed to the ground, he knew someone else was coming. Then he heard his native Russian.

"Soldier, soldier, Polish swine get up."

The boy made a Herculean effort and an agonizing cry as he tried to push himself upright, but he was not fast enough for the soldier. The Russian boot swung up and broke his jaw. The silence of the forest could not muffle the boy's screams as he groped for his hanging jaw. The Russian's answer was just as swift. He reached down and wrapped the boy's hair twice around his hand and pulled him out of line.

"Have mercy," the once beautiful boy cried again as blood filled his mouth. "Please - Mama!"

"Officer? High Polish officer," the Russian soldier said sarcastically as he motioned to the older Polish officer standing behind the fallen boy. The Russian did not want to pick up the boy's feet and drag him all the way to the dirt pile himself. He motioned to the Polish officer to do so.

In the chaos Christian crept back into the small ravine covered with branches and pine needles. He crawled as far as he could through the canopied tunnel until the branches crisscrossed in front of him. He could go no further without breaking them. Dame followed without a sound.

He didn't know what he heard next - the final cry of 'mama' or the crack and sound of crushed bone. He raised his head to see the boy's face or what was left of it. Fixated, he did not take his eyes off those eyes or what was left of those eyes. How long he stared, he did not know. He followed the boy with his eyes as they dragged him past - past him - past Dame - past the line of men - until they reached the front of the line.

The boy made no more cries to his mother. When Christian lifted his eyes from the body, he saw the mound – not of dirt but of corpses stacked to the sky.

The Beginning of That Day – *April of 1940*

In Russia - in April - the snow had not yet disappeared. The intense cold had permeated deeper this winter, perhaps because the heavy plodding of Russian boots followed quickly behind the smart click of German heels. Except for the green swath of giant fir trees cutting across the horizon, the land was still white as far as the eye could see. The dense and dark forest of the Katyn, where only the most courageous ventured, lay north beyond the trees. All the inhabitants of Smolensk, the nearby village, knew the tales of wild boar and bear, but something else compelled them to remain close to their hearths long after the winter had passed.

Those few, who ventured into the Katyn at dusk, never walked out. Sometimes their bodies were found after the snows had melted, but for the most part their remains simply vanished. Some said it was the boar or bear that ravaged those few foolhardy travelers and the 'not quite right in the head' villagers who 'just wanted to see' what the Katyn held. Others knew it was the innate darkness and the spirits that dwelt in that pit of black, which devoured not only their wayward bodies - but also their souls.

Once inside the forest, seasons never came. Hushed, then silenced by the tall overpowering density of firs, spring slid into summer. Fall tumbled into winter, and the mat of pine needles just grew thicker. The floor of the forest mirrored its ceiling - cool and constant. Whether looking up or down, little color or light existed. These prisms of shades of brown darkened to black at night - a black so void of light, even the mind's eye could not shine through it.

It was this total void that drove the foolhardy mad, and the bodies, that once housed the souls of men, became hosts for the spirits and the beasts. Those villagers, who occasionally ventured in and out, knew all this. Perhaps, it was just myth created by those few who wished to appear bolder than the rest. Nonetheless, no one was going to change hundreds of years of tales and legends, and as the world catapulted into a new decade, the moans and voices of the Katyn spoke more loudly and clearly than in other years. Many thought the warmer than usual temperatures of the summer accounted for the intensity of the voices which had begun in the fall and had continued throughout the winter.

The boy on the skis did not worry about the superstitions. He believed his father, the village schoolmaster, who had taught him not only literature and languages but also science. This world was a new one that needed leaders who could speak the truth in several languages and lead their countrymen out of the realm of superstition and into the light of science.

The father had always known that Christian was different. The serenity of Christian Haar's birth seemed but a distant dream as he grew from infancy to boyhood. Before he could talk, he'd awake at night screaming and thrashing. His tiny legs kicked and his body contorted as his hands grabbed his face. His father, Perr, tightly held the baby's hands so that he couldn't scratch his eyes and then he rocked the tiny thrashing body until the exhausted baby fell asleep. When baby Christian awoke in the morning, he cooed and babbled with no memory of the night before.

Throughout his life Christian was placed in situations he felt that he had known before. When those moments occurred, a dizziness would pass over him and a scene would enact itself in front of his mind's eye. He would say how he had that 'feeling' again, but he never could describe what he saw or heard. Because of this Perr Harr developed both his son's intelligence and his intuition.

Since he was a young boy, his father had taken him on a path, far beyond the village, the new farms, the mill along the river Krutz, and the barriers of civilization where they would pick various plants and fungus, said by the villages to hold miraculous cures. His father, too, believed in their powers but for a different reason. He collected them for experiments, delved beneath their stems and leaves, and extracted their healing juices. Throughout spring, summer, and early fall, they collected and categorized the liquid medicines into vials and jars to learn the 'why' of the cures.

It was another spring. Fourteen-year-old Christian Harr laced up his ski boots and strapped them into the bindings. He looked forward to making the first exploration of their familiar route in this predawn April morning. As he pushed each ski in the familiar silent rhythm, he felt the still thick snow and the warmth of the sun. He was ready for spring, but thought about home.

Tied to his waist hung his leather pouch and his knife in its matching leather sheath. On his back lay his bow and quiver, flat against the fur of his jacket - both jacket and quiver were made of silver fox that he had shot, skinned, and tanned. His mother had sewn the soft pelts together and lined the jacket with sheep's wool from the few sheep his father kept in the fields near their small heavy planked home.

Nestled on top of the hills outside the village, their cottage lacked companions; it sat in serene solitude - apart from the townspeople's sturdy houses which squatted like clusters of large brown mushrooms, encircling the bottom of the valley. Each morning Christian and his father had to ski down into the valley, into the small village encased in ice and crystal, like a child's Christmas snow globe, and into the school. Christian enjoyed the ten mile run with the musical clicking of their skis over the hills and fields down into the little valley where the village lay. It quieted his mind and soul. When they reached the door of the one-room schoolhouse, they'd unbuckle the leather straps of the wooden skis and clunk off the cakes of snow in sound clumps. Inside, they would start up the heavy cast iron stove that occupied much of the space of the one-room schoolhouse. Then by its warmth, they would sit, talk, and wait for the students to arrive. Few of the children or villagers skied; instead, they relied on heavy snowshoes to travel during the solitary winter months. For the most part, they were content to remain in isolation, but none considered themselves as outsiders.

However, Perr Harr, the village schoolmaster, had come from Norway, and his heritage and gift of intellectual curiosity made him an oddity and outsider to the Russian peasants of the township. Much like his father, Christian too was considered different. Mostly alone, he'd venture out to fill his satchel with fresh herbs and earthy fungus. He could tell one from the other by simple smell. It was a habit so ingrained that anything he took pleasure in, like his mother's hearty stews and her freshly baked bread, was smelled first. He could remember back into infancy the fresh soap scent of his mother's skin and hair. The gentleness and pleasures of life he derived from her.

From his father he inherited the beauty of words and the truth of science. Yet, his father knew the values the villagers held in esteem, so he made certain his son could not only shoot an arrow straighter and with more accuracy than anyone in the village, but that he could do so on the move - from skis. This quality and skill, inherent in Norwegians, Perr Harr had passed on to his only son. He also passed on the knowledge about the treasures of the oak trees.

Theirs was a search for black gold, succulent earthy truffles, hidden in clusters on tubular growths beneath the roots of black oaks. The money from the truffles, nestled as in a treasure chest, would provide for their escape. Summer would tell which oaks would bear fruit. Until that time, he and his dog would return every week to check on the smells beneath the pine needles that covered the roots of the solitary oaks.

As the days lengthened, the sun of high noon would filter through the dark trees. On these occasional warm days Christian would walk with his Boxer through the fields of green into the mat of the forest. There they would check on the truffles that would buy books and glass vials for their experiments. He was looking forward to those too few summer days that the Russian skies doled out so sparingly, but now Christian wondered how long his days of freedom and exploration would last. War was in the wind.

His schoolmates spoke of Germany in awe. They, like their parents, were enthralled by the power and might of this Aryan race, and made no political or moral judgment about Germany. Like any Cossack, they just admired Germany's ability to conquer. Perr Harr and his son were different. They knew that a Germany with Hitler at her helm would never stop short of total conquest. When Hitler had invaded Czechoslovakia in September of '38, the civilized world stood aside. It believed that Hitler's repossession of Germany's original empire was justifiable and that was all he would take.

Each night Perr and Christian waited for news that this 'peace' would break like a fragile egg. They would lift their heavy metal transmitter/receiver to pick up broadcasts from England as well as Europe. They did not have long to wait. The fervent pleadings, testimonies, and confessions of Poles reverberated throughout the warm September nights of 1939 - before the nothingness of defeat. Warsaw fell, and with her, the voice of Poland. The final silence was complete as September came to an end.

What Perr Harr could not forgive or forget was Russia's compliance with this tyranny, and he was afraid – afraid for his son who would soon be forced to fight alongside the Germans in a war of incessant greed. He could hear the newscasts from France, Germany, England, and Finland. All - he could understand except the ones from Germany, but he was changing that by teaching himself German through books and broadcasts. When he was proficient enough, he would teach Christian, whom he knew, would need it to survive.

The day Russia invaded Poland to fight alongside Germany signaled the end of Perr Harr's adopted homeland. He was no longer a simple Russian school teacher, but rather a man of all nations - with no nation and no allegiance to anything but freedom. The price of freedom was not cheap. Everything in Russia cost. This he had learned well – well enough to concoct an elaborate plan. Truffles held the golden key to their freedom. With financial independence, he and his family could immigrate to England and then perhaps far away to America. There, they would be safe from this war which, he believed, would wreak havoc on all the lands of Europe.

Christian agreed with his father's plan and felt confident that he and his trained Boxer could root the precious treasure buried beneath the oak trees' roots. The rooter's name was Dame - a name, Christian's schoolmates found peculiar and foreign. In fact, even the breed, Boxer, was unusual because it had none of the thick fur and working capacity of neighboring farm dogs.

Dame, however, was quick, intelligent, and protective. Her keen sense of smell, highly refined to locate truffles, also enabled her to track her masters through the thick forests. She knew their smell well, for she had always slept with either the father or the son.

In this new year of 1940 she frolicked without the heavy fox coat Catherine Harr had made to protect her from the harsh Russian winters. She liked her new found freedom and not only dug her nose into the occasional paths of thick black earth but rolled in the snow free patches of ground.

****

As they reached the forest, Dame became more and more excited. Soon the soft pine needles would be beneath her feet, and they would stop to eat the sausage and black bread Christian's mother had packed them for breakfast. Christian thought how she had been coming to the Katyn since she was a pup. Now she was too big to wrap under his fur jacket and press against his beating heart with her muzzle beneath his chin, but that is how she came to love his smell, and he the velvet softness and scent of her loose skin. When the rocking stopped, she knew her job would begin.

Nose to the ground, she would make furrows in the thick pine needles as she made her way from tree to tree. The forest carried no superstition for her. She was aware of only four-legged creatures. Twice she had saved Christian. Once from a boar that had charged him from behind and once from a black bear, hungry and slow from her winter nap. The bear had risen tall and straight in front of them. Dame had come between the bear and her master. Baring her teeth, her primitive growls curdled Christian's blood. She had given him enough time to thread his bow with three arrows and to fire them consecutively should the bear attack. He never had to use them. The bear simply lowered herself and backed away.

Now on this April day, the forest appeared foreboding even to Christian who knew it so well. He stopped to catch his breath when he topped the last hill that separated him from the dense island of trees on the horizon. As far as the eye could, the huge pines loomed, blocking the sun that had barely risen. He never quite knew if he really needed to stop for a rest or if the stop was meant to suppress the rise of fear that might wash over him.

Dame tugged at his pants to pull him along - then bounced ahead and turned to bark at him. Christian felt that he was waiting longer than usual upon this last knoll. Perhaps, it was because the winter felt longer. The realities of war promoted that, or perhaps, it was simply because this was their first outing alone since last summer when everything was green and young.

"What's that?" he spoke out loud for the first time since daybreak. The boxer stood at full stance and pointed toward the forest to give full attention to her master's command.

"It sounds like moaning but too low for men."

Motionless, a still silhouette against the winter white, the boxer stood. None of her prior eager prancing or tugging would cloud her fixation on what her master heard. Like antennas in the wind, her ears moved and her nose sniffed the air as if to place a common name on these uncommon moans.

"I'm getting to act like a villager. Soon, I too will believe the tales of the Katyn. It's only the wind." He started to move forward to commit himself to the idea.

"It's only the wind." he repeated. No conviction came forth with the words. The dog would not move. She still stood motionless facing the forest in front of her. She was trying to recognize the unrecognizable.

"It's O.K., Dame. Let's have mama's fresh bread and sausage, then we'll be ready for the work ahead." He bent down to pat her head. She did not turn her muzzle up to lick his hand.

The dead stalks of the summer's cattails stood bent and gnarled as they poked their tops through the almost melted winter barricades of snow. Christian beheaded dozens of cattails and crisscrossed them into a mat to cover the bare cold ground. They sat in the circle with the sun warming the backs of their necks. The thick bread with the scoops of freshly churned butter his mother had packed in the tin canister tasted especially sweet this morning. Alternately, he cut off a chunk of sausage and broke a piece of bread to dip in the canister - one for him and one for Dame. They sat on this cattail mat and ate in silence.

"The sun gives no warmth," he said out loud as he packed up his satchel.

Gruffly, she answered with a low utterance that was neither a growl nor a bark. She waited for him to signal her to rise and be on their way.

****

Once inside its towering trees, the forest always seemed to welcome Christian and his father. It was as though the forest and they shared a common ground. For them the forest cleared off the superstition it set for the villages and set a new table of serenity. Together they shared laughter and friendship. Today, Christian was not listening for its welcoming laughter, but rather for something he did not want to hear.

"It's my imagination," he thought. "Father sent me to do a job. He said he needs me to be a man." He reached down to the boxer and rubbed her massive head. He held her head in his hands and looked into her face as his father had taught him in training her. He looked into her intelligent eyes. "We have a job to do 'Lady' golden nose."

****

Several hours had passed and they had traveled deeper and deeper into the forest. Christian forced himself not to hear the 'something' that came before the headache and nausea. They had marked the oaks from previous years and noted which ones had produced truffles beneath their roots. Dame diligently sniffed each base and worked her way out to the extremities of the roots. Then in a circle, like a compass, she edged her way around the entire tree, stopping to bury her nose deeper into the thick pine covering that blanketed the entire forest. Five times she had begun to dig religiously into the black Russian soil. Each time Christian motioned her away so that he could investigate. Once satisfied, he covered up the freshly dug earth and took out his book to sketch the particular tree. From his satchel he dug out a salted pig's ear from last fall's pork salting day. It was always her special treat for a job well done.

He enjoyed sketching in his leather bound book filled with blank pages on which to record life's special surprises. Some pages were filled with drawings of plants, others with fields, and some with animals. Interspersed were formulas for medicines and recipes for cures as well as his young observations of life. Each book contained a year's recording of his life and growth.

It was a habit and pleasure he derived from his father. He really could not remember when he hadn't recorded his innermost thoughts on paper, yet once the truffle plan was put into action, the whole family became co-workers in the fight against time for freedom and escape, for all knew war would inevitably touch their soil.

So, he began to keep a record of those trees, which hid buried treasure in their roots. He had a method of shading those special oaks to indicate where the truffles lay and where the oaks stood in relation to the rest of the forest. To anyone who by chance might open the book, they would see nothing but the nature designs of a boy, and his meager observations concerning life. In the corner of certain pages were sketches of faces - faces that appeared in his reoccurring dreams. He had sketched them quickly but in such vivid detail that one would think he had sketched real relatives and friends.

Christian shut his notebook. They had done enough work for the day, and he wanted to push deeper into the Katyn. The wind had been increasing since dawn. Dame would stop on occasion and turn her pointed ears and head in one direction and then another. Like a wind barometer, she would then fix on one side as though intent on hearing something. He, however, could hear nothing but the wind and a crack or two as though limbs were falling or branches breaking but never hitting the ground - so thick and silent was the Katyn's floor of pine needles. He strained to see some movement. He had never been this deep into the Katyn. Its overpowering starkness and solitude was not caused by the distance he had traveled in. It was coming - the 'imbalance' – the deja vu.

****

He didn't know what he heard next - the final cry of 'Mama' or the crack and sound of crushed bone. He raised his head to see the boy or what was left of the boy's face. Fixated, he could not take his eyes off those eyes or what was left of those eyes. How long he stared, he did not know. He followed the boy with his eyes as they dragged him past - past him - past Dame - past the line of men - until they reached the front of the line.

Shocked into looking no more, he turned his head and

vomited into the pine needles. He forced his head down to muffle the wrenching sounds until there was nothing left except a wave of dry heaves. With his eyes closed and face dug deep into the needles and dirt, he could still see the face of the boy, the man, and the mounds of slaughtered faces waiting to be so ceremoniously buried. Neither the images nor the sounds of steady shovelfuls of dirt could mask- in his mind - the noise of his vomiting.

He let Dame clean his face with her long soft pink tongue. She took the same care as she had with her own pups - gently biting their birth sacs and religiously inspecting and cleaning. Curled on his side, he allowed her this rite. As he listened to the steady shuffle of feet and thudding shovelfuls of dirt worked in a rhythm. He could ignore them no longer. He turned and lifted his head.

"Faster," the Russian soldier ordered.

The Polish officer did not even acknowledge the well fed Russian. He simply continued to scatter dirt on the body of the boy he had just called son. The cadavers of officers and other soldiers were piled beneath, behind, to the right and left of him. From one of the piles a hand protruded.

He recognized the hand with its reddish knuckle hair and freckles, a hand that he had wrestled so often - the hand of his best friend, Gigof. He knew it like his own. Now, upright, as though ready for another wrestling match - macabre and obscene, it called from the pile of the dead. Bloodied and only four fingered, the hand seemed to beckon him.

"See! They hacked off my finger - easier than sliding off my gold wedding ring," it seemed to pronounce defiantly.

"When he's covered, you're next Major …. Polski,"
The Russian soldier laughed.

Christian saw the Russian soldier lower his rifle as he bent to light a cigarette. The others in the line never raised their heads but continued to throw one shovelful of dirt after another onto their dead friends and countrymen. Only the one- the old major took notice. Christian saw him clench his jaw, turn his head slowly, and swing the shovel up with all his might.

"Ahhhh," screamed the Russian as his hands went to his

throat – cut by the shovel imbedded in it. He then fell on top of the other corpses. Only his cigarette was left to burn on the ground.

"Kill the Polish swine," the others with the guns yelled.

Christian watched as the men with the shovels had taken the agonizing death of the Russian as a reprieve from their shoveling and imminent death, for they had come up through the parade and now it was their turn in front of the grandstand. He saw them turn in slow motion toward their fellow officer who had dared to raise his shovel and fight. Each felt the shovel in his hand and tightened his grip. Their leader bent down to pick up the cigarette. Placing it between his lips, he walked into the mass grave and took the Russian's gun which lay next to the shovel still imbedded in the soldier's throat.

Christian did not shut his eyes. He knew he needed to remember. The Polish officer with the cigarette did not wait to aim but fired from the hip as the new Russian leader yelled,

"Take him alive. Let's have fun ..."

The new Russian soldier was dead before he could say another word. Whether the shot took off his face or the shovel of the Pole next to him did, it did not matter. Each man had lifted his shovel with whatever strength he had – not as a unified movement, but as acts of courage by individual men and boys. Shots. Screams. Metal against bone. Blood spurting. The moans of the dying. The gurgles of death.

"Kill them all. We have hundreds to finish off," a tall lean Russian officer stated.

A shovel sliced his thigh beneath his groin. The artery flowed red. "Ooo... ahhh... bastard," he smashed his rifle butt into the skull of the shovel-man who was kneeling - too weak to move after his act of defiance.

The Russian took the scarf from his neck to tourniquet his leg as the Polish Major with the gun aimed carefully this time and shot him cleanly through the head.

More shots rang out- this time from machine guns. Most of the men along the ditch, as far as Christian could see lay dead or dying.- Russians as well as Poles. Shovels lay imbedded in Russian guards or simply on the ground from not being raised quickly or powerfully enough to kill.

"Save your ammunition."

More clean well-aimed shots were taken. Christian saw four more of his Russian countrymen killed swiftly. The living marched in a line toward the leader, the Polish Major with the gun, – alone on the dirt rim of the dead or dying. The rest were still in their parade line that had not moved since the rebellion began.

"He's out of ammo," another Russian, a big one in front, yelled as he moved forward – stopping to smash with his rifle butt the skulls of those he passed.

The still living Polish Major impassively looked at him. He raised his rifle.

"You have nothing left," the big Russian laughed. "Know that I will kill you even more slowly than the rest."

"Fool – you cannot even count. For the Eagle," the Major simply stated as he raised the gun again, "and one for you." He pulled the trigger. The man laughed no more, and another coward fell to the ground.

"And one for me," he said as he calmly looked around at all the Russian soldiers. The victorious Major turned the rifle and placed its muzzle beneath his chin.

A shot resounded that Christian knew he would hear for the rest of his life. He did not turn his head as the brave Major crumpled at last – headless, into the grave.

The resistance was over; the methodical massacre continued, and Christian watched transfixed to a moment in history that no one would believe and barely record. Those faces he knew well for they had washed over his mind for as long as he could remember. All he was doing now was matching the reality to images in his dreams. He knew he would survive. It had been willed long before his birth. But why?

There is monotony to the sounds of rifle butts pounding flesh and the flesh falling to the ground and the ground swallowing what once were men. He pillowed his head on Dame and fell into a dreamless sleep.

****

"Chris, Chris." At the sound of his name he turned but did not look up.

"Where am I? What's happening? Did someone call my name?" he thought. "I'm simply there again," he answered himself.

"Chris!"

This time he knew the voice was from the outside. He remembered and grabbed his head to stop the images from coming. Only the sound of his name kept him from screaming. There was something familiar about.

"Chris," the anxious voice called again.

Christian could hear the sounds of footsteps and looked up and over the canopy of branches to see his father standing in the opening where thousands had been slaughtered throughout the day. Darkness had covered the ground, but there was still enough light to make out the outlines of trees. No one was left. The open space looked surprisingly normal. In time no trace would be left.

His father had stopped, and Christian could see him turn his head to scan the area in front of him. Then he turned to the ravine. Chris could feel his eyes on him.

"Chris," he shouted with despair.

Chris wanted to run to his father's arms and be rocked until morning to wake up. To be rocked and soothed as he had been as an infant. To be told all would be right. To be told it was all just a nightmare. But now he knew, it was not – nor ever had been. He released his hold on Dame who bolted at the sound and sight of Perr Haar. Christian was about to follow when he saw the figure step out of the shadows.

This time he knew the voice was from the outside. He remembered and grabbed his head to stop the images from coming. Only the familiar sound of his name kept him from screaming.

"Chris," the anxious voice called again.

A different voice answered.

"You are looking perhaps for someone so far from home."

Perr turned quickly but not without expectancy. Another

Russian soldier stood hatless in back of him with a gun slung over his shoulder and a cigarette dangling from his mouth.

"I have found her," Christian's father said as Dame jumped gleefully around him,

"Chris, is a 'he' is it not?" At his tone Dame stood still.

"We Russians are like that. Are we not? Making names from the father. She is really Dame Christian. Christian was her father. We always come up to the Katyn, but this time she bolted in. After some bear I fear. I've been searching for her for a while."

He firmly cupped her face in his hand as he spoke. "I'm not even sure how to get out," he lied.

Even from afar Christian could detect the forced casualness in his father's manner, but his body language with Dame told a different story. Dame was being set up to attack.

"You are alone then."

"Yes. And you?"

The question was so direct and innocently put that the soldier, who was not used to being questioned by civilians, did not know what to say. Visibly shaken, he knew he had betrayed himself so he used a lie within a lie.

"I guess I too I'm lost. Our unit was on survival missions, and I wandered off." The soldier bent down to pet Dame. She emitted a growl from the pit of her stomach. The soldier stood up abruptly.

"Attends. Pas maintenant," Perr commanded and the dog retreated.

"She's a foreign dog then. That explains it. I have dogs. Good Russian dogs."

The soldier shifted his rifle so that the butt was low on his chest.

Christian could not see this subtle movement because the light was almost gone, but he heard his father say "un moment" to Dame.

"Let's find our way out before we lose the light," he said to the soldier.

They both turned and Perr made the mistake of turning his back first. Christian could not see, but he heard the sound that he had heard throughout that longest day for one more time. The crunch of metal against bone, the guttural spurt, and the collapse of one more body on the soft fragrant pine needles of the Katyn repeated itself..

"Tue!" Christian screamed as he thrashed through the web of branches and out of the ravine, racing to cover the distant between him and the soldier with the gun. He heard its safety click.

Dame threw herself between the bullet and Christian. She had understood the command and was in the air as Christian leaped from his sanctuary. The soldier was dead before he hit the ground. Half his throat was still in Dame's mouth as Christian slid into his father's body and cradled his bleeding head in his arms.

"Keep the secret of the Katyn. Let them think it claimed me," his father choked.

"Papa, thousands were massacred. Poles."

"I know."

"I saw it all. Just like in my nightmares, Papa."

His father's eyes were clouding over, but Christian caught a glimmer of surprise, then acknowledgment. A faint smile crossed his lips.

"Flee to England. Protect your mama and Tatiana. Tell." His skin was cold and his face was turning gray.

"I love you, Papa. Everything will be all right," he lied.

"Yes, you will be alright – now."

Christian held him tight to his chest until he died. Then Christian's head fell back, and from the bowels of his soul he emitted a cry of rage and sorrow so raw that it sought the tops of the trees and then dug back down through their roots to the center of the earth beneath the chilling deadly forest of the Katyn.

****

Night had fallen. The Forest was as quiet as the dead that now lay in their unceremonious graves. When he had no more tears and his throat was stripped, he unclenched his father's fist and pulled out a bloodied emblem of an Eagle insignia. Slipping it into his own pocket, he buried Perr Harr and Dame deep in the Forest of the Katyn.

It was April, and 1940 had barely begun.

<u>Chapter 2 – Poland – August 31, 1939</u>

The family –

"We interrupt Berlin's broadcast of Tchaikovsky's 1812 Overture to bring you news of an overt act of aggression against the Third Reich on this night of the 31st of August 1939. We are broadcasting at the Gdynia radio station just over the Polish border. Patrolling German soldiers and innocent German civilians have been attacked," the announcer reported in rapid fire English.

The announcer repeated the same message in French and then began once more in impeccable Polish. Lastly, he switched to his mother tongue, German. His delivery was rapid, his pitch constantly rising, and his tone one of unmistakable anger. Finished, he turned to his fear stricken guest billeted alongside of him and sequestered high up in the bullet ridden radio tower.

"Why do you, Mr. Videwalski, mayor of Swiecko, think of your countrymen having crossed the border and attacked this insignificant radio station?" he asked in Polish.

"Perhaps," the mayor timidly muttered, "as you suggested, they have become too greedy and want to stretch their holdings to include German soil."

"Spineless acts of aggression would you not say so Mr. Videwalski," the announcer continued to probe in fluent Polish.

Thomas Puratski, sitting in his Warsaw University apartment, could have sworn that he heard the faceless Mr. Videwalski swallow hard before grunting in agreement. Regardless of the language he spoke, his purpose was obvious, and Thomas Puratski, sitting with his son Janusz in the cloistered rooms of their tall tower apartment in the University of Warsaw, could understand it all - in any language - only too well.

He looked across the room at Janusz, with his long thin legs folded beneath him and his cat curled comfortably in his lap. Secure in the bay window seat, Janusz methodically ran his slender fingers down Chopin's back. The cat's purring filled the room.

"I'll have to go, won't I, Papa?" he murmured half to himself as he looked over the city's lights glittering among the branches of the leafy century old chestnut trees and grand oaks that lined the streets, courts, and squares of Warsaw. Through the rustle of their leaves, he could hear the faint cords of an open-air concert still playing in Lazienski Park.

Thomas looked at his son and saw the image of his wife, April. Almost two decades earlier, he had first seen her seated in a window of one of the library towers, a window seat similar to the one Janusz constantly cloistered himself in. Her serene angelic beauty stood in complete contrast to the caustic chaos of a war-torn Europe. The Great War had barely ended, and Europe had just breathed in the air of peace when the rumblings of a future war could again be heard. In the delicate peace between wars Thomas had married April.

Now the peace was beginning to crack like a fragile ostrich egg, etched with web-like fissures. If Europe pressed its ear and listened closely, it would heard the hissing and straining of a fervor that would soon rush forth to change Poland and the world forever. Thomas knew he could not prevent the birth of this demon, but he had been laying a foundation in preparation for the inevitable. He pushed the past from his mind.

"You were to start at the Music Conservatory next week. Your mother was so looking forward to showing you off to all her colleagues." He paused and took a deep breath. "But, it's not to happen."

Janusz turned away from the window. "Why not?"

Thomas kept his voice even and looked in disbelief at this huge child. "When Poland joins this war, as I know she must, you'll be enlisted on the 25th of next month..." Thomas paused to be certain the facts had registered. "because we will be at war by your eighteenth birthday."

"What about Mama and Helena?" Janusz glanced at the closed bedroom doors as he spoke in a loud whisper.

"Your sister is still a child, and your mother, in spite of her delicate looks, has a spine and will of steel. Always a woman without a country - neither English, nor German and never totally Polish, but she could pass for all three."

He paused and looked into his son's face, the boy who had none of his mother's fortitude. "We will not tell them anything tonight. Whatever will be... has already begun. Only morning will speak to the future - for Poland and for us."

****

"Thomas, wake up. German tanks have crossed the border." April Puratski gently pushed her husband's shoulder. He had not intended to fall asleep. He rolled toward the open window and let the lace curtains blow over his bare shoulders as he sat up. He pushed the heavy green shutters all the way open. Leaning out, he looked in both directions at the empty streets below.

"I knew they would not wait long," he murmured.

April began to pace across the bedroom floor. "The radio mentioned an attack on a German radio station by Polish soldiers last night in Gydnia - right over the northern border. Our government says the attack was staged by the Third Reich as an excuse to invade Poland."

"I know, April. Janusz and I stayed up last night and heard the announcement on an emergency broadcast." He turned towards his wife. "What time is it now?"

"A quarter to 5:00."

"Yes, just an excuse to attack. In less than six hours - even." He automatically pushed his arms through the shirt he tossed on the bed just an hour before. Methodically, he buttoned each smooth pearl knotted button and slid each into the hand-sewed buttonholes to give himself time before he fully met his wife's fearful face.

She had stopped her pacing and stood frozen in the doorway. She glanced behind her - towards the children's rooms, and then turned towards the open window. He crossed the room and wrapped her in his arms. He slid his hand over her soft silky hair.

"Everything will be all right," he lied. He felt her body involuntarily shiver.

"No. It will not." She pulled back to face him. "Why did you not tell me last night? We could have begun our plan."

"That is the last resort, the one which can only succeed in a state of chaos." he said gently as he caressed her face. Her fear began to dissipate. "We had decided not to run – remember? To keep our heads when saner men are losing theirs. Wasn't that your line? You were always the true believer in staying in our country."

"I did not want my family – our family – to suffer the humiliation my father did in the war. As a German who married an English woman, he was never at home in England, so he chose to leave."

"That's right," Thomas added. "For you and for your mother. Remember, both English and German blood run through your veins, but the earth beneath your feet is Polish. They raised you here so you would not have to choose like your father did."

"But I am my father's daughter – and so, it is my turn to choose. The circle comes around. Janusz and Helena will be like me – without a country."

"They are Polish and offspring of this rich soil. When this war has ended, God willing – the land will still be here."

"And Janusz's dream of being as great a pianist as Chopin?"

"That will be left for another day – in another time."

"So, we must leave before the 25th." She had come to the same conclusion as her husband. "Why send a lamb to confront a mountain lion?" She reached up and placed her hand on his firm jaw. "And you? The army could take you too."

"I'll be more useful at the Poly Tech. Besides at forty, I'm not exactly infantry material." Thomas laughingly said.

In the doorway Helena appeared, rubbing the sleep from her eyes and pushing her long silky blond hair from her face. Waif like, her thin arms and legs made her seem a child of ten, but as the dawn's light glowed through her long white night gown, the body of a young woman was evident.

"Why is everyone up so early?"

"They've begun, Helena," her father gently answered.

Her body involuntarily shivered against a wind that was just beginning to blow through the land. She stiffened her spine and firmly pressed her right palm against the door frame. She did not ask why.

"Then I'll wake Janusz." Without waiting for a response, she stepped over the threshold and down the hall to her brother's room. In a few moments all were bent over the smooth oak kitchen table as a white enameled pot of coffee brewed on the cast iron stove in the corner.

"It has begun" the leaden voice of the commentator announced. "Germany has attacked us on all fronts. On the southwest below Gdynia, north across the border from East Prussia, and south from Czechoslovakia – have come reports of tanks rolling across Poland's plains, of Stuka Bombers flying in formation above our soil and of German Infantry marching through Polish villages. Wireless reports from other stations, as well as from citizens in the attacked areas, will be broadcast throughout the day. The desecration of our homeland has begun." The announcer paused and swallowed hard before he continued.

"Now is our opportunity to show the world what others have been afraid to do. Sons and daughters of Poland let us not be ground into submission. From 'Warszawa' this is Joseph Kaminski reporting the most current news. Long live Poland."

As the music swelled beneath his trembling voice, the words to Warszawianka, the 110-year-old revolutionary song, filtered through the early morning light. The Puratski family, like thousands across Poland, sat in silence.

After the last refrain, Helena rose, walked to the calendar - hung by a single nail to the whitewashed kitchen wall, and poised a pencil between her index finger and thumb. Before she circled September 1, 1939, she paused, as if to grind the date into her memory. She pressed hard and the scratch of her pencil stopped. The tip broke against the pressure; it fell to the floor in what seemed like slow motion. Hitting the red tile floor, it shattered into black dust.

****

"Are all our provisions ready?"

"They are above us," April answered as she looked over to the pantry, the little nook - almost hidden – by the cast iron stove. The pantry contained shelves on all three sides. Two of which held household provisions and the center back wall of the pantry was lined with five shelves, partitioned to hold individual books. Its upper two shelves held only German novels and the bottom two only British ones. It was the shelf in the center that was reserved for Polish literature and music books – from Chopin to Cole Porter.

April walked over to the center shelf and pulled out Pan Tadeusz by Adam Mickiewicz. Sliding her hand over to the side, she pushed a lever and the entire back wall of books glided forward to reveal a narrow stairway.

"Remember this is where you must hide when the time comes. The book you take with you in order to slide it back in, from the other side, once the door is pulled closed." She directed her words to Janusz, the one who always had to be reminded to place the music books back in their individual grooves once he was finished playing the piano.

"And the satchels are all packed?" Thomas asked as a double check.

"Cousin Wladek sent me the last remnants of canvas. I sewed the final one last week."

"Before we go, we'll check each one - one last time." Thomas said in a monotone as though he were simply thinking out loud, going over each step in his mind - one more time.

As in a game of dominoes, one piece would fall against another and another, snaking their way over the mountains and plains. Thomas knew that when the time came to flee, nothing could be left to chance. Their route and safe houses were locked in place for a journey north to the Baltic Sea where cousin Wladek's small fleet of fishing boats lay in anchor at the port of Gdansk, where the Vistula River met the Baltic Sea. For over a thousand years it provided Poland with a rich heritage. Now this valiant city by the sea would provide an exodus.

Shutters clacked open and swept his thoughts away. Shouts reverberated against the sanctity of stone and the scuffle of feet and hooves of horses punctured the early morning light. The courtyard below was a mass of motion.

"If this tiny university square is filled with such madness, what is the rest of Warsaw like?" Thomas said. "Janusz, you come with me to the Poly Tech, and Helena, you go with your mother to the university meeting scheduled at 9:00. Be back at the apartment no later than 6:00."

They stepped into the elevator and left their turret apartment in the language wing of the university. Janusz pulled the iron grate shut, and they waited in silence as the ancient elevator bumped its way to the ground floor of this great seat of learning. Before Thomas cranked open the gate, he enveloped his wife in his strong arms.

"You are my life, my darling April, so be wise and careful today." He gently kissed her lips and then paused to look into her eyes. They held no fear. He knew they wouldn't.

"Take care of Janusz as I will Helena." Simultaneously, they unlocked from their embrace and opened their arms to include their children.

"We will all take care of one another." Helena stoically proclaimed.

Janusz nodded his head. With that, Thomas slid open the iron grate and walked ahead of his family - into the dark but crowded foyer.

Faculty, students, tenants, and Stanislaw, the old concierge, formed various clusters and were all fervently talking and interrupting one another. Many formed a circle in one corner around a large circular mahogany table on which stood a radio with its tall antenna. The former chess board and pinochle set had been swept aside.

"Over here, Puraski family," a strong voice shouted above the sea of voices. April stepped into the throng towards the sound of Zosia Zapinsky – "Push your way through," Zosia bellowed.

"There she is," Thomas said as he guided his family from behind. He had spotted her mass of auburn curls above the heads of most in the room.

"I see her Papa. Over there Mama," Janusz said although he had forgotten that it was impossible for his mother and his sister to see over this sea of people. Standing behind his mother, he steered her in the direction of Zosia who was now madly waving. Her broad smile and freckled face made him think of all the football matches they had watched together in the university's stadium.

"Good, you made it. I was trying to get up to ring your bell, but the lift has been busy. People are taking out box-loads. They've conceded surrender without having fought." She continued with her usual superlatives and positive principles. Whether a war or a football match, her enthusiasm was contagious. Someone turned up the volume on the radio.

"Polish Divisions have been called up and are marching to each zone of conflict. Already battles are raging in the towns of Skolimow, Grojec, Zamosc, Lesha, Podkowa, and dozens of others near each of our borders. All able-bodied men previously registered in the armed or aviator corps should report to the nearest army base or airfield – immediately. Again, all enlisted men must report to their respective corps now. Most trains are operating and roads are still open. It's imperative that all men report – get there any way you can. This is a civil defense announcement."

The foyer, despite its mass of humanity, was silent. No discussions. No reverie. Someone's hand turned off the radio. Good-byes were said, and two by two, people began to walk or run in different directions. Stanislaus, as though in a daze, limped to his chair just inside the small front vestibule of his building. The front doors were flung open now, and the clean chiseled courtyard of the Language and Humanities sanctuary glistened in the warmth of the early September day.

He had seen many such days from his special seat where his family, the students and professors, entered and exited his life. From them he took his greatest joy, but he had his favorites as any grandparent would. Those were the ones who made him laugh and the ones in whom he saw the face of God. Zosia and the Puratskis came under the former and later category.

"Stanislaus, don't be so pensive. Our hallowed halls made it through the last war, and so they'll survive this one. Count the freckles on just my nose. That's how many days it will take to push the Germans back – perhaps, all the way back to Berlin where we'll lock them all up and throw away the key."

"Ah Zosia, but you have so many tiny ones that I can't possibly see without my glasses. Besides, perhaps each one will stand for a month or God have mercy, a year."

"Always the pessimist old Stas," Zosia ruffled his thinning grey hair to tease him as she constantly did.

Stanislaus looked down at the sun patches beginning to splatter on the stone courtyard floor. Winston, the huge black and white stray, lay as usual at his feet. He had entered Stanislaus' life as a flea ridden morsel of fur, but chose to remain as a constant by Stanislaus' chair instead of roaming the alleys of Warsaw. Stanislaus enjoyed his company especially when he made his rounds. Up and down the corridors, he would talk endlessly to the stray cat. Indeed, it seemed as though Winston understood his master's preferences.

Today, for perhaps the last time, they all stood in the open doorway looking out at the massive stone buildings, which encircled this particular – their own – courtyard.

"Well Stanislaus, we'll see you later," Thomas placed one hand on his shoulder and reached out with his other. Stanislaus shook his hand and placed his other hand over Thomas'.

"Yes, later," he said grimly. "Take care of your beautiful family. The apartment contains only things. I'll watch over that." Stanislaus glanced over the faces he had come to love.

"They are your life," He smiled warmly as he gazed at April, Helena, and Janusz.

The women bent down and hugged him. Janusz shook his hand and then succumbed to the old man's bear hug. Zosia was the last to kiss him.

"If it comes to that, you'll leave with me. I'll even take old Winston," she laughed her throaty laugh. "Come let us go find out what the world has for us - to victory , I pray!"

She slipped her arm under April's and stretched her other hand out to Helena. Like a Roman frieze frozen in the shadow of the doorway, they stopped before they stepped into the light. Without looking back, they hurried to the right while Janusz and his father turned to the left, toward the arch that led to Piekna Street and the Poly Tech.

****

The Beginning of the End: Poland
Afternoon of September 1, 1939

Thomas –

Thomas Puratski held the title of Bureau Chief of Bridge and Road Construction in Warsaw. The decision to replace or repair was his. Juggling dozens of projects at once, he rarely had to look at the detailed blueprints of Warsaw's maze of bridges and roads, for he had worked on each one at one time or another. However, when a bridge was totally new for him, he would bring that particular set of prints home and pour over them until all its intricacies were etched in his mind like the life lines on the palms of the hands.

This innate ability to remember and recall any statistic applied to the number of city blocks between various bridges, the specific soil analyses into which each bridge was girded, the weight limits for each bridge structure, and the amount and type of explosive it would take to blow it. In this year of 1939 his knowledge and its application could ensure defeat or victory.

Thomas was convinced the Poly Tech held the brightest minds in academia. These men and women planned to place Poland well into the 21st century. Some, like Thomas, worked on Poland's inner structure - her bridges, roads, and rail systems. A super train of the greatest speed set to connect Poland's five major cities was planned for the next decade. This, in addition to other projects, would give Poland in the 1940's one of the most modern transportation networks in Europe.

The infrastructure of Poland, as she conducted commerce and generally cohabited with the rest of Europe, was most important to the minds of this department of the Poly Tech. However, all knew the Commerce and Defense Departments were the other two workhorses of this triumvirate. Briefing one another about their projects and progress, Thomas felt that they worked in unison like a troika, and those who were covetous of others' achievements and too secretive with their own successes and failures were eventually left out. The majority worked in tandem with one another and met bi-monthly for half-day reporting. On those days they had an extra hour for lunch and most chose to leave their lunch baskets at home and join one another at a neighborhood restaurant

Thomas enjoyed listening and gleaning ideas from each. Often he'd ask a question or submit a hypothesis to see how others in Defense or Commerce would respond. They had formed a cohesive group: the two chiefs from Defense, three from Commerce and one from Research and Development, and a half a dozen mathematicians and scientists of these respective branches. The numbers remained fairly constant and the faces turned from colleagues into friends as they all, especially the chiefs, approached middle age together. Often the younger members of the lunch would bait their professorial chefs with a particular bothersome question or retort.

Janusz, like his father, preferred to listen. Often he came to these luncheons instead of eating with his own friends on the stone benches of the schoolyard. He enjoyed the company of these men who treated him like a son or younger brother. From them he learned about life and the world outside his schoolroom walls. He especially enjoyed the ploys of the younger colleagues and the reaction or lack of reaction on his father's face. For his father it was like a chess game. Janusz did not watch the face of his father, for no one could tell anything from that. Instead, he looked at the cool blue eyes. They alone spoke the truth. Like a chameleon they turned purplish blue, the color of cornflowers - with joy - or clouded over gray, the color of storm clouds for displeasure.

Today's luncheon was different. After a non-scheduled building meeting of all upper and middle level personnel, employees were told to leave to take care of what they had to do. Many did not go home. Instead, they met for their last meal. They cared about their families, but they counted on the brains and stamina of their friends and colleagues to get them through the dark days that would surely descend on Poland.

'A last supper', Thomas thought as they broke bread together and prayed that its sustenance would enable them to survive.

"Janusz, you don't have to worry about being called to duty," Martin, one of his father's younger colleagues, spoke in a hushed voice to his former school-mate. "For me it's different. I'm neither young enough nor old enough to be exempt. Although this is only my second year at Poly Tech, it could easily be my last."

He paused to swallow the black coffee in front of his still untouched meal. "All my life it was my mother's dream for me to follow my father's footsteps and secure the sought after work that only the Poly Tech could offer young men. Every year following his death that was our promise to him and to one another."

"The dream I know about. Ever since we were little boys, that's all you spoke of. Yet, never once have you told me how your father died." Janusz finally dared to ask.

"You know he was killed in the Great War." He paused and swallowed hard. "What you don't know is that the Germans captured him one night and from that point on, he was forced to fight for them. In his last letter, smuggled in from the western front, he told my mother he planned to escape to Norway and send for her." His voice lowered. "Two months later she got word that he died of mustard gas poisoning. The Poles were always sent into no man's land first – you know, without any gas masks."

"I'm sorry Martin."

"I don't worry about being sent. I worry about dying. With my death, my mother could not go on living. It just seems unjust that now when I can earn a good living so my mother will never have to worry again about food, I just might meet my father's fate – at the hands of the same enemy."

"God is not that unfair," Janusz exclaimed wide-eyed.

"That is one of the things I've always liked about you - your faith."

"Could they take us like they did your father, Martin?" Janusz asked looking openly at his friend. He gazed into his eyes and only saw his own reflection in Martin's thick wire rimmed glasses.

"I agree with you Janusz. God could not be that cruel. Don't worry. You're too young anyway." He deliberately changed the subject. "My sister and I never had such delicious bread."

They each reached for the dark loaf of bread at the same time. They laughed and one broke off a chunk for the other. It was that way between them. Each anticipated the other one's need. Four years separated them - the gulf between boyhood and manhood, but Martin had endured enough hardship and learned enough wisdom for the both of them. Dipping the soft warm dark bread into their ham and pea soup, they turned toward the others.

"Research and Development is going to be crucial during this war. All our efforts must now be channeled into the machinery of war, but I fear we've waited too long," Bernard Berwerksi sadly spoke what the others felt.

"I'm afraid he's right," another chief agreed.
"The question is not why we did not act before, but how Poland can succeed - now that the German Army is practically at her doorstep?" a young man interjected.

Bernard Berwerski shrugged his shoulders.

"With all due respect. Mr. Berwerski had instructed all of our divisions to commit our findings to memory and/or microfilm. For the last year this has been standard procedure," a dark haired young man added. "Yet, he initiated no emergency defense plans or military buildup for a possible invasion."

Everyone at the table turned to get a glimpse of the dark-haired young man who was relatively new to the Bureau.

He continued. "And your branch Mr. Puratski? I understand you have not just done maintenance and peace time construction, but demolition and prefabrication measures, as well."

Thomas took a long steady look at this man. He had so far just listened to the men around him whom he had known so long. This young man was not one of them.

Bernard did not let him answer. He turned to the dark haired young man whom he knew as one from Internal Defense.

"Contrary to your recriminations, all of us have taken measures for this day which is now upon us."

The young man shrugged his shoulders, and leaned back into his chair. The discussion had been open and long. Free speech, as during all their other luncheons, had run as easily as the Polish Vodka. However, no talks had ever been as crucial as this day's. All knew that the future of Poland and their countrymen, friends, and family would be tied in part to the decisions they reached around this huge round oak table.

Thomas began to speak. In deliberate contrast to the fervor of the last two hours of arguments and proclamations, he spoke quietly and slowly.

"Our work has always acknowledged that this day might happen. France could have crushed the German Reichswehr in March of 35' when Hitler thumbed his nose at Versailles and revealed his proclaimed conscript army of 36 divisions. France willingly handed over the Saar with Germany's solemn assurance of no more territorial demands. It's been almost four years since then. Four years for the 'Fatherland'," Thomas Puratski almost spit out that word, "to build up a military force of ships, subs, tanks, and planes. I am afraid no one can stop them now. I'm certain that every other branch and department of the Poly Tech has been making contingent unofficial arrangements for the inevitable. What we do not know are the details of one another's work. I believe the rest of our time - this afternoon and only this afternoon - must be an unveiling of such plans. The invasion has heightened, and we do not know if this meeting we'll be our last. God willing, I'm wrong, and we'll all be laughing and going into work tomorrow morning as usual."

He paused and waited for his words to have their effect. He looked from face to face. Solidarity had been forged – commitment lined the faces of even the youngest, his son - Janusz.

"Go on," Bernard broke the silence.

"Some of us might be called on to join the armed forces. Up to now we have all been exempt because our work has been classified as priority one. If..." he swallowed hard and met their eyes directly, "if ...when the Luftwaffe begins and the Wermarck invades, our priorities will change even if the government does not officially call for such." Some faces shone with a new light; others clouded over in anxiety.

"Therefore, we must disperse our most valuable information, and," he paused and looked round at each man, "any previously held competitive secrets that if kept hidden could change the course of history. We do not know how many of us will survive. Because of that, each of us must know as much as possible and be the voice of knowledge at the moment when it might be needed."

All nodded in agreement and murmurs of 'he's right' 'It's our only hope' What other choice is there?' circled the table.

"Then let us each join hands with the man on either side and raise our arms together to unite and direct us on the same path from this day forth." Thomas proclaimed.

"Yes – 'Tak' " they boomed as one voice with hands clenched tightly.

The quietness returned.

"Then I shall begin. All our work and demolition procedures for mining bridges and blocking roads have been put on microfilm. In addition, our inventions for a metal prefab bridge which could allow for a division of tanks to go over a span of up to 100 meters has also been recorded. Only the key members of that team within our division know where those have been hidden. The three at the table nodded in unison.

"Within the cover of the oldest Polish Bible in the Poly Tech's Library," one said.

"And in the large can of rat poison at the far end of the grounds in the gardener's shed," said another.

"Needless to say, this information could be used for defense or offense. Either way, if it falls into enemy hands it would be used against Poland... and the world."

Thomas again waited for the weight of his words to have their effect. He was almost going to continue and say one last thing. .that, if those copies were destroyed, the plans and statistics were etched indelibly in his mind. He glanced to Bernard who tilted his head - imperceptibly to the others, but nonetheless, noticeable to Thomas Puratski. Thomas tightened his jaw. He stopped talking and instead nodded to Bernard to take his turn.

So the voices and secrets spilled across the solid table and up into the rafters of the old house on Silver Street.

A La Mode de Tanya, Warsaw 1914 – 1918

Zosia -

Zosia's 'joie de vivre' came from her closeness with her mother and her distance from her father. Tanya Zapinski was a talented seamstress with a flair for fabric, but her specialty was her wool designs. She appreciated the finest wool, which in her opinion came from England and the finest fashion couture from France. Since she could not go to Paris, she had Paris come to her. By collecting every possible newspaper advertisement, Parisian society photos, or even an occasional priceless French magazine, she not only taught herself couture finishing but also the French language itself. She even borrowed books from her neighbor's bookstore, Florian's, as a trade for any mending or tailoring that he might need.

What Zosia remembered most about her mother was the laughter in her voice and the bolts of fabric, the reams of wool which attracted one Regina Wentworth. This formidable woman came like a lightning bolt into their lives and stayed by them through the most difficult storms, yet on that fine fall day when she first arrived, the skies were clear - colored with a most auspicious blue, and the train had just pulled into Warsaw. The year was 1913, and the English woman aboard was beginning to tire of her European tour. She did not wait while her trunks were being unloaded but instead decided to just wander the streets of Warsaw. It was in the early afternoon when she spotted the delicate lavender sign of 'La Mode de Tanya'. Crossing the tiny avenue, Regina Wentworth stepped over the threshold of the unique boutique tucked away under the chestnut trees, and her life changed forever.

For both Tanya and Regina it proved to be star-crossed, for fate had plans for them: to meet, to become fast friends, and to be mothers to Zosia. Tanya knew no English and Regina no Polish so they communicated in French. Regina's first purchase was a stunning red and black checkered coat - one that would brighten any drab London winter day. Despite the war, Regina returned frequently for more unique clothes, but it was the chats during the fittings that were the true allure.

Zosia would crawl on the atelier floor and sit contentedly in either woman's lap. Often she would fall asleep in Regina's arms as the middle aged woman sang soft English lullabies to her. She became the daughter Regina had always longed for. Soon the baby listened and understood any word - whether they were Polish, English, or French.

On occasion Regina would visit with a countrywoman who had admired her friend's chic wool walking suits or thick luxurious capes. She would buy whatever Tanya suggested since she was so taken with her style. On these occasions the circle grew and more English was spoken as Mrs. Wentworth translated Tanya's suggestions or commands to her friends.

So it was natural that Zosia, the baby, spoke all three languages. That, along with her flair for fashion, seemed inherent. As a toddler, she layered herself and her porcelain doll with scraps of fabric, for she spent most of her time by her mother's side and avoided her father and his violent outbursts. He terrified her as he sat in the large red parlor chair with his head drooping to his chest. Her father grew more and more remote as he gathered strength from one and only one source - Polish vodka. When he died, neither she nor her mother cried, and oddly enough, Zosia felt totally safe for the first time in her young life.

All that changed, however, when she turned four and went to look in her mother's dresser drawer for the six pennies Tanya would leave her once a fortnight to spend on candy or save for books from Mr. Florian's store. No pennies sat in the drawer. Instead, the parlor drapes were drawn closed, and the sunlight cast a reddish hue on the French tapestry rug. The brocade chairs and love seat had been pulled back to allow for the neighbors' chairs to sit silently in rows viewing the large mahogany box in front of the bay window. Zosia avoided the people who began to enter through the lace covered glass hall doors.

She spent the day in hiding, isolated in the dark, listening to the constant murmuring of voices. In the evening when all had gone home, she finally crept out to check the drawer one more time. Still no pennies slept sweetly in the scented pine drawer. It was then that she wept for the mother she knew was gone. No longer would Zosia be cradled, kissed, and enveloped in the delicate fragrance of lavender. The box now contained the only world she had ever known. The huge terrifying black box squatting in the parlor had devoured her mother. The box now did the holding, and it held for all eternity her beloved mother, another victim of the flu epidemic of 1918.

It was then that Tanya Zapinski's plan was executed. Regina came for the last time on that somber day and found Zosia hiding at night behind a lace curtain in her mother's bedroom. She lifted the little girl up in her strong arms, and the scent of English roses permeated the room. For the first time since the funeral, she felt peace, for the little girl loved the smell almost as much as her mother's lavender scent. Both smelled of love and safety. She had no fear and willingly went with Regina Wentworth - away from the black box, away from her beloved mother and to England, a country her mother had prepared her for.

In time, Zosia grew to love the quirky ways of the English and to realize why her mother had loved Regina so much. As the years passed, Regina never let Zosia forget her Polish heritage and her remarkable strong and talented mother. For Zosia, it was as though her mother were still alive just waiting to open the shop door when she turned the corner of Zakapane Street in Warsaw.

Many years later after Regina had died, Zosia returned to live permanently in Poland. Having lived in London and in Paris, she still regarded Warsaw as home. For six years she had reestablished her roots. It had given her a career at the University, good friends, and a family amongst her own people. It would kill her to leave again, but she was pragmatic. One does what one has to do in order to survive. The living comes afterward.

****

Afternoon of September 1, 1939

The Women-

"We've gone to every store imaginable," Zosia declared to April. "We're set for the duration."

"I hope you're right.'

"It's good we brought our shopping sacks, mama."

"The canvas will hold, Helena. Just slip it over your head and other arm if it gets too uncomfortable."

"One last stop at mother's old shop." Zosia added.

The sign still read 'A la mode de Tanya' and Zosia looked over the blue letters and for an instant remembered the crisp whiteness of the sign with her mother directing the sign man in the art of calligraphy. The letters had been lavender then.

"She has them all ready?" April asked.

"Yes," Zosia answered, "according to the original design - reversible capes, full raglan sleeves, two lamb's wool frogs in the front with an extra frog and snap under the collar, and a reversible detachable hood. The capes' wool was muted like the landscape with a reversible side of khaki canvas treated with paraffin to waterproof it. The seamstress had also made a snap on white canvas hood for the snows of winter.

"Perfect" April said.

When Zosia closed the door to her late mother's shop, she turned and looked up at the lettering. Her eyes traced the letters 'Tanya' and tears ran down her face. She knew in her heart she would not be going home again. Wiping her tears with her hands, she concentrated on the future and patted the brown paper bundle tied with cord which she slid beneath her arm. It was 4:00 in the afternoon of September 1ˢᵗ 1939.

****

Dinner was set on the table when Thomas and Janusz returned home, but the family, including Zosia and Stanislaus, were sitting in front of an open parlor window listening to the radio perched on the wide stone windowsill. Their faces reflected none of the glow from the warm evening sun. In silence they listened.

"The Polish army is in retreat. The lightening war that the Wermarcht had used against Czechoslovakia has been turned against us. They have blazed through some 75 kilometers on our north, west, and south borders. The Luftwaffe has begun attacks on Polish air force." His voice droned on with reports from nearby areas. It all amounted to the same - devastation of Poland.

That night over what would be their last normal meal they heard the bombs like thunder accompanying a warm summer rain. Far in the distance their countrymen felt the wrath of that German thunder. Stanislaus sat in silence as the others talked about their day and the days to come - their role and responsibility, yet only Stanislaus truly knew the horror that would follow. In the last war his wife and only son were killed, and he could do nothing to stop it.

"This time will be different," he thought as he looked around the table. He would gladly give his life for theirs. They were his family now. The pain of his personal loss, always just below the surface, had dulled with time. These new faces were almost clearer than those he had lost. Each one was dear to him - especially those of the women whose mannerisms reminded him of his wife's.

"Will they come tonight?" Helena asked.

The question shocked Stanislaus out of his silent reverie. More than two decades earlier, when his family had lived in the little town of Osinow Dolny near the German border, his wife had asked the same question.

"Nie, not tonight puski dear. You can sleep soundly," Thomas answered his daughter.

An involuntary shudder ran through Stanislaus' body. Word for word, it was the same question his wife had asked the night before the Germans came, and word for word, he had given her the same answer.

In the morning - she and their son lay dead.

Chapter 3- September - The Fall of Warsaw

Zosia's faculty apartment received a direct hit the fourteenth of September and Warsaw, now surrounded by German troops, was being starved into submission if it did not surrender. The Polish Capital's answer came through the mouth of civilian governor-general Walerian Czuma' - "never". Hitler's retort came swiftly - round-the-clock artillery fire and bombs, unleashed by the Luftwaffe, Relentlessly, they pounded Zosia's mother's shop, her childhood home, and all the stores where she, April, and Helena had gathered the last of their provisions just three weeks before. Now they were but piles of ash and much of the University lay in ruin, but the courtyard and the tower of the Puratski apartment, high above the rubble, pierced the sky as though in defiance. What had been the seat of wisdom for Poland's best and brightest no longer existed.

Throughout the nights of endless bombings, the agonizing cries of those buried beneath the stones could be heard, but as daylight came the cries diminished. Through the dust of each new day another search for friends and food began. People helped one another when the bombings first began, but as chaos became a way of life, each person's circle shrank.

Immediate family counted. The others – friends and neighbors did not. Like canny foxes they crept out of their dens to journey out for food or fuel - to detour or stop their quest was unthinkable.

Zosia now lived with Stanislaus in his basement rooms beneath the wing which still anchored the Puratskis' tower. The courtyard, however, had disappeared a few days after Zosia had arrived with her knapsack of belongings and her hair so short that only a singular curl stuck out from beneath her cap. Stanislaus, looking out into his empty courtyard, was seated in the foyer door of the department building.

For late September the days were so warm and the evenings refreshingly cool that the leaves of the giant chestnut trees had no hint of the orange and yellow of autumn. The sun was setting, casting a hue of red across the empty classrooms and the few occupied apartments across the yard. Winston meowed and meandered next to Stanislaw who bent down to cradle up the cat as he had done each night since the bombings began. Usually they sat until the moonlight crossed the threshold and the first bomb lit up the sky somewhere near the north border of the city where many of the factories lay, but this evening was early.

Zosia's pot of stuffed cabbage smelled sweetly pungent and the old man's stomach growled even more than usual. He was getting use to one meal a day – cooked early in the daylight and left to simmer from the embers on the tin stove. The gas had been cut off for weeks and families throughout Warsaw were adjusting to rooms darkened by blankets thrown over windows, one lukewarm meal a day, and constant confinement. They scurried out only during the early morning light to forage for whatever nuggets, like manna from heaven, the bombs had burst forth from the rubble.

Winston's meows were so persistent that Stanislaus acquiesced and shuffled down the ancient corridors, down the cool stone steps to the basement halls below. He had passed the furnace room when he heard the sharp drone cut through the September eve; the birds were still singing when the explosion followed. As his shoulder hit the stone wall, Winston jumped from his arms and ran to the gray door at the end of the hall. The door flung open and Zosia rushed out.

"Na, I am not hurt," Stanislaus groaned as he motioned her aside and pointed to the opposite stairs.

As Winston returned to lick the old man's scraped elbow, Zosia ran to the tower steps; taking them three at a time, she quickly passed the first level window and glanced out to see nothing but a wall of rubble where the window's courtyard view used to be. As she rounded the third flight of stairs, she could see the light from that floor's window. At that moment Janusz nearly knocked her over. She grabbed his arm to keep from falling, and he easily supported her.

"We're all right," he uttered as the rest of his family soon appeared.

"It's no longer safe to stay up there. Who knows how long that tower will stand? You must sleep down here at night," Zosia ordered her friends.

"We had just reached that decision the moment before," Thomas answered. Looking around he added, "and Stanislaus?"

"Winston must have hurried him in. He was already in the downstairs corridor when the bomb exploded."

"April, you and Helena go with Zosia and stay below. Janusz and I will see if anyone survived from across the courtyard." Thomas said as he peered out of the top third of the window to see the tops of the chestnut trees, broken and twisted like shadows through a mirror.

Janusz read his father's mind. "Only the Steins and Leibers are living there. Zosia and I saw Aaron Stein this morning. He said they were planning to leave soon and make their way to Holland where his son is now living."

Like soldiers on rounds, they separated. The women quickly filed down the steps to care for Stanislaus, who they found seated, with a wet cloth to his head and a pillow behind his shoulder in the small front room's overstuffed chair. Winston, seated in his lap, was licking Stanislaus' limp hand.

When Thomas and Janusz returned, Stanislaus was lying on the sofa with Zosia spoon feeding him chunks of stuffed cabbage.

"Are you all right?" Thomas asked as he shut and bolted the gray metal door behind him.

"Tak, Tak - yes I am good. Just like a baby they treat me. And Mr. Stein?" Stanislaus looked up at Thomas.

"And - Anna Leiber and her family?" Zosia held the spoon frozen in mid-air.

Janusz shook his head. His face was drained of color.

"The Steins?" April added.

"If anyone was home, no one survived. All that remains is a pile of stone." Thomas stated.

"Maybe they left for Holland?" Helena in her childish optimism added.

"That's a good thought, darling," Stanislaus smiled as he reached up to caress her face. Behind her stood April; her jaw clenched as she swallowed.

"Come. We've set the table. Let us take of Zosia's fine golabkis."

Each one found their seat on either side of the long table set in the hall between the kitchen and the two small bedrooms which connected in railroad fashion to the sitting room at the other end of the caretaker's apartment. It was spacious for one person, but cramped for six. Zosia placed a bowl of steaming cabbage leaves filled with rice and bits of sausage and two smaller plates of baked apples drizzled with brown sugar in the middle of the table. Thomas sat at the far end behind one of the tall white candles that he bent over to light. The glow cast over his face, and soon spread to illuminate the narrow wooden table and those around it.

"This will be our last dinner within these hallowed halls that we have lived and loved so well. God willing, we will have many more together," Thomas said as he stood above the white candle. His face showed no fear, but rather held a sense of relief. Finally, they could take action. With precision, he broke the brown bread and passed the split halves to either side of him.

They ate in silence except for the loud booms that shook the earth and reverberated within the subterranean walls. There was no concern for being seen since the only half window, high near the ceiling above the sink, was shuttered closed. Deep in the catacombs of the University they would not be found.

Although bound fast to one another, each held his own individual thoughts. Like waves, they crashed into through their minds, unable to be turned back – thoughts of death, separation, famine, loss, and of the tomorrows – how many would be left to each?

When all had finished eating, April took the dishes to the tiny kitchen and placed them in the deep concrete laundry sink. She turned around to touch the black stove's cast iron coffeepot to make certain it was still hot. Satisfied, she stepped towards the icebox and extracted from its one shelf a lemon meringue pie. Its stiff white peaks, tipped ginger brown, were just the right consistency and blended sweetly into an amber hue.

****

April had spent most of the day searching for eggs and a lemon, and when she found them she quickly returned to her tower home to spend the last few hours of safe light baking at her beloved cast iron stove. Once the iron door was shut and the brass hinge secure, she slowly moved under the archway of the front parlor and let her eyes gaze from one memory to another. They halted on the piano of rich mahogany that she had polished each day for the last eighteen years. Hesitantly, she moved behind the keyboard and allowed her fingers to touch the ivory and ebony keys, lounging like black panthers in the sunlight streaming in through the lace curtains.

She looked over her beloved Warsaw and gently pressed her fingers to the keys. Soon the notes of Chopin filled the sunlit room as the smell of sweet lemon tinged the air. She played with abandon and let the chords of music - rise, crest, and fall over her to strengthen and steel her for what she knew the future held. The ruins, which lay before her, were only the beginning. As far as her eyes could see, charred buildings and trees defaced the skyline of what was once a noble city. Since it could no longer be so, she would carry it as it had been – in its glory – before this brutal assault. Proud, strong, and stately it would always live in her memory.

April stood up from the piano bench and walked to the windows. She lifted her silver necklace and let her fingers feel the rough texture of the intricate silver leaves before sliding them over the cool smooth stone they encompassed. She raised the amber stone to eye level and looked through it, over her city, colored in patina like an old masterpiece. Her eyes came to rest on the courtyard below and the chestnut trees whose fruit was nearly ripe. For one more time, she held her Warsaw in forever amber. Letting the cool necklace drop between her breasts, she returned to the kitchen and Janusz' birthday pie.

****

"Oh Mama, it's so beautiful. So delicious looking." Helena exclaimed.

"It's all those days without sweets my love that make this seem so extraordinary." April chided, yet she was proud of this accomplishment. This simple act, one that she had always enjoyed and one that her family totally appreciated, she had taken for granted like so many other common pleasures of life. Now, it seemed special – god given.

"No, it's incredible. The delicate meringue reminds me of my mother's shop and all those cream colored laces," Zosia remarked until the bombs made her remember that it was all in the past.

"So let us put a candle on it, make a wish, and eat it all!" Stanislaus bellowed.

"I see the bump on your head didn't affect your appetite." Zosia teased.

"There you go my son – the tallest candle ever," Thomas pulled the candle from its holder and placed it in the center of the pie.

"Happy Birthday Janusz." they all chorused.

"But the 25th is not until tomorrow." Janusz replied.

"Let us take advantage of today," Thomas tried not to let the impatience edge into his voice. Had he himself been so self-centered and childlike at eighteen? He knew the answer. The edge crept into his voice.

"Tomorrow we must leave. Warsaw is surrounded, and the Russians have crossed the eastern frontier. The French and the English could have crossed into Poland from the West. They have chosen not to." he paused and whispered. "They will not come to our defense at this late date."

"The talk on the streets is that German soldiers have entered and are going from block to block." Helena added.

Thomas continued, "We cannot endure any more. Today's attack was too close. There can be no more trips upstairs to our home, for the time is ripe to start our journey out. Once Poland officially surrenders, total chaos will follow."

"But, for one more night let us have our dreams of yesterday," April gently added looking at Janucz.

"And our cabbages and pie," Zosia laughed. "Happy Birthday, Janusz, the brother I always wished I had." She hugged him and placed a red parcel with a silver ribbon next to the lemon pie.

"From Winston and me," Stanislaus pushed a small thin old narrow rectangular wooden box in front of him. With the other hand, he smoothed down the cat's ruffled fur until Winston's purrs began to fill the room.

"And from me," Helena put a light object tied in a flowered cloth napkin into his palm.

The gift from his parents lay in a flat brown parcel tied with a black string, the kind Thomas used to tie up the paper rolls of city plans.

The dessert and coffee held no more talk of what might be, but rather of what had been. They reminisced about the Poland of old, their youth, and Helena and Janusz's childhood. The lemon pie plate held a few remaining crumbs so Zosia placed it on the floor for Winston to greedily lick in between loud purrs. The papers from Janusz's gifts littered the stark table. Zosia's gift of a brown flat leather pouch with a thin leather strip fastening one end to the other for easy concealment around the neck and under a shirt lay opened on the table. In it Janusz placed the harmonica Helena had purchased for him and the polished Swiss army knife that had been Stanislaus' father's gift to him as a boy. Lastly, he gently unfolded his favorite sheet music his mother had selected, and the ivory middle C from their piano.

His father's small package he opened last. A rusty key fell out, and Janusz held it up, puzzled at first. Then his eyes met his father's. His father mouthed only one word –"shed".

****

Thomas slid the bedding underneath the sofa some time before the sun rose and after the last bomb had fallen. He had tiptoed into the bedroom where April, Helena, and Zosia were sleeping.

Janusz could hear his father whispering to his mother. He knew he would remember everything on this first day of his eighteenth year; the early morning hours held the worse bombings since it all began, and the putrid odor of death and debris overpowered the sweet smells of the last days of summer. Perhaps, those smells of summer only existed in his fond memories of what 'used to be'. The line between the present and the past cut thin like a razor's edge - so thin that 'What was' and 'what is' blurred his sense of reality. He felt sorry for himself; his seat in the University's privileged music conservatory, the beginning of a promising career as a classical musician - both consumed by the burning acrid smoke of the constant bombs.

Turning his back on his father as though he were to blame for this overwhelming hardship, Janusz did not want Thomas to see the shame in his eyes. Thomas placed a firm hand on his son's shoulder and forced him to turn around.

"Take care of the women. I will return by noon. Have everything ready to leave - with or without me. Janusz, do you understand?" he did not move until Janusz looked him in the eyes.

"With - or without me. 'Zakiada sie.' It is understood?"

"Yak, Papa" And like a young child he threw his arms around his father's neck. "I understand"

Thomas rubbed his hand through his son's fine blond hair and pressed his lips to his cheek. "God will give you - will give us the strength to carry our burden."

He left without looking back and by mid-morning he had not returned. April paced the floor.

"I am going to find him. He said he was saying his last good-bye's to Bernard before detonating the key entrance points into the city."

"I know some of the names of those bridges and roads. They talked about them on Silver Street Restaurant the day after the radio broadcast from Gdynia." Janusz said.

"I'm not leaving without him, and you're not going off yourself. I don't want to lose both of you." April's statement was more to herself than to Janusz.

Zosia could see her dear friend was trying to push down the panic she felt. "We will all go together." Zosia knew that April was thinking with her heart, not with her head.

"I take care of Helena. My radio still is working." Stanislaus assured them all.

"We'll all go to his office first maybe he had to..." her voice trailed off. They had not planned it this way. They needed to have left by now. 'The answer lies somewhere out there in what is left of Warsaw. If we cannot find him by nightfall, we'll have to leave without him.' She thought of his warning this morning. Thomas had told her twice to leave without him - by noon. It was already well past noon on this 25th day of September 1939.

The Round Up

"Schnell, Schnell," the colonel with the tall leather-riding boots yelled as he used his riding croup to beat those Polish civilians nearest him.

Bernard Berwerski whispered to Thomas. Thomas looked at his friend and colleague and realized for the first time that Bernard was no longer the young man with whom he had begun his career at the Poly Tech. Both were closer to middle age now. Thomas said nothing as he saw the colonel whip his horse and send it plundering through the crowd.

"He's killing us," an old man yelled as the horse trampled those not quick enough to run from the powerful hooves and flanks. A half dozen men fell, writhing in the dirt and dust, as the colonel, croup in hand, let it whip across the face of Bernard.

"Ahh", Bernard screamed and automatically covered his face with his hands. When he pulled them away, they were wet with blood.

"Into the stable. Into the stable." Another soldier ordered.

"No talking or this will happen to you," the colonel reached down from his horse and pulled Bernard up from his collar and let him fall back into the dirt.

"Pick your friend up. Carry him in." another soldier ordered.- In the stable the odor of manure, musk, and morning dew held itself in a tight fist, but there was another smell that permeated the hay beneath their feet. Just at that moment when his eyes got accustomed to the dark, he felt his shoe touch something soft. He looked down to avoid stumbling and saw beneath the hay - a leg. As the others pushed him forward, he saw hundreds of men lying face down in the straw from one end of the stable to the other. The smell of urine wafted up from the hay as each new man shuffled in.

Soldiers with machine guns at their hips lined the stable walls. In front of each cord of men lying face down was another upright man in an impeccable gray uniform with shiny buttons and a stiff black collar at the throat. What amazed Thomas was their youth, and handsome faces, marred by vacant pure blue eyes and expressionless mouths.

One of them prodded him with the barrel of his gun, "You, lie down. Over there with the others." Thomas walked over to the mid-section of the stable near the front of a stall. He noticed that most of the horses had been taken from their stalls and in their place were the wounded, the dying, or the dead. His stall just smelled of manure, and the horse in it shifted restlessly.

The same soldier grabbed Bernard by the shoulder, pulled his hand away from his face, and said something to the solder behind him. Thomas could not hear, but he did hear the universal derisive laugh, which followed.

"Yah, put him with them. He be of use for a time."

Bernard fell on his knees next to Thomas and the soldier pressed him the rest of the way down with the hobnailed heel of his leather boot. This time Bernard said nothing. Thomas looked at his face, painted with panic, and gave him a sideward calming glance before looking beyond his head to the rest of the men filing in.

The bludgeoning and beatings continued as the soldiers forced the men into the dank dark stable. They separated the men according to age, and Thomas, by turning his head slightly, could observe the far end of the stable. He noticed the young were made to lie in the middle of the stable in a circle whereas the old sat near the stalls of the unusable.

As the hours passed, the oven-like heat baked those in the stable. "How many more can they fit in and for what purpose?" His mind tried to put time into perspective. He had arrived at the Poly Tech at 5:00 this morning and found to his surprise many of his colleagues already there. Each had their own agenda and the only words spoken were "good luck", "be careful", "God go with you," each uttered as the men sorted through personal and professional papers. Thomas had taken care of everything prior to their final luncheon four weeks ago. The weeks had passed as years. Their well-ordered lives had vanished.

Thomas came to give his last good-byes to a place he had loved and to which he had given his youth. He walked through the remaining corridors, laboratories, meeting rooms, and archives. In a daze he nodded out of habit, yet his face held a certain frozen grimace. He continued to nod at all the faces he had known through the years and all the ghosts of those who were no longer there. Had they left that first day in September or had they been killed in the bombings which followed? He already knew that this was only the beginning of thousands of unanswerable questions. Before he had left that morning, he had heard rumors of round-ups. German troops were rounding up men – in or out of uniform. "Keep Janusz inside with the others. I will return before noon, and we will make our way to the northwest corner of the city." He had told her. "I have two things to do before our escape."

When he turned up the stairs into the wing of the infrastructure departments, all was quiet. The offices he passed were empty including those on either side of his office. He stepped over the threshold and closed the door behind him. Crossing over to the bookcase, he pulled out one of the red leather bounded books on the far end near the window. Behind it slept a German Luger. He lifted up his right trouser leg and strapped it into the special holster that accompanied the gun that had belonged to April's father. He was looking out the window when the knock came on the door. He reached down for the gun.

"Thomas, you are in there?"

"Yak, Bernard. It is me."

Bernard gently pushed open the door. A smile flashed

across his face. "So good to see you my friend," Bernard placed two hands on Thomas' shoulders and pulled him forward in a firm bear hug. He patted his back and then looked into Thomas' eyes.

"So, you will leave tonight, yes?"

"Yes, we must. And you?"

"My wife wants to stay. Her mother and sister are here. And where are we to run?" He said powerlessly.

"The question remains – what will become of Warsaw once they take over for good?" he paused to once again look out onto the charred ruins. "Our courtyard was bombed last night. The Steins and the Leibers didn't survive. No sounds last night. Nothing. And nothing this morning."

He pulled Thomas again to his chest and tightly squeezed him. Over the years, the bear-like hug had lost its intensity but not its warmth.

"You need to take care of your own," he said. "Why are you still here? Go!"

"One last thing, Bernard. Come with me." He began to walk toward the library.

"I've already checked, Thomas. The plans are still there."

"And the shed?"

"Yes. I've left my key under the large stone at the end of the path. I told Martin, for he too will remain in Warsaw. We've all moved into the stone house at the end of Arbor Road. There are rooms underground from an old vegetable store room."

"Good. After this is over I want to know where to find you." Thomas did not add… "and we will be in London.".

And Bernard did not ask. If tortured, a man could not divulge any information that he did not know.

Neither spoke, for the question was unspeakable. How long will after be? They walked in silence toward the Poly Tech Library. In their minds the tasks were turning. Step by step, they went over what had to be done before the heavy-booted Germans marched in. They entered the last corridor of cool marble and ancient artwork that bridged the working domains from the privileged world of knowledge.

They swung open the oak library doors and the light

from the corridor flooded in. Thomas turned around and looked
back down the corridor. Was that a dark head or just a shadow?
He looked at Bernard who showed no concern. Thomas
shrugged his shoulders in annoyance over his reaction and
closed the doors behind him.

He took measured steps to the bookshelf and extracted
the Bible. Afterward, he tried to recollect how long it took to tell
Bernard which bridges had already been detonated. They had
unfolded the tissue paper thin maps from inside the Bible, and
section by section Thomas pointed to the exact spot where the
sleeping fuses lie. These were the bridges and thoroughfares that
were wide enough and strong enough to hold the venomous
Panzer division tanks Hitler had unleashed. Thomas had agreed
to detonate all those bridges and roads in the north and
northwest sectors. Dividing up the blueprints, each man took
what they had agreed upon and reviewed it one more time.

Thomas left after Bernard. He placed the Bible back on
its shelf, walked over to the massive stone fireplace, and carefully
dropped his blue print sections into the embers from Bernard's
sheets. As Bernard had done, Thomas waited for each sheet to
catch fire before he added the next one.

Then he walked into the sunlight and into the waiting
arms of the Gestapo.
****

"Age? Rank? Address? Profession?"
'"Yah, the intelligentsia. Take him!"
`More and more tumbled into the mass of men being
forced through the streets and marched to the far corners of the
Warsaw's periphery. As they were herded through Oak Tree
Square, he saw Bernard at the corner of Gold Street - being
pushed into the center of the mass. Thomas pushed forward and
Bernard forced himself back until they were side by side. Neither
looked nor spoke to the other. Only two hours before, they had
embraced and said their good-byes.

Now they were lying on the floor of the stable. Bernard
reached his hand under the hay to press against Thomas.
Thomas turned his head slightly to the left to see Martin stumble
in and fall to his knees in the middle of the circle. Next to him
was the dark haired young man from the same department. He

remained standing, talking to the tall soldier in charge of the middle circle.

"Nein", the German soldier shouted, and as he kicked the dark haired man down, a book fell out from beneath his jacket. As the tall soldier bent to pick it up, the dark haired man nodded his head and pointed to it.

Thomas could not hear what was being said, but the audible gasp from Bernard was clear. The soldier turned his head and the dark haired man peered across the stable to see Bernard's and Thomas' eyes fixed on the Bible in the soldier's hand.

"Get up!" the tall soldier shouted to Martin and motioned to two soldiers by the back wall. Their heavy footsteps sounded through the hay as they ran with guns pointed at Thomas and Bernard, lying motionless side by side in the hay. Neither soldier noticed the imperceptible movement of Thomas' far hand as it slid down his leg to rest on his shin.

"Cowardly swine. Son of a bitch." Bernard screamed as he leapt to his feet and sprung on the traitor from his department that he had nurtured. "I'll kill you."

In the shuffle the tall soldier dropped the Bible and fell backward. Martin had his opportunity. He spun around, kicked the soldier in the side, and pulled the gun from the German's holster. Thomas heard the click of a safety release and saw Martin lunge for the Bible now buried in the hay.

****

The Search

The twenty-minute walk from their courtyard to the Poly Tech had cost April, Zosia, and Janusz two hours. The face of the huge clock affixed to the Poly Tech's main entrance rang two heavy strokes as half its hour pointed to the two and the rest dangled somewhere between the five and the six. The stress of finding every other road blocked by fallen stone and the eerie emptiness of the remaining buildings and streets had unsettled the three of them. They had inched their way through a living graveyard towards where they hoped Thomas would be found.

No one was inside the Poly Tech. Doors stood open. The buzzing of flies mingled with the heat of the once cool corridors. A metallic burning odor permeated the air. They tried to listen, but the sound of their footsteps echoed too loudly in their ears. Janusz advanced to the lead position some time during their journey. Not even he could recall the exact moment when he had positioned himself in front of the women. Like people discovering a new frontier, they tiptoed up the stone steps leading to the Infrastructure wing where Thomas' office lay – vulnerably in the middle of the last corridor.

"Mama, stand back. I'll open the door," Janusz whispered. He held his breath to steady himself for what might be. April heard his audible sigh of relief and knew the worst was not there, but neither was Thomas.

She walked over to the bookshelf and pulled out the red book at the far end of the shelf. She reached her hand up and felt the empty space. "He was here."

Neither Janusz nor Zosia questioned her statement.

"Mama, there's one more place he might have gone. Stay here, but keep the door open like the rest of the offices. If you hear anything, just stand behind the open door."

"Your father might be home by now. We're running out of time, Janusz." Zosia added.

"He might be in the library. Give me ten minutes."

Janusz tiptoed through the corridor then to the halls that led to the library. As he inched his way along the wall, his hand felt the smooth shut doors of the library. He put his ear to the doors and then flung them open - half in anger, half in despair. He grabbed the back of a chair to swing it against someone, but no one was there. He ran across the marble floor to the far-left wall to ceiling mahogany bookcases. Several empty spaces gaped out. Had his father pulled out all of these to conceal one empty space or had others borrowed them during normal times? His hands touched the empty spaces and the books on either side. He was certain. The Bible was gone.

Quickly, he glanced at the tables around the room. All were empty. He ran past the heavy draped windows to the opposite end of the library to check the shelves beneath the two tables on either side of the fireplace. Just before the last window he stopped to look out. He pulled back the gold drapes and jumped back.

"Have they seen me?" he thought.

He crawled back to another window and peered out. There on either side of the shed near the back entrance through the garden stood two German soldiers. One was smoking while the other appeared to be talking. With machine guns tucked under their arms and Lugers still in their holsters, they stood. Janusz involuntarily clutched at the leather pouch beneath his shirt and felt the key in the corner next to the knife.

Stepping backwards, he passed the fireplace and felt a bit of warmth from the charred remains. He peered into the embers and saw the curved silhouettes of what appeared to be pages curled over a chunk of partially burnt wood. With the iron poker he stabbed at the remains until they disintegrated in a gray puff. He stood up slowly and stared into the fireplace. Abruptly, he ran from the room. He did not shut the door.

****

Approaching the courtyard of the former language wing, Janusz felt some of the tenseness in his neck dissipate. "We're back home. Safe as long as we can continue to evade the German patrols." He thought.

In silence they quickly pressed their backs into the hot stone of the wall. The trio, blending into the fallen stone and broken trees, watched as groups of Polish men were herded past them at gunpoint. None were Thomas.

"Where are you father? Sealed safely within our tower walls?" Janusz thought. "If not, we'll have to leave without you." Janusz raised his hand and motioned for April and Zosia to follow.

When they reached the largest of the uprooted chestnut trees, Janusz spoke out loud, "Stay hidden beneath these branches. I will come back for you after I make certain the halls are clear."

"I must go too." A sharp unfamiliar edge had crept into his mother's voice. In the past he never would have contradicted her.

This time he softly said, "We do not want to lead any of them to Helena or Stanislaus. If father is already home, I will return."

"April, let Janusz go. He's right." Zosia urged her friend. She saw the calculated sense of reason in his eyes.

April nodded and Janusz began his climb through the rubble and into a shattered classroom window hidden by one of the broken defeated chestnut trees.

****

The Women

"He's been gone too long."

"Not more than twenty minutes, April. It just seems interminable."

"Ten more minutes. That's all." April said as she pulled off her cap and twisted her blond hair into a knot on the top of her head. She pulled the cap back over her head and pushed in the strands of wet hair that lay plastered to her neck and forehead. She scanned the windows of each room hoping to see something or someone, anything to indicate what course they should take.

She reached into her back pocket and pulled out a handkerchief to mop her forehead and pat the sweat from her eyes. She peered up into the windows of the tower. Her hand stopped and the handkerchief paused.

"Look up, Zosia. Someone passed by the bedroom window." Both began to move toward the rubble which was once their home.

"What roads lead out?" she thought. "Those streets that curl through Warsaw and out through the country- how many have turned to rubble like this courtyard? What other routes exist? Thomas would know. But Thomas is not here." She forced such thoughts out of her mind. She stepped inside the building now and began to creep towards the tower.

Through the connecting rooms they passed, pausing first in order to detect any unusual noise. It was not until they climbed the second staircase that they heard a heavy object fall somewhere above their heads.

"Let's separate." April said as she motioned that she was going up. Zosia nodded in agreement and began her descent toward the basement to Stanislaus and Helena.

As she inched her way up to her home, April strained to hear any other sounds. She thought she heard the shuffling of feet, but perhaps it was the trees brushing against the broken glass. Intermittently, a soft wail like that of a trapped animal emitted from the other noises. She did not know if it was Winston, the wind, or simply her imagination.

The apartment door was open. She stopped in her tracks and pressed her back against the stone of the stairwell. A wail echoed within the narrow corridor and with it a chill went through her heart. It was a human cry. Then she heard the harsh German voices.

"Why torture her more. She's no good to us."

"Perhaps, she know where there is money and jewelry."

"She knows nothing. Polish dirt. Let's do her now."

"If the others find out, they'll kill us for screwing a Polish slut."

"They won't find out. I'll hold a knife to her throat, and when you're finished, it's my turn. Then we'll cut her throat when we don't want any more."

April froze. They spoke in German, dressed in German uniforms, but their accents were Russian. Russians, speaking a German Helena found difficult to understand. Then she heard Helena scream. April crossed the threshold into what was once her home.

"What's going on in here?" She shouted out in English. She waited until one of the soldiers appeared. Big and stout his red face glared at her, and he shouted in German for his friend to come.

April did not acknowledge that she understood what he said.

"Get out of my house. I am an English citizen." She stepped forward toward the bedroom and from the open door she saw Helena curled in a fetal position of the bed, her fingers gripping the ripped blouse around her breasts.

"Ah this is better. We have an 'anglez' with more experience." The fat one laughed coarsely. "She won't scream."

"We'll rip through her 'anglez' snootiness. She'll be begging us for more," the other said without moving his thin razor straight lips.

"What do you want from us? I live across the hall and work at the English Embassy." April said in slow English, as they stood frozen in front of her in a twisted Grecian frieze. She repeated her lie again in Polish, but again there was no response.

"What the hell is she saying? Goddamn foreigners can't speak German. Try Russian."

"It doesn't matter. They'll blame it all on the Germans. Let's smile and move toward her."

April gripped the door jam and said smiling in slow deliberate Polish, "Stand up and move toward the outside hall doorway, Helena. Then run. Find Janusz or Zosia. Don't look back."

"Maybe she's a whore."

"They'll all whores," the fat one grunted. His strong hand grabbed and twisted her wrist. "Now we'll see what you can do 'anglez' whore." He yanked her into the room.

Helena lunged for the door – but her half way effort was blocked by the other Russian who pulled her back by her hair as the fat one ripped off April's blouse with his free hand. April made no move to cover her nakedness. She stared defiantly into his small pig like eyes and said in English, "Let her go. You can't want a child in place of a woman." She motioned her arm toward Helena as she spoke

"Take the young one to the kitchen. Don't contaminate yourself again with the Polish one...yet." We'll see what this one can do." The fat one let the harsh words like grease slide out of his mouth.

"Don't fight for me. Look for your one moment of escape. Kill him if you can." April spat the words out in hatred… and in Polish.

****

The Russian soldier bound Helena to a kitchen chair with the lace curtains he had ripped off the window so he could settle down for a snack. A large kitchen knife stood straight up in the kitchen table as he slid out a kielbasa from the icebox. He put the sausage to his nose and sniffed before digging his teeth into it and hungrily bit off chunks.

Helena gazed in shock into the empty doorway that led to the outer hall. She clenched her jaws and wished her hands were free to block out her mother's moans that penetrated the thick warm air of a September. As the moans turned into a piercing cry, something in the hall caught Helena's eye.

"Come, Wilhelm," a guttural panting command came from the bedroom. "The English whore is losing her fire. Let's both heat her up. Then I'll leave her just to you before we kill them both." he said in Russian.

He wiped his mouth on the sleeve of his uniform before pushing his chair away from the table. As he passed into the bedroom door, Janusz's face appeared in the darken hall. Helena gasped, but the Russians were too busy to hear. Janusz placed a finger in front of his lips to silence her and crept to peer into the bedroom. He froze at the debauchery he saw. His mother's dazed eyes locked into his, and she pulled her head to the side beneath the fat one's legs to motion her son back to Helena.

He stepped backwards and across to the kitchen table. With shaking hands he pulled the knife from the table and cut Helena's bonds. In both arms he lifted he up and carried her to the bookshelf. Gently, he rested her against the wall and slid out the book to open the secret passage. She moaned as he pushed her into the opening. He heard one of the Russians shout, and quickly he jumped in beside her and shut the case. With one hand over his sister's mouth, he fumbled with the other, searching for his pouch and Stanislaus' gift. "Had he left the other knife in the table or resting on it?"

Heavy footsteps clamored across the wood planked kitchen floor. "She's gone," he called back to Wilhelm in the bedroom. "One less bitch to kill," he muttered as he lifted up the butcher's knife on the table and sliced off another piece of sausage.

****

Zosia found her way back down to the cellar apartment and Stanislaus' badly beaten body. She hardly recognized his face - so bluish and beaten that it sickened her, but she lovingly washed the blood from his eyes and mouth as it kept oozing despite her cleanings. She knew he was bleeding internally. It did not take him long to die. Afterward she took Winston off his chest and wrapped a wet towel dipped in vodka around the knife wound that had almost severed the cat's front leg. She opened the door with a bundled Winston. Holding him tight to her chest, she began the slow climb up to find April.

The apartment door was open. Without hesitation she walked into the kitchen and came face to face with the soldier whose stained sweaty T-shirt barely covered his fat stomach. She noticed his right arm was streaked with claw marks and held Winston even tighter.

"Have you come to join us?" the Russian smirked, advancing toward her as she circled behind the table. "We got another one, Wilhelm. Perhaps, another 'anglez'. Cat got your tongue pretty one?"

Russian swine", Zosia spat out in Polish.

"Speak only Polish," the faint voice of April called out. Zosia turned toward the hall. At that moment, the fat Russian leaned over the table, grabbed her arm, and Winston was set free to dig his claws again into the Russian's flesh.

Putting his hand to his face, the Russian yelled, "Bastard cat. This time I'll make sure you're dead." With his left arm, the soldier groped for the cat as he tried to keep his hold on Zosia, but his balance shifted, In that moment she reached for the knife and drove it into his neck.

"Polish whore" he yelled as he fell to the floor,

Zosia knew she had cut his aorta, but what she did not know was that Janusz was inside the hidden room. At the Russian's cry, Janusz jumped from behind the bookcase and motioned Zosia back into the dark hidden room. He flattened himself to the far side of the kitchen door just as the other Russian soldier stepped into the kitchen. At the sight of his dead friend, he automatically lowered the Luger.

He did not see Janusz lunge for his wrist, but he did feel the gift from Stanislaus plunge into his side. In a scream of agony the Russian with his free hand pulled the knife from his bleeding side. With his two hands now on the Russian's wrist,

Janusz flipped his hand and the Luger backward until it fell halfway down the hall toward the bedroom.

"You snot-nosed kid. I kill you before I die," he yelled as he forced his bleeding stomach into Janusz and pushed him into the wall.

Janusz brought both his hands into one fist and swung up into the Russian's groin. Screaming in pain and rage, the remaining Russian forced his hands up to encircle Janusz's neck.

"Son of a pig. You Russian trash," Janusz choked out in German as he fought against the pressure crushing his throat.

"So, you speak German," he panted out in measured breaths. He held his side with one hand and with the other lifted Janusz up by the throat. "Then let me tell you what I do to you before I let you die." He laughed as he spit up blood into Janusz's face.

"Nein. Let me tell you in German that your Lugar is pointed at your head."

Both glanced sideways to see the naked woman fiercely steadying the Lugar with both hands. "Release the boy," April spat out in precise German.

In shock from loss of blood and from the realization that she had understood everything, he lost his grip on Janusz. Janusz, not taking his eyes off his mother, fell to the ground.

"Now die – at the hands of 'one less bitch to kill'."

Janusz never saw the shock on the Russian's face, for his eyes never left his mother's, glowing in hatred – painted into a porcelain calm rage, as she coldly pulled trigger.

****

When Thomas Puratski opened Stanislaus' apartment door, he did not expect to hear the click of a Luger – or to see it in the firm grasp of his son. Zosia and Helena were crouched behind the chairs ready to spring like young lionesses. He learned soon enough that they acted as a lair of cats, against a pair of wolves, now. In those hours of his absence he learned the horrible truth. His son was no longer a boy, his daughter no longer a child, and his wife, no longer whole. She lay crushed in the darkness in the bedroom at the end of the hall.

When he came out, his face was ashen and in a monotone he asked Zosia where they had buried Stanislaus. She told him that he, along with Winston, were beneath the only remaining courtyard chestnut tree. They had placed rubble from the fallen buildings as a headstone to mark the spot.

"If only I had never gone...our family... our lives would still be ....intact." he bent his head and covered his face and began a senseless monologue. "They rounded us up like cattle from their lists with our names and herded us to the riding stables on the outskirts of the city. Many, I recognized many – librarians, teachers, officers, politicians, and many from the Polytech.... Martin and Bernard."

He lifted his head and wiped his eyes "Both probably dead...Martin instantly... trying to grab the Bible that no longer held the blueprints. A wasted effort... like mine. To go for what... the pages we ripped out and burned ... all the blueprints. And Bernard... shot following me out of the stables. I could not even turn around at the thud of his body hitting the ground."

****

It was 8:00 p.m. and what was left of the city skyline was shrouded in gray smoke when they left through the North of the city. Janusz and Thomas took turns carrying April as she tried not to cry out in pain. Through the side streets and bombed out buildings, they crept - halting when they saw uniformed men or lines of timid civilians. As a diversion and no longer as a patriot, Thomas backtracked to detonate the shed. The key he had given Janusz the night before - a lifetime ago - no longer had any use. No clues would remain to be used by the enemy against the Poles or against those parts of the world still free. He pushed down the thoughts of those free countries that had just stood by waiting - watching.

The shed detonated. Thomas did turn back to see if the guards were left alive. He continued forward, wreaking havoc on this enemy he now hated with a vengeance. As he detonated the last bridges of his beloved city, he led his family through this last act upon the darkened stage of Warsaw. All the way to the sea, none would look back.

Chapter 4 – April 1940 France

Luc Dubois looked out over la Manche. On this day the English Channel appeared steel gray cold, but unusually calm for April. He looked down the steep slope to the sand where miles of coastline stretched until the cliffs to the east jaggedly cut through the horizon. He could not see the isle of Great Britain nor beyond to the United States of America. "Those immense powers," he spoke to the void. "Why don't they stop Hitler?"

He, along with millions of Frenchmen, wondered why neither had come to Poland's aid last fall when the screams of Warsaw slashed the September skies. Yet, he knew the reasons. Division. Every French family had relatives lining up on different sides. Those who believed that flinging themselves in front of the German war machine would stop it in its tracks before it began to gnaw its way through France, and those who believed that by stepping aside, Poland would be the last sacrifice for Germany's plate. His own brother, Denis, stood with the latter.

A sardonic smirk crossed Luc's lips as he thought of Denis and his comment. "If France in turn becomes 'le dessert' – the dessert, so be it." According to his brother, Germany had a lot to offer. "If France could be France without the Jews, then maybe that's all the machine wants. Once its belly is full, it will be satiated. And anyway, why worry, 'le vieux general' Petain feels the fortified line along France's northeast border will keep the Germans out" was what he and so many other Frenchmen were saying.

Luc clenched his jaw whenever he heard that logic. The wind blew his black hair across his face. He pushed it back, revealing a strikingly beautiful solemn face. His delicate features and full sensuous lips contrasted with a strong jaw, but when he smiled his entire face glowed with an angelic beauty so extreme that it stopped strangers – drop-dead in their path. Luc, however, was totally void of vanity, dismissing his looks long ago. His luminous fair skinned face, kissed with freckles, belied a devastating determination which existed just below the surface of his portrait-perfect profile.

He spoke out loud to the sea, 'Damn the Maginot Line – just how long can it keep the Boche out!"

"Dis donc, Luc – tu fais quoi?" his father shouted as he crossed over the pasture to the hill where Luc stood defined against the dark blue cloudless April sky.

"Rien, papa," Luc shouted back to his father as he turned to watch him cross the land that he and his father, grandfather, and great-grandfathers had owned   long before records had been kept. Luc knew that he, like his father, were called 'paysans'. In Normandy it held an endearing ring to be called 'farmer' 'countryman' by one's neighbors and friends. In Paris, to be called 'paysan' was an insult, yet Luc didn't mind the good natured joking by his Parisian friends. He was proud of his heritage and could fence with Parisian snobbery and slang alongside the city's most sophisticated – for his mother, Francoise, had taught him well. His father's heritage, however, gave him roots, dug deep into this rich farm land, high on the Normandy coast.

"You are always doing nothing, mon petit chou," Benoit Dubois chuckled as he placed both his large soil-worked hands on his son's shoulders and kissed one cheek and then the other. Luc let his head be moved from side to side as he had always done for most of his twenty-one years.

They stood side by side, each one's arm across the shoulder of the other – looking out to the Atlantic. Luc, taller by a head, had none of his father's breath or massive chest of the strong stout Norman stock, but rather his mother's Parisian agile lithe frame. Parisian born and bred, he was Norman by choice.

Benoit was the first to break the silence.

"Ever since you were a boy, you'd come out here, yes. To see the vastness of life, To see what lay beyond our hedges."

"I'm no longer a boy, Papa, yet I still come for the peace it brings my soul and the answers it gives my mind. But Now, I wonder for how long. How long will all this still be here? How long before tanks cross our pastures and soldiers step over our thresholds ...only to wait on these cliffs for the world to arrive on our beaches?"

"Always the questions and thoughts of tomorrow. You never seem to just enjoy today."

He might have responded 'only fools enjoy today without thinking about tomorrow' and jump into the ready-made arguments that he always had with Denis, his older brother, and sometimes when he lost patience – with his father. He would not let himself do that on this day, his last at home.

"War is all around us papa, and I fear our way of life will be no longer. Why they have not come to stop the Germans? Are they waiting for French blood to run across this land again?" He stopped and dug his fingers into the dirt, throwing a clump out to the sea.

Silently, Benoit Dubois turned his back to the sea and faced his vast rambling stone house with its barns and calvados 'cidrerie'. For generations their Dubois 'quarante ans', a venerable brandy was aged for 40 years in tightly crafted oak barrels. Their largest clientele were the Germans, with the English, and the Americans coming in second and third. Most of France considered it a coarse mediocre nectar.

"This land, this home is what kept me in one piece during the Great War. I cannot think of another war in which this time my sons might fight. It is too 'terrible' to contemplate. So I keep my mind on my home and let the politicians figure out the rest of the world."

With the old guard Benoit Dubois was comfortable believing the rhetoric of Marshall Petain and War Minister Edouard Daladier that the fortified line built on France's border would keep their northern neighbor, Germany out. The trench fighting of the Great War would be needed again. Benoit Dubois did not or chose not to understand that this war would not be kept out by a wall, for tanks were the new feet on which this war would tread. However, Luc's beliefs and faith lay in Charles de Gaulle, a young lieutenant who understood the future by learning from the past. What he wrote and what he spoke was that the Maginot Line would not restrain the new German war machine. Only tanks would.

He looked to the cold sea. A lone fisherman from Brittany was returning home with his day's catch. Steering his boat around the cliffs toward home, he waved to the two figures on the hill, high behind this flat stretch of beach beyond the coastal town of Colleville. One had his strong back to him gazing at the land, the other crouched at his side, looking out to the sea. Neither returned the wave.

"Paysans," the fisherman muttered to himself as he chugged on east to Arromanches.

****

Almost packed, Luc had wanted to finish before his mother called them for dinner. One last meal together before they had to again - pull apart. Placing his hands on the rough-hewed timber sill, he paused at the window. The smell of the sea filled his small room and the crisp cotton curtain caressed his hands as the wind blew across the wide planked floors. He breathed deeply of the fresh sea air and marveled at the darkness of the sea once the sun went down. Tonight though, a full moon and its rays played on the caps of the waves as they hit the beach. He could clearly see the edge of the beach as it met the ocean, and the white expanse from there to the cliffs.

He turned abruptly and folded the last of his cotton shirts neatly into his brown leather suitcase. His thoughts from this afternoon washed away. Ready for tomorrow's return to Paris and the final completions for this season's show, he had needed the fortnight back home to make ready for the hectic days of July.

"Ca suffit. That's it." He said out loud. "Three months until all the couturiers show their line. Then I'll be more than ready for an entire month back here." He firmly snapped the brass closings on the suitcase and buckled the two large supple leather straps to secure it shut.

"A table, Luc – tout le monde," his mother shouted from below.

"Oui, maman," he answered.

"D'accord, Francoise," Benoit answered his wife. "J'ai faim comme d'habitude."

She smiled to herself. She regarded his hunger as a complement to her cooking.

Denis was already at the table as his sister and mother were bringing in the 'salade mixte' and the red bowl of 'oeufs durs'. By the time his father and brother came to the table he was half finished with the delicately arranged green lettuce leaves Francoise had artistically arranged.

"Denis," his father admonished. "You could not wait for us? Or perhaps for your mother and Juliette to be seated, non?"

'Ouais,' he abruptly said with egg oozing from the corner of his mouth. "I could not wait."

"Bon! Denis. You will wait for the next course." Francoise curtly said to her oldest son. "You will not spoil another meal. This one especially."

"You are returning to Paris, oui? That is good. Normal we can be. No more fancy meals. She can leave us real men behind." He waved his hairy bare arm across the expanse of the lace tablecloth which covered the polished burled walnut table. Nearly knocking over his crystal glass of red wine, he lunged with his other hand and grabbed it with primitive agility. Hungrily, he swilled it down.

A slow rage crept across Benoit's face.

"'She'... 'she' is your mother. The best table in this province she sets for us. Look around you," he gestured with his first two fingers at the matching armoire with its intricate apple blossoms carved into the headpiece and legs, and the equally exquisite table and chairs with their turquoise brocade cushions – dotted with pink and white blossoms. The matching table and chairs sat on the Chinese rug that had been in the Morneau's Paris home along with the blue and white vases, gracefully sitting on the long sideboard above which hung a muted oil painting of the Seine at Argenteuil that gazed serenely over the room.

"All this is home. Elegant. Peaceful, Filled with beauty. After a day's work in the pastures and barns I need to feel 'civilized'," he smiled at Francoise as he said this.

It had always been a joke between them from long ago when he first saw the beautiful young girl whose parents had rented the 'gite' on the other side of the main road which led to Colleville. His mother had sent him over with a bottle of their Calvados, a circle of camembert packaged in the round thin wooded case labeled 'Maison des Dubois' like the Calvados, and a trio of baguettes wrapped in brown paper to whomever leased the old Deneuve gite for the summer

That particular summer he had turned eighteen, not much older than Juliette who now sat across from him. Almost twenty-five summers had passed since then, and now they not only had two sons but this sixteen-year-old daughter, with her ivory skin and dark hair who resembled Francoise – even down to her mannerisms.

"We know Papa," Juliette cajoled. "The civilization story again." She pretended to pout and took a sideways glance at Luc. She always managed to defuse the tension with her constant high spirits and pantomime. She caught his eye.

"Maman was so lovely..so..so..'parisienne', 'chic', talented – a breath of springtime." She paused for effect, waving her fork gracefully in front as though it were a baton. "and how she could prepare a 'pot-au-feu' and such 'tartes des pommes' – exquisite." She popped her fork into her mouth.

Luc's tight mouth broke into a wide grin and lit up his face.

"Such an actress,' her mother laughed.

"So, I will tell again the 'civilization story' as you call it, one more time – for me was well as for the 'uncivilized' one, your brother, Denis." Juliette finished chewing a few leaves of the 'salade mixte' turning the fork over before she removed it from her small perfectly porcelain mouth. She looked at her father intently as he began to tell the story she loved and had heard so often.

Denis just snorted as he sullenly looked at his empty salad dish. He poured another glass of wine and refused to meet his brother's stare.

"Naturally, when I was invited into the old Deneuve house, I was 'etonne'. So surprised was I to see all the changes. From a Norman farmhouse to a Paris home – the transformation, 'incroyable'! Beautiful flower filled vases in every room and shiny silver lamps with delicate fluted glass shades. No heavy brown drapes to keep out the cold sea winds but fragile lace curtains blowing inward from the sea breeze. Lace everywhere –tables, settees, chairs. When Madame Morneau, votre grand-mere offered me a seat, I did not know where to sit. My pants were dirty from milking the cows and cleaning the barns.'

"You sat quickly enough. Next to maman's 'petits gateaux', Francoise laughingly said. "How hungry yet polite he was – this big, strong boy. And such enthusiasm, he listened to Maman's stories of Paris life and of her husband's work as a tailor 'extraordinaire'. Art, fabric. Life... cuisine, he was interested in all."

"And you, most of all, ma cherie'.

""Oh, la, la', you did not even notice me," Francoise teasingly pouted.

"'Mais si, cherie' how could I not."

And so the story filled the five course meal. Each dish reminded one or the other of something they had seen or experienced in Paris or Normandy. Her love of the land and of the ocean was equaled by his desire to see beyond his limited acres, town, and province. Each anecdote was lifted to its peak by the questions and reminisces of Luc and Juliette. Even Denis began to add his memories after the pork dish and his fifth glass of Bordeaux.

Nothing in Luc's life equaled the bond that his parents shared. That summer of 1915 - during their youth - began as fast friends and ended - much later- as lovers. This commitment, nurtured in the fertile soil of Normandy, blossomed in the worldly air of Paris.

"Perhaps, this summer in Paris will be special for me, and I will find 'mon amour' my special someone," Luc thought as he looked across at his parents.

****

"'C'est l'heure'", his mother gently whispered as she knocked on his door.

"'Oui, je sais bien'", Luc answered as he rolled over and looked out the window to see the sun barely kissing the horizon. The waves still lapped the shore as a reminder that time would not wait.

His mother peeked in. "You are awake, 'non'?"

"'Oui', I am awake – but up 'non'." She crossed over to his bed and placed her hand on his unkempt dark hair. She sat down on the side and out of habit brushed the hair out of his eyes. Her scent of parfum de rose filled the room as it had since he was a little boy. He loved her smell and the feel of her soft cheek as she bent down to kiss him.

"Juliette has a hot bowl of 'café au lait' and fresh 'pain au chocolat'. She made them especially for you."

"Can't we take her with us this summer? She's tall enough now. We could use an extra model for the show."

"I know you want her to experience the Fall couture, but this will be her last summer here, home. This September begins her 'rentree' at your old college in Paris."

"Why did she not begin, as I at the lycee at thirteen?"

"Because you are you, and Juliette is Juliette."

"Always the same answer."

"Always the same question. 'Allons-y, cherie'; 'le pain et le chocolat' are getting cold, and we have a long drive to Paris." She rose from the bed, clicked across the room in her black high-heels, and gently shut the door as she left.

He lingered for a moment – a moment to shut his eyes – and to taste once again his childhood. Perhaps, his mother was right in wanting one last moment for Juliette. His job was in Paris; his sister's was here in Normandy, with their father. He could help take care of his mother; she would do the same for their father. Denis, as usual, would take care of no one but himself. With that last uncomfortable thought, Luc placed his bare feet on the floor, crossed to the porcelain wash stand, and poured cold water into the basin. He bent down and cupped his hands, letting the water splash down his face and chest.

****

Once in the car on the road to Paris all thoughts of their life in Normandy were slowly replaced with concerns about their profession in the city renowned for its haute couture. Luc, as his mother before him, had known that fashion would be his life. Francoise brought her sons to Paris after Christmas when she would accompany her own mother and father back after their long holiday in Normandy. Genevieve, his grandmother, doted on both boys, but his grandfather, Michel, had a particular fondness for Luc – perhaps, because he was more open and appreciative of their lives than Denis.

Even as a child, Denis was firm in his ways and stuck deeper than any tree in his Norman roots. He was out of his element in Paris and paced like a caged panther across the Chinese rugs in his grandparents' house on Avenue Georges V. His only interest was the walk up to the Pont de l'Alma to gaze at the water that ran beneath the bridge. Michel Morneu used to tell him of the Great flood in January of 1910 when the waters of the Seine had risen so high as to cover the chin of a Polish Second Empire soldier statue which decorated the base of this Napolean lll bridge.

Since this apparently was the only allure Paris had for him, and because he always taunted his younger and thinner brother, Francoise had begun to leave Denis home to help Benoit. She only took Luc for the two month stay when she helped 'grand-pere Michel' design, select fabric, and cut the suits for the spring and summer line.

Michel Morneau had been a tailor like his father, grand-father, and great grand-fathers before him. He of his ancestors who cut the cloth for the kings of France, but it was his only child, Francoise, who persuaded him to venture into the domain of the current 'queens' of France – those rich fashionable women who wanted a change after the end of the Great War. The 1920's provided that decade of change.

Francoise persuaded her father to include a line of 'little dresses; - basic, simple, chic, short, and black. Their work was done in the basement – a downstairs 'atelier' in their three hundred year old home on the chic avenue just off the Champs Elysees. In these workrooms little Luc would mimic the seamstresses' job. With the silk, cotton, and wool scraps he'd make his own clothing for his metal soldiers.

He grew to love the scent of women – their laughter and softness and constant chatter. He would quietly listen to their quarrels, gossip and minor conspiracies and watch how they'd interact with the men who would enter the atelier to have their waists remeasured to see if too much 'fois gras' had done its deed. At an early age Luc was aware that the women were no longer direct and self-assured in their presence, but became coquettish and submissive. They coyly asked the men's opinions and pretended to accept them without reservation. Only after they left would the women laugh at this monsieur or that monsieur. Like cats, preening and playing with their mice before they decapitated them, they toyed with these men.

Luc loved all the women and girls of the 'atelier' on Avenue George V. To these mother and sister cats he was their kitten and taken into their lair as one of their own. So therefore, it was expected that he would eventually leave the beaches and pastures of Normandy and make his way permanently to the streets and avenues of Paris. It was grand-pere 'Mich' who would teach him the intricacies of 'couture' after Genevieve's death.

****

By mid-afternoon they were packing up the remains of their lunch under the shady willow on the banks of the Seine south of Rouen. After a delicious 'dejeuner' of mushroom brioche, spinach salad peppered with orange slices, and crisp white chardonnay, they had finished with ribbons of apples from their orchards and fresh chunks of camembert.

"I'll drive now 'mon fils'," she said to him as he placed the basket in the trunk of the car. She had taken over the road, for she thought better when she drove. Hugging the narrow roads, the silver Renault curved and swayed as it followed the route of the Seine into Paris. She took the curves quickly and sharply judging each one with precision as she did her designs – sleek, yet shapely. as she approached.

The sun shot its last warm April rays across the roof tops of Paris, the Dome of Sacre Coeur, and all the way down the Butte of Montmartre.

"'Reveille-toi Luc," she said but did not need to. Luc, ever since he was a little boy, always awoke just as they passed through the outskirts of Paris. It was as if he could smell the scent of Paris and did not want to miss a moment of her promise. In late afternoon, Paris seemed to dress herself in Champagne-colored light. Francoise was driving more slowly now, down the Boulevard Malesherbes across the wide Boulevard Haussemann, just to the Place de la Madeline with its ancient church. The steeple glimmered gold in the last rays of the sun, as they crossed Avenue Saint Honore toward the Seine and down the Avenue Montaigne. He could see the bridge of Alma ahead as Francoise cut down Georges V past two great houses until they pulled in front of theirs, 'numero 9 Avenue Georges V'.

****

Six frantic weeks had passed since Normandy and Paris was dressed in her glorious robes of spring, but Luc Dubois barely had time to notice. He sat alone in a small café on the Rue des Freres Perrier - waiting for Simon, his boyhood friend from his first days in Paris. For a moment his mind slipped back in time as he enjoyed the view of the Eiffel Tower and the Seine which had slid her way into his heart and flooded into his memories like the great Atlantic of his Normandy had.

Today, on this particular May day, the light reflected off the Seine as though she were a diamond displaying her many facets, shimmering in indescribable beauty, yet he found himself gazing upward, following the sunlight as it trekked its way through the iron work of 'la Tour Eiffel'. He still marveled at this mass of metal erected more than fifty years ago and detested at first by every Parisian.

"'Boff'", he laughed out loud.

This supreme gadget of copper with its symmetry and intricacies appealed to the French mind of his generation. On its green plot of land since 1889, it was not until now that the Tower was considered a part of Paris' history. Ironically, it now served an even greater purpose. In the last six weeks few tourists were allowed to climb into its elevator. Instead, civil servants and military personnel paraded up and down her stairs. They recognized the Tower's superior height and construction as an ideal radio communication center.

Those few tourists who came to Paris this season arrived early and left early with their purchases. They could not wait until July for the couture shows, or more accurately, they feared there would be none. All of Europe could hear via the airways the news of Hitler's conquests and the declaration for peace that England and America promised, but few believed. How much his mother and grandfather believed Luc did not know, but he did know they had worked to make the collection accessible to their customers two months ahead of schedule.

Brief 'café au laits' rendez-vous's early in the morning on street corners in front of the 'kiosks' to trade information with friends became his only social connection. They had read all the headlines and believed Finland had been kept at war by Russia, to provide Germany with time to develop a plan to enter Denmark and Norway which it did later on April 9, 1940 about one month short of Finland's peace agreement with Russia. Countries could be gulped up in fewer than thirty days. Only Holland, Belgium, and Luxembourg remained as a buttress to France's north.

"How long would it be until Germany turns its eyes to France?" Luc continued to think as he gazed at the Eiffel Tower. "The connections need to be in place when that moment comes...when the unimaginable would inevitably be forced upon each citizen of France." Luc's dark thoughts etched into his face. When Simon simply appeared before him, Luc was caught off guard.

"'Ca va, mon vieux'", he reached out and grabbed Luc's hand to shake. He looked directly into his face. "But I can see you are not fine," Simon Delacroix said as he pulled up a café chair and waved to the garcon to come around.

"You will have to learn to conceal your thoughts better than that."

Luc shrugged his shoulders but said nothing as the waiter approached. The middle aged Parisian waiter with an air of authority whipped the linen napkin off his arm and adeptly brushed off the crumbs of the previous customer and handed two menus to the men.

"'Premierement, une bouteille de Saint-Emillion rouge'", Simon ordered as the waiter smiled his approval and then realized it was Simon and Luc who had their backs to him.

"To celebrate the finishing of your fall/winter collection. non?"

Luc's eyebrows went up as he heard Henri Galet's voice and felt his hand on his shoulder.

"Maman and Grand-pere's," Luc interjected.

"I will find you a good year for such a feat in these times, 'mes jeunes hommes'", the waiter of twenty-five years said. He had known his clientele all of those years, and he also knew his profession. Discretely, he left.

"The House will be yours one day. They have been grooming you for it since you were a 'petit enfant'", Simon said.

"Perhaps,.. if the war doesn't change all this," Luc gestured toward the Seine and upward to the top of the Tower.

Henri Gallet, the waiter and 'patron', returned and uncorked a bottle of St Emillon. With napkin over his arm, he poured and twisted the bottle upward so that just a mouthful was in Luc's glass. Luc swished the deep blood red liquid in his long stemmed glass, smelled its bouquet, and then let the nectar rest in his palate before swallowing slowly

"Superbe, monsieur Henri.. merci bien." Luc complimented the man who was a fixture for his family's Sunday restaurant dinners. Henri Gallet smiled broadly, left the bottle of wine uncorked in the sunlight, and moved on to his other customers.

"Thank you 'cher copain' for this excellent wine and for your dear friendship." Luc said. "You've been with me during the best of times and will be... God willing, for these worst of times that will soon be on our doorstep. May we survive... mon frère."

Each young man in the sunlight of the shimmering May early afternoon lifted his glass to the other and... to Paris. The sun shot through the glasses and the wine, like liquid fire, stopped time and branded the moment into their memories.

Luc lifted his knife and skillfully rotated the green apple as the skin peeled off in one long ribbon. "Do you think they will all act as each has spoken or are some just talk and no action?" He put down the skinned apple and sliced a thick piece of camembert.

"We can count on Jean-Paul, Robert, and Pierre, Gustave and their sisters Catherine, Elizabet, and Lucie." Simon rattled off the names of their childhood friends. "Also Laure - her brothers and sisters – and the Boileau brothers, Philippe and Gerard. Do not forget the nephews of Monsieur and Madame Claiborne – Matthieu and Jean-Philippe. These would lay down their lives. Of this, I am certain."

"'Ouais'. I am in agreement with you on that."

"However, some there are who are on the fence, so to speak. They might go one way or the other depending on what the future deals them. You know the ones I speak of?"

"Oui Simon, perhaps Pierre Lafayette, Richard Rimbaud. Laurent Givenchy, or Lisette Roche. These I do not trust. Even in our childhood they were weak and changeable as the wind. We cannot count on them."

"I have told them nothing of our plans. Have you, Luc?"

Luc looked at him in amazement. "'Mais non-certainement non'. I am not a fool."

"I never said you were. I just wanted to state it clearly. No room for error –or for false pride – can there be."

"You're right. Always direct. We'll need that in the months to come. To be certain we all know and communicate the correct and most essential information."

"I've left nothing out. Yes, I am certain I've listened more than talked to them The talk has been general.. to see how they sit with certain issues. I know they do not sit with us... at least, 'pas encore'."

"Even if that 'not yet' becomes a 'yes' in time, we cannot trust them. Their past has shown that they act on what is good for them. What profits only them. They are users not givers.. and 'bien sur' – certainly, not idealists nor even patriots. Simply put... they are 'egoistes'.

Luc realized, as he looked across the table at Simon, that all of the characteristics he had as a child were in the man. That sense of directness without effrontery, commitment without deviation, and moral fiber with fairness for all, as long as one did not cross him, were at the center of Simon. Luc knew, as he knew his own name, that this brown haired, brown eyed unassuming young man was more like a brother to him than Denis. Times and places would change, but people would not. Very few would change their core – perhaps, only their appearance like a chameleon.

Simon could detect this change, and this gift, Luc knew, would serve them well in the times ahead. Luc did not have Simon's instant ability to read a person and see the truth. He would have to learn. In the meantime, he would rely on Simon's uncanny discernment as he had when they first met in the lycee courtyard. Surrounded by the century old wings of the Lycee Henri IV, Simon had chosen him first in that cold stone courtyard. From all of his friends from previous years, Simon had wanted Luc on his team. As the game began, Simon quickly set Luc up with two skillful passes to kick the ball in for goals during the first five minutes of the game. It was at that moment that the partnership of a lifetime began – at noon on a cool summer day.

As though reading his mind, Simon said, "I chose well that September day so many years ago."

Some, at first, judged Luc on his physical beauty and refined mannerisms and interests, but the clever ones never made that mistake twice. In time, Luc's strength, fairness, and breeding were obvious to even the coarsest of the lycee boys in the 18th arrondissement. For once Luc had the facts, he was like steel. The judgments quickly followed. One either had to fight him or follow him. Most chose to follow. Few put him to the test, and if they did, they never did again. He was a natural leader.

Simon knew his friend was ready. The late afternoon sun lay low over the Seine. Sipping his coffee, he said, "The safe houses are set."

"All?" Luc's eyes locked with Simon's

"'Ouais'. Except for one in the 18ᵗʰ and the 10ᵗʰ."

"All the various metro stops we had agreed on are set: Abbesses,Concord,Denfert-Rochereau, Pere Lachaise, Alexandre Dumas, Emile Zola, and the rest. Jean-Paul even got Chatelet and Cite. With Notre Dame on our doorstep the Germans will have a bit of God's fear put in them. Pierre arranged for certain trains on each line that will jump the schedule or delay it for up to three minutes. He has access to keys for the connecting passages underground and even extra 'controleur' uniforms and 'comptoir' hats and shirts." Luc stated.

Simon knew the ticket men uniforms and countermen accoutrements would be lifesavers. He then stated what he arranged on street level – above ground. "The Claibornes have a safe apartment on the Rue de Kleber. Their nephews, Mathieu and Jean-Philippe, have set up a radio receiver and transmitter in the maid's room which has a tree high view of the Arc de Triomphe. Other apartments and rooms from Montmartre to les Tuilleries to les Jardins de Luxembourg to Bois de Boulogne are in place."

"Three more additional ones are set thanks to our seamstresses: La place de la Concorde from Rue de Rivoli, L'Etoile from la Rue de Haussemann, and south of Jardin du Luxembourg on Boulevard Saint Jacques. If the Germans come, that will be the place their generals will select. The most chic – non?"

Luc laughed as he thought of all the models and seamstresses that had befriended and even loved him. At first, as the 'petit-fils' of Michel Morneau and the 'fils' of Francoise Dubois, but then as a young man in his own right. Now he enjoyed their camaraderie and laughter at the men who came to the salon with the beautiful women who controlled them. The German military would be at their mercy – if it came to that.

"So, it seems that all is ready." Simon said.

"All we need to do now is wait." Luc steadied his gaze on his friend.

Their eyes met and they lifted their glasses with the last remains of wine. The sun glistened in the blood red dregs as each swirled the contents, clinked one another's glass, and swallowed in one gulp.

****

-

<u>1940</u>
<u>May 9</u>

The airwaves in Paris reverberated like lightening. "At 11:15 p.m. a general state of emergency has been declared in Belgium. Both England and France have been officially notified.

<u>May 13</u>

"Germany's lst and 10th armored divisions headed by General Guderian have crossed the Meuse River in Belgium. France's First Army and British divisions are poised to counter-attack. The Dutch Army in Holland is fortifying its defense to a fortress position."

The radio waves struck and slashed through each building, apartment, and room in France. But Luc and Simon's coterie got a different message than the official news reports. A communiqué from French headquarters stated that the 'enemy' had established strongholds at Namu, Dinant, Montherme and Sedan. The Maginot Line had been circumvented and the enemy occupied the center of Belgium.

That afternoon Luc, his mother, and grandfather heard the news from the BBC. The Dutch army was collapsing and Queen Wilhelmina and her government had taken refuge in London. Part of Churchill's speech from the House of Commons burrowed into his mind and chilled his soul: "I have nothing to offer but blood and toil and tears and sweat".

That too, he knew was all he could offer.

<u>May 16</u>

"Attention, attention citoyens, citoyennes de France.. ecoutez – Attention every French man and woman citizen..

listen. German General Rommel's 7th armored division has penetrated 90 kilometers into French territory toward Cambrai and has captured 10,000 French soldiers and 100 French tanks."

Luc turned off the radio in his black Renault convertible as he crossed onto Pont d'Alma. Once over the bridge, he turned left onto Avenue Georges V, slid the car onto the sidewalk right in front of number 9 and catapulted over the side of the car. Running past the design house front windows and entrance, he flung open the heavy iron gate on the side and ran through the courtyard and up the stairs to their apartment, over the main rooms of his grandfather's store front. He knew they all would be there close to the rooftops where the radio and transmitter picked up broadcasts from England and all over Europe.

The door to the living room was open as were the ancient floor to ceiling windows of the large iron gated balcony that faced the front of Avenue Georges V. His grandfather, mother, and six models and seamstresses sat or stood frozen, as though waiting for the curtain to end the act against the backdrop of the clear blue Paris sky. The sound effects, supplied by a large black radio with intricate glass bulbs and tubes, rested on a Chinese lacquer desk.

Francoise stepped out of the scene and came to kiss him.

"'Mon cher fils', you have hear the news?"

"'Oui maman,' the expected has arrived."

His grandfather rose from his chair and Colette, the new young model, helped him up. Simon crossed the room to him and his grandfather kissed him on both cheeks. "I have heard from an old and trusted client, one with inner circle connections with Premier Reynaud that the road to Paris is open."

"The fool has not yet declared Paris an open city has he?"

"That 'fool' is still France's leader, mon petit-fils," his grandfather gently reprimanded.

"Oui, I know grand-pere, but he should have listened to de Gaulle. The Maginot Line would have succeeded in the last war but not in this one - tanks and planes – yes, trenches- no."

Some of the women nodded in agreement. Others wept quietly.

"'Ecoute', Luc. Your grandfather has not yet said the "unannounced' news."

"Churchill is arriving this afternoon. The meeting will be at the Quai d'Orsay". Michel Morneau simply said as he returned to his chair with its view of his beloved city.

Francoise walked to the window and looked down the Avenue where French flags colored the street and flurried from balconies.

Who will be at the Foreign Ministry, Madame?" Colette murmured with her beautiful passive face.

"Reynaud, Daladier, and General Gamelin," Francoise answered.

"Daladier! What a Minister of National Defense he has been!" Gabrielle, the oldest and most valued seamstress, spat. "'Boff'". She walked to the window and stood next to Francoise. The street below was empty.

<u>May 17</u>

"Attention, we bring you crucial news of Colonel de Gaulle's 4th Armored Division counter attacks on the Third Reich's barbaric and flagrant military force on France."

Luc and Francoise had been up all night trying to get and send as much information as possible. They first contacted Benoit, Denis, and Juliette who were continuing to make all necessary preparations for the imminent German occupancy.

"These attacks have not halted Germany's assault on our soil,' the radio announcer continued. 'La Marseillaise', the national anthem, resounded in the background. Another voice began.

"This is Prime Minister Reynaud. Germany has been within our borders for more than twenty-four hours. As of yet, despite our treaties, there is no indication that Germany will withdraw. England is fighting along our side. Together we will fight on and push Germany back."

Luc turned to his grand-pere. "He'll call back Petain."

"'Petain', I spit on that name," Michel Morneau said from his chair. "The old have no business conducting this war.

He barely got us through the last one. Too many French sons lie in Flanders. I cannot live through another." He stopped in mid-sentence and looked out onto the Paris sky that held no trace of war. Only the outline of the rooftops, like a singular black silhouette, cut sharp against this mid-May day.

June 3

"Monsieur Morneau, you must come down, Madame Francoise has sent me, and Madame Gabrielle has threatened to box my ears if I do not return with you," Colette teasingly coaxed.

The blue May sky, like so many of her citizens, had fled Paris, and in its place clouds had appeared and darkness descended. The much needed rain, however, had not fallen. In its place were ink black clouds, carrying the thunder and decimation of the Luftwaffe.

"I feel comfortable here. I would rather face what is to be than hide."

"It is not hiding to return to your own home. Madame Francoise and Madame Gabrielle have been working hard all day making adjustments for next month's show."

Colette did not tell him of all the other preparations, overseen by Luc who spent the day with Simon. The two organized all last minute arrangements and ironed out any flaws in their system. She was not privy to the inner workings but knew they were taking 'precautions' as Madame Francoise had told her.

"There will be no show next month, and I think, 'ma petite', and these booms and lights in the sky will be our 'quatorze juillet', our Bastille Day celebration."

"Do not say such things. We will celebrate our independence day as Paris as always does. The flags will fly; the soldiers will parade down the Champs Elysees, and the planes will fly over la Tour Eiffel!"

Another boom resounded in the sky and an even darker cloud appeared on the horizon.

"I wonder whose soldiers and planes they will be?" he said softly to himself as he pushed himself out of the chair and away from the city, not yet dressed in defeat.

June 4-5

The free air waves burned like high tension wires with the news. Every home clamored with England's announcement. Every ear listened.

"Dunkirk has been evacuated."

Through his network Luc knew that between May 27 and up until the night of June 4 more than 338,000 men had been rescued from French soil, 120,000 French and Belgium. Every available ship dodged the Luftwaffe's bombs over the strip of channel between France and England. Private yachts, fishing boats, and the smallest dingy rescued men and only men. Guns, trucks, ammunition, fuel, and supplies were left on the French beaches. Men were the priority. Those weapons not destroyed were left, for the Third Reich to pick up like seashells –for their collection of machines of war.

Churchill's speech to the House of Commons rung out over the free world:

"We shall fight on the beaches; we shall fight in the fields... we shall never surrender."

June 10

Italy joined Germany in a state of war. France is now blocked to her south.

June 14

"Attention, attention ecoutez bien francais et francaises...

"Paris has been declared an open city. I repeat Paris has been declared an open city. There are no more available divisions and air support to stop the Third Reich. We will be occupied in a matter of hours. The bombings of last night were specifically aimed on our industrial sites in the suburbs of Paris. We are still transmitting from La Tour Eiffel..."

Luc seated on the Rue des Freres Perrier could not only hear but could see 'L'Eiffel. The French flag was still flying; Monsieur Henri had silently put a red bottle of Bordeaux on his table and sat by himself at one of the empty tables. As they both looked upward, the French tricolor on the Eiffel Tower was being lowered. Quickly, with fury and force the German flag ascended the tower. Black and orange marred the once free blue air.

The airwaves too turned to German. The official language took over, German phrases punctuated the Paris sky, and most Frenchmen turned off their radios.

Chapter 5 - June 1943 England

The British airborne company commander in blue and gray camouflage appeared more like a dapper Harrods's mannequin right off of King's Row than a British officer, yet his impeccable mustache and crisp British English conveyed without a doubt that he was in command. He spoke rapidly in a clipped staccato manner as he pointed to various marked areas on the large map behind him.

"You few men of the 6th Airborne division have been chosen because you are the best paratroopers. Of course chaps, you also have volunteered."

The dozen men in front of him laughed nervously. Sandy Johnson looked around at his mates. For the most part they were small men – compact and muscular. Their common denominator was agility and nerve. He knew they would need both this night.

The air borne division company commander continued.

"You will be dropped in at 800 feet along the coastline of Haute Normandie. Others have gone before you – three years ago to the month. That's how long we've been at this." He pointed to the map and continued. "According to our contacts the Germans have not yet fortified this area. You've trained for months so you know the drill. Disconnect and roll up your parachute as soon as you hit the beach. Get your sand samples and get off the beach. Your contact will find you. Listen for the mocking bird whistle. Whistle back. Then wait for him to whistle back twice."

Sandy and the other men knew that this was a dangerous mission; one they hoped would hasten the war's end. He thought about going home to the docks of Liverpool and being with his girl Beatrice, the Betty Gable of Liverpool he called her.

"Thanks to the bloody Yanks, she might have jumped the fence," Sandy thought. In London the British soldiers were lorded over by the bloody Yanks who were issued more than three times a British soldier's pay. All the English birds fell for them. "Maybe a few metals on me chest would make them see the light."

He was bored being confined to pastures and fields to practice jump after jump or to metal hangers on rainy days to jerry-rig bridges – build them and then tear them down, but the worse tedium was the classroom where some old frog lady taught them French day in and day out. He had hoped they could'a at least got a pretty 'mamsell'.

"Are there any questions?" he looked around at the solemn faces before him and wondered who would not come back. He did not mention the cyanide capsules again. Each man knew he could not risk being caught.

"O.K. then, this gentleman will fill you in on the rest." He took one last look at the map of the Normandy Coastline and that dotted area with the code name that only he knew: Sword Beach.

Sandy eyed the man standing before them. About his age but definitely an Irishman. Dressed like a farmer, he somehow had a European flair, and when he began to speak, Sandy detected an accent – not much of one, but to an Englishman or a Yank he wouldn't pass mustard.

"These towns - Langrune, Luc, and Ouistrerham Lion marked with red flags border this section of the French coast. You will be found as soon as you clear the beach by a man or woman from one of these towns. They will pass you through the underground and get you back to England. If by chance, you overshoot your landing mark and have no platoon, make your way to one of these towns and find a house or a farm with a carved rooster on its door. Tell them you come from the dressmaker – or 'le couturier'." He looked over the dozen men's faces. There were no questions.

At twenty-four, Luc was now taller and heavier by twenty pounds of sheer muscle. Once France had fallen he had wasted no time in joining the Free French Forces. As he looked over the heads of most of these English paratroopers, he saw the essence of a nationality, he had come to admire in the last three years.

"Now mates, let's see how much French you know,." he grinned as he began to speak in rapid fire French.

****

Every man, woman, and child on the isle of England could feel the shortages this year more than last, and last year more than the year before. They did what they had to do and did without – all for the 'war effort', all for the 'boys' who had to be well fed, clothed, and equipped. Luc admired their 'stiff upper lip' attitude. After Dunkirk in June of 1940 each Englishman and woman felt that one of the 'boys' evacuated ... one of the 'boys' left behind was their boy. Each household knew directly or indirectly a son, who had stood on the sand at Dunkirk, looked out across the Channel to his England and waited for Churchill to bring him home... and bring them home he did – alive or dead. In most Englishmen's eyes, Churchill could do no wrong.

Luc Dubois sat at his solid cherry davenport desk. His fingers traced the gold gilded metal which bordered the desk's elevated top compartment. He placed the small glass vase which held a single spring of holly on the window sill. Although it was frigid, he still had the window opened a crack to let the December wind blow its frost through his small flat in the Sloane Square section of London. He liked the way the wind moved the red and black brocade curtains. It reminded him of Normandy.

He lifted the lid of the davenport's compartment and saw the neatly placed pink envelopes from Juliette in one divider and the green and lavender ones, Francoise's from Paris and Saint Honorine, in another. Next to them was a bottle of ink. He moved it. The letters, his only connection to home, were too precious to warrant a careless spill of blue black ink.

Le 23 decembre, 1943

Chere maman et grand-pere,

"The winter feels much colder to me this year. Perhaps that is because my family is missing to me. Your tasty pot-au-feu I can smell as I sit here gazing out my window. My view is of a quiet park, tucked down a small street where barely one car can pass. Of course, there are few cars on the streets. The petrol is rationed, and hardly anyone takes his car out of London."

Luc knew his letter would take a long time to reach his mother and grandfather who he hoped had left their 'Champs Elysees' quarters for their Norman farmhouse. Although the letter was not going through the 'Post', it had to seem harmless if intercepted. One of Luc's 'people' would carry it over, via a network which consisted of thousands of bands of men and women. Throughout every country in Europe they were scattered but united together in the common cause of resistance. Luc and Simon's embryonic seed conceived in Paris cafes, Norman farmhouses, and Calvados orchards before the German Occupation had grown from infancy into manhood in two and a half years. Now it included the free French in England and through them the English themselves. Back and forth across the English Channel they went – transporting and ferreting out messages and men.

"I have found some delightful fabrics for our designs. Flowered and 'gaie' – a synthetic blend, it is light and strong. I feel it will appeal to our mostly German clientele. It hugs the body but creates a drape appearance depending on the cut. The thinner 'fraulines' and our French women will look appealingly fresh, and the heavier ones can conceal their girth within the drape-like fabric. The English call it rayon. I'm placing some sample scrapes within this letter."

Luc thought of the real reason for the rayon fabric. He gazed out at Sloane Square – so bare and isolated in December and thought how the Germans had become more cunning and ruthless in their skill at finding and convincing people to disclose information. Because very few could withstand the Gestapo's torture, each man or woman within a band of resistance fighters knew only certain information. However, within these cells of fighters were many key figures who could unlock an infinite number of doors. It was for these men and women that Luc Dubois had found this 'paradise' fabric called rayon. It was perfect, for it could conceal the cyanide capsules which held their salvation – if captured. Loosely sewn into scrapes of rayon in pockets or under labels and lapels, the pill and fabric could be ripped free and swallowed whole. He forced his eyes back to the letter in front of him and placed his pen to the parchment like paper. He continued to write.

"How is father? My sister? My brother? They are missed by me. The apple orchards do survive without my care? The branches do not gnarl together and form grotesque intrusions one into the other, do they? I do hope Denis is keeping them in shape. And 'les vaches' is he still milking them or have cows died because of him? I am sending this to Normandy since I think you have taken grand-pere with you out of Paris for the holidays. The lycee of my sister must too be closed. I will be back in Paris by the end of January with the designs I have made to accompany the rayon fabric. I have additional patterns and materials which will aid us with July's show."

He wanted Francoise to get this letter by mid-January. Not so much as a reassurance that all was well with the Free French forces in England, but to let her know he'd be returning early. He was concerned for his father, alone in his own home with the Germans who now occupied it. His brother, cut from the same cloth as the Nazis, was content to have them live under his roof. Luc was certain Denis would have worn the authoritative German uniform and even the tall leather boots if he could have done so without getting a bullet in the back of his head from a Norman neighbor.

The question was if his brother was maintaining the farm, protecting it from the Germans, or was it overrun by them. Was he wrong about Denis? Had he killed any 'vache' meaning 'Boche' or were the Germans as prolific as the cows of Normandy?

Luc let his thoughts come back to what he could control. He wanted Benoit, Francoise, Juliette, and grand-pere Michel to know that the end was coming. More and more Americans were on the streets of London and in and out of official British headquarters. Having direct access to the middle levels of command, Luc had the occasion to see the high level officials of all the Allied Forces.

Frequently, his path had crossed General de Gaulle's, who had been conferring more and more with the American high command. Luc was always impressed by this atypically tall Frenchman with the typical 'gaulois' nose which seemed to take up his entire thin face. His commanding appearance had nothing to do with his promotion from Colonel to General. De Gaulle had received the rank of General after the Germans invaded Paris. Luc and the Free French believed that his tactical abilities and knowledge of military history placed him ahead of his times. However, it was his commitment to France that placed de Gaulle a head above the crowd.

Since the textile factories along the Thames were still producing the wool fabric of England, Luc could easily go from one to the other via the tubes and make his connections to the unofficial offices of the Resistance. He was one of the inner few spies who knew the term, 'Operation Overlord', the code name for the landing in Europe of the Allied Forces. He also knew that it would occur in the New Year; The Designated Day (D-Day) held the only hope for Europe. He let his mother know by mentioning the "July Show' and that all the 'rayon' samples needed to be in place for this final effort. Rayon too, had a double meaning – the cyanide coverings and the nylon parachute rip cords of those airborne soldiers who would be dropped in.

Thousands of parachutes were needed to drop the American, British, and Canadian airborne units into France, and England's factories were working around the clock in triple shifts. From midnight to 6:00 a.m. with floor to ceiling blackout curtains and leaky exhaust pipes which led from the machines to a series of tunnel-like mazes opening out to bombed out factory and rubble sites. The workers toiled like galley slaves amidst the Luftwaffe's nightly bombings that did not need the advantage of a factory smoke stack target.

Only the most trusted workers and resistance men and women worked in these catacombs of textile factories. During the day green, brown, and red plaid bolts of wool fabric for the civilian population were produced from the lambs' wool of Scotland and England. Scattered among these, bolts of solid blue, green, and brown which at night were brought down to the cellars where men and women, both Irish and English worked next to one another sewing blankets and uniforms for the British Royal Navy, Army, and Air Force. Alongside each station were others who produced nylon for parachutes – hundreds were made each night and shipped out to areas beyond London and into lorries which, at dawn, would travel down the roads into the English countryside. The stock piling of supplies for the invasion of Europe had begun long ago.

Luc knew they were ready.

"I hope grand-pere's health is better. Can he survive the cold and deprivation of another Paris winter?"

Mille grosses bises, xoxoxoxo ton fils, Luc"

Although he missed the pastures, hedges, and the 'bocage' of his beloved Haute-Normandie with its vista of the sea, the bustle of London reminded him of Paris. Looking out his window at the sleepy peaceful park across the street behind the iron metal fence, it was hard to equate the two cities, yet beneath the confining order there was the same stance. Even the people were similar beneath the surface. Although the British tailors were not like the haute couturiers of Paris, their love and care for their profession was the same. He had learned much from them in the last few years. For they readily shared their tricks of the trade with him, Many of course knew this young Frenchman as they knew Francoise and before her, Michel and Geneviève Morneau for whom they had great respect.

Others, of course, were privy to his other life, his network. On Fleet Street there were Frenchmen who crossed the channel delivering messages to those waiting in Caen or Calais. From there the word was spread across the Norman countryside and across to Paris.

He enjoyed the bustle and determination of London, for in part, its attitude paralleled the Parisian tenacity and sense of superiority. The business and purpose of Londoners gave him a sense of belonging, and he marveled at their civility. Only the English, even during air raids, could queue up so politely. Yet, what he could never get used to was their cuisine – or rather lack of it. Although shortages were everywhere, Frenchwomen could make delicious stews even out of cats and moldy carrots and potatoes over their 'rechaudfages'.

When he did return to Paris, his mother or Gabrielle would cook him a meal on one of these mini burners made from squares of folded metal assembled to make a metal box with a flat heavier tin top surface. Under the box they would place folded compressed paper. When lit, this burned and functioned as a mini stove. Most Parisians were used to cooking in this manner, British women especially those in the country had wood burning stoves and their food shortages were not as sever, but still a decent meal seemed impossible.

The only good food he could get in London without cooking it himself was at Chez Tanya, his one refuge in a stormy sea. He could sit at Zosia's red, white, and blue oilskin covered tables and always be assured of fresh flowers, fine food, and friendship. This family was his second one, and their escape from Poland in September of 39 was as miraculous as it was ingenious.

Luc walked across his room to the blue ceramic coffee pot that simmered on his little cast iron stove. He poured a fresh steaming cup, added hot milk and thought again of his new friends' odyssey. Walking only at night, north to the sea, they made the journey in less than a week. Once there, they crossed the square of the Port of Gdansk and under the direction of Janusz's Uncle Arthur, they climbed into his boat, one of the last ones out of the Port of Gdansk. Janusz told him that his mother had survived the journey across her precious Polish soil.

Thomas, during a later conversation, said it was as though she willed herself to the coast. – willed herself to see that her family's freedom was in sight then died on the eve they were to set sail for England. Thomas confided that part of his being died with her that night. He chose to inter her in her homeland and hoped that one day he could return and be buried next to her. All this and much more Luc had learned slowly and cautiously as he became a frequenter of their café on Grove Street.

The café had opened in April of 40'. At first Luc stopped in for a morning croissant and cafe au lait, and then as he felt more comfortable, he began to stop for dinner in the evening.

It was the beautiful Zosia that he first noticed. Somehow she was connected to them by circumstance and choice, a stronger bond than blood. She served as the center of their circle and her love for them had held fast through the eye of many a storm. He heard Zosia tutoring them in English. She insisted that they to speak only English, but when alone or if they wished no one to understand them, they spoke Polish.

Luc found himself stopping in more and more after his long days, and looking forward to his talks with Thomas and especially with Zosia. He was forming friendships with all of them, something he had not done since his schoolyard days, yet ultimate trust only came when he heard her voice speaking French one day at French headquarters on Hyde Street. He passes through the wide reception area as Zosia's words stopped him right in front of the lower offices. In amazement, he realized it was Zosia having a conversation about military operations in French with one of de Gaulle's liaisons.

When she saw him in the doorway, she smiled – a smile he thought much like 'La Jaconde', the Mona Lisa's. As she brushed by him, the scent of roses followed, and all she said was 'Tu n'as jamais demande' – 'You never asked'.

The trust was established. Often they could be seen with heads together, speaking in French. To anyone who entered the café they might have seemed like two lovers, murmuring their secrets into one another's ears. Thomas saw both of their mirrored reflections and in Zosia's movements and actions he recalled April, the beloved strong, April of his youth. He was happy for them but ached in his own loneliness.

****

London, England   December 23, 1943
    Dear Mommy –

Papa would be amused; perhaps proud is a better word that all his language instruction has made me a 'tip top' linguist. London, England is so different. It's still so strange – a city, a foreign language. English, of course, is so easy for me now. My accent is definitely a British one. By the time I kiss you again, dear mommy (very British – do they use Mommy in American?), you'll both sound like the Americans you now are.

Terribly I miss you – every day, but especially this time of year. I have no open fields to forge through, - no flowers and trees to sketch, no forests. Well, never mind. Here I am now. Not back in another time and place that exist no longer.

Many Londoners have placed their children with strangers in the country since we have air raids most nights. I am in charge of a certain sector. My job is to get all the children in my block of buildings down into the tubes. Often we sleep the entire night on the subway floors. It is incredibly clean – the British are like that. It is also very safe. Don't worry. I too am safe and get plenty to eat. I work in the restaurant I keep telling you about. It's called Chez Tanya.

I will tell you that story someday. We serve solid Polish food with a smattering of French cuisine. It's run by good people, as you know, and Zosia and Helena's dishes are much akin to Russian food.

I am no longer your little boy. I have grown. I am taller than Papa is – was. You know I cannot write of that day – nor really speak of it – to you or to anyone. I did what Papa asked of me. Our truffle money set you free. I know how difficult that was .. to leave the home Papa had built for you, and you had born us in. I also realize, now that everything has a price, and that there is a destiny that we must follow once God has shown us the path.

I have found my purpose. The price was high – my dreams, my deja-vu, my separation from you and Tatianna, and the loss of father. However, you and Tatianna are now free. I take comfort in knowing that you are doing well in your new country. I see and hear of America's resources and open strong men. Many say I look like an American. I take that as a compliment. I am ashamed mother Russia only switched sides when she realized the way the winds of war were blowing... and for that other unspeakable reason.

In fact, I do not speak Russian at all – just English and French to the free French here in London who buy my herbs. I am picking up Polish, yet I understand much more than I speak. But that is how it is with languages. I now understand Papa's love of these different tongues. These are the people I hear and speak to every day.

I miss our traditions this time of year. Our food, the beautiful table set for Christmas Eve, the midnight mass, and the cutting down of the tallest best tree we could find. How Tatianna and you would make us go over one more hill to find that perfect tree! Papa, Dame, and I would complain and want to choose any of the trees since they were all lovely. It makes me sad to remember... yet happy to have had those memories.

But do not worry about me. My family here is good – very good to me. Thomas is as close as I'll ever get to having another 'papa'. He treats me like a second son, and Janusz is the brother I never had. Aunt Zosia says we'll get to a woods outside of London and cut down a Christmas tree.

They too have their memories and losses. Thomas rarely speaks of April, his wife and Janusz's mother. She died in the Port of Gdansk. That's all they can say. However, Helena, the daughter, is more open. She's a year younger than me and has a mind of her own. She has an iron spine and acts as though she has nothing to lose. I think she must take after her mother.

Enough of me. I do not know when you will get this letter... or if you will get it. Know that I write every week. I tell you that in each letter. One never knows who reads and blacks out what. I try to keep it general if any eyes here or there are censoring communications. They do it for security. I am quite aware of what that means.

America has been in this war for two years. With all their resources they will end it soon. Then we can be a family once more. Merry Christmas! Happy New Year! May this be the last year of our separation?

Love and kisses,
xoxoxoxoxoxo Christian

He signed the letter and licked the envelope shut. He looked around the restaurant remembering when he had first entered its doors.

It was April of 41, the first anniversary of his father's murder. Feeling very alone and to escape the rain, he entered in. It was ironic or perhaps fate that the first words he heard were in Polish. There was no desperation in the words or the faces. They were not his tormented ghosts which played over and over again in his mind's eye. The warmth and spirit of the little restaurant embraced him with its European flavor and hearty Slavic food like his mother's. It was only until much later that he learned that Janusz's mother was named April. Perhaps, her ghost directed him to her family – to heal the wounds of that other April in the Katyn.

It had been a long year, and despite his fragility and loneliness he never let down his guard. He entered in because he felt that they too had a past, and perhaps, could be trusted. In time, Zosia and Helena took the place of his mother and sister, and with them he felt cared for, and with Thomas he felt secure and safe. Perhaps, it was the methodical analytical mind of Thomas that made him so dependable in Christian's eyes – and for the interest that Thomas took in the medicinal potions that Christian concocted and sold all over London. By the end of that spring he was living in the back of Chez Tanya's and working for room and board.

Soon Thomas realized Christian's gifts went beyond medicinal cures. To the Free French Forces he had been giving another of his gifts - his skill at making explosives and designing detonators. It was then that Janusz, Thomas, and Christian began to work as a team. It reminded Thomas of his other life in Poland at the Polytech, but now the common language was English. As they spoke, Christian's attention would wander over to Luc's French conversations with Zosia. Luc had at first thought he was eavesdropping, but that was impossible. This young Russian boy who spoke English perfectly could not possibly know French. Luc noticed his face was passive and gave no indication that he understood. It was only until much later that Luc realized Christian could understand every French word he and Zosia had spoken.

****

Of all of them, it was just Luc who was free to come and go. Twice a year as 'head' of the House, he had to cross over the Channel. The German authorities in Paris had acknowledged his business as a buyer of wool in England and silk from Italy and the eastern markets. The wives and mistresses of the German hierarchy wanted Paris Fashion so those in charge saw no harm in letting this pretty boy Frenchman mingle with their women. Luc was amazed at what their women would reveal to him. He could even get information about troop maneuvers so he could secretly cross the Channel. If he were caught, he might not be able to talk his way out

Francoise delegated her position to her son and let him assume the role of head of the firm. As its head, his power and prestige affected women of all ages and created the subterfuge needed to connect with Free French activists across the Channel. It was through Francoise, Gabrielle and Colette's silent movements among the German wives and French mistresses that the women picked up information to be relayed to Luc or Simon and in turn to Paul (Renaud), Luc's boyhood friend in Normandy.

July was the last time Luc had seen Paris. The city, whose heat hung over her like a cowl, showed its fashion show finery only to Axis members and collaborators. To Luc it did not matter, for all the clients regarded him basically as one of the girls – a fixture, a man in a woman's business. The Germans viewed him as such and made the grave error of talking in front of him. Because of this, he was a constant conduit of information.

In August he went home to Haute Normandie.

****

Janusz looked at Christian and in many ways saw himself. Tall and thin without the breath of manhood, Christian appeared as Janusz had been a little over three years ago, but now at twenty-one Janusz was hardened. It wasn't just his physical power and strength but the defining of his character. He gathered strength from the key his mother had taken from the piano in their living room of the University tower. Now it was kept in the secret compartment of his dresser. When difficult times came, he would pick it up and feel its coolness in the palm of his hand, but he had neither the time nor the heart to play the piano.

He was not that selfish boy – unhappy with not being able to pursue his beloved music- pouting because his mother and family made him an early birthday party. It was so long ago. Those gifts that night wrapped and forged from the last days of complete 'family' would come to his dreams at night. The knife – the key- April's amber necklace cut sharply through those last sunny September days. The knife, Stanislaus' gift, had saved his sister's but not his mother's life.

He suffered her loss in silence, much like Martin had suffered the loss of a father he barely knew. Time had reversed the roles. As Martin had been for him over the oak tables of the restaurant near the Polytech; now he was the mentor for Christian. At the time, Janusz had not been able to truly comprehend Martin's pessimistic attitude nor the sadness that overtook him at times. He had seemed much older than his years.

Now, Janusz understood. He understood too that Martin would not have to worry about the Germans enlisting him. Life was not that cruel, but cruel enough for him to have died that day in the stable. His father had told him that Martin had shot the Germans first and then... himself.

Janusz knew that Christian at seventeen had the strength – no hesitations – to do that now. He had more courage than he himself had at that age. A deep sense of order, practicality, and common sense cut to the core of Christian's being – all the things that had never been a part of Janusz's ephemeral life. He learned the hard way that his head had been in the clouds; whereas, Christian had his feet rooted firmly to the ground. At an early age, life had forced Christian to act.

Each had lost a parent in indescribable horror. Janusz had gotten through another September, but Christian's month would be April - the April of his nightmares- the April of daylight deja-vus. Neither would talk to the other about it. Thomas was the only one who knew some of the pieces of the puzzle.

****

They sat across from one another at the back corner table near the kitchen door. The small round table with a view of two streets fit in just beneath the window. Christian gingerly placed his brown leather satchel on the floor and opened the top flap to adjust the wrapping on each cork topped bottle.

"I have three more to deliver," he said as he buckled his satchel shut.

"How many potions did you sell today?" Janusz asked.

"Four – two for burns, one for scaring prevention, and one for strength. Neil White, the old man on Dorchester Street, uses that. It's full of vitamins and minerals."

As he said this, he took out his sketch book and checked off his neatly written list. There were no names but simply pictures or designs to indicate a person's identity. For Neil White there was a small sketch of a bent gnarled tree. His precautions were habit. Even in England one could never be complacent about freedom.

Out of his book he slid two small folded pieces of paper. He covered these with his large palm and casually looked around before pushing them across the table to Janusz. Chez Tanya was nearly empty. The early morning laborers had come and gone, and only two elderly women chatted over hot cups of tea. A middle-aged woman counted out her purchases from a tartan plaid cloth bag as she sat near the coal burning stove. Without opening the slips of paper, Janusz slid them into his pouch around his neck.

"I'll see that the heavy one gets these," Janusz said to Christian as he lifted the spoon of steamy leek and potato soup to his lips.

With no need for further discussion, Christian simply changed the conversation to the mundane. "We will get our Christmas tree tomorrow."

Janusz smiled. Despite the organization and mind of a scientist, Christian was still a boy with a boy's emotions of home and Christmas.

"Yes, I know. Zosia promised you a real cutting down ceremony. That we will have –tomorrow, Christmas Eve."

"Tip top," he exclaimed with the delight of a child. He liked using his new English expressions. He took another sip of his soup. "By the way, your father said we were to meet him at Polish headquarters at 4:00 this afternoon."

"Yes, he told me before he left this morning."

He and his father had often conferred together with officials, but rarely, had the three been asked together. Janusz wondered at the urgency of this meeting two days before Christmas.

"As usual, we'll get to Chestnut Street separately. I'll arrive a half hour early. Then you come," Janusz added in a forced matter-of-fact manner before savoring his soup.

****

In Polish headquarters on Chestnut Street a baby grand piano stood on the ground floor off the foyer. Whenever Janusz climbed up the stairs to see Major Morganski, he glanced sideways at its silent keys. He had never heard it played and could never pass it without wondering, yet for him to play was unthinkable. His wounds would open raw, never to be sutured shut again. As he reached the top of the stairs and passed by the two sentries on either side of the major's door, he wondered what could be so important to discuss just before Christmas.

"Dobry popoludnie, pani Pazdaski ... Bozego Narodzenie" Janusz greeted Mrs. Pazdaski, the keeper of the gate to Major Morganski. Morganski was the key advisor and boyhood friend of General Sikorski, head of the Polish Forces in England.

"Good afternoon and Merry Christmas to you too my little one, Janusz Puratski." she rounded the corner of her desk and enveloped him in a big warm hug. Holding his face in her large hands, she planted a kiss on his cheek. "You've grown so much since the last time I saw you. And not so thin, this is good."

Lilcha Pazdaski had lost both her husband and her only son in the roundups of 39'. She missed her men, but she sought to deaden the sharp pain by devoting herself to motherless Polish boys.

"Sit. Sit." She pointed to one of the large arm chairs and she herself eased her ample hips into her chair behind the desk, near the door. She resumed typing her stack of letters and memos. Fast and efficient, capable of doing several tasks at one time, she made herself indispensable to both the Major and the General.

Janusz looked out the picture window that had been specifically treated to withstand the vibrations of the bombings. Each time he came he noticed new networks of cracks near its corners behind the heavy gold drapes. Like their tower living room window in Warsaw this room too had an aerial view of the tree lined street. Glancing down at the street below, he saw Christian slowly walking and looking at everything as though his eyes were the lens of a camera.

"Christian is coming," he remarked to Mrs. Pazdaski.

Never taking her eyes off the page she was typing, she simply nodded in his direction. Her plump fingers hit each black key with precision and when the bell of the huge black Royal typewriter rang, she forcefully hit the return handle which swung the carriage onto its next line.

Soon Janusz heard Christian's light footsteps, taking the stairs two at a time and then saw his head lean into the open door.

"Hello, Mrs. Pazdaski," he said rather formally as his eyes glanced over her. Janucz noticed that he never seemed to be able to look at her face or into her tired blue eyes, and she, in turn, was always cordial but never warm to him.

"Christian, hello. Take a seat." She responded. "You are still too thin. You must eat more of Zosia's Polish food."

Christian looked at her in surprise, for her unusual personal comment caught him off guard. "Yes," was all he could say. He crossed the room to a chair near Janusz. No one else was in the office to notice the awkward exchange. Janusz, alone, took notice.

Although Christian was Russian, that still did not entirely account for her aloofness She knew he was an orphan and obviously too young to have had anything to do with the round-up of her husband and son. The Russians had switched their allegiance since then, but Lilcha Pazdaski hated and did not trust them. They were not like the English or the French, and miles apart from the bold irreverent Americans. As Janusz thought about it, their relationship seemed to have more to do with Christian's demeanor than hers. He seemed guilty in her presence – like a child caught with his hand in the cookie jar.

The buzzer rang.

"Yes Major. They are both here."

Over the intercom the Major spoke, "Wpuscici-ich Tomas Puratski – to gotowy ."

The Major's office was large and comfortable, and like him, it had the appearance of home. Within its walls, one felt safe. Perhaps that was the purpose of it – to provide a refuge from the chaotic war – to make its visitors be willing to face insurmountable odds in their fight to end this war. Whatever its façade, neither young man could mistake the softness of the armchairs with the tall broad gray haired man in front of them.

"Welcome boys," Morganski rose up his massive frame and extended his hand. Thomas, ashen, did not bother to rise. The young men shook hands with the Major but their eyes were on Thomas who suddenly seemed frail.

"Sit down, please. I've asked you all to come at once, so that we can work together on a newly discovered circumstance of the war. I think this is the most crucial event... at least for Poland even though she no longer exists as a free nation."

Thomas was staring blankly out the window. His mind was on another day at another place. He had deliberately suppressed all memories of his last day in Warsaw when his beloved family was ripped apart. Now the stench of the stable filled his nostrils as he recalled the memory of Martin's gallant effort to grab the Bible and kill the German officer and the dark-haired traitor from the Poly Tech. In quick consecutive movements Martin had killed both, threw the Bible to Bernard and allowed both Bernard and Thomas to escape. As they ran, he shot the two guards at the stable door. He had saved the last bullet for himself, Thomas turned to see Martin's brains splatter on the soldiers who flung themselves on him.

"During September of 39' as Warsaw was being bombed into submission, a concentrated premeditative plan was put into action. As you know Janusz, your father was rounded up along with other members of the 'intelligentsia' and Polish military leaders. The plan was to kill them all."

As the Major spoke, Thomas looked at Janusz and knew that he had gone back into time – not to the putrid stench of death in the stable, not the desperate run to freedom, not the barrage of gunfire and the thud of Bernard's body as it hit the ground – but to the animal like moans and wails of April and Helena. Janusz was there for that. Closeted in the secret annex, he had hidden until he could lunge out in fury and cut the life out of the Russian pig who raped his sister and mother.

The Major's words interrupted their thoughts. "Those who were not immediately shot escaped. Some like you and your father made it across Poland and the Channel in those early days of war. Others were not so lucky. They found themselves trapped. Polish fighting units chose the lesser of two evils. Caught between the German Army on one side and the Russian on the other, we now know they surrendered to the Russian Army."

The major looked to Christian as he stated the facts that they all knew but never mentioned. Christian knew immediately the end of the Major's report, and he also knew that he, Christian Harr, had told no one. The details of what he had seen in the forest of the Katyn had never been revealed. In the beginning he was in shock and could only concentrate on getting his mother and sister out of Russia and to America and himself to England. And once he arrived in London, he could only survive by suppressing the nightmare.

In his dreams it still came – the muffled sounds of footsteps, the silent moans, the blue eyes in the death masks – but added to it was the face of his father and the lunge of Dame – and the shovelfuls of dirt, this time for them. He had buried them both well. He had told Thomas only that he had seen his father killed by the Russians and that he had buried him in a forest near his home of Smolensk.

"We'll go to the General's office. He wants to tell you about some highly classified information we just discovered. This way gentlemen." Morganski ushered them into the adjoining rooms of General Sikorski.

****

"And so Thomas, Janusz, and Christian that is what we know." the General finished.

Janusz was as gray as his father when the General finished his detailed account of the mass graves that had been found in the Katyn. The General went into detail about the atrocities that must have accounted for the dismembered skeletons. Janusz placed his hand over his mouth and bolted for the WC. His retching and flushing occupied the silence of the room. Christian sat stone still. He had done it all before.

When Janusz returned, The General continued. "The British have been continually monitoring the German airwaves and breaking their code with the enciphering machine, ENIGMA. Pertinent intelligence that affects our operations is passed immediately to our headquarters. These intercepts of German radio traffic and other secret information have been recoded ULTRA by the British and passed on as so deemed. Early on in the war the British have had access to all communications. All communications within Poland during September and October of 39' have been documented and analyzed, yet only recently did a new discovery shed light on this entire mystery. For the last three years we have been trying to determine who was killed by German firing squads. The numbers did not add up. Thousands were unaccounted for."

Abruptly, Christian interrupted the General and asked the question he had never asked before.

"How many were found in the Katyn?"

"The Russian Army killed more than 4,000. Let me clarify that. The mass graves contained some 4,000 officers and civilians. 11,000 have never been accounted for. Certain double agents discovered this last April. We've been trying to confirm it since. We asked the Russian government to investigate. They have refused and broken diplomatic relations with us."

They all sat in silence. Christian had bowed his head. He pressed his fists into his eye sockets. Thomas, turning to

Christian and placing his hand on his shoulder, was the first to speak.

"When the general informed me, I told him perhaps you knew something, Christian. The place and perhaps the time connected with your arrival in England. We do not know when these massacres occurred, but we do know that the Polish Army was running for its life in October of 39'.

Christian's head came up slowly. He looked straight ahead as if in a trance. All the men's eyes were riveted on him. He began his story with an unimaginable precision. His photographic memory, like the clacking of the outer office typewriter, began with one fact following another – in constant staccato...

He began with..

"It was April of 1940...."

And ended with...

"I buried my father with Dame in a grave so deep that they could never touch them again." He let his head fall back to stare at the cracks on the ceiling.

The men's faces turned white – their heads dropped forward, and they cupped their tear lined faces in their hands. For thirty minutes, Christian Harr had recounted every detail with the precision of a typewriter ringing at the end of every very line. He enumerated for the first time the events that changed his life forever as Mrs. Pazdaski's black Royal machine continued to click clack on.

Chapter 6 - May 31, 1944 - Somewhere in England

Just England   May 31, 1944

Hi Mama and Pop

Bet you're surprised at all the mail I send you. It's not that I'm lonesome. They keep us plenty busy. I just figured that you, especially mama, want to be sure your 'bambino' is O.K. That's why I sent you that post card book last week. It's got all the stuff each American military branch does plus all those razzle dazzle pics of the boys' 'indoor' activities. As you seen, there was that colored photo of some guy writing home. It's crazy, but we all write like we're a bunch of friggin' authors!

Another shot was of the mess where we eat three squares a day. It's like being home with Angelo, Giuseppe, Ricardo, and Caesarea. These guys here remind me of my brothers. The only time we wait to eat is when the chaplain says grace every night. After that it's every man for himself, just like at home. But mama, it's sure ain't your home cookin'. What I'd give for a big plate of your homemade pasta and sauce with Papa's homegrown tomatoes, oregano, and basil.

Hey Pop, have you finally gotten your vegetable garden staked out according to your specs or is old Mr. DeAngelo still trying to grab another foot for himself? Christ, he's been doing that since I was a Kid. Why it is every wop in Brooklyn fighting over his 'tomato' turf? Thank you FDR. Now the rest of the good old USA has jumped on the band wagon with their 'victory' gardens. I'll come back to the middle of a tomato war!

Speaking of Brooklyn, I miss the bums. When I get home, the next thing I want after mama's pasta is a cold beer, a hot dog, and a seat behind home plate so I can hear firsthand... Babe Phelps curse at the ump.

Well, I gotta go now. More training. One picture they didn't have on that postcard book was the paratroopers. Most of those pics look like the first war. I figure they don't want the Krauts, Japs, and Wops to know what we really got. This paratrooper and supply build up stuff is a pretty well-kept secret.. I don't know how many of my letters get to you or if a bunch of stuff is blacked. I don't throw in too many details since I want you to have something to read.

Anyway, I've told you I'm in the 82nd Airborne Division. I know there're other divisions, but to see us practice day in and day out you'd think we're the only ones! They've picked up the pace. I've lost only one tooth in the jumps. State side, we had those great towers to practice on, but here they started us off jumping out of aerial balloons. The ground comes up awful fast, and many guys lose a bunch of teeth. If you lose more than six, you get discharged cause they got to get you false teeth. No man can jump with a set of artificial choppers cause he'd could choke to death if they dislodge when he hits the ground. Would you believe, I've seen a couple of yellow bellies deliberately hit the ground face first to be sent home!

Me, I can't wait to pulverize those Nazi Krauts. I've trained enough. I just want to put what they taught me to use and kill as many of those bastards as I can. Red white and blue through and through – I am. Remember our rides on the Staten Island ferry" Summer picnics on Lady Liberty's lawn with Aunt Celeste and Uncle Gorgio? How cousin Roberto and Sofia and I would run to see who would be the first to get up to Lady Liberty's torch. God, we could see all of New York from her. What a view!

I'm fightin for that view – the view that the entire world deserves. You brought us to the land of opportunity and freedom. I'm gonna see you get to keep it.

Enough of this stuff. I'm getting teary eyed just writing it. Saw General Ike today. Actually shook his hand. He asked me how it was going and really listened to my answer. He's a regular Joe.

A bunch of xxxxx your 'bambino' –
Anthony Joseph Martino.

"Hey Tony, you finished that letter yet? We gotta go. The sergeant is chomping at the bit. Says we gotta move on"

"Yeah, yeah. Don't piss your pants, Billy. I'm comin."

"Listen up men." The sergeant bellowed over the engines of the C-47's. "You've heard it all before, but you'll hear it again. – and again until it's for real."

Tony felt his heavy pack with the two chutes as he pushed back against the cold metal of the plane. The weight dug into his shoulders. He reached down to adjust his leather high jumper's boots. He didn't want to snap an ankle when he hit the ground.

"When you jump it will be at night. This is your last daytime one. Beginning – D-4 you'll have only night time jumps."

"What about D-5, Sarge," Tony's friend, Billy asked,

"Tonight you got a night on the town, boys. So there'll be no jumping tomorrow. We don't want any hung over boys making errors."

The 'boys' – for they were just that – laughed nervously. Even the old married man in their unit, twenty-one- year- old college graduate Lieutenant Sidney Smith joined in.

"Remember you'll be standing in the 'stick' ten minutes before jump time. You've attached your webbing tail of your chute to this overhead cable," The Sargent grabbed the cable to get their attention. "I'll go down the 'stick' to make sure you're all attached. We'll be flying in low so as to catch as little enemy fire as possible. I'll tell you when we're one mile before our designated drop zone."

The sergeant tuned to the man on his left. "How much time will that give you, soldier?"

"Thirty seconds, sir!"

"Affirmative. And in that thirty seconds you're going to put yourself in God's hands and the hands of the 82nd Airborne, Right!"

"Yes sir, Sargent, Sir." They all shouted back.

Tony Martino just hoped he would not be the one to freeze in the open door of the plane. The sergeant had told them all to grasp the sides of the door with thumbs outside. If anyone froze, the man behind would 'thaw' him out with a push. He did not want to be pushed into the black night of Normandy, France. He wanted to freely fall and begin it right.

The sergeant's words broke into his train of thought.

"Remember the U. S. of A. Air Corps has provided you with an extra chute. You begin counting the moment you leap from this door... one thousand and one, one thousand and two, one thousand and three. If you haven't felt the opening shock of your back chute by the count, pull your emergency ring." He paused for emphasis and glanced down the line of seated men on each side of the cylinder like tunnel of the C-47.

"You'll fall 500 feet in 8 seconds with an unopened main chute. You got 3 seconds to count before it opens. You got 1 to 2 seconds to pull the reserve chute, 1 or 2 to open. That uses up 7 seconds. Remember soldier, that leaves 1 second, and that's all the time you got for daydreaming."

He looked down the aisle once more and hoped to God they all had it. "O.K. men 10 minutes to drop zone. Stand up, form the stick from the man in front of you. Reach and hook up to the cable as you go."

****

Tony, Billy, Sidney and the youngest, sixteen-year-old Tim hit the streets of London together. Sidney hadn't wanted to go. He felt he should rest as much as possible for what lay ahead. Like the rest of the men, he knew the invasion was finally on its way. Not gun-ho like Tony, he had enlisted because he felt it was the right thing to do. All his life he had done the right thing. He had a plan and was sticking to it. College, marriage, war – in that order. He had accomplished the first two, and now all he wanted was to finish the last and return home in one piece.

Marjorie was a great girl. He had fallen in love with her in the first grade and was true to her all through high school and college at the State University while she did double shifts in her father's hardware store in Hannibal, Missouri and the small restaurant attached to the back of it. He was thinking of her now... she was probably putting in a new screen on the back door for Mrs. Wilson whose household of dogs and cats always ran amuck. In the middle of stapling she'd be running back across the restaurant's linoleum floor to wipe up the Formica counter top and to make a fresh pot of coffee for the customers who'd be stopping by for breakfast after the grave yard shift at the airplane factory. He knew many of the assembly line workers and riveters were women stopping for a bit of chatter and java before going home to their second job – a house full of kids. Like the rest of the women, Marge would be wearing one of those red bandannas tied back over her soft dirty blonde hair.

Sidney felt he didn't need the hoopla of London, but he had to make sure his 'boys' came back in one piece.

"You know, the only reason I'm going is to make sure you guys don't get your heads busted in some pub," he told them as he drove the jeep through the streets of London

"Jezz, we appreciate it Sid. The Sarge would'a never given us a jeep," Billy commented.

"Crap, I would've just took it. What can they do to us - throw us in the brig?" Tony said as he took his last Lucky Strike out of the pack. He crumpled the empty pack of cigarettes and tossed it out of the Jeep. Cupping his hands, he lit the match from the matchbook, turning it over as he did so.

"'Suzy's Strippers'", he read. "Let's go guys. Our last free 24 hour leave should be a doozer, and this sounds right up our alley," Tony tossed the matchbook to Tim. "Your education starts tonight kid."

Sidney smiled. He liked Tony. A streetwise kid – 19 years to his 21, yet in many ways Tony knew a lot more than Sid. Nonetheless, Sidney would never let on. It didn't bother him that Tony called him the Professor. It was a compliment, and he didn't mind that Tony had twisted his arm into coming tonight. Sidney was glad he did. He didn't need to stay behind and think about what tomorrow or the next few days would bring. Too many thoughts. Besides, he convinced himself to play big brother to these guys – especially Tim. The kid had the guts to escape the clutches of his father who had put him in an orphanage after his mother died. The old man kept the older sisters at home to clean, cook and do God knows whatever else. Sid thought of the story In order to enlist he had lied about his age and paid some drunk to pretend to be his father and say that he was eighteen.

"He gets a drunk to sign his enlistment papers, so he can get his head blow off at sixteen. He's got guts," Tony had told him.

"Suzy's it is", Sidney said as he veered the jeep to the right, down Venice Street to Dolphin Street where Suzy's joint stood. He figured they all had a right and a need for female companionship. "Hell, we all might be dead in a couple of days as you so eloquently put it, Tony," Sidney said, but figured at least he'd be there tonight to make sure they didn't get thrown in the brig for disorderly conduct or for revealing any military information. A second thought flashed into his mind.; maybe they'd be better off if they were in the brig and missed the invasion. Nothing to tell their grandkids, but at least they'd be alive.

As they pulled up to the curb, Tony noticed the American and British MP's. They were everywhere. Tony glanced over at Sid. He was surprised that he caved in so easily.

****

She twisted her fingers in the dark curls that fell across Tony's forehead. No amount of Brill Cream and pomade could keep them glued back – only his cap, rakishly pushed back and off to the side did the trick. Military regulation wasn't forcing him to wear it right now, so it rested on the bar next to his drink. The warmth inside the club and her breath down his neck couldn't keep his hair or anything in place. He had a hard on as soon as he walked in the door of Suzy's strippers.

The girls who pranced in silks and feathers in front of a room of American and British soldiers came in all sizes and shapes. They bumped, grinded, and tossed their sweaty curls to the beat of the drums and an occasional saxophone. Tony had the impression that the Brits were like those few kids on his block – Sam, Harry, and Pat who knew the music but not the dance. He had never seen an Englishman who had rhythm and these girls were no exceptions. The beat and movement of swing somehow swept right over them, and the feeling of down home Dixie Jazz that he would take the subway to Harlem for must have jumped skipped across the Atlantic, missed England altogether and landed in France. He heard the 'Frogs' clicked to the 'jive'.

Josephine Baker and her boys had written their ticket in Paris after the First World War. They went everywhere and got the royal treatment, but back home the 'coloreds' just stayed below 125th Street. Tony never cared. A colored's a colored, a wop's a wop, a mick's a mick – if they held their own and could bat or throw, they'd meet at the sandlot for a game or two of baseball. As far back as he could remember, baseball was his passion.   When he got home, maybe he'd try out for the Brooklyn Bums.

"Hey, where are you luv? Didn't you like me dancing?"

Underneath all that rouge and red lipstick she was just a kid like himself... maybe even a year or two younger. He took a gulp of the warm watered down scotch and soda the waitresses kept lining up in front of all the GI's. "Sure babe," he placed his hand on her knee. "I was just thinking how you could be a Rockette. You were the only one who can move to the beat of the music."

He really meant it. Somehow this kid could move like she had all the answers, yet her face was that of an angel. Beneath the heavy coat of face powder, he could see whispers of freckles on her nose and cheeks. She reminded him of Theresa, Angelo's sister, the first girl who let him go all the way with her. In fact, it was in the back seat of Angelo's father's Desoto that his manhood was initiated. It came so quick that he hardly knew that was it. He was embarrassed, but she just laughed and showed him what she wanted and how to slow down the second time around. At eighteen, she was the older woman. Afterwards, she couldn't believe he was only fourteen. "Christ, it's like doing it with my kid brother."

Of course, she told Angelo, and he came looking for Tony. Tears of anger and shame ran down his friend's face as he swung a bat at Tony's head. Tony had ducked and landed a right to the side of Angelo's face. Both knew Teresa wasn't worth a fight, but Angelo had to defend his sister's tarnished honor, and Tony had to prevent being killed. Angelo forgave Tony and the mess he had to clean up in his father's car, and Tony forgave Angelo for having an 'easy lay' for a sister.

Although this girl looked like Theresa and there had been a few Theresas since, she did not have her edge. She played the game, but it was like a little girl acting. Unlike Theresa, whose angel face concealed a hard heart, this girl seemed like the 'genuine McCoy'. He almost didn't want to take advantage of her.

"Well ya know, I do want to be a real dancer. A Ginger Roger's type with those long white dresses and gardenias in my hair. I take tap lessons with the money I earn here. Most goes to me mum, but I get to keep a few shillings for me lessons." She moved in closer and hadn't taken his hand away. "Have you ever seen a real life movie star?"

"Nah." He laughed.

Why did they all think America was like friggin Hollywood with big cars and streets paved with gold? he thought. Why should she think different? America – land of opportunity – her dream was as good as anyone else's. He looked at her face as he moved his hand up her leg.

"I just thought." she stammered.

"I've never been to Illinois let alone California, but Hollywood.. yeah, I'd like to see that." He softly lied.

She smiled. Tony thought it was a real sweet one.

"I'm from Brooklyn."

Little furrows appeared beneath her brown bangs.

"New York," he clarified. "Can't you tell by my accent?"

"All you Yanks have an accent."

"That's right, you must get every God damn G.I. that come to England." He took his hand off her thigh and reached for a fresh pack of Luckies. He pulled the red cellophane strip from the top of the pack and opened up a silver corner. He crumbled the papers up and tossed them on the bar. Hitting the pack against the back of his hand, he shook out two cigarettes. He offered the first to her and put his mouth to the pack and pulled out the second for himself. He flicked out a piece of tobacco that got stuck to his lip as he lit the match and offered it to her.

She cupped her hand around his as she bent her head over the match. "Your accent is cuter than them other Yanks." She smiled wide. "They just come to look first and grab second. Me mum hates me working her, but the war changes things. Anyway she still gives me lots of advice."

The room was loud. The cheering and clapping of the men, the too brassy laughs of the girls and the incessant boom, swish of the drums. It was like an out of hand New Year's Eve bash without the promise and hope of change. There was a frantic nature, a manic frenzy among these men. They couldn't count on the promise of another year.

Billy and Tim, part of the cheering and two finger whistling section, sat with two platinum blonds at a front row table. The 'girls', considerably older, enjoyed the endless rounds of drinks and packs of American cigarettes the boys provided.

Sidney sat at the far end of the bar in the back of the smoke filled room. Detached from the raucous circus, he passed no judgment, but kept his ears and eyes open for anyone who seemed too curious about why they were here or when they would leave. Security was tight, but with so much whiskey men's tongues loosen up. Like the director of a play he paid acute attention. He didn't mind. It was part of his role as big brother to make sure his motley crew made it through the war. Besides, he was glad to be out and not confined to the barracks. This way he couldn't think too much about his wife and his life stateside. He focused in on keeping them safe for now.

Tony, too, was aware. He could never turn off his antennas – 'you could take the guy out of Brooklyn but never Brooklyn out of the guy,' he always said. The streets and pubs of London had the same dangers as the corners, alleys, and bars of New York City. Sidney was covering his backside from the end of the bar and watching out for the country boys in front. It made Tony feel comfortable. He especially hoped Tim would get a piece tonight. If he was old enough to get killed, he was old enough to get laid.

"Let's get outta here.." Tony realized he didn't even know her name.

"Maggie, that's what they call me here, but Margaret is my name."

She hopped off her stool, and he stepped down. Placing her hand on his arm, she said, "Give me a minute to get into my street clothes. O.K..."

"Anthony", my name's Anthony."

She smiled. "That's a nice name."

He watched her adeptly sidestep all the soldiers who blocked the way to the backstage area. Then he caught Sidney's eye and walked towards him.

Chapter 7 – June 1, 1944 – The Americans

Falmouth, England   June 1, 1944

Dear Dad,

I'm sure you've gotten my other letters, but just in case, I'm letting you know I made second lieutenant. I'm proud of that, although you might not be. I had to beat out a lot of other men in C Company and believe me the infantry is hard work. Sure, I know you think all the prestige is with the 'fly boys', but I didn't want to be a pilot. So Herbert's a pilot. I'm happy for him and for his father, but the guy's short. I couldn't stand to have my legs all crammed up in the nose of a B-24 – too claustrophobic for me. If you can't stand Manny coming over from his Deli to your store and boasting about his 'Herbie', tell him his pastrami odor permeates your suits. That'll keep him out!

Seriously Dad, the least of your concerns – my concerns – should be Manny and his fly boy Herbie. It's going to be rough – that they keep drilling into us. I wonder what sort of courage it will take to scramble out of our LCVPs (Landing Craft Vehicle Personnel), hit the beach, and move inland. The paratroopers will clear the way, and our B-26s' bombs are supposed to take out the big guns on the cliffs and the bunkers lined up every 100 yards all the way down the coast, but we'll be the ones hitting the beach and having to hold it. What will matter is whether the men in the first wave can get out of their tin cans, wade ashore, cross the beach, and fight their way inland.

"I've memorized every inch of our beach – the one they keep telling us we'll land on and move out of in order to secure it for the next wave. Every time they drill it into us, they pull the map out of a long tube and tack it up on the board. I've looked in my German grammar book and in the French book they've been teaching us out of to see the rest of the coast line. If the Krauts blindfold me, I can find my way out of that beach or any other within a forty mile radius.

You know, what C Company calls me?. 'The Kraut'. Don't know whether it's because I know German or because the name Melvin doesn't have enough grit to it. In all honesty, I don't think they like me much. Intelligence and persistence always kept me on track in 'civie' life, but here, I'm not high on the totem pole. They don't have to like me. They just have to obey orders, and that they do. So if they call me kraut behind my back, so be it. We're all fighting to grind those Nazis to dust, besides they know the irony. I'm the only Jew, yet I look the most 'Aryan' of the entire company. If the krauts capture me, they'll never take me for a Jew – too tall, too blond, and too blue-eyed.

You won't get this letter until after the invasion is underway. By the time you do, I'll either be left for dead on the beach or have walked through Hell and be the road to Berlin. Dead or alive, I'll have found out if I had the stuff or if I was too scared to move. One thing is certain; I know I won't turn and run. There'll be nowhere to run except back into the English Channel and the cold Atlantic. A swimmer I am not!

I figure I got the luck of the draw.

Number one, I'm going in on the 2nd wave. The US of A's Navy big guns will have shot that beach to oblivion. That means the guys ahead of me will have jumped from shell crater to shell crater and will be off the beach to provide artillery cover for the rest of us. Number two, the Army has code named the beach after all Nebraska boys like me – **Omaha Beach** –

Number three, my specific sector of Omaha is called – **Easy Red.** 'Easy' I can live with.

So, I know someone up there is looking out for me. I'll make it home. I'll make you proud.

Your loving, son, Melvin G. Baron

****

Far from the beaches on the other side of the Channel two Generals, Omar Bradley, U.S. First Army, and his Lieutenant-General, Courtney H. Hodges had passed on orders to 29th Infantry Division Commander, General Norman 'Dutch' Cota and 4th Infantry Commander, Major General Raymond 'Tubby' Barton. These two men continued to talk.

"Our divisions have the toughest beach." 29th Infantry Division Commander Cota commented.

"That seems to sum it up Dutch. Ike assigned two divisions to Omaha, Mine – veteran fighters, battle tried, worn in and yours – green, well trained, iron men. Mine know what steel they have; yours will find out." 4th Infantry Division Commander Barton stated.

Dutch Cota stood up and walked over to the worn stained map which stretched across the entire wall behind him.

"We know ours is the crucial beach, the link between Utah on the west flank and the British beaches of Sword, Juno, and Gold on the east. I keep looking at that damn coast between Utah and Omaha – an 18 mile stretch of rock, cliff, and marsh. Our boys will have to move forward at top speed. Christ, the only place to link up is inland."

Tubby Barton swiveled in his chair and answered his old friend by simply reiterating the facts one more time. "The leaders of each division and their Company know thi, but the officers and enlisted men know only their beach heads, their section of this 7,000 yards. The American high command has christened this crucial 7,000 yard stretch 'Omaha' and sectioned it - from west to east as 'Dog Green", 'Dog White', 'Dog Red',

'Easy Green'and 'Easy Red'. Each company A through E is assigned a specific colored sector of that 7,000 yards. All know the first wave of men has the toughest job."

"Not only that," Barton continued, "these bluffs are like god damn Mount Everest. The American sectors are not flat like Gold, Juno, and Sword. Of course, they give that flaming Montgomery the easy ground while our 'Yanks' get the beach backed by bluffs 100 feet high. Our boys will have to go uphill to take the Kraut fortifications."

Cota lit another cigarette and extended his hand across the map's expanse of cliffs. "At least Tubby, our latest info has it that General Rommel's 352nd Division is twenty-five miles inland at St. Lo."

"Yeah Dutch, we're going to hit so fast we'll be over those cliffs before he even gets there." Cota answered.

"Jesus, my boys are itching to go."

"Mine too," Cota echoed as he looked out the ground floor windows of the English country estate so removed from the cold Normandy Beaches. "But as you said, they're green. Waiting is always the worst part. Time wreaks havoc with their confidence. Fear and second guessing begins to work its way in." He paused and whispered, "Cry havoc.. and let slip the dogs of war..."

"D-Day minus 4 and counting." Barton answered.

Cota murmured, "On June 5 when the tide is low and the moon is full. June 5, the beginning of the end... God willing."

Each general looked again at the map whose names: Pointe de la Percee, Vierville, Les Moulins, St Laurent, and Colleville – French towns, etched in their minds and more familiar than their own boyhood hometowns. Each one knew there were only five roads off Omaha – five paths of hell to crawl, walk, or run through to get off the beach in order to move inland to the towns that would eventually lead to Paris – to Berlin – and to freedom that the world was waiting for.

****

Night – southwest coast of England

"O.K. men, one more time. We're going out, once again in the dark," 2nd Lieutenant Melvin Baron barked at his crew of thirty men. With himself and the lieutenant that made thirty-two – not counting the medics, a standard unit obliged to cram itself into a LCVP. Lieutenant Wilson let Baron lead the manoeuvers as he had done many times. In fact, any one of the thirty men, if he had the guts, could do the same. Lieutenant Wilson and 2nd Lieutenant Baron felt sure about their men. They'd put them against any other infantry unit that was hitting the beach on D-Day.

"Yeah, that's what the Kraut always says," O'Brien, one of the four mean special wire cutting team, mumbled.

"You got a problem with that O'Brien, you obstinate Mick?" Baron shot back.

"No Sir, Second Lieutenant Baron Sir." He shouted in force. Melvin Baron thought he detected a wry smile of approval on O'Brien's face.

Regardless, Baron wasn't there for a popularity contest. He was there to get the job done. He had stopped worrying about his nickname months ago. They all had names for one another. His just had more of a slap to it.

Wilson stayed out of the confrontation. Baron had learned to let it roll off his back and to give as well as get. He knew the men didn't have to like him but had to just do what he said. Wilson made sure they did just that. He had let Baron command many more dry runs than the other LCVP units. The men could separate the man from the uniform. They did what the uniform ordered, and by now, except for O'Brien, they did it without any flack. Wilson knew that if he was killed, Baron would take over, and if Baron was killed then O'Brien or Russo or Stone. Any man in any American team would do his job even if there was no officer shouting commands. Get the job done or die on the beach – those were the only choices.

Baron looked out from the bow of the small transport ship, camouflaged to look like any other fishing ship out for a catch off England's southwest coast. For months the men had been practicing climbing down huge rope cargo net ladders hung from the inside of the steel hangars which dotted the English countryside like ugly mushrooms – not far from any English coastal shore. This time they would not be practicing on dry land, but in the rough waters they would soon be crossing. The Atlantic seemed colder and more treacherous than normal this time of year. Baron had heard of men swimming the English Channel, but he dismissed them as fanatics. The currents went fast and chaotic in this stretch of waters – this twenty-six mile alley of freedom. He didn't want their assault boat to flood with freezing water coming over the gunnels. With ninety pound sacks, no one could swim. He'd rather take his chances with the Germans on the cliffs than the icy waters of the Channel.

"Men, you'll never get use to the dark, and if the water's choppy, pick a morning star to focus on. Don't look at the waves. Go by touch. Riflemen, feel for your Garands, extra clips, and grenades. Check you left hand pocket of your assault jacket. Is the block of TNT and the fuse there?"

"AOK, Second Lieutenant." Russo shouted out.

Baron nodded in his direction.

"O'Brien and you other men of the wire cutting team, check for semi-automatics and ammunition belts. Each one of you four has his big cutter, right."

"Mine's big alright Baron." O'Brien quipped.

"Sure it is O'Brien. See that it doesn't get shot off." Baron retorted. The men laughed. They were a team setting up the batting order for the biggest game of their lives.

"Remember. There's four of you and four Big Ones – wire cutters that is." Baron waited for the laughter to subside. "If one of you drops his cutters, there's backup to carry on. Each one of you is crucial to the operation. You're the guys that are going to open up those gaps in the barbed wire for us to run through."

Baron looked over to Stone and Anderson.

"Now you, two-men teams carrying those Browning Automatic Rifles and bazookas. You four are our homerun hitters. You're carrying the big guns. The BAR men, check that you got all 900 rounds of ammunition."

"Yes sir, Second Lieutenant," both men answered in unison. "We'll spray those rounds and get those sons of bitches."

"Stone, make sure your bazooka is steady and held tightly when you pass it down into the LCVP and when you run out with it. Follow us – running – right onto the beach when the ramp slaps down."

"Got it, Shirley's ready and willing." Stone shot back as he hugged the big weapon that was the length of a stovepipe. Big black letters spelled out Shirley down the length of pipe. Neither Baron nor Wilson remarked that he had defaced Army issued equipment. It was now a 'non-regulation' issue. At this stage of the game, it didn't matter.

"And you Anderson, as his partner, make sure you stay with Stone. You're carrying the extra rockets and the carbine to protect him as he sets up Shirley to take out any bunkers or guns left standing from our Navy and Air Force early morning bombings and barrages. Remember to have your carbine loaded and ready to take out any enemy as he's setting up."

Anderson nodded in the affirmative and patted the light rifle which hung over his neck and right shoulder. Although they were anchored offshore, the vessel rocked and had to keep steadying themselves along the rail. Every so often, one of them would look down into the darkness to try to catch sight of one of the waves which they could hear slapping against the LCVP securely tied against the large transport ship. They could feel the cargo net strapped to the side of the ship's outer hull.

'You four men with the mortars check and double check. Are your twenty mortar shells secured? You're the men with what many think is our most effective weapon. Hang on to it and use it well. We'll need all the firing power we've got. And our flame-throwing team? All set to follow the mortar section?"

"Yes Sir. Our jelly gas will spurt all over those pill boxes, and my man Harold loves to light that fire," Jimmy, the kid of the thirty-two man team nervously joked.

"Be sure you don't set us on fire, Harold," Baron kidded back. But he was uncertain about these two – too green – too young.

It was like an overnight boy scout trip for them. He couldn't allow himself to think too much about what he considered the weak link of his team. If possible, he'd try to keep an eye on them after they got to the base of the cliffs. He looked back at the last section which would be in the LCVP - his five men demolition team. He would not have to worry about them. They were the ones that carried square packages and long poles charged with TNT.

In order to carry out their job they had to advance to the base of the concrete walls of any German pill boxes or gun emplacements left standing. To get that close they had to count on the others – Russo and the other men with the Garand rifles and grenades, Stone and Anderson with the BAR's and the bazookas, the four with the mortars, and lastly and most importantly on the two kids, Jimmy and Harold, with the flame thrower. These two had to douse any strong points with fire before the TNT team could plant its explosives. With the Germans stunned, the demolition men could make their final rush to set off the fuse and in the remaining three seconds hurl themselves out of the line of the blast. Baron knew they were ready.

They started to climb down the cargo net. Baron thought of how - once they hit the beach - he would need the two medics with their first aid supplies and helmets, blazoned with big red crosses. Now they sat in the rear of the boat. Baron looked at their helmets and wondered if the Germans would give a damn. After killing every Jew they could find, why should they abide by any rules of war? After all, did this grand absurdity, named World War 11, have rules? In a few days from now, they would all find out.

****

Luc, crossing the Channel at almost the same time that first day of June, heard the BBC's news bulletin. "A personal message to Marianne – from Pierre:

'Les sanglots longs.. Des violone.. de l'automne.'"

'The long sighing of the violins of autumn' Luc said out loud. He was in shock. They had endured and waited years for these lines of poetry to set in motion Resistance cells in Normandy. The invasion was imminent. He looked at Zosia's face turned toward the wind of France. The British would not broadcast this refrain again on the 15th of June as planned. He was certain the second half of Paul Verlaine's verse would be transmitted well before then. When the second half of

Verlaine's' famous poem was transmitted, the French in this sector of France would know the invasion would occur within 48 hours. They could finally spring into action.

Luc thought of Sainte Honorine as the waves splashed over the gunnels of the small boat. Saint Honorine, the simple name of his village, which enclosed a home and homeland that had been forever changed by these winds of war. Each time he carried dispatches in an out or smuggled British pilots back to England, he realized the Resistance fighters were becoming more determined and daring, and with their acts the Germans retaliated more ruthlessly. Each time he made his way in and out of France the changes ran through him like an electric current. Common landmarks and landscapes were eroded like the beach by the tides after a storm. People shattered like shards of glass. Some just disappeared. The Gestapo was good at that, and Hitler, excellent at selecting these disciples of Satan who made Europe and France a Hell on Earth.

Luc personally knew Hitler's manic defense of France. From the Cap de la Hague to Honfleur, Hitler had created his Atlantic Wall of 1,800 blockhouses spaced 100 yards apart. Built by Frenchmen forced to dig up their land and replace the rich earth with tons of cement, this fortified wall was meant to keep the free world out and them in. Pay and extra food was the incentive, but the Frenchmen saw neither. Guarded by German soldiers ready to shoot or beat to death any collaborator, resistance fighter or indifferent Frenchmen who labored in their own soil for nothing. Even the collaborators, who worked willingly, began to be more negative as the German promises turned to dust.

Denis Dubois and his father, Benoit, worked on the fortified gun turrets overlooking the beach near Colleville. For months they had dug a foundation and then poured cement to build this encircled prison of firepower. High on the bluff, its heavy guns faced the stretch of beach in front of it. Dozens of Frenchmen and thirty-five Polish prisoners were forced to build it. The prisoners and captured Frenchmen lived in trenches strategically placed all the way along the Atlantic Wall. . Along with the trenches were teller mines at the water's edge. German soldiers would be manning the big 88mil guns from the blockhouses, riddling the beaches with their MG-42 machine guns. Any man, caught in the crossfire patterns, set up from their safe deep trenches would face immediate death. Hitler just played a waiting game. The invading forces would be blown up as they approached or cut down if they hit the beach. The tide would take care of the rest. This Luc knew.

He thought of Raphael, the lead counter espionage agent inside of France who also had several cells with de Gaulle's Free French in England. The orders to take out the guns at Colleville and bring back German troop locations came directly from him. To work 'prudemment' was the understatement Luc thought. Of course, he'd be careful. He looked at Zosia and knew her life was his hands.

On these cold waters, he also thought of his father and sister who were part of one of dozens of Resistance cells in Normandy and Brittany. Working on the lines during the day, Benoit Dubois was allowed to return to his farm at night. Although strong for his forty-four years, he had become thinner and weaker as the months turned into years. He had been on the lines since the Spring of 43 and during that time he kept his ears open and mouth shut. Any information he passed to his resistance cell.

Every farmhouse and home of substance was occupied. At first the French were allowed to live on the ground floor with the German officers occupying bedrooms upstairs. In time, the owners were confined to one or two bedrooms upstairs, as the German officers took over the downstairs and any other room in the house. Finally, as the war progressed, the French land owners with barely the clothes on their backs, were pushed out into the fields and streets.

Luc had learned the specifics about his own farm from Francoise and Juliette. Both gave him information when he came to Paris for the business and what they could not provide, he got from Simon, Gustave, Pierre, and Lucie who were still alive. He was the conduit for many cells – from the coast of Normandy to the hub of Paris. He never ever told his mother that he was one of the ones who had pieces of rayon sewn beneath his lapel, shirt collars and inside his pants pocket. If one or the other was taken or ripped from him, he had another. He knew too much. He could not be taken alive.

Francoise and Juliette had been in Saint Honorine since Christmas. Francoise Dubois had remained in Paris to allow Juliette to go to school – to give her as much normalcy as possible, to continue the business, and most importantly to care for her father. The winters, since the Occupation, had turned more and more severe. Food and fuel shortages made the death rate soar. The young and the old were the most affected. She tried to get Michel Morneau to come to Normandy for Christmas and to remain there, but he was too frail and set in his ways. Born in Paris, he was determined to die in Pairs. The Boche had not displaced him in the first war, and he refused to let them do so in this second one. Openly defiant of the Germans, Michel Morneau wanted to die with honor and courage.

Luc knew she decided to stay in Paris and send Juliette home – for good. She was concerned about Benoit and knew that Denis was not caring for him – Juliette would. Juliette would also help with her father's dispatches. It was she who would slip out of her tiny attic room, since her own bedroom was now taken over by a German Colonel, and down through the hedgerows to locate the pigeon cage dropped by the RAF. Each time she found it, she would turn off its small battery light and carry it to the barn. She slid the slender tubes and pulled out the thin paper sheets rolled up inside. These she put in her sweater pocket. She set free the pigeons inside the barn and hid the cage under the hay. All the way back to the house she would touch the slim glass tubes and wonder what words they would now write to put in them. Often she or her father would write just one word, the name of a pilot they had found who would stay hidden until the time was right to send him through the underground and back to London. These missions were her contributions against the iron hand which squeezed France dry month by month. After January of 1944 her actions had become more and more defiant.

Too many would be lost if he let his mind race ahead. Instead, he had to focus on perhaps his final mission. In London he was told he would need a partner. He had always worked alone. He was doubly shocked, when he walked into de Gaulle's office and saw the back of a woman's head – full of soft auburn curls. A shiver went through his spine as he realized, before she turned her head, that it was Zosia.

"Je crois que vous connaissiez cette dame," the general had said.

"Oui, je la connais bien, mon general." Luc answered.

"Doc, vous savez qu'elle parle anglais, polonais, francais, et allemande," de Gaulle continued.

"Non, je n'ai pas su ca."

"O.K. Since we are in England, we speak the English." de Gaulle said.

Luc took the chair next to Zosia, and although she smiled briefly, his face remained frozen. He had told the general that he knew Zosia well, but not so well to know that she spoke German.. He had learned to separate his feelings from his actions. He did not think he could do so now.

"You know one another. This I know. This is one reason you work together. Trust and confidence there must be, non?"

"Yes", Zosia answered.

"Her polish is necessary and the German goes without saying. Some who worked on the Atlantic Wall fortifications are Polish - some Russian. She can hear and understand all. Yes, she is too tall for a Frenchwoman –but we falsified some papers with Norman-Anglo roots. Her French is impeccable. The Germans will believe she is French. She will be your fashion model girlfriend if questioned. Home to meet Maman. And who am I to say she is too tall to be French?" he stood up to his full atypical French height and laughed.

"Now, let us go next door. Raphael and the Americans will brief you on the guns of Colleville. The Germans have contrived three areas of defense from the water to the beach to the bluff where the blockhouse is situated.. Allons-y mes soldats."

And so they both followed the general as he led them out the door.

****

There was no doubt in his mind that Zosia was cut from the same cloth as Francoise and Juliette. He had never met anyone with their strength until he walked into Chez Tanya. Zosia, totally Polish in her allegiance to her country, nonetheless held a love for the English and an appreciation for the French. Her zest for life was limitless. She seemed so different to him., but it was not until he saw her come out of the Free French Headquarters and heard her speak French, that he knew she was one of them. A true Joan of Arc – full of fire and fury. At that moment that he knew he had met his match.

Now weeks later, he glanced at her in the dim moonlight reflecting off the sea and wondered if he could keep her alive. He had never felt that way before. Up to this moment, he had functioned and survived by erasing from his mind and heart all those who had fallen into the hands of the enemy. To think of their torture and suffering would uselessly cloud the present and make the future unattainable. He wasn't cold. He was the opposite – he felt too much. The mourning for the faces of friends in squalid rooms, prison cells, concentration camps or proudly standing in front of a firing squad would come when the war was over.

Luc now had to decide. He was bringing her into occupied France. If anything happened to her, could he tear her from his heart – isolate his emotions as he had done for the past three years in order to keep the network alive? With friends and family he had been able to draw the line between his heart and his head so many times before. Could he do it again? He thought about the last time – less than five months ago, which had proved to be the truest test – a homecoming of sorts.

****

The third week in January of 1944 brought more snow. Its blanket of white, however, could not hide the black oppression which smothered his country in its iron grip. As he walked through the hedgerows and apple orchards of the Dubois Farm, the six inches of fine fresh powdery snow provided the same silence as it had through the streets of Bayeux. A member of the resistance network had driven Luc by horse in his farm wagon for this last stage of his trip back home to Normandy.

Luc was amazed by the quietness of this once large town which had become more and more silent as the months turned into years. Businesses and homes had ceased to exist and many which remained had boards in place of windows and tarps on their roofs to block out the cold winds and snow from entering the gaping holes. He went to a safe house, the one of his oldest and best childhood friend, Paul 'Renard' Fortin.

"Assieds-toi, cher Luc. Madame Fortin said to him as soon as he entered the warmest room in the house, the kitchen. He sat next to Paul, the seat he always took in his Madame Fortin's house.

"Voila un beau pot-au-feu, mais malheuresement pas de viande." Paul's mother said as she placed a steamy bowl of stew and hot fresh crusty bread to dip in the 'pot-au-feu'.

"Merci il est delicieux. On n'a pas de plat special en Angleterre." Luc said with a wide smile, the smile that had endeared him to her since he was a little boy.

She cradled his face in both her coarse hands and kissed him on one cheek and then another. "Bienvenue chez nous et ton retour en France."

He kissed her back and told her the stew was so good with its thick stock of potatoes and parsnips. He knew all the food cupboards were almost bare and that she had probably dug in the frozen earth for whatever was still buried from the summer. Luc and Renard reminisced about their boyhood summer days on the beaches and in the fields of Normandy. They told one another it would be the same again, soon.., yet all knew, except 'petit' Claude, Paul's younger brother, that it would never be the same.

Renard told Luc all the information he had gathered from his cell: troop stations and movements, artillery locations, munitions supplies, occupied houses, fortified bridges, flooded fields. Renard had memorized every foot within a hundred kilometer radius. Most importantly, he knew every fortification that lined the coast and beaches from Port-au-Bassin to Pointe du Hoc. Renard, like Benoit Dubois and many other able bodied Frenchmen, was forced to work on the "Atlantic Wall'.

The pay that would have helped his mother and brother never came. He never thought it would. Without adequate nourishment, he barely had enough strength to do the work. He rarely spoke and kept to himself. He avoided eye contact with the German soldiers who stood guard with their machine guns at their hips. They began to assume he was deaf and dumb like his brother, little Claude.

Although a dozen years apart, Paul and Claude worked separately but in unison. Claude's job was to carry water along the line. Hour after hour he walked or took his bike down narrow dirt paths to the thirsty men neck deep in a trench or bent over a foundation of freshly poured cement. Claude could not speak and just nodded or smiled blankly at the men. Whatever they said, he kept filed in his incredible memory to tell his brother or his school master at night.

Born with hearing and sight, 'petit' Claude woke up one night after a burning fever, with no ability to hear and vision to see only milky shadows. The sight returned, sharper than a hawk, but he still could hear nothing except deep thunderous noises. The loss itself and its shocking entrance into his life took away six-year-old Claude's ability to speak.

The Germans assumed he was dumb as well as deaf and never censored their talk in front of him, but he could read lips perfectly from any distance because his mother and a German cousin used to talk incessantly to him. Yet, in school he was taunted by the other boys so he was kept at home where they could teach him to read and write. Monsieur Ross, Bayeux's schoolmaster, came weekly to drop off books for him and to show his mother and cousin what he needed to learn next.

Little did they know that Claude's brilliant intelligence and his deafness were really a gift from God – a gift that would be desperately needed within the next five years. By the time Germany had overrun France this twelve-year-old boy would become the actor of his life and in doing so would save hundreds of lives.

After lunch Renard began to speak of the latest news. "Petit Claude saw some high ranking German officers just after the New Year that he had never seen them before."

Claude smiled his knowing smile, and his eyes glistened. He signed for his mother to bring a scrap of paper. As he began to write a few words on the paper, Luc put his arm around

Claude's slender shoulders and said, "When the invasion comes, our allies cannot be driven back into the sea. The feet they place on French soil must be firmly planted like the roots of oaks. Only then can they carve their way to Paris and on to Berlin."

Claude proudly gave the note to Luc whom he admired and loved like another brother. It was Luc who had taught him to sail, shoot, and climb apple trees and never treated him as anything less than a complete person.

"General Rommel – un plan de Cherbourg a Honfleur," Luc read in amazement.

"When I questioned him about the General he saw, every detail fit the description of the Dessert Fox. Also in Claude's mind is the plan of all the coastal defenses from practically the tip of France to the mouth of the Seine." Renard added excitedly.

"Incroyable, mon vieux," he slapped the back of Renard and lifted Claude up in a joyous hug.

"That copy we must get. For three weeks, my cell and others have been searching. We narrowed it to Caen. By the time you leave, you'll have it in your hands to take back to England."

"Excellent, Renard and especially you, Claude."

"Luc, to you I must say again. Trust your brother with nothing." Renard looked to his mother and his own brother before he said what he had never spoken before. "Things have changed under your father's roof. I've heard it from Juliette, and I see it in your mother's eyes. Lead with your head and not your heart."

He searched his old friend's face, the face he had known from childhood and did not ask any questions because if Renard had wanted to tell the stories he would have, and Luc, himself, knew he could not cloud his mind with shadows of what might be or what might have been if he had never left. He simply nodded in agreement and focused on the task at hand.

"With that map, Renard, and the sword of God we'll lessen the hemorrhaging of blood on our beaches. Whatever blood is to be spilled, let's pray it be theirs," Luc lifted his glass to toast.

"All, including Madame Fortin, lifted their glasses as Claude took the slip of paper dropped on the table and ripped it up into several pieces before he threw it on the fire. Glancing at Luc, Claude's expression exhibited sorrow, as though Luc was the one to be pitied – not he.

Borrowing back his own bicycle from Claude, he traveled the narrow snow covered roads that were still passable to Vaucelles, Fosse Soucy, Etreham, and then up to St. Honorine where his home faced the cold Atlantic waters of the English Channel and the snow covered pastures of Normandy. Cutting across pasture land with its borders of familiar mazes of mammoth hedges, he had to side step ice filled troths dug into the soil. He kept his eyes riveted for any German patrols.

As he came closer to home, he could put names on the maimed houses and farms which blighted the white frosty skyline. Windows had no panes; houses had no doors; roofs gaped open like the mouths of the dead. The only visitors to enter these once convivial homes of neighbors and friends were the snow, rain, and the German soldiers. Suddenly, he heard what he expected to hear – the heavy slide-slap-click of a carbine.

"Qui etes-vous? Ou allez-vous?" said a voice with a German accent.

"Je suis Luc Dubois." Luc answered, carefully turning and letting his hands remain on the bicycle at his side. "My family lives over the next few hills."

The German soldier's eyes looked at him from head to toe and saw the clothes and stance of a Norman farmer but a face too pretty and delicate for one. "I haven't seen you before."

Luc just shrugged his shoulders in the typical fashion of his countrymen. The German took his lethargic attitude for weakness and lack of discipline. He was tired of questioning these obstinate Frenchmen and felt he was just another foolish one making the traditional rounds of New Year's greetings to his relatives and friends. He let him go on his way, but not without looking in what direction he was heading.

Along the way, Luc had stopped at two small houses – one the owner of a bakery in Etreham and another of a blacksmith outside of Fosse Soucy. Each man had told him how the average German soldier was sick of the war but too rigid and conditioned to alter their fate. They still followed orders perfectly, but without the zeal and perseverance of earlier days. However, the Gestapo and devote Nazis were more fanatical than ever. They had stripped off their mask of guile and now with ruthlessness and total abandon they tortured and killed at the least provocation. As the Resistance increased their sabotage activities, the Gestapo increased its retaliation.

****

As Luc came across the last field, he could see the two chimneys of his house jutting into the darkening sky. Since the fields were pitted with holes, he had left Claude's bike in the secondary wood shed hidden among the hedgerows bordering the eastern field. The lock was still on the door, and Luc found its key hidden in the secret knothole of one of the apple trees. He put the bike inside and glanced around the shed. Nothing seemed changed but there was an air of secrecy within its sturdy walls.

This had always been his and Juliette's childhood rendezvous place. It seemed untouched by time. Unused for years, nonetheless it was in pristine order. Even the two bunk beds he and Juliette had made from apple tree boughs were polished and spread with clean blankets. He left quickly and relocked the shed – placing the key back in the designated knothole.

Passing through the last of the bordering hedges, he stared at the familiar face of his home. Although more weathered, it appeared the same despite a few shutters hanging from a singular hinge. He glanced upward toward his bedroom window and noticed the window half way open with the curtains blowing outward. That – along with the figure he had first thought was standing by the window, surprised him. He bent his head and continued to trudge ahead.

"Luc, mon cher fils, tu es arrive!" his mother greeted him with just the right amount of expected surprise as she came, hatless and coatless, down the front path. She kissed him the customary greeting – adding an additional kiss on both cheeks. He returned her kisses and a strong hug that he learned from the English and the Americans. As Francoise leaned into him, she whispered, "Do nothing rash. Wait for the opportunity."

As he looked over his mother's head, he saw Denis' huge frame blocking the doorway with a German Colonel behind him. Both were expressionless. The Germans stopped the charade of friendliness in their occupied 'country' thirty-six months ago. When in the South, Petain's puppet Vichy Court ruled by an iron hand. The "Free Zone' was a misnomer. No one was free. He had made his way through Madrid and into the Free Zone which was the customary way if one had the right papers. What would have taken days, now took weeks. From his mother's warning Luc knew that his Christmas letter had been received and that his hopes for family unity and health were not to be.

"Oh la la, I have missed you so." Juliette threw herself into his arms and hugged him with a fierceness he had never experienced. She whispered just three words into his ear as he swung her around as he so often did in their childhood. "Revenge – in time."

He pulled her away and set her down so as to look into her face. Her smile was forced, and her lifeless eyes held an immeasurable sadness and weariness. With an arm around the shoulders of his mother and the waist of his sister, they walked up in a triumvirate to the forms waiting at the threshold.

****

"You could have done nothing for him. It was not just the lack of food and fuel that killed him, but the occupation." Francoise told Luc as he sat in his parents' bedroom in a chair from the downstairs parlor. The once beautiful room was packed floor to ceiling with his mother's favorite possessions. From every room in the house she had gleaned the objects she loved the most. Pillows, fabric, bric-a-brac, love seats, tables, chairs, photo books, paintings – every inch of wall and floor space was utilized. The large four poster mahogany bed, that he had jumped into when the lightening came with too much force for his childhood ears, still stood in the middle of the room.

Luc listened to his mother's words, how much could he tolerate and shelve to the back of his mind. "Did he suffer?"

His spine had hardened to match the times. He looked across the room at his sister, gazing out a window toward the sea, letting the words flow over her so as not to drown.

"Non, mon fils. He died quietly in his sleep."

"Before or after Christmas?"

"Before. Gabrielle, Colette, Juliette, and I had prepared a gourmet feast for him... all of his favorite foods. We had been scourging Paris for weeks. The Patisserie aux Framboises had shaved chocolate off the chunks used to make the German officers' 'gateau au chocolat'. Monsieur l'epicier had taken one pig's foot out of each jar he had in stock to make a special jar for your grandfather, and monsieur Henri provided a plate of his favorite pate and 'fromage' taken right from under the noses of the German command."

"I should have gotten you all out of Paris and out of this house," Luc spate out in dismay. "To live like prisoners in our own home – to die from the cold as the Germans use our fuel – to die from lack of food as they take our best to fatten their frauleins and their own expansive waistlines., Look how thin you two are, while Denis and that Colonel downstairs are specimens of health!"

"A Frenchwoman is never too thin, mon fils," his mother tried to joke lightly as his sister's face clouded over.

"So, he never came here for the holiday?"

"Non. After our feast I sent Juliette home with 'Baudelaire'.

Luc noticed how his mother used the code names for his Paris boyhood friends. Even in their own home, she felt she could not speak freely. This was not the time for any false slips of the tongue.

"I wanted to make certain there'd be enough provisions and heat for your grandfather while we were gone, so 'Baudelaire' took your sister as far as Argentan and 'Rimbaud' took her to Caen. From there Renard brought her home."

"I would have liked to say good-bye."

"Yes, I know. But he was so proud of you and Juliette. Proud of how you fight for France and for his beloved Paris. He was sick, Luc. Not just from lack of food and fuel, but sick at heart. The cloud of darkness and terror that permeates Paris suffocated him. When the joy and laughter left Paris, it also left his heart."

Luc gazed at the two women. Juliette could not be labeled as a child anymore. She had not just grown up physically, but there was something different about her nature. Pensiveness had replaced exuberance, sadness... happiness, and selfishness... selflessness. She was more giving yet more reticent and closed, had the occupation crushed her under its heel? Whatever the cause, Luc realized that the coltishness in her had vanished and in its place was a young cat... with a lair to hide in and claws and fangs for protection.

He looked intently at the faces of both of them as though to commit them to memory before he spoke again. There was only one other woman's face which was edging its way into his heart – that of Zosia's. He concentrated on those faces in front of him.

"There have been too many goodbyes."

His mother crossed over to him and placed her hands over his shoulders. She cradled his head and gently touched his black silky hair as she had done when he was a child. Juliette, hesitating at first, left her window and crossed like a panther to his feet and leaned against his leg. He caressed her long brown hair and rested his hand on top of her head. Silently, she stayed.

A moment in time – each did not want to be the first to move. By moving, the unity and strength would be broken and none of them wanted this close familiarity – this safe feeling to end. Stilled like a photograph before the picture is clicked, they did not hear the soft movements by the door, but only the knock which shattered the serene silence.

The door swung open without the intruder waiting for an answer. However, in that fraction of a second the three separated themselves and froze. In the door frame stood Denis. All he saw were three people separated by space and frozen in what appeared to be their own thoughts.

Francoise and Luc casually turned their heads toward the door. Juliette turned hers in the opposite direction toward the open window. Her back was turned against him.

"Sorry to disturb this family reunion," he said sarcastically, "but 'father' has returned from his daily surveillance."

Luc stared at him before he spoke in a low voice.

"And how is 'father', Denis?" he said with a gentleness that was absent in Denis' cold word. "Have you been taking care of Papa?"

"He takes care of himself, as usual... and his property," he retorted.

"Of course, it's 'our' property, yes? And don't you go with him to check the hedges and walls to keep the cows in and to make sure the apple trees are still upright and don't need staking?"

Luc knew the answer to this before he asked. He knew by Denis' presence, still blocking the doorway – going neither in nor out – that he had no desire for intimacy. He had chosen his side and just said, "I've been sent by him to tell you he's returned and hungry for diner."

Denis turned and walked down the hall. He waited in the hallway for a moment before moving on. They did not speak until they heard his footsteps going down the stairs.

"Your father did not send him up. The Colonel did. But your Papa is home. They cover truths with bold lies until no one can tell the difference."

"The difference is... that we can."

"And we always will," Juliette remarked to Luc. "I will tell you what 'our' two cells have accomplished – both in Paris and here in our sector of Normandy – since we spoke in July."

Luc knew he would have to wait until their walk in the morning mist. Then she could tell him what had happened in Paris. He had deliberately not stopped on his way from Madrid and only received pieces of information from his cells on route from the south to the north. Juliette and Francoise would relate any change and developments in Paris, and his father and Juliette would tell him about the last months in Normandy. With what Renard and Claude had told him about the continued fortification along the coast, he needed whatever other information they could supply.

His mind worked quickly. Did they know of the 'map'? Had they disrupted any fortification construction or delayed German progress in any way? He had to get the 'map' back to England as soon as possible, yet still give this new Colonel' and

Denis the impression that he was a weak Parisian – concerned only about fashion and the 'good' life.

These new 'Germans' along with the forced Polish/Russian troops now occupied the Dubois' farm had been taught about the standing arrangement he had with the main occupied forces in Paris. They had heard from command that Luc was here to see his family – for the holiday he could not make because of the delays war caused – but also for business reasons to talk about the spring summer line. The Colonel wanted for a long time to see Luc for himself to confirm the impression that Denis and others before him had given that it was the 'pretty' brother, the 'cannot make a decision' brother – the Parisian bred brother who needed to show 'maman' the fabric samples from Italy and Spain for her approval. The Colonel had been told that she controlled the business – especially now that the grandfather had died.

Neither cared who really controlled 'the business'. They only cared that their enemies believed their charade. Luc would show his mother the designs and fabric for a clientele of Germans and collaborators. For this season of 1944 there was even less fabric but enough style for the German wives and collaborator mistresses who still had money to buy such frivolity as fashion while their countrymen died of famine.

****

Out of sight of the Colonel and the sleeping troops, Luc, Benoit, and Juliette walked arm in arm across the once vast green pasture that now contained but a few cows. Benoit gently had touched the cows' soft wet noses in the mist of January. Their breath was warm on his hands. It was a sensation that he had always taken for granted. Now, he realized the most precious and simple things in life brought the most joy. Juliette swatted the emptiness with a dead apple branch she had picked up from the frozen ground, and Luc stared at both of them.

"Your sister and I have accomplished cells. She finds the pigeons the British let loose at night or the ones they bring through the lines by rubber boat off the little islands near Moursaline. Those she brings back one by one underneath her coat when she walks or rides her bike back from the contact point."

"Right under the nose of the Gestapo at times," Juliette mused.

"You must be more careful. A carrier pigeon without a message is not worth the risk."

"But the men we occasionally hide and send back to fight are."

"Choose your battles my sister."

"Her band of young people poured sand into the oil of the gear boxes of the tanks which line the flat cars between Caen and Falaise. These Tiger tanks are enough for a division. They've been sitting on a secondary railroad track since December. The Resistance believes they're designated for Calais."

"Their engines start just fine. They warm them up every day but don't take them off the flat cars. The Boche will never know they can't move until they try to get them into action. Then it will be too late." Juliette proudly stated.

"And petit Claude is one of your 'men'?"

"One of the best. No one ever suspects him. They think he's deaf and dumb, but he's the smartest boy. When he is close enough, he can read the lips of the Krauts in charge then translates any key information into French. He's saved at least a dozen of our people by getting them out before the Gestapo came in."

"Papa, I know you're in contact with Renard." Luc paused before he continued. "My job is to get the Allies into France by way of our beaches and off before the Germans spray them with their big 88's. Claude saw a map – a map outlining German defenses along our coast. When the invasion starts, our allies need to know in advance what fortifications, artillery, and troops they'll be facing. This map indicates that. It will determine whether the world wins or loses. While the world still waits, I must find it and get it out of France."

They continued to walk toward the sea and away from the secret shed where any downed British or American airmen, any Jews or sought after Resistance fighters were kept until they could be smuggled out of France. The only one in the family who was not aware of the shed's existence was Denis. Never privy to their childhood games, Juliette and Luc had kept it a secret.

Benoit stopped on the second to last hill from the beach – the Atlantic seemed relatively calm. He prayed that it would be that way the day the invasion came. He also prayed for strength – the strength to maintain the charade that he and his family were forced to live. Could he still continue to restrain himself from killing the Colonel who slept like a viper beneath his roof?

Shutting his eyes before he turned to look at Luc standing next to him, he paused and then turned to face Luc's profile, etched like a beautiful Grecian head against the gray clouds off the Channel's Coast.

"That Colonel, who now sleeps in your bedroom, raped your sister."

Juliette turned her head quickly to look at her brother's face. Her eyes had no shame – just hatred. She had to see what passed over his face in that instant. Accusation? Pity? Hatred?

His eyes closed for a long time and tears rolled silently down his face. Then he clenched his jaw, opened his blue eyes, and turned them toward his sister's. What she saw in his eyes amazed her as it always had. She could see them turn color like a chameleon – from cornflower blue to a steel gray as cold as the Atlantic in front of them. The hatred she read in them scared her as nothing had before. It seemed that the very veins, which carried their warm filial blood, was syphoning in the icy waters from below the cliffs. She had her answer before he blanketed her in his hard muscular arms and broad shoulders.

Benoit touched his son's shoulder and let go the tears he had kept hidden from his wife and daughter. His heart broke every time he thought of the Colonel's hideous act of violence. To defile his daughter ... to take her innocence, trust, and love of life in one lustful act of indecency was more than he could bear. Now, he had a man to share the burden with. His shoulders were tiring from the weight of German indignities.

How long they stood a frozen trio silhouetted against the January morning of another new year they did not know. Benoit had been the first to speak again. A man of few words, he spoke of despair and fury at not being able to kill this man. The shame he felt for himself, his wife, and his daughter had no end. To remain in their home which was now simply just a house was further cruelty. His ancestral home only covered them from the outside elements – there was no safety or sanctity inside.

"You chose the only course of action possible, Papa. Otherwise, you'd all be dead." He looked his father in his eyes. "By doing nothing you also protected the Resistance. By choosing not to kill this one German, you have killed others and saved the lives of allies and Frenchmen. Your personal revenge will come.... in time...soon."

Juliette waited until her father was half way back to the house. Then she spoke. "There are two things you must know that no one else knows." She took her brother's hands in hers and held them tight. "Before I tell you, you must promise not to take any action – as you have told Papa...until after."

Now he would know what else he needed to understood what his mother had whispered when she greeted him yesterday afternoon. Twenty-four hours had not yet passed and his once secure place in this chaotic world was upside down. Now, what would his sister add to Francoise's three words of yesterday..." Revenge... in time".

She squeezed his hands tight. He nodded, 'yes'.

"When the Colonel raped me, Denis was outside the door – the entire time."

Luc's hands shook with fury and clawed the thick air. He leaned his head back and let out a primeval yell that matched the vastness of the empty landscape around him.

She grabbed his hands and forced him to look in her eyes. "Only petit Claude knows about Denis. Claude had seen him whispering to the Colonel- making a deal with him for 'his sister a few days later."

"Salaud. Bestial traitor," Luc screamed at the heavens.

Calmly, Juliette continued. "I've used his lust against them all. The Colonel and I ... have met. He thinks he has seduced me with his charms – that I am filled with desire for him. Because of his vanity, I get much military information which I pass on to the Resistance."

"Ma chere Juliette, I am in such pain for you."

"I know 'mon cher frere'." She allowed the tears to come to her eyes. Not for herself but for him and her father and mother. "I've told mother that the German sneaks into my room when I've indicated all is clear. I think he realizes father would kill him... this time, if he knew. Denis thinks I am a whore who he rightly sold to the Germans. Mother knows I am a patriot and am doing what I need to do... have to do to have us all survive."

She continued with eyes downcast, "Besides when I shut my eyes, the fool takes it for passion.. not sheer hatred."

"As God is my judge, when the time comes, I will kill them both." Luc declared.

'Until that time – let neither of them trap you to unmask your true feelings."

"I feel like 'The Man in the Iron Mask', concealing the good along with the bad. When this ends I hope I will be set free."

Juliette had never seen her brother so broken. To touch him could crack him completely. She steeled ahead. "Maman and Papa are cold to Denis and cannot hide their disdain. For them it is because of his camaraderie with the Germans- nothing more. He does as they wish so they will grant him favors. When he and Papa worked on the 'Wall', he was one of the few who got paid and was given for his work free bottles of looted wine and circles of camembert. These of course, he never shared with any of us – not even Papa. Instead, he drank his loot after a day of digging alongside the piles of dirt and in the company of German infantrymen."

Luc had cleared off a patch of ice for himself and Juliette. He motioned for her to sit down next to him. It was as though she was telling him a 'bedtime' story like the ones he used to tell when she could not fall asleep at night. She sat down next to him and continued.

"He left Papa to walk all the way home by himself since he had taken his bike to 'lend' to a new found friend, a German officer. It was Renard and Claude who saw Papa walking home alone that day. He spoke few words about his feelings but when they saw Denis early the next morning neck deep in the trenches – digging furiously, Renard realized by his stench and attitude that he had spent the night with the Parisian whores the Germans had brought in for their officers.

"When did this happen?"

"In November, it was the last week they worked on the 'Wall'."

"And the rape," Luc said in a softer voice.

"23 of November. Maman had sent me home while she stayed in Paris with 'grand-pere'. I left on the fifteenth and did not get home until the twentieth. She spent Christmas in Paris, for he died the day she was to leave – on the twenty first. His burial could not take place until after Christmas."

"Merde", Luc muttered. "Cette guerre est terrible."

They each faced the sea, side by side, but lost in their own individual thoughts. If one could avoid looking to the west and the block house at Colleville and not let one's gaze fall down to the beach and the mined obstacles clearly visible at low tide, the coast line and channel seemed the same, as though war had not touched the face of France. The snow covered the marred land pitted with holes and the trenches with mole mounds of cancerous earth.

Juliette broke the silence.

"I know where in Caen the map is."

Luc looked at his sister in surprise. Her adversity had killed the child in her, but had bound the woman in steel.

"Not only do I know where it is, but I have figured out how you will be dressed and where you must conceal the map in order to get it out through the South and then to England."

He had underestimated her resourcefulness and resilience. It seemed that she had learned much in Paris."

"So tell me your plan." He turned now to listen to her tell a different story as he and the rest of the world waited.

Chapter 8 – June 1, 1944

To Caen

His sister's plan that Paul and Claude would carry out was ingenuous. Renard had accompanied his brother to La Blanche Herbe, a little village to the west of Caen. Although Claude had taken this route many times before on the pretext of trading his mother's 'comfiture de pommes ' for whatever items Madame Fortin had written down on a torn off section of brown paper, this time he appreciated the ears and eyes of his older brother. On this most important mission nothing could be left to chance.

Most of the soldiers he met along the way had either seen him before and simply dismissed his presence or waved in a gesture of normalcy. By afternoon of the second day he and Renard arrived at La Blanche Herbe, where they spent the night with Father Etienne who was one of his mother's cousins. They attended the evening mass in his small stone church where they had been baptized as infants. It was home to them and to his congregation. The members of the Church of La Blanche Herbe always marveled at both boys' growth and fervently prayed for hearing and speech for 'le pauvre petit Claude'. Old women with tears in their eyes kissed the top of his head and the young women with children touched his cheeks but seemed to keep their children at arms' length from him.

On this particular Thursday both brothers scanned the faces of the congregation to detect any signs of collaborators. There could be no one to prevent them from getting the map, locked in a metal box in a prestigious house on Rue de Saint Francois, the best street in Caen. The current occupant was a German commander who opened the locked bottom desk drawer of the ancient desk in the front salon each morning and every night. Each time he patted the metal box with his plump hand.

Except Father Etienne none of the people in the Church of La Blanche this cold February week day of 1944 knew of this map or of the box. Each member had their own transgressions and sins Father Etienne willingly heard. The war had made every day a Sunday. He gave them penance and blessings in the name of the Lord. And of the Lord he asked guidance as he passed the most important of these sins onto the Resistance. After the service all three knelt before the cross in the small cold stone church and prayed for strength and guidance to carry out this most dangerous and crucial mission.

Renard and Etienne slept restlessly that night and between fitful bouts of sleep, Renard lay awake staring at the wooden beams in Etienne's small spare bedroom. When he would turn to gaze upon the sleeping Claude, he would often see Etienne standing in the doorway looking at them both and making the sign of the cross.

Early the next morning Renard kissed his brother on both cheeks and fiercely hugged him to his chest. Cousin Etienne made the sign of the cross with holy water on his forehead. Both made certain he had his satchel filled with the two dozen jars of jam securely cushioned against one another and the smaller brown leather sack filled with the biscuit tin, one tiny jar of jam, a small knife, and a bottle of mineral water. Then Claude bicycled alone toward Caen. He stopped at all the normal places where his mother's homemade apple jam was welcomed and would show each customer his mother's list. They, in turn, would put the traded item into his large brown leather satchel.

Since no one had seen him in this New Year, each visit took longer than usual. They greeted him exuberantly and all wished to share a little something with him whether it be a precious piece of taffy, a fresh chunk of bread, or a pause by the warmth of a fire. When he left the security of each house, he'd make his way through the maze of narrow streets. Some he would begin down, then have to circumvent because the rubble of stone from destroyed buildings blocked his path. On occasion he would come upon a German patrol who would yell at him and then angrily motion for him to empty his satchel. This he would gingerly do so as not to break the jars of apple jam. He would show them the list his mother had written and the checks to indicate what he was doing on the streets of Caen in the middle of winter.

When they were satisfied usually in mid search, he would offer the head soldier a biscuit from the brown sack he carried. He would carefully open the tin and let them select just one. He was so precise in his mannerisms and his face so expressionless, except for that first smile he always gave them, that they were shocked into following his hand directions.

At last he returned to a small church on the edge of Caen leading back to La Blanche Herbe. In the safe sanctuary he sat praying. A tall priest stood at the open door when petit Claude had entered. For several minutes he continued to stand there adjusting the large wool shawl he wore over his shoulders. Then he slowly and deliberately shut the heavy oak door of the church.

Walking down the aisle of his church, he passed the boy sitting in the pew who was carefully lifting out biscuits from a tin. Like toy soldiers he was making a line of them on the pew next to him. He smoothed out the multi-colored rayon fabric with its little fleur de lis pattern that acted as a liner for the tin and then carefully selected one of the biscuits to eat.

When Claude saw the priest's robes passing by he looked up. The priest mouthed. "Maintenant, on attend. Now we wait."

By the time Claude was chewing his last bite, he felt the pew move beneath him. The few parishioners in the church ran out to see if the ear deafening explosion was their house this time. The street was full of German soldiers racing toward the center of town. Fire trucks sounded; shouts were heard, orders given. The boy heard nothing. He lifted his head up to view the cross in the front of the altar. From the corner of his eye he saw a figure in the shadows brush into the priest who still stood erect. In what seemed to be an act of straightening his robes the priest pressed a square brown envelope into the inside pocket of his robe. With slow precision, he then walked to Claude and bent over him. His tall figure masked the envelope he passed to the boy as he said in a loud voice.

"You must go home my son. There was an explosion again."

Claude looked up into his eyes as he took the envelope. He fitted it into a slim secret water proof pouch which matched the fleur de lis pattern of the tin's liner.

The priest gently motioned the boy to go. In response, Claude simply nodded his head at the priest and began to meticulously pack up his biscuits. One by one he placed each inside the tin again, making them fit like the pieces of a puzzle. He slid the tin once again into his brown leather satchel and left the church through the side door.

By the time he was bicycling down the main street out of Caen, no German soldier took the time to stop or even question him. Many had seen him that morning, and those who had not were too busy aiding the call from Commandant Holfestedder's housekeeper. She had waited until the fire was already an inferno before she ran out into the street screaming.

It was not until evening that the fire was contained. By that time the formidable house of Monsieur Huglois was a skeleton of charred posts and two burnt black chimneys. Monsieur Huglois himself stood outside shaking his head in utter despair, but his eyes held another emotion... that of victory. This had not been his home since the Germans had taken control, and the commandant, who had given him the edict to leave, was lying, charred to oblivion next to what had been the twelfth century walnut desk of Monsieur Huglois. Its bottom right hand drawer secret compartment had collapsed and along with it, the German high command map of the Atlantic Wall.

After strangling the commandant, Monsieur Huglois waited for the explosion. He had taken his spare key to open the desk's drawer before setting fire to the room. He stepped over the body on his way out the door, passed the map to the housekeeper who slid it into the diaper of a baby being pushed in a carriage by her young sister on the kitchen side entrance of the house. Afterwards, the housekeeper pretended to look frantically for a German officer. She waited until the fire spread completely before she began to scream.

Claude, Renard, and Father Etienne slept soundly that night as the biscuit tin sat boldly on the priest's kitchen table. Early the next morning Claude and Renard refilled the tin with a parishioner's tasty apple caramel tarts to offer to any officers on the way pack to Saint Honorine.

****

Somewhere in the Channel,
West of Pointe du Hoc

Now four months later Luc looked at Zosia's face blackened with tar to match the night air of this cold June night. Their mission was based on the reliability of the map he had carried back to England in March. Many times he had thought of Juliette's plan which had worked without a hitch. Dressed in priest's robes and carrying a Bible in his hand, Luc was passed into the hands of only the most able of Juliette's and Renard's men and women until he reached the Benedictine monks of Mont Saint Michel. In such robes he traveled through Colleville, St. Lo, Avranches, and across to Nante. At Mont Saint Michel he had rested, and took solace in the cold high stone walls of the Monastery with the peace that it afforded.

On his last morning he stood inside the Monastery garden high on the mound of this little island, separated only by the high tidal waters which surrounded it twice a day. The rose bushes stood as sticks waiting to bloom in the warm salt air and rich fertile soil of this enclosed sanctuary. Luc looked over the high strong thick walls of Mont Saint Michel and the expanse of Atlantic that separated this far point of French soil from free English air.

Where along this expansive coast would the Allies land? At Calais, the most narrow crossing or as far west as where he now stood? Would this Monastere-Forteresse from the 1200's survive the bombings that would soon destroy dozens of towns and thousands of people or would Mont Saint Michel crumble like the Maginot Line had? Would its Archangel Michael wrestle again on the rocks of the Mont with the devil, this time in the form of Nazi Germany. Could he like Michael win once more for God and the people of France? Luc prayed for the strength of Michael in order to fool the German war machine and slide this map right out from under its nose.

Luc brushed his left hand over the bib of his Benedictine priest's robe as his right hand he held the Bible tightly. Inside its back cover rested the freedom of the world. Juliette had sewn the map inside the black leather cover. He remembered thinking, "I've made it this far and have collected information along the way to be set in motion once the invasion began. God willing, I'll make it to the sailor's boat off the coast of Spain.

For once Luc was glad that his face was pretty, since that along with the robes had allowed him to gain passage through the rest of France's coastline and over the border into Catholic Spain and the coastal town of Saint-Jean-de-Luz. His years of Catholic training had let him pass as a man of the cloth. As he moved from village to village, he looked into the eyes of the men he had known only by their code names, but never into the eyes of those German soldiers who stopped him or whom he saw crossing his path. He kept his eyes obediently subservient. This absurdity was clear.

"After all, I only have to fool the Germans, not the Italians."

****

Four months had passed, and he was again in a boat crossing the same Channel – but going back – again, to his France. He was returning to destroy one of the most powerful fortifications on Hitler's Atlantic Wall, the guns of Colleville. The fishing boat, whose captain Luc had known since childhood, cut its motors one mile from the coastal point of Pointe du Hoc. He was letting Luc and the girl out beyond the Roches de Grandcamp, the deadly rocks which made up the natural fortification for this part of France's coastline. They would attempt their landing at high tide on the area that was the most desolate between the towns of Maisy and Gefosse. With no villages and only four connecting roads, it was far enough east of the River Vivre which opened up into a salt water inlet and a bay.

"Luc, I do not like leaving you to the mercy of Les Roches de Grandchamp,' the old fisherman said.

"We have no choice Guillaume. Besides my worries are the Germans. This coastline I know, almost as well as you," he said with a smile and a Gallic shrug to defuse the worry on his old friend's face.

"Guillaume grunted. "'Ouais. The rubber dinghy is ready. I have put additional waterproof mesh netting on your satchels."

"'Merci', Guillaume. This fog and the night will cover us as securely was your wrappings for out satchels."

"I hope so my young friend", the fisherman said as he kissed him on both cheeks and did the same to Zosia. "Take care of one another."

"Pas de problem," Luc answered lightly as he hugged the fisherman a brief strong good-bye.

They carefully climbed down the netting on the side of the boat and into the dingy which lay suspended like a big green cocoon in the cold calm Atlantic. As they paddled toward shore, they heard Guillaume say, "Aille le bon dieu avec vous' – May God go with you."

****

When they got over the last rocks near the shore, they still could not see land. Luc not only knew when they would hit land but approximately where they were in the huge expanse of hidden cliffs which towered above them. As the crashing of the waves on land became louder, neither spoke until the sharp bump was felt beneath the bottom to the dingy. "Get ready to jump, crouch, feet first," Luc whispered. On the next sharp bump the hiss of air punctured the night and the fog cleared at the base of the cliffs.

"Jump."

Her heart was thumping, but she did as he commanded. With total trust she followed him. Bobbing in the surf, she kept her head above water and her arms outstretched to protect her from the rocks in front and below. Her hands, protected by thick rubber gloves strapped at the wrist, paused over their slippery sharp surface. She could feel the occasional cut from the razor-like rocks which sliced through to her palms and fingers. Suddenly, Luc stood up in front of her and reached back for her hand. She grabbed it, and as she stood up, she felt her boots hit the solid rock shelf beneath her feet. They walked out of the cold Atlantic at the highest tide mark onto a mere path of sand two feet wide beneath the dark cliffs. Breathing hard, they flattened their backs against the rocks and slide down onto the wet sand.

Without a word Luc stood up and took off his satchel. Pressing it against the cliff, he opened it and took out a small sharp pick, coil of thin parachute rope, and a fold up shovel which he handed to Zosia. The first ten feet were the most difficult. He climbed above as she worked below.

Luc reached up. The sheer smooth wet surface provided very few edges or crannies to get a toe or finger hold on. Cautiously, he made his way up to the top where he wedged two metal pins in adjacent crevices to secure the rope that he tossed down to Zosia. She tugged on the rope to indicate that she had buried the rubber remains of the dingy. She had no difficulty, for the night was clear and the stars sharp. The moon would be full in the next week, but for now there was enough visibility for both to see. On this expanse of empty cliff and pasture land, Luc already knew exactly where he was.

He lay flat on the ground so as not to create a target. His sources had said no patrols or guns existed in this sector, but he took no chances. He looked over the side as Zosia climbed her way up the face of the cliff. As she neared him, he grabbed her by the shoulders and lifted her over the ledge.

Flopping over like a large fish, she flipped on her back panting for air. Her wool black hat and wool black jersey made her appearance even more incongruent. Regardless, Luc leaned over her blackened face and kissed her full open mouth. Her taste was a pleasant salty sweetness that filled him with warmth and desire. She put her arms around his neck and pulled his torso on top of hers. His strong sinewy muscles pressed against her firm full chest, and they both were never as alive as at this moment between promised life and prospective death. She looked into his eyes – a blueness that still shone through the dark.

"Was that the French version of mouth to mouth resuscitation?" she laughed.

"'Non', that is my version of what is to come if we ever get out of this alive."

"Then, that will give me a further incentive 'mon plus cher Luc'."

"I always separated my head from my heart. But I now cannot. I tried 'ma belle'. But there are no rules now. Zosia, no matter what happens, I need for you to know - simplement, je t'aime'".

She gazed into his eyes to etch this moment in time forever. "I love you too with all my heart. 'Je t'aime, Luc'", she said as she pulled his head down to feel the fullness of his lips again.

They were alone on this stretch of land, seemingly at the end of the universe. The silence. The stars. The oneness with all that surrounded them. They wanted to abandon themselves to their passion, but both knew this was neither the time nor the place. De Gaulle had chosen them well as a team. They matched one another in size, spirit, and commitment. As they had come together willingly, they separated from one another at the moment the kiss ended and before another one began. Falling back, they clasped hands and looked up at the dark heavens. Nothing was said until the rat-ta-tats of a machine gun rattled them out of their reverie and back into a time and place that would never be again.

"Allons-y, ma camarade," Luc whispered as he motioned her to follow him into the darkness.

Their initial movements were slow as he crawled ahead of her and jabbed his eight inch knife in the ground in front of him. The soil was stiff and pebble-like, not conducive to placing mines, but the Germans were thorough. He could take no chances. Once they were over the two hundred yards that separated them from the first stone wall and the hedges that bordered them, he would be certain of their exact location.

Throughout history this sector had been impassable because of its rugged rocky terrain. Few farms or houses occupied this barren stretch of coast, for only the most hardy or foolish would choose this land to live on.

Zosia followed him as they inched their way forward in the dirt finally coming to rest at the stone wall. It was a relief to sit up against the rough stone of the wall to scratch the wet wool itching her skin.

"The farm of the DeVanchers is to our right, and the house of Madame Blanche is to our left."

Zosia peered over the wall to look at Luc's explanations. She could barely see anything in the darkness, just two darker squares, book ended by taller thinner forms on either side. The horizon appeared far away, and it would take them hours if they had to crawl on their bellies, but they both knew from their briefings that this pasture land between was not mined but rather had traps called 'Rommel's asparagus', another insidious device of the German tank General. Luc could clearly see their outlines, for no Norman farmer would plant trees to grow in the center of pastures. These tall thin vertical forms were ten-foot high poles with wires across the top which were linked to explosives and buried mines. If any gliders carrying paratroopers tried to land, they would hit the wire and explode on landing.

"See Rommel's asparagus," Luc said as he pointed to the tall thin shadows in a hexagonal patter in the center of the pasture.

"So we cross on the outside," Zosia confirmed the obvious.

Slowly, they walked along the peripheral with Luc as the lead man. He had taken out three cylindrical metal tubes and screwed them together to form a cane. In the first section lay a blade hidden within the tube which worked on a spring trigger. If the cane was slapped hard against a straight surface, the knife shot out and locked in place as a lethal weapon. In silence they made their way within fifty yards of two more walls which bordered a small road between the properties of Madame Blanche and the DeVanchers.

They heard distinct footsteps on the pebbled surface of the road and the whistling of a tune that sounded sad to Luc but brought a flood of memories to Zosia. They both froze in place, black silhouettes against the velvet dark of a night jeweled by only a few stars. Luc began to lower himself. He lost his balance. His back foot came down hard on a twig and the crack resounded in the silence. The whistling stopped, and the footsteps changed direction. Suddenly, a click of a rifle cut through the night air.

"Who goes there?" a young voice said in French.

By this time Luc was flat against the ground hidden in the stubble of grass that was just beginning to grow. The cane lay flat against his side Luc turned his head to see if Zosia's movements indicated her position flat on the ground behind him. Instead, he was surprised to see her feet – bare without the rugged boots of the landing – step in front of him.

She cried out as though in pain and staggered fully exposed, straight ahead of him. He looked ahead and saw her strong bare back facing him with her black men's trousers falling slightly off the curve of her full hips.

"Oh, my countryman, help me I have been raped," she cried out in Polish as she ran her hands bloodied from the rocks over her face, neck, and breasts.

The soldier's flashlight found her form and cast a light white against the whiteness of her skin.

"Oh my God" the young soldier reverted to Polish. "How are you here so far from home?'

'You know we have no home," was Zosia's anguished answer.

The boy dropped his gun and helped Zosia over the wall. Luc could see him take off his jacket and place it over her shoulders. He wet a cloth with water from his canteen and wiped the blood from her face and neck. He kept murmuring in Polish to her as though she were the child and he the adult. All the while Luc inched his way forward with the cane, level at his side.'

"Who did this to you?" Luc heard him ask in Polish

"You don't know the answer to that?'

"That disgusting German Major, non? I thought he had enough Parisian whores for his amusement."

He was going to say more, but before he spoke again he asked, "How did you know I was Polish?"

"That melody you were whistling is a Polish lullaby my mother used to sing to me."

"So sing it to me then," the boy responded as he wet the cloth and gave it to her before he picked up the rifle. He waited for her to answer.

Luc was at the foot of the wall. All he had to do was slap the cane against the wall and vault over. In one movement the knife would be in the boy's chest. In that moment he heard Zosia's throaty voice, wafting through the night air singing of nightingales in May in the lush fields of a free Poland.

The boy put down his rifle and openly wept. He placed his head on Zosia's shoulder and sobbed for the mother and sisters raped and killed by the Germans for whom he now had to fight. Zosia held him fiercely to her bare breasts and tears flowed freely down her dirty blood stained face as the buried memories – too joyful and too painful – of her dear April came to the surface. She thought of April, who had lived with beauty and fought with courage and in death, had given Zosia her gift of freedom from fear. When she buried her closest friend, April's fearlessness escaped the grave and was instead interred in Zosia's bones. It was for her friend's daughter, Helena, and her son, Janucz, that she now fought. Although they no longer had the country their mother had chosen for them, they had the freedom she had so courageously paid for – with her life.

Looking over the boy's head, she saw Luc climb over the wall.

"C'est d'accord – je suis francais." Luc said to the boy as he turned abruptly like a young animal backed against the wall.

He looked at Zosia and then back at Luc.

"Yes, it's o.k. He's really Polish. My God, he looks like.."

"Janucz... oui, c'est clair," in amazement Luc finished her sentence.

"He can be no more than fifteen – just a boy, and just like Janucz at that age. I remember well; perhaps, too well our other lives which seem like mirrors, jagged with images through time." Zosia said with sadness.

The boy could not understand English, but realized Luc was truly French, for that language he had learned fairly well. His face was calm and a certain sign of hope seemed to appear in his blue eyes.

"Let us remember Warsaw." the boy said softly and slowly in Polish

"... and never forget the Forests of the Katyn." Zosia methodically finished the phrase, and added..."out of the graves..."

"....the eagle will fly.' The boy with a big smile on his face finished the sentence this time.

Luc could clearly understand the entire discourse, for he too had memorized the passwords in Polish, in French, and in English to identify any real Pole who was part of the Resistance in France. Too many Russians who still had allegiance to Germany or were taken as part of the German labor force were trying to pass themselves off as Polish. Those free Polish forces who now knew about Katyn hated the Russians even more than the Germans. They would shoot any Russian who tried to trade on Poland's good name.

"You are one of us then. You are the ones I've been waiting for. You are fine – no German raped you?" the boy asked both of them in simple French.

"Yes, we do not know who our contacts are – only the codes by which to find them." Zosia answered.

"As you know, that way it's best for all – no names.. no nationalities." Luc added.

"They just told me to whistle Polish tunes. No words – except the passwords I would need for contact. I patrol every night

"To think I might have killed you." The boy said to Zosia.

"And I, you.' Luc added. "That is one reason why 'nightingale' is here. She is one of you." Luc told the young boy who knew only Zosia's code name, but never knew if it referred to a man or a woman. Luc knew the boy never expected an introduction to himself – other than 'Dumas'.

"And, I am..." the boy began to add.

"Freedom... 'la liberte'", Luc finished in both languages.

"I like the sound of the English although I know none," the boy laughed like a child who just discovered something new and wonderful.

There, the three crouched incongruously by the side of this narrow dirt road in the silence of a starry June night – three individuals thrown together perhaps by destiny as well as chance. The boy took them to Madame Blanche who was waiting as she did most nights with warm hard apple cider and bread spread with camembert for those who had come on difficult journeys.

'Liberte' had gone back to his nightly patrols for the Germans. The French did not bother him because they knew he was Polish and the Germans made no note of him because he was just 'expendable foreign labor'. Because he was young, blond, and blue-eyed, they thought in time he would become one of them. They were wrong.

****

Madame Blanche had shown them to their room, hidden under the eaves of one of the many rafters in the large Norman farmhouse Her great-grandfather had built his home onto existing foundations and walls dating back from the times of the Norman Invasion. During the last century Madame Blanche had been born in this very house, and during the new century she had lost her husband and two sons in the First World War, and now in the Second she had given her two grandsons. Her fight, whether her grandsons survived this war or not, was to save as many sons and grandsons of the free world as possible. Whenever the Resistance asked, she simply nodded yes. All they had to give her was the time, place, and code name of whomever she needed to hide. If the polish boy brought them, she needed no names for he was like another grandson to her.

She took them to an oddly shaped dark room hidden behind a secret passage of an existing upper story bedroom. The large armoire bolted to the wall had a sliding back portion which opened up onto another room. The ceiling was very tall in the center and high up in one corner stood a shuttered window, large enough for a thin man to climb through. The steep pitch of the roof forced both Luc and Zosia to bend their heads. A large feathered mattress, layered with quilts, took up the center floor and in the corner opposite the window was a decorative screen covered with soft paint strokes of apple blossoms. A wash basin with lavender soap and towels and a chamber pot stood behind it. Two glass lamps with candles were placed on either side of the bedding.

It did not take them long to tumble into the feathered bed. Now was the time, perhaps the first and last time that they would ever be together. The cold fresh night air blew on their naked bodies illuminated like streaks of white lightening in the dimly lit room. Intoxicated by the calvados, by fear, and by the beauty of one another's strong lean bodies, they each let their fingers glide over the smooth muscles and soft lips of the other.

She let her fingers side through his black silky hair that was beginning to curl up at the nape and around his perfectly shaped ears. As though molding a Grecian head, she let her thumbs cover over his high cheek bones and across and down his aquiline nose. She brought his face to hers and with the softness of her full wide mouth kissed his eyes and tasted the salt of his eyelashes and gently slid her kisses down his beautiful face to his firm waiting mouth.

He slid his hands up to cup her chin, and she let her hands fall down to his chest which pressed against hers. She felt his strong hard torso, smooth against her soft full breasts and marveled at the perfectness of his body. As he pulled her body into his, her arms wrapped beneath his arms. He caressed her strong back. A shiver went through her being as his fingers like a pianist played down her spine, across the small of her back and over her high soft buttocks. In turn, his buttocks were hard and small, in direct contrast to his wide shoulders and long lean torso. They fit perfectly, each like the matching puzzle piece of the other. Slowly, they made love, for they had waited a long time for this moment. Each one wanted to savor it. They eagerly and passionately met one another at the same moment and opened their mouths to one another in an effort to muffle the moans of passion.

No one could have heard their cries, for Madame was already fast asleep in her room at the far corner first floor of the house and the pastures and beach, resting at nearly low tide, had no ears to hear. As the ocean moved to its own rhythms, so did they. After so many months of longing, they rose and crashed like the waves upon the beach until exhaustion pushed them into a heavy sleep each wrapped in the other's arms.

It was the discrete gently rapping on the wall of the armoire that woke them after too brief a sleep. The morning light had flooded the pastures and was playing gently on the waves which lapped the shore beneath the cliffs.

"Mes enfants, reveillez-vous. Are you awake?"

"Oui Madame, we are awake." Luc answered

"Bon, I left a breakfast tray on the table in the outer bedroom. Come down when you are finished." She said without waiting for a response and shuffled out of the room.

He turned to her. "Bon matin, mon amour. No matter what happens you must never doubt that."

She looked into his cornflower blue eyes, so blue that she could lose her being in their coolness and serenity. An overlay of white, like a few fluffy clouds on a perfect summer's day, passed over his gaze.

"You need not tell me. I know that." She said as she intently looked into his clear face. "I'm not going to lose you. We've come in together, and we'll leave together. No matter what."

He felt a complete responsibility for her. He was not the same person of twenty-four hours ago. He had crossed the line and could not go back. In order to keep her safe he had to treat her as a nonentity. To act without emotion but with instinct and intellect would keep them alive

As though reading his thoughts, she said, "I can take care of myself. I'm a survivor. Don't forget that."

He looked at her as she sat up and walked over to the screen. She turned and stood, tall and naked and pure as Eve must have first looked to Adam. Her auburn curls fell loosely around her full round face. With no self-consciousness she tilted her head back and ran her fingers through her wet knotted hair. Her breasts were like round pink grapefruits in the morning light and the line of her body flowed strongly into her flat stomach and long legs. She walked behind the screen and Luc could hear the splashing of water like a lioness in the veldt. Totally content, she called from behind the flowered screen.

"How about getting our breakfast. I'm ravenous."

He laughed. He had always liked a woman with an appetite.

Madame Blanche greeted them in the vast timbered kitchen with hearty talk and more hot café au lait. Like a concierge, she talked to them of country roads and houses of 'good people'. She would be setting them on to their next contact. She did not know their ultimate destination was Colleville, and like any good concierge, she did not ask – and like any good resistance fighter, she knew they night not come back alive.

****

The day before Juliette had returned to the main house, and nearly dropped to her knees when Luc walked brazenly through the front door before breakfast. Neither the German Colonel nor Denis said a word. Luc was clean from head to toe like the true "Parisian fob" they presumed he was.

Luc had brought Zosia to the secret shed and now all of them had set out with the "Caen' map committed to memory. Coming through the last hedgerow in pitch darkness of June 3 was their worst nightmare. They were all lost in an enormous field, and Renard, who led the way, realized they had passed the same barbed-wire entanglements several times. Like a blind man trying to see, he led with his fingers, and the piercing ragged sharpness of the wire ripped open his fingers no matter how gently he placed them in front of his face. Juliette who was following close behind tugged at his sleeve in order to go ahead of him. Having traveled this area by bicycle, north of Le Hamel but south of Colleville, she remembered where the hedgerows ended and the vineyards began.

Renard, Luc, and Juliette knew that nothing was more treacherous at night than the network of wires on which the vines grew. They had all grown up and played as children in these very fields, but this game was most deadly, and Zosia had not the advantage of knowing the terrain in better times. Even though she had the end position in their single file line which snaked around hedgerows, barbed wire fences, Rommel's asparagus bombs, and fields deliberately flooded to drown any paratroopers that the Allies might drop into France, it was she who tripped on these invisible wires meant for the climbing vines. Occasionally, Luc went in front of her to break her fall. None had an easy time.

At times the rain, coming down like bullets, cut their visibility to zero. At these times they tightened the distance between them, but if someone didn't stay in line and veered two steps to the right or left, they'd often fall into holes left by the Germans. Wet to the core, all sank knee deep in mud before they finally stopped on the south side of the block house. The rain had let up, hopefully just enough to allow them to drop their packs of TNT into the air vents of the bunker which overlooked the Colleville draw.

Suddenly, one of the windows in a nearby house lit up and the barking of dogs could be heard. Perhaps, it was the thunder or lightening that had woken the inhabitants at 2:00 a.m... The line of four flattened themselves into the mud as they saw a figure standing in the doorway. His jacket was unbuttoned and the ample flesh from his bare belly hung over the unbuttoned pants and unfastened belt of the German soldier. His form, silhouetted by the kitchen lit against the black sky entertained them like a silent movie reel. Leaning up against the door, the comedian clumsily unzipped his fly and barely held onto his crotch as a stream of urine arched through the already wet night. When he shook himself, his whole torso shook like a huge jellyfish. His last salute to the night was a resounding belch. He turned off the kitchen light and told the dogs to be quiet before taking out his flashlight to find his way on the path he was to have patrolled.

"The German drinking house for this sector," Juliette whispered to Renard to pass down the line.

That was all the talking they did as they crossed over a road to the west of Le Grand Hameau and into another area of pastures and hedgerows. Renard stepped back in front of the line as they neared the beach, for even in the rain and darkness; he knew the location of the trenches that he and Luc's father had helped dig. In front of the blockhouses the trenches were dug deep into the face of the cliffs. The Germans had placed all their eggs in one basket. From the beaches to the blockhouses every type of mine was planted and every type of gun fixed on the wide expanse of sand in front of each. Set up to crisscross the beaches in deadly fire, no enemy could run, walk, or even crawl across them without being cut down. Of the three who knew the most, only one led Luc, Juliette and Zosia this night. One was too young – the other too old for this mission. Juliette and Renard had told neither that they were leaving on this mission to blow up the blockhouse at Colleville. When.. if they succeeded in blowing it up, then they'd be told.

The plan was to come up from the one blind spot of the pill box – the secondary entrance door on the side of the massive half buried globe of concrete. No recessed rectangles of windows were slashed out of the three foot thick wall at this section. The face of the rounded cement stronghold commanded an incredible panorama of the beaches below onto which were trained the long heavy muzzles of what they believed to be 210 mm Skoda guns. Renard and Luc were to climb up the sides to the dome shaped roof. Despite the rain drenched walls, the concrete was very rough and provided more than enough texture to prevent any slipping in this torrential rain. The women would stay on ground level to take out – with any means possible – soldiers coming out for a necessary stroll.

They crossed through the last hedgerows south of Sainte Honorine. From that point to the cliffs was a good 500 yards.

"Let's fan out, ten meters apart, If there's danger, 'hoot' like an owl," Luc said as they each crouched to advance.

Hidden by darkness, the wind and incessant rain muffled their movements. They were near the connecting path and fifty yards from the trenches beyond when Luc almost ran into a patrolling soldier. He stopped abruptly, a foot in mid-step because the match lit by the soldier for his cigarette glowed in the helmet he used to shelter the match from the rain. His back was turned to Luc. He finished his step, snapped the knife out of the cane and drove it under the soldier's arm and into his heart.

Luc 'hooted' to the others as he crouched in a frozen position. They were already flat against the ground, for each had heard the knife's snap and the slight grunt of the soldier before Luc lowered him to the ground. He proceeded ahead and peered into the empty trench on the slight incline of the sand and rocky cliff which led steeply to the beach. He knew the tide was beginning to go out, and he had a change in plans.

****

"I know what I need to do Luc. Just give me your tools and pack of TNT." Juliette said to her brother who was now dressed as the German patrol infantryman. He pulled the strap of the helmet under his chin and the hood of the rain cape over that. The boots were too big and the gray pants too short, but no one would notice in the rain, especially since they wore the pants inside the laced up boots. The Sturmgewehr 45 asssault rifle he slung over his shoulder.

"Be careful. Don't slip on the roof. Clip the wires gently off those ventilator shafts. You don't need to drop the explosives all the way down, just wedge it in below the roof line, so when it blows, the whole building will go. We'll detonate the stacks with timers. Set them for fifteen minutes."

"She'll do it right, Luc. I'll stand guard in back of the trenches in case we have more night time patrols." Zosia said.

Everything's clear on the other side." Renard said as he lifted Zosia's sack of TNT from her back.

"Four sacks, four stacks. Let's go Renard," Juliette directed.

Like cats climbing trees, both shimmied up the corner iron poles which riveted each side of the hexagonal bunker in the soft sand of the cliff. Luc proceed on his patrol and noticed no movement on either side of the path. The rain continued to pour, yet in spite of it, he still heard the heavy snores of men sleeping in the cold wet trenches. Pitched tarps covered the sections in which the men slept. He stopped when he heard the snores break and continued when they began again. He could not look back at the pill box to see if Juliette and Renard were standing by the stacks. Even if he did, he could see nothing in this rain. The large search lights which mainly shone into the sea only slightly cut through the black rain. They scanned over the bunker every three minutes. They had plenty of time to start and then lie flat and restart and finish before moving onto the next stack and beginning the process once again. All had timed themselves for the job that Renard and Juliette would now do.

Luc had confidence in his sister. They all knew she had ten minutes and no more.

The search lights had made their pass twice when Zosia noticed movement from one of the pitched tarps to her far left. She saw a figure look out of the trench and stumble toward her. She rolled over toward the wall of the pill box and came to a sitting position. Back flat against the concrete, she pushed herself into one of the hexagonal corners. She heard him stumble and curse in Polish.

"God damn it, they treat us like swine. Having to climb out of this hell hole to go piss in the rain.... with all their frigging military might- a toilet would be such a challenge." He kept mumbling as he came closer. Zosia put down her knife and was about to speak Polish to him.

"I'll show them. I'll kill so many English and Americans Hitler himself will give me the iron cross." He said and then stopped in front of Zosia and looked up at the roof of the pill box. His mouth opened in awe and in the search light that passed, she could see in his face an expression of delight. She picked up her knife and drove it into his heart.

"Done. Let's go." Juliette said as she hit the ground. She glanced at the body by Zosia's feet, put her hand on her shoulder, and pushed her forward back the way they had come. As they crossed the path, they turned back and saw Luc with his rifle in hand standing on the path until they crossed back into the hedgerows. Both waited in silence for the men. The time seemed interminable.

"They should have been here by now." Juliette said in a worried tone.

"Luc was on the path – protecting the rear, and Renard should have been on the far flank. They'll be here." Zosia tried to sound reassuring.

They could not wait much longer a minute more passed.

"Who was he?" Juliette asked to interrupt her own thoughts.

"A Pole."

"I'm sorry."

I'm not. He was a traitor." Zosia answered. "We must go. Luc said never to wait beyond the zone of safety. We're passed that zone. Let's go," Zosia said this time as she pushed Juliette ahead to lead the way to Saint Honorine.

Exhausted, they trudged through the mud to get enough distance between themselves and the explosion which would come in less than five minutes. Two lives for hundreds. Was it worth the price when those two lives were the men they loved? Would the invasion come before they could rebuild the blockhouse at Colleville.

No one had heard the second verse of Verlaine's poem.

Thirty-six hours had passed since Zosia and Luc had heard the BBC's broadcast coming over the Channel. The waters had been calm on the first of June, but now with June 3rd having just begun, the idea of an invasion seemed remote. Who would send an armada out in these seas?

<u>Chapter 9 – June 2/3 1944</u>

New haven, England   June 2, 1944

Dear Sweetheart,

God, I miss the heat of Texas. Despite that it's June, the weather here is miserable misty rain. In fact, it always seems to be raining – one sort of precipitation or another. Today, it's a colder rain. How can that be for June? I'd take just one day of our hot wonderful Texas sun!

But I miss you most of all, darling. I'd trade a lucky seven days of Texas sun for one of your long warm kisses. Every time I'm in a crap game or poker game I twist my solid gold wedding band. You bring me luck, darling. You always have. I've wired you all my winnings from this past week. I can't take it with me – that's for sure. Buy yourself some pretty frocks and a gold bracelet – I hope they wired you that note along with the moolah. It's an early June 6th birthday present. Happy 28th sweetheart! I'll be thinking of you.

I'll probably still be sitting in this God forsaken town on your birthday – imagining how pretty you look – prettier than lovely Lucille! How is my prize longhorn? I'd give anything to be riding the range again. Sitting high on my horse with my nice wide rimmed felt cowboy hat instead of an army green helmet. All we do lately is catch rain in em'! Life by the sea is not bliss for me! Hey, I'm a poet and I don't know it!

I've had enough taste of the sea to last me a lifetime. How can anyone live wet like a fish day in and day out is beyond me. We've been confined to barracks which makes matters worse. Mail comes in, but none goes out, so I know you won't be receiving this letter for some time. Tension is really running high. The waiting is the worse for all the men.

When you see the newsreels, look for me with the enlisted men playing craps or poker. So far, I've not come up with snake eyes. I hope my luck holds out. Here have been lots of army 'movie men' shooting film not guns. Good for morale at home I guess to see us guys having a 'fun time'. They'll be filming when we hit the beaches too!

"I'm cutting to the end zone now. I was briefed this morning on our mission. Follow my company and division when those news clips come up in the movie theaters you'll be seeing it long after it actually happens. I'm proud of my company, Company C of the 2nd ranger Battalion. There's sixty-three of us – the toughest sons of bitches (pardon my French, Cherie) you ever did see.

We're going to scale the cliffs of Pointe de la Percee west of the town of Vierville. Another two hundred specially trained men, part of our provisional ranger force, will climb the godforsaken French cliffs at Point du Hoc – straight up to take out the 155 millimeter guns seeped in concrete before they level our men who'll hit the flat stretches on the west end of the beach which they've told me is called Omaha. I would have thought they'd at least call it Houston or Dallas. I could see why Alamo doesn't have a good ring to it; yet Dallas would've been great.

Anyway, our objective is to take out the gun battery at Point de la Percee. I guess we have it easy – our cliffs are ninety feet, theirs are one hundred high! You know when I first heard it from our Colonel who got it straight from the horse's mouth, Lieutenant General Bradley, I thought he was just trying to scare us Texas boys. Half our unit is from Texas; the other half is from the rest of the good old U.S. of A. I don't want to scare you, hon, but just to give you the facts. You'll be getting this letter after it all begins. You'll know exactly where I'm fighting for you and junior. Kiss my boy for me. I'll make both of you proud of me and of Texas.

When I get to Paris, I'll buy you some of that French perfume I've heard so much about. They're sending us over with rations, French francs, and a little blue book full of French words to help us communicate with the natives. – such as 'Quelle armee est ici"? What army is here? As if we didn't know. If there's fighting going on it's obviously the Kraut army. Anyway, I picked up so much French in the North African campaign, I feel like an honorary 'frog'. Besides the French francs in my pocket, I've got American dollars taped in a waterproof pouch inside my helmet. That way I'll be sure never to take off my hat – no matter how uncomfortable it feels. That's my 'pin' money since I know the French francs won't be enough for the Channel Number 5 I'm going to buy you. I got the word that's the cat's meow.

Besides the extra loot from the poker games, I got something more practical in my helmet – a map, printed on silk, that an English paratrooper used to raise the ante in last night's game. After I get off the beach and over the cliff, I'll know how to get to 'Paree'.

Enough, for now hon. By the way, did Mama get the V-Mail for mother's day? The army issued it to all of us. The only one who didn't send it was Sal, the guy from the Bronx, New York. I get the impression he doesn't have a family. He certainly asks enough questions about mine and my life. Getting back to the V-Mail, the army must have a heart since one of their poets included a banner on the face of the "Greeting on this Mother's Day, 1944" which said:

"Though we are a world apart,

You are always in my heart."
I hoped she liked it. I miss all of you and that little poem goes
for both my girls – from the bottom of my heart.

Love always, xoxoxoxo Hank*
*AKA Captain Paul Hudson or the 'old man' by my men
p.s. love again, sweetheart... moi (French for me)
p.p.s. I'm getting good at their lingo

.*******************

    "Hey Captain, you in or out of this game," shouted Sal
from Hoboken.
    "Keep your britches on partner. I'm just finishing this
letter to my Missus."
    "Just cause you can't write Sal, doesn't mean no one else
can," Jimmy from West Virginia twanged.
    "Yeah, yeah, Mr. Einstein," Sal looked at his cards. He
had a pair of tens and kept the king as a kicker. "Hit me two," he
continued as he placed the two discards off to the right.
    "I'll have you know I'm the first of my family to
graduate." Jimmy said proudly.
    "From where, grammar school?" James Earl from
Alabama teased as he discarded three.
    "Now, now. Leave the man be. Just because Sal chooses
not to write... we all know how he loves to read." Aaron from
California added as he studied the spades that he held tight to his
chest. A possible straight he'd like. "He peruses his foot locker
from head to toe three times a day."
    "Yeah, I can read Betty Gable from head to toe
anytime," Sal laughed. "Rita's my best reading. You guys know
that. When I lift the lid on her, you're 'perusing' over my
shoulder.
    "You all got any girls like her in the Bronx, Sal?" Jimmy
asked.
.   "Christ Jimmy, if there were, I'd even write. You staying
or what, Hollywood boy." Sal retorted.
    "Dealer takes just one, gentlemen." Aaron discarded his
queen of hearts and picked up an ace of spades.

"You're bluffing. I bet a fiver," James Earl said as he looked at his three sevens.

"Ma didn't raise no fool. I'm out." Sal threw face down his pair of tens and looked over at the 'old man' as he was rereading his letter again.

Sal definitely considered the Captain as one of the boys. He never pulled rank. Sal listened to him and never bucked his orders because he just seemed to know more than the others. Sal always tried to get him to open up – to reveal his past campaign because he had to have had one. 'The army just doesn't make a man a captain for no reason. Where had he been for the last two years? A guy just doesn't 'join up' at twenty-eight.' Sal thought, but kept his suspicions to himself. As a buddy, Sal like Paul Hudson; as a soldier and leader, he didn't know. His street antennas were up, and they'd stay up – until all of them hit the beach, climbed the cliffs, and moved out.

"I meet ya. I only picked up one you know," Jimmy added as he got nothing more than the two pair he had been dealt.

"No fooling Jimmy boy," James Earl laughed.

"I realize the innate possibilities of your hand, Jimmy... but, I hasten to add, I must raise. You've peaked my curiosity." Aaron added. "Raise you ten."

"Man, I can hear him making his movie picture deals, now, Metro Golden Mayer step aside; Aaron Axelrod is next in line." Sal joked, but in his heart he knew that Aaron had the balls and the brains to play with the big guys. He'd stick with him – during and after the war. If they made it, he'd be his ticket to the Rita Haywards of this world.

"Well, you boys in or out." Aaron said to Jimmy and James Earl.

Jimmy looked at his pairs of threes and tens. He frowned. Maybe Aaron was bluffing. Maybe not. Either way, James Earl probably had three of a kind, Maybe. Maybe not. Without lookin at either man, he said, "I wanna see." He added his ten.

"I still think you're bluffing," James Earl said. "Call you." He placed his ten in the pot.

"Read em and weep – as they say," Aaron said as he carefully laid down his royal spade straight.

"Looks like hillbilly and nigger have been taken to the cleaners again by Jew boy," Sal laughed loudly.

All three looked at him - not with malice nor surprise, for all were used to the words. – those words used to generalize their status, race, and religion. They had heard it all their lives, in all forms. They certainly had heard it all from Sal who talked about everyone in categories. There was no bigotry intended, for they knew Sal would lay down his life for theirs. If a guy needed someone to cover his ass, he'd chose Sal Marchese. Without looking at one another, Jimmy, James Earl, and Aaron simultaneously came to the same conclusion – those epithets had begun this war and would end it one way or another.

Captain Hank Paul Hudson heard Sal's three in one hit. Hank thought that he himself had said it all – with bravado, with self-consciousness, and in self-protection, but never with camaraderie or courage. Sal said it with the former and during the invasion he'd probably say it with the latter. The captain knew Sal had the 'stuff', just as he knew that he, Hank Hudson from the great state of Texas, did not. He sealed shut his letter.

James Earl was the first to speak.

"Man, I don't like them spades. It's bad luck. What did you throw away," he said as turned over Aaron's discard. "Lordy, the queen of hearts, 'lucky lady'."

"None of that mumbo jumbo talk, James Earl," said Sal, who was superstitious. He wanted to suffocate the fire of fear before it began. "Next you'll be sticking in pins in some sort of voodoo doll."

"No, the cards mean nothing," Aaron added. "They're only cards. If the 'wop' is superstitious, here's another interpretation for Sal. We're sharply trained like the points on these spades. We're black like death because that's what we'll bring to the enemy, and we're carrying spades to bury them. The lady that was discarded is lying face down because she's in our hearts – she is our heart. We not only have luck... we have God's will in each of our hearts.'

"Amen, Aaron my brother." James Earl added with a smile on his face.

"I like your version," Jimmy said.

"You could out talk and out reason the devil himself." Sal laughed.

Hank Hudson pulled up a foot locker to join the game. He said nothing. He knew they'd need all the luck and divine intervention possible. He hoped this time God would be on his side and give him the courage to lead these men. He could not fail again.

****

His thoughts went back to North Africa and another invasion. This one was on November 8, 1942. He was one of thousands of crack combat troops, airborne rangers, marines and sailors who began the Allied invasion of French North Africa. Hudson, an infantryman assigned to land at Casablanca, had gone sleep with his company at four that afternoon and got up at ten to arrange his pack: bayonet and combat knife honed to a keen edge, emergency escape packet with practical boy scout and extra things : a tiny compass, water purifying tablets, a metal file, unlimited amo clips of .30 caliber bullets for his M-1 rifles, his Colt 45 plus amo, grenades, and condoms which had been issued by the thousands. He remembered Charlie and Sam and dozens of others who were blowing them up into balloons and filling them with water for a fight of a different sort. Most men, however, put them over the muzzles of their M-1's to keep out sand or water during the landing. He even stuck his watch and two dozen franc coins he had won in a crap game in a few condoms and knotted the end to make tiny waterproof sacks. All the men imagined that after the landing, they'd use the 'rubbers' for their intended use.

He hoped this new D-Day landing scheduled for June 5 would be easier than Operation Torch in North Africa. He expected the ride to be as miserable and wet. On that night the booming shells had dropped in the water and made huge geysers. His boat had gotten lost in the waves. When the waterfalls cleared and the Navy's counter attacks fell silent, he could see everyone who had first landed on the beach casually standing around smoking, laughing, and taking the condoms off their guns. Then the enemy guns opened fire on them.

When his boat hit the beach, he didn't know who crawled up the beach first Charlie, Sam, or himself. Screaming shell fragments careened through the air and artillery fire razed the beach. He was so scared he never fired his rifle but simply got up and started running off the narrow beach. Then the bombers came. He threw himself into a hole and never realized he was lying in camel dung until the planes dropped the last of their bombs and circled back to their inland base.

The commander of his company had been hit, setting up a bazooka. At that moment Hank stood up in fright and fled the last of the beach head. Charlie, Sam, and the others who weren't pinned down already, followed him thinking he had taken the initiative after their lieutenant was hit. Instead, Hank found the first crater and threw his enormous frame into it. Lying in the dung listening to the constant barrage of enemy fire off to his left, he peered over the hole and saw the fire was directed at the rest of his company who were still pinned down on the beach.

"Hudson", Charlie had called from what seemed like a distant fog behind him. "Can you see where it's coming from? I've got a grenade in my hand. Just give me the word."

"Charlie... Hank. I'm off to your left." Sam yelled. "I got no hole. I'm flat on my belly. I can reach a grenade in my belt though. Are they ahead of me, Hank?"

The words of his friends passed over him like in a distant dream. He heard their voices, understood what they said, but could take no action. His body was like lead and not a part of him. It shook and his teeth chattered. He pulled his six foot four inch frame into a fetal position and hugged his knees to his chest.

"Hudson, do you read me. Are you hit?" Charlie whispered.

"Charlie, how far ahead of me are you? Can you see their position?" Sam asked

Hudson heard their voices. To stop the guns, to stop the voices he motioned his arm above the hole before wrapping his head in his hands. They took his motion as a signal to go and raised their bodies upward before letting loose their grenades.

Hudson first heard Charlie's piercing scream then Sam's as the machine guns swung around and riddled their chests. It was then he uncurled his body and raised it up to see Sam's headless torso and Charlie's throat and chest spouting blood like a lawn sprinkler. In that split second he knew he had sent them to their deaths without firing a shot. After death their grenades had found their targets. The blasts sent dirt and body parts into his hole. An arm with a sleeve and insignia attached fell into the camel dung beside him. In shock, he read the markings of a German major and then threw it out of the hole as though it were a live grenade. His body wracked with spasms. He ripped off his helmet and vomited into it until only the dry heaves came in waves.

Bodies rotted out quickly in the North Africa sun, even in November. After four hours the smell was so intense that their pungent odor made even the strongest men spill their guts. Those who watched Hank Hudson go from body to body, whether German or American, wondered at this immense mountain of a man, helmetless in the hot North African sun and covered in camel dung. Amid the rotting putrid corpses, he dug hole after hole. He didn't stop to puke, to drink, or to wash off his own stench in the roped off section of the ocean.

Word spread that it was he who had taken out the German machine gun nest and taken it upon himself to bury his dead comrades in arms. As the sun was beginning to set, he stopped his mechanical digging. A lieutenant from another company pried the shovel out of his hands and pushed him toward the sea sanctuary, the baptismal-like font for those still alive, not for the bloated bodies already dead. The lieutenant, who pushed him toward the sea, wanted to see if the blood on Paul Hank Hudson came from his own wounds. Almost reverently, a medic held Hank's head in his hands and let Hank's body extend itself. The sea salt saturated his army greens, and the medic made tiny rivulets of water to gently wash the blood off his face.

Floating on his back, Hudson looked over at the setting sun with its golden shafts of light like banners still waving across the horizon. Its golden radiance still fought to dominate from the rim of the earth, challenging the moon and stars soon to illuminate the wide expanse of another North African night for those still alive to see it. He shut his eyes to the last light of the sun and to the serene light of the night which promised redemption.

He had failed in his baptism of fire. He had failed his friends, his company, and himself. He had failed on French soil. And for it, Hank Hudson received the Silver and Bronze stars and a commission. He never fired a shot. He never lobbed a grenade. He never was courageous and was only gallant to the ladies of Texas.

****

Sitting not on a ship deck but in a tent, cramped into one of the sausage like lanes with tent after tent sealed behind long narrow fencing, Hank Hudson waited for the 'green' light to begin the invasion. He looked around at these men – none of whom knew of his previous duty, the Allied invasion of North Africa which had set the stage for this invasion of Europe. They had pushed the 'dessert fox', General Rommel out of Africa and left the territory to the French and now Hudson would see Rommel's massive tanks again, and the General's uncanny ability to crush anything and everyone within range of the deadly treads.

He had seen Rommel's Tiger tanks from afar and made it through the African campaign by sitting in combat towers. Because of his sharp shooting ability and because of his 'effort' on the beach head, he was given a sniper position. Amazingly agile for a man so big, he could get his huge frame up any tower, precipice, or tree; it was as though the devil himself was on his heels. Perhaps, it was.

His thoughts came back to the present. The faces of Sam and Charlie became the faces of Sal and Aaron. This time he promised himself it would be different. He would kill or be killed. He would not lose another company.

"Hey Cap, they gonna give us another great meal again. I feel like a pig getting ready for slaughter." James Earl joked.

"That could be the idea," Sal retorted. "All I know is I can't take another steak, and I'm sick of being cooped up."

"Them's fighting words, Sal. There's never enough steak for a Texan. Anyway, when we get back home, 'yawl' invited for a real down home Texas barbecue. Aaron, you can swing by on your way out to California, and Jimmy, you can forget going home to that puny state of West Virginia. After seeing the great expanse of Texas, you'll never want to go back again." Hank said as he picked up the cards Aaron had dealt for him.

"And I'm to find the cash to get there all the way from New York City?" Sal sneered "You know what they say, 'How you gonna keep them down in the slums, after they've seen Paree.'"

"Don't you mean the farm?"

Maybe in your case James Earl, but in mine, it's not like we want to stay there; it's that we ain't got a choice.' Sal answered.

"Choice. You're 'bitchin', city boy? Look at my skin if you're talking about choice." He dropped down his three aces and pulled in the pot. "I notice I don't get no invite, Captain."

"It goes without saying. You're invited. None of those Texan sons of bitches will even blink twice at you when you're by my side. That's the one thing this damn war might do. I don't look at color or..." Hudson glanced at Aaron Axelrod. "Religion, any more. I've seen half breeds fighting harder than ten whites. As long as they're doing their job, they're O.K. by me."

Sal looked into Hank Hudson's face. "Where did you fight before, Captain?" he said with feigned casualness.

He looked up from his hand of kings. "North Africa", he answered with matched nonchalance. "Let's play cards."

****

:

Everything was on the move. From May 31 on – from the west to the east of England – jeeps, trucks, tanks, artillery, and even bicycles were going to their embarkation point. Eisenhower had set D-Day for June 5. Each regiment of each division had marched to its assembly area, and like Hank Hudson's Company, were confined to their 'sausages'. Tent cities had been set up in a line configuration, connected only by gravel paths and camouflaged under wire netting, sprung up on the sides of roads. From the air they looked like sausages, and the men were allowed neither in nor out of them. The MP's saw to that.

Everything they needed, except alcohol and women, was issued to them. Those who snuck in or out to go to local pubs were arrested and thrown in the brig. The only booze was in each medic's canteen. Most of which never reached the beaches of Normandy. The medical issued alcohol was poured into other containers and in its place good old Scotch or English whiskey was filled. What they did not drink to calm their nerves before the invasion, they used for consumption or sterilization on the beaches of Normandy.

Nonstop poker and crap games helped pass the time. Boredom, anticipation, and fear were their enemies so each sausage contained a library and sports area. Hank Hudson got a football game going with his men, and Sal Marchese played his game, baseball, and threw the ball with the fervor of one of his beloved Yankees. When it got too rough and bones were broken, they switched to softball or went to the sausage library.

Many chose to read and pass their hours passively, They'd pick up a paperback Dell or Avon and save their energy for battle. In time, Private Sal Marchese from Company C, 2nd Ranger Battalion and Private Anthony Martino from the 82 airborne had tired of baseball and the poker games. Each had walked down the gravel paths to their sausage's library and selected <u>A Tree Grows in Brooklyn.</u> It didn't matter that it was about a girl; they liked the title and the fact that it was about home life in a city that typified America. It took their minds off this little island, called England, and of the foreign soil they knew little about, had no affinity for, and on which they were about to land and probably die. Even the officers felt that way. Lieutenant Sidney Smith and Second Lieutenant Melvin Baron strolled over and selected The Pocket Book of Verse whose short poems spoke to them and evoked the emotions they kept hidden from their men.

Most had trained together for more than two years, and had seen the best and the worst in one another as only those who live together can. Having trained, worked, slept, and eaten with one another, each company was like a family and each accepted the guy next to him with all his faults and all his strengths. They played, kidded, and fought with one another and knew details that make up the fabric of life – down to how each one drank his coffee. Each knew his life might depend on the guy in the next bunk.

If they were afraid, they didn't tell one another, but those who were catholic were lucky. They had confession and the confession booths were kept busy with their sins and fears in those late days of May 1944. If they were afraid that they'd turn and run, they never told their buddies. Fear of dying was secondary to fear of failure and cowardice in front of these men who had become their brothers.

****

"Pick up those feet, men. A walk in the park, this isn't." Second Lieutenant Melvin Baron yelled to his men on a designated country road.

"I never thought I'd be happy to march," Russo mumbled to O'Brien.

"Yeah, I got to give it to the Kraut. I need to get the ants out of my pants." O'Brien answered.

"Keep moving fast. Think of the beach head you're going to cross. And will cross in force, right men?" Baron shouted.

"Yes Sir," Russo, O'Brien, Anderson, and the rest of Company C shouted back as they marched through England's southeast countryside and saw the stock piles of equipment – from Navy wet suits, to ration tins, to tanks to aircraft. All tucked under football fields of netted tarp. They passed by the sausages of other American units and those of every nationality ready to fight. The Poles, the Australians, the Dutch, the Belgians, the New Zealanders as well as the British, Canadians, and French set to go by kicking a ball, dealing a hand of cards, reading a book or going over their bit in the Invasion. It was like a mini Europe – a preliminary run through – for all were speaking in their mother tongues or speaking English with their particular accent. Regardless, the might of the Free World was ready. Baron and other officers knew the men needed to see that and their marches reflected more than just a release for pent up energy and maintaining of mass.

****

For Sidney and his men from the 82nd Airborne their night in London seemed two months not two days ago.

"The pot's mine men," nineteen-year-old Tony Martino said as he took a French 500 Franc note out of the middle. "Which wise guy threw this in?" he asked.

"It's probably a forgery, Tony." Sidney joked. "You know de Gaulle didn't want us Yanks to be issued any French money. I guess were uninvited guests so to speak."

"They want us. Right Billy?" Sixteen-year-old Tim asked.

"You bet they do!" Billy answered

"Just as long as we don't stay too long." Sid added.

"Tell you what, guys. I want a souvenir. Pass the bill round so every guy in the 82nd signs it." Tony said.

"You tell me I'm a kid. Even I know one of em will swipe it." Tim said.

"Not when I go around with it... after it leaves you guys that is. I'll get the exercise and a memento from all yous." Tony stuffed his winnings in his pockets and stretched his legs. He intended to mail seventy-five percent of it to his mom and the rest to Margaret. "Maybe with a note too." He thought.

****

"Are sure every one of these babies is waterproofed?" another company sergeant in the 29th Division told his men.

"I got enough Cosmo line on her to make her slide all the way into Paree,' the mechanic answered.

"Don't worry Sarge. Nothing's gonna corrode this LCVP."

"When I pull my M3 submarine gun down the landing ramp and head for the beach, it ain't gonna stall." The driver said.

"And, if I'm going to shoot it, you can make sure the breeches have been covered with rubber cloth and its edges sealed with rubber cement," the gunner added. "No sand and water in my guns!"

"Your lives depend on it men," the Sergeant said as he inspected each MI Garand.30 caliber semi-automatic rifle, 38 and 45 caliber revolvers, 37 mm flare pistol , and M-3 fighting knives.

****

On the British side the men reacted the same as their American Allies. They too were ready to jump in before the actual battle – to be the forerunners for freedom or early arrivals to Hell. Each had his own perspective.

"So, you know what I heard one of them Yanks do," Sandy from the Airborne said. "What mate?" "Gave gum to a little English girl as he was marching with his unit. He had stopped to talk to her Mum." Sandy remarked.

"So?" another one of the British paratroopers said.

"Don't you think that's starting a bit young?" Sandy angrily retorted.

"Bloody Yanks. Not enough they get the rest of our British birds," A paratrooper commiserated.

"Right O?" Sandy liked to be agreed with.

"Crap. It's not them. It's their money. The birds go with who has the heftier bankroll." Another man from the 6th Airborne added.

"If they help us get out of this alive, they can have all the 'dames', as they call them, in England or the rest of the continent for all I care," the shortest man said.

"Give me a big fighting-do-all Yank by my side any day." another one added.

"Once I'm dropped in France a few nights from tonight, I want to find one of them in the dark – not some ugly Jerry with a G43 87mm semi-automatic rifle." Some guy said.

****

Back from their mission in the morning hours of June 3rd, Luc and Zosia sat on the small narrow bed in the hidden shed on the Dubois Norman farm. The secret radio removed from the trap door behind the wood pile rested beside them. The BBC was broadcasting the last stanza of Verlaine's poem. These common words brought an uncommon feeling, a feeling that the end was here – an end to tyranny and a beginning to freedom. In two days, June 5th the Invasion would begin, but Renard had not returned.

On French soil the battle had already begun. Every resistance fighter was putting into place his or her final act of retaliation and revenge. Their long ago freedom taken for granted would be taken back in blood, and the blood had already spilled in the early operation of the secret four. All but one of them had returned.

But, as the day of June 3 lengthened, the clear weather became overcast and the winds began to blow. The Allied mine sweepers had done their job of sweeping the English coast in case the Luftwaffe and E-boats had dropped mines in the area. The 245 vessels on which they were aboard had cleared five channels for the assault forces to enter. Lit with buoys at one mile intervals along the channel, these sea highways marked the way for an invasion Armada that the world would never see again. The last step had been to clear the area where the transports would be anchored off each separate beach.

All they had to do now was wait. Wait as the wind and waves grew stronger, Wait for the weather to break. Wait for D-Day, 'Jour-J', to be that designated day that the world had been waiting for – for too long.

The thousands of men huddled in the south of England in their individual sausages wanted to begin the fight of a generation. Too many fears and too little to do contributed to their nerves. They had Two options: to run across a 100 yard stretch of French sand or to drop through 300 yards of French air. The second part was to fight and live through it. That was the only way they could walk again on the soil of their own lands.

Chapter 10 – June 4/5 1944

British 6th Airborne parachutist Sandy Johnson already knew the terrain first hand. He thought about last June - almost a year to the day. He, along with seventeen volunteer paratroopers, had been dropped in directly northeast of Caen on a beach called Colleville-Montgomercy Plage. They had lost a man. He had broken his leg when the Dakota, an American C-47, dropped its stick of eighteen. Although it was a night landing, there was no wind. They landed within yards of one another... everyone except Dan, who jumped last out of the plane.

Landing on the roof of a farm house, his right leg fell through the weak roofing and wedged between the rafters. The Resistance fighters, who had been waiting for them, cut him loose, shredded his parachute, and divided its pieces for each to conceal and carry out from the barn. They took five different routes with one French guide per group to lead the Americans down to the beach. Their objective was to get sand samples from the beach sectors. Each group scooped up small vials of sand from separate sections. As soon as their mission was complete, they were ushered into small black rubber boats whose rowers took them hundreds of yards off shore to an armada of five small fishing boats. These nightly fishing rites had been systematically established by the French fisherman ever since the Occupation in 1941.

To the Germans these boats were part of the scenery. They went unnoticed as they floated 500 yards apart from one another. To those in the Resistance each one signaled freedom, for the majority were part of Resistance cells that carried men and messages in and out of Occupied France. This mission like the others was never explained to the fishermen. None, even the most courageous, could withstand Gestapo interrogation. Everyone knew that it was better that they were literally kept in the dark.

There were times when an escapee was below deck in the hole covered with 'les fruits de mer' – fruit of the sea as the Norman or Brittany fisherman called all the fish, oysters, and lobsters they caught in the sea. These piles of nightly catches hid the men they transported. Many times a man was in the hole when hundreds of fish rained upon his head. If a man had become curious and was not in the coffin like box drilled with holes, fitted with a metal breathing tube to the outside, and covered with netting, his neck would be broken or he would suffocate from the weight and mass of the wet squirming fish.

On this particular night the engineers wanted samples of sand to be certain the beach could hold the weight of the LCVP's loaded with men and equipment and the DUKW's. These amphibian dual rear axle vehicles would be called 'Ducks' by the men driving these two and a half ton vehicles off the beach. The Army and the Navy wanted to be certain these boat/trucks did not stop or sink into the wet shallow water sands of the beaches. The sand needed to be hard so they could drive off the beach head. The proof, that it could or could not hold the weight, was in the samples these eighteen men would bring back.

Sandy and the two other paratroopers had scrambled into their boxes in the hole of their fishing boat when they heard the engines of an approaching boat. As he shut the cage door, the fish fell in thuds on top, and he could hear nothing more. Although he could breathe, the stench of mackerel made him feel trapped underwater. He felt like he had only so much time before he drowned, the oxygen would not last forever.

He remained perfectly still and said a prayer. The German patrol had probably come aboard and was poking the barrels of fish with their rifles to see if a man was hiding. Whether this was a routine check or a more vigorous one due to information from a collaborator or from a tortured man, Sandy did not know. Had Dan not been able to escape? Had they tortured him? Had he revealed their mission? These unthinkable thoughts Sandy tried push out of his mind. What had been Dan's choice – death through torture by the hands of the Gestapo or death by his own hand with the cyanide capsule ripped from his shirt?

Minutes seemed like hours. Soon it was over. The boat's engines started and he could feel the rocking motion of the waves of the English Channel. The box was pulled upward through the mass of mackerel and up and out of the hole into the salty fresh night air. He rested suspended over the hole but below the deck as the evening breeze cooled the sweat and smell from his body. He felt the engines move westward.

When he was transferred in mid channel to the English boat, he learned that the check was routine. The Germans used such techniques to keep the French off balance. The terror of the unknown and unexpected – to always be afraid was how they wanted the rest of the world to live.

Dan did not live. He had been hidden by a mound of hay in the barn as two of the men went into town to bring back the local doctor. Dan had been placed near a cow that was carrying her calf. If anyone had entered, he would look like a normal French farmhand waiting for the cow's time to birth. However, the German on patrol that night took more than a passing interest in this cow. He was the son of a farmer from the Rhine and thought Dan was a Frenchman, but knew he was no farmer. His answers, although in perfect French were not correct. Dan read the disbelief in the soldier's eyes, and when he said he had to continue on his rounds; Dan knew the soldier did not believe him.

A boy skirted behind the soldier and paused in the recesses of the barn door's shadow. He saw the man wince in pain as he turned his body sideways to frantically pull the shirt out inch by inch from his pants. Exhausted from his effort, he weakly felt for the bottom edge of the shirt and stopped when he found what he needed. Dan ripped the capsule from his shirt tail and let it rest flat in the palm of his hand. The silent boy with the passive face saw him looking at it. The boy nodded 'yes' to Dan and walked over to him and wrote something in the sawdust of the barn floor. The man's face turned ashen. The boy took his hand, and Dan bit hard and decisively into the capsule. Each made the sign of the cross before the spasms of death racked the paratrooper's body. The boy held his hand tight. Afterwards, he needed to use his other hand to release the iron clad grasp of the dead man. When the German soldier returned with two Gestapo officers, Dan lay dead in the straw.

Now a year later Sandy thought of Dan and wondered how many in this stick and in this company would not be going home. This was the jump that counted. There'd be no second chance. This was his last jump into France, but this time the entire British 6th and lst Airborne would be at his heels: his mission – to land behind the Beach called Sword, to create pandemonium, and to confuse the Germans stationed there. Bridges were to be secured. Gun turret emplacements destroyed. Machine gun batteries taken and mines deactivated.

This was his final decisive mission – the definitive mission – the mission which would begin D-Day. He and his men were part of the British and American paratrooper companies who had to be dropped in before the infantry waves hit the beaches. It was their job to make the landing of men and machinery on the British beaches of Gold, Juno, and Sword as smooth as possible before the designated landing H-Hour of 6:30 a.m. June 5, 1944.

****

All day on June 3 the rains had poured incessantly onto the streets of London. Londoners awoke to another day of deprivation and destruction. Each day brought more change, another commodity gone, and another building or apartment in ruin. The bombings had diminished; the backbone of the

German Air force was broken. With America in the war their seemingly endless runs of B-25 and B-27 bombers had leveled German munitions plants, refineries, and airfields. The American flying fortresses also dropped their tonnage on railroads, and the Liberators took care of the rest. Wherever the Germans were transporting weapons and supplies, the American and British air force were taking them out. French, Belgian, Dutch and Polish Resistance men and women supplied the invaluable information about German activities within their borders. This information on supplies, troop movement, and capabilities along with some decoded messages from "Enigma' about major German battle plans paved the way for the invasion to begin.

All the Allied Generals knew that within forty-eight hours, they would know the answer. Would the fruit of their labors of the last two years pay out? Either they would have a foothold on the beaches or would be driven back into the sea as at Dunkirk. For the British and the French another Dunkirk or Waterloo was unacceptable. The freedom of the world rested on their shoulders. If they were pushed into the sea this time, they could never again amass such an amount of men and equipment. The war might continue for another four years or more. And who would win? Hitler?

In the Polish headquarters three generals and a newly commissioned fourth, General Morganski, were meeting. The rains and winds beat the window panes outside of General Wladyslaw Sikorski's office. Morganski still called it Sikorski's office although he had been dead for almost a year. His plane had crashed at Gibraltar of the 4th of July, 1943. Morganski thought how they had learned about the 'Katyn' from the Russian boy that April. Two months later the General was dead. Now, with victory so near, he had his thoughts on the years after the war. He counted on victory for the Allies, yet knew such a victory was hollow for him and his country. He and Wladyslaw Sikorski had often talked about politics, but the General had not lived long enough to see his beloved Poland tossed aside – in November of 43.

At Teheran, Churchill, Roosevelt, and Stalin had bartered Poland away. The men of the western free world had handed over a tidbit to the Russian dictator in order to bring him to the

European table. That appetizer was Poland. England and America could not win the war in Europe without Russia's armies on the eastern front. After the war Morganski, Churchill, Roosevelt, and De Gaulle knew the fight would be communist Russia. Morganski was preparing now – for that day.

"As you know, the invasion begins in less than forty-eight hours. That is the most important element on our minds, yet we must look to what will come after. After Nazi Germany – the world will have to deal with the Russians and their new Soviet Union. They began their conquests with my country – Poland."

The other three generals in the room nodded their heads in agreement as Morganski continued.

"We've had information concerning the massacre of more than 4,000 Polish officers and Polish intelligentsia at Katyn, one of the darkest forests in Russia. For over four years the 'pride' of Poland has been lying in mass graves, and it was only by accident that this gravesite was discovered a year ago. At that time Poland was still free and our Polish government in exile demanded an investigation concerning this massacre which occurred in April of 1940 when the Russians were Germany's ally. Germany attacked Poland from the east and Russia covered the western front. They methodically marched these men to the deep dark Katyn and massacred them all,... but one, a Russian boy." He stopped to let his words sink in.

"Now, they are your allies, and not only have they denied any accountability for the killings at Katyn, but they cut off diplomatic relations with us – and then six months ago, they 'officially' took over Poland."

"Out of sight, out of mind. The dirty bastards," George Patton, the American General, muttered...

"They cannot be trusted. The French communists in Paris are being spurred on this very moment by their Russian comrades," General de Gaulle added.

"There's that other adage gentlemen," English General George Montgomery said, "War makes strange bedfellows."

They all looked at one another and knew that this was true. Politically, culturally, and socially they differed dramatically from one another, but their one common denominator was their fervent desire to bury the German war machine, to end the Nazi reign of terror and dominance in Europe, and in doing so concentrate on Japan and the ultimate end of the war.

"What are you asking of us Antoine." Patton used Morganski's given name.

"I want to send in a team at the time of the invasion. Their mission is to get to Paris and secure documents which are now in the hands of the German General commanding Paris."

"What do these documents entail?" Montgomery asked.

General Morganski stood up and walked to the front of the room. Between the two large windows which o overlooked Hyde Park there was a large scroll. He pulled the scroll down and on it were two maps – one showing the face of Europe with delineations on what countries were now in Germany's hands and the other, an enlarged map of Poland and Russia.

"This is the Katyn." He said pointing to the map. "And the documents I want have detailed accounts of the march from here," he pointed to Warsaw, "to here," he said pointing to the Katyn.

"And the names, Antoine? Do these documents list the names of the men and the method of their deaths," Patton asked.

"Yes," Morganski answered.

"This team, it desires to arrive in Paris before we get there?" De Gaulle asked.

"Yes. Once the Germans know for a fact that they will lose Paris, they'll destroy all documents." Morganski stated.

"Eisenhower doesn't' want to head straight for Paris. He thinks there's not enough petrol." Montgomery quipped.

"Monty, you know Ike wouldn't hesitate for a second, but the Germans will fight like hell to hold Paris. All our men and resources will be blocked in for weeks and the Germans will have time to regroup for one last stance before we drive to Berlin." Patton argued. "I could swoop my 3rd Army down the West coast through Avranches and across to Paris in no time..., but that's not the plan."

"Paris is France, messieurs. She cannot be circumvented. Like Rome she is to Italy." De Gaulle looked at Patton as he said this.

"I know my history, mon general." Patton wryly commented.

"And besides, you are right General Morganski. The Communists they have plans." De Gaulle added.

"Right-O. Churchill knows they'll be our next threat." Montgomery interjected.

"We all know that gentlemen – from Roosevelt to Ike, from Churchill to you Monty. So, it seems there is nothing to lose, but everything to gain when this team goes in and finds the evidence of the Russian atrocities. The world will know they are no better than the Germans." Patton said.

"Good. This team is non-military."

They're all civilians who are fighting for different reasons. Like us, No? The information will help all of us – especially the Polish people and the French," the Polish General said, and as he did so he could feel Sikorski's presence.

"We have had Paris and the rest of our cities occupied for over four years. We cannot tolerate – C'est insupportable' to have it begin again with new invaders. When Paris is being liberated, the French communists will be in place, ready to seize power. There I must be when the hour of Freedom comes. If this team can change the course of history, I will help. My vote is given – 'Allez aux barricades' – any true Frenchman will cry out!" De Gaulle emphatically shouted.

"Ike's going to have to face the Russians in Berlin. He doesn't want to battle them now. It would break our effort against the Germans. He knows the Russian Army is essential to our fight against Hitler. But, he doesn't want France, our allies since the American Revolution, to fall into enemy hands. He wants a free France too, 'mon general. Nous allons aux barricades avec vous. He'll agree to the team. We will go to the barricades with you" Patton spoke. "1776 and 1796 – together this time"

"We're all aboard. It goes without saying." Monty added.

"The Polish people thank you generals. We know we have no country now, but perhaps we'll have vengeance. 'Mine eyes have seen the glory of the coming of the Lord'." General Morganski bowed his head for all of them.

****

That afternoon of June 4th the commanding General of the 1st American Army summoned Lieutenant Sidney Smith from Hannibal, Missouri and now from the 82nd Airborne, into Allied headquarters.

"Sid, I'm putting two extra men for your stick." General Bradley directed. "Your 82nd Airborne unit will now have Christian and Janusz – a Russian and a Pole. They'll be jumping in civilian clothes; one is fluent in Russian and French, the other, Polish and German, and naturally in English. They are on a crucial mission approved and given high priority by the General Staff of all armies – including de Gaulle's. Their mission is to get to Paris and secure documents about the Russian atrocities in the Katyn. The documents have detailed accounts of the massacres of Polish intelligentsia and military in April of 1940.

Sidney swallowed hard. "Can they jump, Sir?"

"They've been training outside of London. The other part of the team, who will meet you inside France at Saint-Mere-Eglise, includes a Polish woman fluent in English, German, and French, and a Frenchman who knows English as well as German. They were dropped in by a fishing boat June 1st. We've gotten word that they made it safely back from their sabotage mission and are somewhere near Colleville. By June 5 they will be in Sainte-Mere-Eglise." Bradley stated.

"How will we recognize them?"

"He's known by the code name, 'the dress maker' primarily in Normandy or 'Dumas' in Paris She is called 'Tanya' or the 'nightingale'.

"Physical description?"

"He's tall for a Frenchman – six feet, dark hair, fair complexion, blue eyes, and mid-twenties – basically he looks like an Irishman. They say is a pretty boy, but don't let appearances fool you. Be glad he's on our side. She's also tall: five feet ten – a beauty with auburn curly hair and blue eyes." Bradley read from the paper in his hands. It also says top priority. Crucial to the long range effort for the post war world."

"Do my two new passengers know the rest of their team?"

"Absolutely." They met in London. Not only do they know one another, they trust one another – which is essential for the success of this mission. De Gaulle himself recommended the Frenchman and Sikorski recommended the Poles and the Russian. You are to get them to Paris before the rest."

"Meaning?"

"Before the French, American, and British armies converge on Paris. They have to be there prior to – in fact, days before. I repeat, days before any Allied Army approaches Paris.

All Sid could do was whistle. He had to drop his men in at night, accomplish his military mission to ensure the success of the troops who would land on his designated beach that same morning, fight his way to Sainte-Mere-Eglise, locate the two in the chaos that had to follow this night raid, and then manage to get four novices through German lines all the way to Paris.

"You need to land east of the Merderet River and secure the causeway and bridge at Chef-du-Pont. It's one of the two crossways over the river which leads to the West and through the Cotentin."

"So, our first mission stands. We're to secure and hold the bridge until reinforcements come."

"Yes. In addition, here's a written order to round up and incorporate any stray men from any other units, especially, for the purpose of taking and holding that bridge. On your mission to Paris you're to have no more than eighteen men and no fewer than twelve. An even dozen including the team of four would be the ideal. Too many would cause undue attention, and too few would not be able to get the job done. If reinforcements do not come at Chef-du-Pont, give the letter to your four best men and have them get those two civilians to Saint-Mere-Eglise. When you or they get there, it should be almost clear. Come look at this map."

Bradley indicated a model in plaster that took up most of the room. They walked around the table to the side closest to the two beaches which were labeled Utah and Omaha.

"As you know, you're landing here – the Merderet River runs here toward the Channel. The two bridges are yours at Chef—du-Pont and over here to the west at La Fiere. Here is Saint-Mere-Eglise and through it runs N-13. This route runs through the village north to Cherbourg, south to Varentan, then east to Caen and on to Paris." Bradley used a long wooded pointer.

"And without Sainte-Mere-Eglise the men landing on this beach, Sid looked over and read the name, 'Utah' – 4th Infantry Division will be cut off- unable to move west and north."

"Also, without the use of N-`13, the Germans will be cut off from the north and unable to attack the 82nd Airborne paratroopers of the 4th Infantry Division." the General concluded.

"So, this little village holds the key. Where are these two – the 'dressmaker' and the 'nightingale' supposed to be holding up while all this is going on?" the Lieutenant asked.

"In the cellar of the church in the center of Sainte-Mere-Eglise." Bradley answered.

****

Renard had lost track of time – in two days an eternity had passed. His body and mind were beyond pain, yet he was aware that their plan had failed. The annihilation of the main pill box at Colleville on the cliffs of the beach never happened. The first round of TNT had exploded, but the other three rain soaked satchels had failed to detonate. He knew he would die, and die for nothing because Coleville's large guns were still intact. Hundreds...maybe thousands of Americans and British would also die in the cross fire – caught on the beach – between the sea and the sand.

Renard had learned more from his torturers than they from him, but for what good? His mind and spirit floated above his mutilated body. He went in and out of consciousness. The Gestapo had stopped their beatings; it was too strenuous for them. They need a cigarette; their voices foggy in the smoke and blood. He heard them say, "... the invasion will not happen here or now. No one will land in this gale of wind and rain. No one will make the crossing here when it is shorter from Pas de Calais to the coast of England... After all, Rommel left the Normandy

Coast this morning to return to Germany for his wife's birthday."

****

She had listened for the explosion and hoped that the thick torrents of rain had blocked out the sound of the blast at Colleville. She did not want to think of the alternative. Although bone-chilled and exhausted from her middle of the night excursion, she feigned pleasure in the arms of her German Colonel and learned of a 'foolhardy group of resistance Frenchmen who had attempted to blow up the Colleville bunker".

She thought to herself, "The mission has failed. All that for nothing."

"Can you imagine their stupidity? A few of them against an army on the cliffs. What were the fools thinking?'

"Who cares 'mon cheri'," Juliette murmured, yet she thought 'as long as we are all safe'.

"True. But we have one of them. He will talk. They always do. Then we'll round up the others." The Colonel said as he turned his head to receive Juliette's warm lips.

"Perhaps, he'll die from the elements," she kissed him full on the lips and real shivers racked her body.

"No, my dear. The Gestapo knows its trade. They have him in the cellar of the bunker. Deep beneath the earth. Closer to the grave. It makes it easier for them."

She shut her eyes so he would not see the hatred burning in them.

When he was spent, Juliette slipped from the sheets and crept up to the rafters of the attic. Beneath the eaves, pigeons slept. She selected the sturdiest one and tied her cryptic message to his leg. Plan G beneath the Earth D/R."

****

Claude had waited up all night for his brother to return. Even if the explosion did occur, he would not have been able to hear it. He kept looking toward the sea, for a flash of light. When that did not happen, he searched the landscape for any shadows or movement, It was not until daylight that he saw the pigeon, struggling against the wind, flying through the rain and into the hole in the barn's roof to land in its nest.

His slender fingers unwrapped the compact message. He knew 'Plan G' meant grenade and "Beneath the earth' – the lowest room in the Colleville Bunker, but he was confused about the rest since the message was in English this time. Was 'D' for the 'dressmaker' – Luc, his friend', or "R' for 'Renard', his brother'. Who had been caught? Who was still being tortured at this very moment – if the 'who'... is still alive?" Claude thought as he forced himself to think of neither name. How could he choose?

He took all three grenades that he had hidden under the hay in the barn a year ago on that other night when the British paratrooper had fallen from the clear calm dark sky and crashed through the roof of the barn. If Claude could have heard as well, the stronger sharper sound that night was the crack, like a huge match stick, of the paratrooper's leg as he plummeted to the floor of the barn. By the time Claude ran across the fields and around Rommel's asparagus detonators, which loomed like innocent young trees in the night air, the man lie half hidden by a birthing cow near a large mound of hay.

Claude had stepped behind the barn door when a German soldier came into the barn, and he followed the soldier when he left. Claude returned to the barn when he knew the British soldier must escape. He had tried to help him walk, but Claude was too slight, and the man called Dan too big to be able to walk down to the beach. Claude wrote one word in the sawdust of the barn – 'Gestapo'. He looked into the English paratrooper's face as the color drained from his cheeks and his face turned gray, and although Claude was just a boy, he had seen too much and been taught too well. He had delivered him a verdict of death – without a judge and without a jury.

The paratrooper had motioned to him where he had hidden his pack and told him to leave, but Claude stayed, nodded grimly, and held his hand. With his other hand, the Englishman threw the capsule, the 'deliver of death', that he had ripped from his shirt tail into his mouth. Claude could not hear his teeth grind decisively into the cyanide, but he saw the grimace on his face. Claude stayed and shut the man's eyelids when death came. He slid out the side door before the German soldier returned with two Gestapo officers.

Now, Claude held not his hand but the three grenades. Sadness filled his heart as he thought that all that remained from this man's life were the grenades from his paratrooper satchel. His rations and bottled water had been consumed long ago, and throughout the past year his knife, gun, canteen, maps, book, and all those things he had carried into France that night had been dispersed as needed to various resistance fighters.

****

Claude followed the same path that Luc, Zosia, Juliette and Renard had made two nights before. The pill box at Colleville loomed on the horizon – a black blight, blocking the view to the sea below. There was no view this night, nor had there been any for the last three. Rain, wind, and an unbelievable cold lashed the Norman Coast these first few days of June.

Despite the cold, Claude lay sweating on the ground near the dimly lit window on the northeast side of the bunker. It was almost the sixth of June, and he could finally see a break in the ink black clouds which covered the night sky. The rain had stopped, but he lay soaked to the bone in the mud near the bunker.

He felt the grenades attached to his belt. No matter who was in this tiny basement room of one of the strongest fortifications ever built, he would have to pull the pins from all three grenades. To kill him... to save him from further torture. He did not want to look to see either his dear friend Luc or his only brother, Renard.

He laid the grenades on the ground beside him like tiny tin soldiers. He touched them before removing the tape from the pins. "The English paratrooper must have done this so they would not accidently explode,' Claude thought as he steadied himself to pull out all three pins simultaneously. He had heard of hands being torn off or men killed because grenades left no margin for error.

Before he pulled the pins out precisely and dropped them down the airshaft all at once, he forced himself to look through the tiny dimly lit window. In that moment as if by destiny, the bloody man chained to the chair lifted up his bent battered head to the window. Claude could not recognize the swollen face, but the eyes he knew. Paul's eyes looked into his from that pulverized mass. The head nodded downward, and the remained lip of the faceless face forced a pursed 'oui'. With tears streaming down his face, Claude knew the 'D' had been for 'death' and the "R' for 'Renard'. He nodded yes in response and let loose his deliverance. He dropped the live grenades down the air shaft and ran.

Chapter 11 – June 5 & 6, 1944

In England on the coast they had dug in for another day and night of interminable cold rain. The word had come down yesterday that it was a 'no go'. The American and British troops of the greatest Armada ever to be assembled could only wait again. The free passes to London, the trips into nearby coastal villages, and even the mingling among the sausages had been canceled or kept to a minimum for the last three days. The card games, the radio, the social paring lacked the convivial spirit of the past months. Trained to a keen edge, nothing could dull their desire to get on with it.

The French, Poles, Canadians as well as the Brits and Yanks had been told it was set. They had waited in their hammocks, bunks, trucks, tanks, planes, and ships double checking their battle dress and gear. Most were quiet – thinking of 'what if's, writing letters home 'just in case', telling buddies what to do 'in case they didn't make it back', giving things away:

records, booze, pin up pictures – whatever they would not be taking with them, and running all the 'battle plans' and 'maneuvers' through their minds one more time. Many were kept busy painting 'war paint' – three bands of white paint around every allied plane's fuselage and wings. No one wanted the D-day planes to be mistaken and shot down as enemy planes. No one wanted a repeat of Sicily. Then, the word came down – D-day was a 'no-go' – "I repeat a no go" was said from the lips of every officer.

Like many of his commanders and men, Dwight D. Eisenhower had been up all night, yet as Supreme Commander of Operation Overlord it was he and only he who would make the ultimate decision. Eisenhower had conferred with all his Generals and those of this British and French Allies. Whatever he decided, the world would critique and judge after the fact. The British great white General Montgomery, and the Free French General, de Gaulle, would add their own perspective and no doubt twist history into their image regardless of his decision. If his decision was successful, that was because they had advised and supported him; if it failed, that was because they had been adamantly opposed it. Eisenhower knew all this when he made the decision to call off the Invasion.

All his advisors had agreed it would have been lunacy to send thousands of troops into the cold rough waters of the Channel. The air support would have failed in the high winds and zero visibility of those late night hours of June 3. Once the difficult decision was made and even more difficult one had to follow – if not now, when?

****

Forty more hours had now passed – forty hours of wind, rain, and fury. The decision had to be made again this late afternoon of June 5th. Eisenhower stood at the front center of the large square table. The map of the coast of France, color coded and labeled with flags to indicate which country was responsible for each sector marked with division and company markers, was fixed to the wall behind him. The Americans had Omaha and Utah beaches along with the sheer cliffs of Pointe de la Percee and Pointe du Hoc. The British were responsible for Gold, Sword, and Juno beaches. Eisenhower knew the American rangers and infantry had drawn the harder hands, but this was much more than a game of poker. In front, spread out were various weather maps and teletype reports which changed by the hour. A dozen men, billeted in for the last twenty-four hours, had received, gone over, and discussed all weather, troop positions and possibilities. Men and women in all sorts of uniforms came in and out of the room with donuts, scones, sausage pies black coffee, cigarettes, and updated information.

"So that is it gentlemen. Either the invasion begins now – with the paratroopers laying the ground work for D-day," Eisenhower looked at the large luminous dial of the clock on the wall behind him as it turned to five, "at seventeen hundred, or we wait two weeks for the tides to be the same again. Two questions need to be asked. Two and only two," he looked at each general in front of him. "Can we believe the weather predictions of a twenty-four hour window of clearing or can we believe we can maintain our buildup capacities on this island for another two weeks without being detected? Can the lid be maintained on our crucial information of when, where, and how?"

He waited for the impact of his words to register with each major Allied General and to be translated if necessary. Eisenhower turned his back and looked at the colored sectioned beaches on the map. He visualized the number of men landing on each beach head – from the sea and from the air. Whatever vote they would give him, the ultimate decision was his and his alone. He had already written a letter for a press release for the annals of history, for this is how he would be remembered – taking full responsibility – either way. He could not see the words anymore, just the faces – the faces of these alive young Americans, Englishmen, Frenchmen, Canadians, and Poles that he was about to send into the 'valley of the shadow of death'.

Had he taken all precautions? Had he made the right decision concerning the conditions at this moment in time – as the word waited to exhale? Would their sacrifice be for naught or for the freedom the world had been waiting for? The

Supreme Commander of the Allied Forces turned to face his generals.

"What is your decision – 'Yes' to go today after H-hour at twenty-four hundred – and have the land forces begin tomorrow- D-day the 6th of June, or 'No' to delay, a delay of a fortnight."

The room resounded with 'yes's' and 'no's". There was no right answer. He could not play God, yet that was what he had to do with thousands of lives. He had prayed to God for the 'right' choice. He had heard each of the Generals and had looked them in the eyes when they answered. Now, he shut his eyes to block out theirs, and the eyes of the soldiers, sailors, and airmen he saw every night in his sleep. A warm serenity spread over him, enveloped him in a wave of white gold. He had already decided. He opened his eyes and spoke.

"Yes, it will be now... the Day – the designated day for the greatest land invasion the world will ever see. God be with us all."

When he walked out of the cigarette filled rooms, a cool clear evening breeze was starting to sweep the clouds away and with it the cobwebs of doubt hiding in the attic corners of his mind. He looked upward and saw two black clouds part and the last rays of the sun shine through. He thought of the poem by a nineteen-year-old American aviator killed in action with the Royal Canadian Air Force on December 11, 1941. Breathing in the cool air, he repeated the words of one John Gillespie Magee Jr. who had joined the war his country had not.

"Oh, I have slipped the surly bonds of earth,
And danced the skies on laughter-silvered wings,
 Sunward I've climbed and joined the tumbling mirth
Of sun-split clouds – and done a hundred things
 You have not dreamed of – wheeled and soared and swung
High in the sun lit silence. Hovring there...
    Put out my hand, and touched the Face of God."

Then he bowed his head and prayed – prayed that the airmen of the United States 82nd and 101st Airborne Divisions and the British Airmen of the 1st and 6th Divisions might feel in their fine young manhood – the vigor, optimism, and pride of this American Airman, and that his words would take them through the horrors they would have to face before they'd 'touch the face of God' and 'slip the surly bonds of earth' when their time came. All his hopes were pinned on their courage and strength – tonight and tomorrow. All he could do was wait.

Standing alone on the only free soil left on this side of the Atlantic, he knew he was placing his faith in the nearly 20,000 men who would be falling into France tonight – this 5th day of June of 1944 and into the dark morning of the 6th. From the beginning of Operation Overlord, he had been going against the advice of many, including Sir Trafford Leigh-Mallory, Commander of the Allied Air Forces, who held the belief that it was suicidal to drop inexperienced paratroopers eight miles behind the Atlantic Wall right into the lairs of veteran German divisions.

Eisenhower had answered him as he had answered all the others, "These paratroopers have had three years of training. Never in the history of mankind have soldiers been so prepared. They must go ahead of their sea borne soldiers crossing the Channel. Holding off the paratroopers would subject their brother soldiers struggling up the beaches to an even greater probability of disaster."

So, he turned to make preparations to walk among those 20,000 who would be lined up on the airfields of England – of those and others who had and would 'fight in the air, on the sea, and on the land', as a man he respected had said a lifetime ago, or so it seemed to him. He and Winston Churchill saw eye to eye and with a determination that was almost clairvoyant.

Churchill had a tenacity and fearlessness edged by a sharp reason which had carried the Brits through their long years of night bombings and deprivations. Although many a Brit had said, "One more Yank tank and we'll sink into the sea." Eisenhower and the Americans – Churchill and the British, had also said through actions as well as words, "We're all in this together".

Soon his tour in these evening hours of June 5th would begin. He had to count on his three Airborne Divisions, parachute troops, and gliders to land behind the Atlantic Wall fortifications close to Sainte-Mere-Eglise and Caen. The British 6th Airborne would be getting the additional attention of General Montgomery, Eisenhower's counterpart for command of the 231st Army group. Under Montgomery's direct command was British Army General Dempsey who could cover the left flank of the operation when they hit the beach tomorrow morning. Eisenhower counted on Dempsey and the 2nd British Army to land successfully on the beaches of Gold, Juno, and Sword and fight their way off the beaches and into Caen.

Eisenhower thought of his right flank coverage by General Omar Bradley, Commander of the 1st American Army. Although both flanks had the same amount of companies, the British had an extra division to cover the same footage of sand. Last night he had to tell Bradley that the mission to take out the guns at Colleville had failed and the mission for the guns at Pointe du Hoc depended on the success of the 82nd and 101st Airborne glider and paratrooper forces. Those were the men he had to visit first in order to look them straight in the eye and acknowledge their fire, as well as their fear.

The success of the men on the beaches directly correlated to their success in the air and their ability to cause significant damage behind the lines. The plan was for Allied Air and naval support to take out the German guns jaggedly positioned to form barrages of cross fire on the French beaches. The Allied bombs from the air and from the sea would begin only after the British 6th Airborne and the American 82nd and 101st were dropped. If all went according to plan, the first troops to set foot on the sands of Normandy could claim the beachheads quickly without too many casualties. The big guns at Colleville would have to be eliminated by naval barrage and Allied bombs since the four man special mission team had failed to do so. Once the land forces were in, a supply port could be built at Arromanches – right between the 1st and 2nd Armies.

His mind was jumping ahead, as usual. He took a deep breath of the early evening air and felt a wave of calmness. The decision had been made. It passed from his hands – into the hands of God. This he had to believe – for his own sanity and for the future of mankind.

****

They were so young – such boys he thought as he looked over a sea of men line up as far as the eye could see. He had to walk among them until they all had taken off in flight across the Channel – each stick of men, in each and every company, in each and every division were geared for their specific mission.

"Where are you from soldier?" Ike asked a boy with a blond forelock sticking out of his helmet and partially covering his oiled face.

"Omaha, Sir."

"And you?" Ike asked the tall lean tanned soldier next to him.

"Los Angeles, General!"

The short dark haired soldier across from him didn't wait to be asked by Commander General Dwight D. Eisenhower.

"Brooklyn, New York.. Ike... I mean General... I mean Sir," he stammered with a grin on his face.

"That's O.K. Brooklyn. We Midwest boys know where New York is – especially Brooklyn." Ike grinned back. What's your name?"

"Tony, Sir."

"Throw the bum out; he's probably got a lousy arm," a freckled face broad shouldered redhead countered half way down the line. "Leave it to us Bronx boys to throw a grenade across a fuckin field...damn field.. Excuse me General Sir... darn field."

"Where you're going and what you are about to do entitles you to speak as 'colorfully' as you want. Right soldier?" he looked to the soldier on his right.

"Damn right, General," he smiled as he licked the cocoa and linseed oil off his greased lips.

"Looks like hell. I hope the stuff tastes good." Ike countered.

"Mighty good," the paratrooper said with a grin as he looked at the faces of his buddies, each covered with the 'army issued' face paint to camouflage and protect them from the elements and from the Germans.

He walked down row upon row, asking each the same easy questions- the personal ones that showed that each and every one of them was important. As he looked into each paratrooper's face, he knew that he might be one of the last ones who would see him as a person and not as a number on a dog tag. They all knew, but no one said it – that within the next four hours they might be lying dead on the sand or soil of France with only their dog tags to speak for them.

He walked up the steps of a platform to the right of the airfields. Above the revving engines of the planes, he pulled the standing microphone closer to his mouth.

"I'm proud of each and every one of you. America, England and the free world is proud of you. You are the finest trained men the world has ever seen. I have confidence that by tomorrow the Germans will be pulling back from their strongholds on the coast of France – the tide will turn. You are the force that will turn it, and it will be their time to run. Are you ready?"

"Yes" roared from the mouths of the men as one strong vibrant voice – so loud that it droned out and floated over the sounds of the B-24's, B-27's, and C-47's taking off down the runways and over the fields.

"We're with you Ike" was heard in waves as the affirmation of faith sounded from column to column of men.

****

Sandy's eighteen men and the entire 6th British Airborne Division heard the voices which built to tidal force by the time it reached the ears of the British airmen. Somewhere along a column a word had changed, 'we're with you Monty!" was the British airmen's response.

Sandy smiled in appreciation of all things English and General Bernard Law Montgomery was certainly that. In these last rays of light fighting the darkness Sandy could see the straight lines of drab Brownish olive jumpsuits and the new Pattern 37 short wool brownish olive battle jacket/blouse with its exposed pockets and frontal buttons. Hats capped over their ears, many held their helmets in one hand or the other. Their backs carried the weight of the ninety pound sacks needed for their mission and for their survival.

The C-47 transports, each heading for their specific beach, taxied up and down – preparing for tonight's take off. They reminded Sandy of the daily traffic in Trafalgar Square – or at least how it used to be before the war. With few cars and fewer tanks of petrol the congestion was no longer a problem. In fact, it was like a walk in the park now. He wondered if this drop of theirs would be 'a walk in the park'. "What did the Yanks say?' he thought "Three strikes and you're out."

For the men in his stick this would be their first official drop behind enemy line, for him it was the third. The Third Infantry Division of the British 2nd Army would be landing tomorrow on Sword beach, the code name for the beaches at Luc, Lion, and Ouistreham. From his other two missions he understood that the sand would hold the debarking vehicles. Tonight his mission was different. Now, he could fight. All these men were more than ready 'to let slip the dogs of war' on the German war machine. To take out bunkers and machine gun nests, and to secure all bridges on the way to Caen was their goal. Through the military grapevine he had heard British Commander Leigh-Mallory say it was a suicide mission.

"What does that old fart know?" Sandy continued to think as a blend of "America the Beautiful" and "God Save the King" reached his ears. "He's just pissed Ike sees us paratroopers as the king pins in the plan."

He smiled as he thought of these brash – but likeable Yanks, he had to admit. They would be covering his right flank and perhaps even his backside. "And we all speak the King's English... although they mutilate it," Sandy mused. "And we have the same song, so even if they take our birds or 'gals' as they would say, it's all for one and one for all. The British birds go where the money is. Who's to blame them? Besides, with a Yank you know where you stand. None of this polite upper crust Brit talk of the aristos who just as soon cut your legs out from under you."

****

Later that evening inside the metal cocoon of the British transport carrier, Sandy felt anything but secure. His thoughts focused on the beaches the troops would land on early tomorrow morning. Perhaps, the French name for this beach, 'Lion-sur-Mer' is a good omen. Richard the Lion Hearted had been the prideful courageous King of England. He had fought a war of another sort – a religious war that had also spanned across today's Europe. The fact that the code name 'Sword' was one of the British beach heads also conjured up the images of Merlin and King Arthur of the Round Table. Theirs was a fight for the inhabitants of England – to create a Camelot, an ideal civilization.

Sandy looked around at the faces deep in thought, crammed shoulder to shoulder to the right, left, and in front of him in this noisy little plane. For them the civilization of the entire free world rested on these same shoulders. Personally, it would be life or death. They would land in a different arena, fight with different swords, yet the purpose was the same age old honorable one – a fight for fairness and personal freedoms.

The loud drone of the engines reverberating in the metal cocoon made talk nearly impossible. The first formations of planes had taken off at eleven o'clock with the last of the daylight to begin their flight across the Channel. Like geese in V shape formations they followed one another. The men near the round encased windows could see the ships of the invasion – like small rubber boats in the rough bathtub of the English Channel below.

By the time Sandy's plane had taken off night had come. Nothing could be seen below and only tiny purple wing tip lights guiding each plane over the Channel kept them apart, and beckoned them onward. Close to the French Coast they could see bright blasts of color. No one spoke, but all had the same thought "was that a buddy's plane? Will it be me next?"

The tension grew as they began to see the explosions and artillery fire like 'Boxer Day' sparklers and feel the jolts and bumps of explosions that had just missed them. No one said anything about the plane on the starboard side of their formation. Like a fireball from Hell it had burned. Their friends and fellow paratroopers in it had no choice but to jump into the Channel below or be burned to death in the air. The youngster across from him put his fingers under his helmet to block his ears from their screams which cut through the engine roar of the planes. Sandy turned to look out the window and saw one man pull his chute too soon. A chunk of burning metal hit the top of it and the flames took big white fluffy licks out of the chute and then slide down the cords until the man was consumed like a marshmallow over a camp fire.

"Hail Mary, Full of Grace, God be with them," someone near him murmured.

"Our father who art in Heaven hallowed be thy name..." another joined in.

"Yea, though I walk through the valley of the shadows of death, thou art with me..." the boy with the blocked ears repeated in a trance-like mantra.

Sandy couldn't discern if the boy heard the sounds of the exploding shrapnel as it fell like hail onto the roof of their transport. 'Perhaps it's better that he not hear. Perhaps it doesn't matter to him. Terror has already frozen him in her grip,' he thought.

The plane, which had begun to rock from the violent explosions, was beginning to veer and zigzag erratically like a pinball in a Brighton Beach amusement park game. The five minutes from the French Coast, directly over Hitler's Atlantic Wall, to the drop zones eight miles beyond was becoming the Valley of Death for hundreds of paratroopers, pilots, medics, and chaplains. In order to avoid crashing into an exploding plane in front, to the right or to the left of them, the pilots were breaking orders and veering out of formation. Each instinctive avoidance by a pilot had a domino effect on every other pilot and plane.

"Is everyone O.K.," Sandy's sergeant Big Al, boomed as he stood up with his head bent in the flying can of sardines. Men had been thrown to the floor, and as they tried to get up, they slipped on the slick vomit of their sardine mates.

From air sickness or fear their retching filled the plane. They all had to shake the smell from their noses and throats or they'd be frozen into inaction. Big Al had seen men so afraid they couldn't move out of an enemy tank's path. Fear had such a powerful grip that they were locked in place, and only the treads of the tank as it crushed their bodies beneath four tons of metal could pull their feet from the earth.

"Slap the man next to you." He bellowed. "That's an order. Pull him off the floor if you have to, but slap him hard." He pulled up the paratrooper in front of him. "The green light's on. Go you son of a bitch." He pushed him onward.

They pulled one another up, stumbled, and in some cases crawled to the open door of the plane. Big Sal made sure all of his men had clipped onto the overhead jump cable. Like a subway strap each nylon tether held the men in line ready for their jump – a jump into a night lit by fire and heralded by jarring explosions and the staccato repetition of artillery fire. The green light continued to blink as the plane swerved to miss a shell so close they could reach out and touch it.

"Go." Big Al yelled as he pushed each man out the door.

The youngster who had plugged his ears was the third to go. He jumped with his hand to his chest pocket where he kept the pictures of his mother and girlfriend and a lucky rabbit's foot.

"Hail Mary full of Grace." another said as he touched his neck where his gold confirmation cross hung from its 22k gold chain.

"Our Father who art in heaven, hallowed be thy name..." placed his right hand on the chest pocked where he kept a small Bible as fate pulled him into the night.

Sandy was the second to last to go. Big Al would follow him. Sandy jiggled the silver dollars, ten franc coins, Canadian quarters and English pounds he had won in his first London poker game. He had cleaned out two American soldiers, three free Frenchmen, a Canadian and four British Airmen in that lucky game so he kept the winnings in his pockets for the first two jumps. He would take no chances for this third jump.

"If anything happens to me or the Lieutenant, you're in charge of the boys."

"I know Sarge. It's in the bag." Sandy answered with a nod of his head toward the TNT in the ninety pound load strapped to his front and back.

He didn't wait for a push. The cold wind hit his face as he yelled "Big Al". Sandy could hear the jump yells of 'Winston' 'England Forever' 'Mum' echo through the corridor of wind, rain, and fire. He looked up at the plane above him and saw Al outlined by the green blinking light and the purple wing tip lights. Right before Al's turn to jump a direct hit burst the plane into jagged flames, and Al stood but a glowing shape in the disintegrating door frame. Sandy instinctively covered his eyes from the blinding light and when he opened them fragments of fire glowed in the air and the plane was a falling comet heading toward the ground.

He could see some of the men who had jumped ahead of him.' Though I walk through the Valley of Shadow of Death' had a palm size cross sewn on the right corner of his pack. Sandy knew it was him when he saw a flash of fire cut through his right back pant pocket and up through his groin. His unearthly scream was cut short when a second flash hit him directly in the chest.

As he floated through the night air, the sights and sounds around him were worse than any of his nightmares. Like Dante's inferno every grotesque shape took on a satanic form as it gurgled and choked. Like hideous marionettes dancing on the devil's stage, they dangled and shook on invisible strings. To survive he blocked out the fact that these were his countrymen, his fellow paratroopers, his friends.

The ground was coming up fast. He could see it in bursts as someone or something on fire illuminated the forms on the ground below. Before he hit the ground, he wondered if the Lieutenant was still alive.

****

In another space of air, over another piece of Channel, approaching another piece of beach of the Atlantic Wall, Anthony Joseph Martino of the 82nd Airborne wondered if his Lieutenant Sidney Smith, the professor from Iowa who would be the first to jump, would get it the worse. He really liked the guy – he'd use the word love, but his Brooklyn buddies would have called him a fag. He had wanted to say something to Sid before they boarded, but he hadn't and now it would be too awkward. He wanted the guy to make it – not only because they needed his lead, but because he had a wife, Marjorie – Marge, who he talked about all the time. He was real proud of her. Anyway, Lieutenant Smith was AOK in his book.

Tony looked to his far right and saw the faces of the two strangers Sid had told them about. Their entire stick of eighteen would have two more, a Pole and a Russian, – on top secret Generals' (plural) orders. Sidney and the Sergeant knew their names but had introduced them to the paratroopers of the American 82nd Airborne as simply the Pole and the Russian. They understood their secondary mission was to get them to Sainte-Mere-Eglise. Their primary objective for this stick of American paratroopers along with the rest of the 82nd and 101st was to bomb out or secure the main bridges, roads, and arteries eight miles behind the American beach heads of Omaha and Utah. Sid's men specifically had to secure and hold the bridge at Chef-du-Pont over the Merderet River until there were enough reinforcement troops to leave it in their hands.

No one except the Sergeant and the Lieutenant, was privy to, the two foreigners' mission, to get to Paris at all cost, and only Sidney Smith knew that General Bradley's orders were to commandeer any men possible to get them to Paris before the American and French Armies liberated it. These orders were secured in a water proof envelope inside a thin titanium pouch on a cord hung over his neck and inside his shirt and jacket – close to his heart.

Tony glanced over at the Lieutenant and noticed that he frequently touched his chest. He wondered what lucky medallion he had hung from his neck. "It's probably a picture of his wife, Marge," he thought.

Tony touched his pocket, outside was his army regulation Colt 45 and inside was his 'lucky lady', the 500 franc note that he won in the last poker game. After he had gotten all of his stick's John Hancocks, he went from sausage to sausage two nights ago collecting as many of the rest of the signatures of the 82nd that would fit on the large colorful French bill. All around the head of Marianne, some French dame, he made sure they wrote their names. Some even squeezed in the names of their companies or hometowns. That was the last night of real partying, for as June 3rd ended and another early rainy morning began most had gotten down to the serious business of sleeping, writing their last letters home, putting their things in order, and setting their minds to the business ahead.

Now, two nights later they were on their way. Tony wondered what each of these guys thought – these men who were as close as brothers or Brooklyn block buddies to him. He smiled at Billy and Tim who were sitting across from him, staring blankly ahead. They sheepishly returned Tony's grin, for they knew he was thinking of their ride home in the jeep that the Lieutenant had 'commandeered' for their last real night out in London. Tony couldn't tell who was happier – sixteen-year-old Tim or his buddy Billy. Each had found a girl who had, for a price, made his last night as a free man memorable. Tony looked at Tim and thought he had aged since then – what would happen to him after tonight?

Tony was aware that two years earlier Tim had gotten some drunk to pose as his father and sign the enlistment papers. Tim had told the guys in the unit that his real father had put him in an orphanage when he was a kid but used to visit him on the weekends. The old man had kept his sisters at home to cook and clean for him and do 'who knew what else'. Tim had said many times that after the war he wanted to go back to Kentucky and get his sisters out. Too thin and slight despite his chiseled face, his jaw line was firmly clenched. Tony wondered if he didn't regret his hasty enlistment. If he had stayed, at least he would have had food and a roof over his head until the war ended.

In contrast, Tony thought "the two new guys seemed relaxed like this was just another "walk in the park'. The blond blue eyed Pole can't be more than three or four years older than me, but the brown haired one is around my age, nineteen. They're both too young to have had any real war experience."

Tony Martino knew that even Sid, the oldest of them at twenty-one, had seen no combat. "The Pole," he thought "had to be twenty-one tops – too young to have been in the Polish Army when it fought for its country's freedom in September of 39' or to have had any combat experience anywhere else. So what could make them so self-contained – so at ease with what we're going to face," Tony thought as he turned his head to look at them.

Janusz's and Christian's thoughts were focused on what lay ahead. Word had gotten back to them in London that the destruction of the guns at Coleville had failed. Luc, Juliette, and

Zosia were safe. Someone had been caught. They did not know who, yet Janusz and Christian both knew firsthand what torture could do to a man or a woman. They had to cut those thoughts out of their minds and keep nothing but cold passion in their hearts. To be fearless equaled success.

They had experienced raw unparalleled fear and walked away alive. God had taken them by the hand and walked each one through their unique valley of the shadow of death. What was to be would be. They would never again worry about that which they had no control.

Both knew there was a reason why they had been spared. To jump from an airplane in the middle of the night behind enemy lines in the company of strangers seemed normal to them. Strangers had provided for them in the past, and they would again. Each recognized the destiny of these particular strangers would be linked from this time forward to theirs.

Sidney looked over at them. "I wish I could be as calm as these two"," he thought. "What they have to do in Paris is so important that I had to be brought face to face with Omar Bradley, General of the entire First Army. They must be damn good."

The plane was beginning to rock as it got closer to the French Coast. Sidney felt he should have told Tony in addition to the Sargent about the Pole and Russian's objective to get to Paris at all costs. He'd tell him about the pouch as soon as they hit the ground. Changing his mind, he edged out of his seat.

It was at that moment that the plane began to twist and turn. Sidney held onto an overhead strap, but Billy and Tim were thrown to the floor. Bullets ripped through the fuselage. One cut through Tim's Adam's apple. It took him but a few blood gurgling minutes to die.

Christian pulled Billy back to his seat by his jacket collar. "You're going to be O.K. Your friend is in no pain now." Christian forced Billy to look at him "Jump and fight for him... and no one else. That'll keep you alive."

Sidney nodded at Janusz and slid into Tim's position across from Tony. Over them a C-47 took a direct hit and burst into flames. It rocked their plane even more. With engines wide open Sidney shouted what he had to say – to Tony.

****

Sandy hit the ground running. His plane had climbed too high when the artillery barrages began. To him it seemed to take a hundred years before the ground came up. His battalion had not been the first to arrive nor would they be the last, but what he saw he did not expect. Not able to see his hand in front of his face, he hit, rolled, and ran into pitch black. Cutting through the night were unearthly moans of 'mommy', 'Oh God' 'help me' followed by the sound of burp guns firing. Their burst of light allowed Sandy to see glimpses of scenery and movement like a shuffle of picture cards where each movement was in slow motion and only remotely connected to the previous card. It took him twenty minutes to be free of his chute. His first thought afterwards was to roll up the stick, find his other men.

He landed in a small clearing and once free he took out his compass, looked at its luminous arrow, and headed southeast toward Caen. Suddenly, he heard German voices and flattened himself into the marshy ground. The cacophony of guns – of all chaotic calibers – shattered his ear drums. He could see the boots of Germans with rifles at their hip shooting at whatever was in the sky or on the ground. His lightweight assembled M-1 was in his sack. He only had time to reach for the knife in his belt.

As tracers, forming beautiful arches of red, yellow, blue, and orange continued to shoot through the dark, the paratroopers from the rest of Sandy's battalion dropped out like puffs of cotton into the chaotic carnival of death. He wondered how he had survived. Planes were flying at a mere 500 feet above the marsh, dropping with loads too fast and low - so low he could hear the bullets ripping through wings and fuselage like a popcorn carnie machine.

A German's boot almost stepped right on his face. Sandy turned on his back and pulled the soldier down with his gun still blazing. He flipped back on his stomach, saddled the soldier, pinned him down, and felt for his face. Pushing it back into the soft marsh, he drove the knife through his throat. His death rattle could not be heard over the mayhem of the marshes and the screams from the sky.

Sandy crawled through the wet marsh towards the shadow of hedges he could see through the bursts of artillery flak and the fireballs of planes in the sky. His hand with the bloody knife reached out ahead as he slid quickly through the deepening marsh water.

"They've flooded the bloody fields," he almost said out loud. "Jesus, I'm going to drown on land."

Halfway to the hedges his hand felt a warm body. He instinctively pulled his hand up before his training kicked in, and he plunged his knife into the mass. He felt no movement and flipped the body over. Just then a paratrooper lit up the sky directly above him. His torched chute came screaming down, and in its light Sandy saw the body's uniform. Its color was British olive brown with the insignia for 6th Airborne. The rank was that of lieutenant – his lieutenant, who had taken a mortar in what was left of his intestines. Sandy turned away to vomit in the waters around him.

****

"Let's go." Sidney Smith's jump master sergeant shouted as the men in the back of the Dakota began to call off their numbers as they had practiced – jump after jump in England.

"Twenty," Janusz shouted.

"Nineteen," Christian followed.

"Eighteen," Tony responded as he nudged Billy to call out "Sixteen."

The three Americans thought about Tim, number seventeen, lying dead on the floor of the Dakota. He had said seventeen was his lucky number, and he intended to celebrate it somewhere in France – hopefully with a French girl. 'Might -have –been's had to be swept aside. All could feel the change in altitude. They crossed the Channel at 500 feet to escape radar then climbed to avoid anti-aircraft fire, then swooped down to 700 feet for the drop. Standing in line, hooked up to go, they all saw the searchlights, tracers, and explosions cutting down C-47's to the right and left of them. Above and

below, planes continued to disappear in fiery balls like moths
hitting flames. They twisted and turned to avoid the 20mm shells
and the heavier 88mm ones.

"God, as a good catholic... as a catholic, just get me alive
and in one piece to the ground." Tony shut his eyes and made
the sign of the cross.

Janusz and Christian looked at him and did the same.

At that moment they took a direct hit – up through the floor
and out the jump door – taking out the green lighting panel, the
jump master and the first three paratroopers. In a blink of an eye
the destiny of four men was determined by a number in line.
The remaining sixteen men hugged onto their lines to avoid the
four foot hole through the center of the plane. Despite what
they had already seen, many hesitated at the opening – where the
door had been. Nothing had prepared them to jump into a wall
of tracer bullets. If they paused in the darkness of the Normandy
sky somewhere over the Cotentin, Sidney pushed them out.
Through this chaotic circus Tony and the last two men of the
stick, Janusz and Christian, were literally thrown out of the hole
head first as their plane took another hit in its left wing.
Mesmerized by lights, sounds, and sights all around him, he
glimpsed up to see his plane turn back toward the Channel.
"Maybe he'll make it home," Sidney thought as he saw the two
chutes of the foreigners open slightly above and to the far left of
him. Other planes were dropping or tumbling men out like balls
onto a green billiard table, yet these balls were flesh and blood
who made themselves known, perhaps for their last moment of
life by shouting: "Geronimo'" "Rita baby..." "The Alamo..."
"Give em Hell, Ike'"

Below two 20 mm guns in a flak wagon pumped up shells
into the night. They ripped through his chute, and Sidney
instinctively pulled up his legs. Dead paratroopers floated down
beside him, their bodies jerking like marionettes from the impact
of the shells. One was torn loose from his chute by a heavy
bundle of equipment attached to its cord minus the chute. Other
equipment bundles with half opened chutes hurled past him like
Mack trucks without any brakes. Solidary helmets, knocked off

the heads of paratroopers by the opening shock of their chutes, rolled like bowling balls.

Through the mist and debris, Tony looked at the luminous dial of his watch- 1:30 a.m. "What a bitchin hour for a man do be doing this," he said out loud and then laughed at his inane action and reaction. The common place act of looking at his watch knocked him out of his dazed detachment from the reality of the horror. Below he could see the frantic movements of the Germans as some leapt for the equipment bundles and others stayed fixed in fear or fury until their guns glowed red from the heat of constant fire. In the last moment before he hit the ground he still could not see Sidney or any other from his stick.

"Christ, I'm going right into a machine gun nest," he thought as back draft from a plane falling fast to his right blew him into a grove of apple trees. His chute floated through the branches, and stopped with a jerk as it caught the thick gnarled fingers of an ancient apple tree. He thudded to a stop ten feet off the ground as the scent of apple blossoms filled his nostrils.

He pulled out his trench knife from its sheath at the bottom of his pack. Quickly, he cut through the lines which held him helplessly dangling from the tree. He dropped to the ground –flipped the knife to his left hand, unsnapped his revolver holster, and found his clicker. His eyes had become accustomed to the night. Quietly, he headed out through the north side of the grove. He kept low and looked steadily around him as he sought out the rest of his stick... or the enemy.

As he cleared the grove, he had seen neither friend nor foe. He had stopped looking up since he could not help the continuous flow of men being dropped or glided in this early morning of June 6. What he did see hidden by hedges thirty yards to his right was a wagon of four 20 mil guns red hot from firing rainbows of bullets into the sky. What he heard were the screams and death gurgles of the 82[n] Airborne paratroopers who were like sitting ducks in a shooting gallery.

He reached into his pack for a grenade. Its pineapple rough leafed top fit snug in his palm. He carefully pulled off the tape he had placed over the pin. Although it was not regulation, he had to keep his eyes straight ahead, as he gently moved the grenade toward his mouth. He let it caress his lips to find the point of the pin. All the while his eyes scanned to the right and left of the guns. In one continuous movement he clenched the pin in his teeth and pulled. The grenade sailed out of his hand like poetry – a slow curve ball over the plate before it dropped. The wagon blew up in a flash of fragments and the bodies of the German soldiers flew out like rag dolls into the night.

"Thank you Joe DiMaggio wherever you," a voice yelled as he floated down.

"That 'a boy", echoed through the night.

Tony could not help but smile to himself. They should see me in Brooklyn – now that I've turned into a Yankee. He picked up his clicker and crawled ahead to the hedges in front of him. He heard a noise to his left and clicked his clicker and waited to hear the two click response. None came. He clicked again. He clicked for the third time. When he heard movement again, he reached for his gun.

"Flash," a voice said.

Tony was so shocked that he did not answer.

"Flash," the unfamiliar voice said again.

Then Tony heard a click. He responded with two clicks and added, "Thunder". Just then he saw a shape appear directly out of the hedge row in front of him. He recognized the Russian – number 'nineteen' – in his stick. "Why the hell didn't you click twice. I could've killed you." Tony said.

"They never gave me a clicker. Just the password."

"So what did I hear after you said 'flash'?"

"This," Christian answered as he lifted up the MI carbine 30 caliber semi-automatic with his bayonet attached.

"That'a been swell!" Tony sarcastically said. Then he looked into the Russian's cold blue eyes and added nothing more. "What gives this guy this edge of steel." he thought but didn't say.

Christian kept looking at this American, shorter that most he had seen in England but definitely 'tough'. That was a word he knew the street meaning of. "Swell' was different. He hadn't comprehended this soldier's meaning of the word, but he recognized the tone.

"On y va!" Christian used a colloquial French phrase he knew the American didn't know. He kept a straight face, yet a faint smirk passed over his lips.

"It's nice to be in the game again," Tony thought. "And what's your name 'Ruskie'?"

"Let's go. And the name's Christian."

"Christ, that's jive. I'm in hell with Jesus. Now, I know I'm gonna make it."

Christian had moved out ahead. He had a sixth sense as he slid among the hedgerows which bordered the fields in this part of France. He felt at home. It had been four years since he fled the Katyn, but it had never left the marrow of his bones or his soul. He was at home in the darkness and the web like mass of the hedges. Tony followed him – relinquishing the lead position without a fight. There was something about this kid that gave him an aura of confidence, of trust. Instinctively, the kid moved to the right or to the left. He knelt down to listen; for what, Tony did not know since the guns, bombs, and screeches of what used to be human filled the night. He quickly became aware the kid seemed to know things he could not possibly know at his age. How could this kid possess the experience and field intelligence of a Rommel or a Patton?

Christian stopped short in front of him, reached behind to push him down, and slid his knife, long and slim like a hat pin out of his boot. In the darkness Tony could not see what happened next, but he heard a slicing sound followed by gurgling chokes – like someone drowning. Tony had taken out his thick blade service knife, but realized his cumbersome weapon was better for cutting a chunk of bread than slitting a man's throat. Tony felt Christian's hand tap him twice, and he began to follow him once again. He looked down as a flash of a downed plane hit the open field in the center of the rows of hedges. There stuffed in a hedge was a young German with his helmet still on his head, a cigarette burning in his mouth, and his eyes were still open. Except for the red slice from ear to ear, he appeared alive.

This time it was his turn to pat Christian twice – not because of the dead German but because of a large mass among the asparagus in the field. In the ball of flames of the downed

Dakota Tony had seen a shape move between the ten foot high wired poles. They both buried themselves in the hedgerows as they peered across the open space. The Merderet River was to their west and paratroopers had dropped in it and drowned from the weight of their packs, but these Norman fields were more insidious. Built to separate one farmer's land from the other, they now they hid the enemy. The open fields in the middle looked like a walk in the park to Tony – easier than inching around all the bordering tall hedges to get to the other side he had thought. Christian knew they could face hidden mines or be easy targets in the open empty space.

Tony reached for another grenade, but before he even touched it, a swish slid through the air. In less than five seconds a blast of light and explosion filled the field. They heard a 'moo' and a dark form take flight into the air.

"Oh shit," a voice just a stone's throw from where Tony and Christian were crouched, exclaimed. Christian said 'flash' at the moment when Tony clicked his clicker once.

"Thunder" was the response – shortly followed by a mad set of clicks. They stepped out of the hedges simultaneously – each with a weapon pointed at the other.

"Oh shit," Tony stood downwind of the manure covered form in front of him.

"Yeah, I'm off to a great start. Landed in pile of it – haven't killed a German...just a cow." the smelly shape said.

"What the hell, that can only be you, Billy."

"Tony! Sweet Jesus, I could hug you." Billy happily answered.

"Well don't. You got a great camouflage outfit going for you." Tony quipped. "The Krauts will just think a cow is near them."

"Who's with you?

"Christian, the Russian –is the only one of our stick. The last time I saw the Lieutenant he was in the air next to me."

A rustle in the hedgerow behind them made them instinctively turn. Tony clicked the safety off his MI Garand. They heard two clicks.

"Flash", they said in unison.

"Thunder", Sidney answered from the hedges as he stepped out grinning and sopping wet.

<u>Chapter 12 – June 6 – Between 0100 and Dawn</u>

They had jumped into the night – over thirty thousand American, British, and Canadian paratroopers. Dropped into the sea, the marshes, the fields, many were to be interred into the soil of Normandy forever. From Cabourg to beyond Carentan they were scattered across miles – long and deep. Few could roll up their sticks, and they joined whatever American or British units they found. Their original objectives, for which they had trained months, were of little use. From different companies, different regiments – even different divisions they merged into fighting units with officers telling them to advance on targets they knew nothing about. It was hard to take orders from strangers and to trust that the enlisted man on one's right, left, or rear would do his job – but, that is what each pocket of paratroopers did.

Through the early morning hours of June 6th the British 6th Airborne moved toward Caen – cutting off communication, bombing German transport lines, capturing locks and securing bridges as they went. The Americans from the 82nd and 101s did the same. In the cold corridor of one plane had sat an American unit along with one Pole and one Russian ready to be dropped. In the chaos which followed, the Germans did not know if this was the real invasion they had expected. They thought it would come at Pas-de-Calais. These raids or diversions were not far enough north, and without direct orders from General Rommel the troops protecting the Atlantic Wall could not counterattack.

As fate would have it, Rommel left the day before, Monday June 5, to spend the day with his wife. It was her birthday, and in his absence one of his chiefs of staff was having his own party at Chateau Chambord in La Roche-Guy. So, on the day of the greatest invasion the world would ever see only German patrols were sent out. The Panzers were already on night maneuvers and a Company of Colonel Luck's 21st was on a night exercise just outside of Caen. No one was there to give the order to stop the invasion they had waited so long for, and no one wanted to wake up Hitler.

****

After his drop Sandy was one of the many who found none of the men in his stick except the Lieutenant who lay dead in the marsh. Creeping through the fields, he found lone paratroopers to form a fighting unit: a pathfinder, another engineer like himself with a sack of TNT, a lad from Stafford, a Yorkshire man, three street fighters from Liverpool - all from other units of the British 6th Airborne. They joined together in a cluster of eight behind a barn where Sandy took out his small flashlight as the other engineer took out a map.

"We're supposed to blow this bridge here – five kilometers west of Caen," the engineer said.

"Our mission was to secure this village at Bayeux – near Route N13 and wait for those who hit Gold Beach this morning so they'd have a road to Caen," one of the Liverpool lads stated.

"To move as far east as possible and clear the way for the Canadians landing on Juno by cutting the roads between Courseulles-sur-Mer that run from Arromanches to Ouistreham," the Yorkshire man added as the boy from Stafford nodded in agreement.

"Well, we all have different objectives, and I figure we're here," Sandy pointed to a little village far to the southwest of any of their objectives. "If we knock out the communications from here, here, and here," he showed them the cutoff points on the map. "We'll help those landing on Omaha as well as Gold."

"Right mate! The Germans won't know what hit'em." the big Yorkshire man agreed.

"Fine, but I'm setting up my 'Becky'," the pathfinder said.

As he set up his Eurkeka/Rebecca Radar Beacon System, the others huddled smoking one of the Liverpool lad's dry pack of Lucky Strike cigarettes he had won in a card game with a Yank two nights – two lifetimes ago. The pathfinder cursed and complained as he fought with his 'Becky' to get her ready to send a signal up to any C-47's looking for a drop zone.

"Here," he said to the farmer, the lad from Stafford. "You look like you know something about critters. Take one of the pigeons out of this container and put a note with our coordinates into the capsule on his leg."

Sandy handed a pencil to the boy and pointed to the coordinates on the map. No one argued with Sandy. In truth, Sandy was just taking an educated guess that was no better or worse than anyone else's – except that no one else came forward. By default, he was now in command.

"We better get out of here," the boy said as he let go two pigeons.

"Why," one of the Liverpool lads asked as he took a deep drag from his Lucky Strike.

"Yeah, let's have a breather, mate," his pal countered.

"See the way those cows are standing and turning toward that tree over there," the boy said.

Sandy and the others looked in the direction he pointed. The others could barely see in the sporadic bursts of light, but Sandy, more accustomed to night drops, made out the shape of the tree and the mass of cows in the night.

"Cows always turn that way when they see someone – because they think they'll be fed," the boy matter-of-factly said.

"In the middle of the God Damn night!" the big Yorkshire man exclaimed.

"'Well, we can bet it's no French farmer at this hour. Let's move out of here." Sandy ordered.

"This God damn Radar system isn't set yet," the pathfinder said.

"Leave it or take it, but get out of here." Sandy barked.

"Who died and left you boss. I don't need any more god damn orders." The pathfinder growled in frustration.

"Righto mate. Move out." Sandy countered as the Stafford boy led the way on Sandy's first command. The rest had stubbed out their cigarettes and followed. Sandy and the pathfinder were the last ones near the barn.

"Go."

"Yeah, ... in a minute." The pathfinder grumbled as Sandy crouched low and moved out.

No sooner had he caught up to the others when he heard the click. Immediately, he hit the ground. A round of machine gun clatter let loose, and a cry and explosion pierced the night. Sandy turned to see a burst of light and feathers flying in the air where the pathfinder had been. The machine gunner was still spinning shells from the nest directly in front of where the cows had been. A few were split wide open. The rest mooed frantically and ran in the opposite direction when the gunner opened up.

Over the heads of the cows, a glider silently swished across the pasture heading toward the pocket of fire behind the barn. Incapable of steering their motorless plane, they hit the barn and its flames which had spread from the hay on the barn's floor. Trapped inside when the door near the glider's nose crushed shut, they cried for help.

"They're done for," Sandy thought. "Another French barn – another death trap."

No one could get them out. The flames enveloped them quickly as their yells turned to agonizing screams. The men, even the big Yorkshire man, covered their ears to deafen the cries they could do nothing about. The barn where they had minutes before huddled in safety was now an inferno, raging on the bodies of the pathfinder and a dozen British airmen in the glider.

Sandy looked up and saw C-47's dropping their men into the drop zone. Before exploding, the pathfinder's "Becky' must have sent out enough signals to communicate to the planes above that their paratroopers could jump into a secured area.

Floating like moths to a flame, they had nowhere to land but into the burning barn. If the flames didn't reach up and lick them out of the sky, then the machine gunner, still hidden in his nest, shot them helplessly out of the sky. Lifelessly, they fell into the crematory below.

"Let's go," Sandy said. He motioned for them to follow him into the shadow of the trees bordering the pasture. The apple trees sent out a sweet scent – a promise of another time, hidden within their pink and white blossoms. One of the Liverpool lads found his voice and hummed the refrain, 'Don't sit under the apple tree with anyone else but me. Anyone else but me.'

"Stupidity, Fantasy, Reality,' Sandy thought as they passed by the trunks and branches of the apple trees to circle the machine gun nest. "What is real? The hell of this night or the apple trees of springtime in the French countryside." Sandy did not know anymore.

The seven men crept cautiously, clicking their clickers and waiting for an answer before moving ahead. They moved as fast as they could, and none glanced up at the sky to see the helpless stream of parachutes- floating white like ghosts – somewhere between heaven and hell.

Sandy's men tried to block out the paratroopers' cries as bullets rained into them or as flames consumed their flesh. Periodically, the thud of a man landing on the ground indicated contact – dead or alive. Those 'lucky' thuds had missed the inferno, but had they missed the aim of the German soldier firing relentlessly from his secure nest?

The staccato bursts were louder and more visible as they approached. Sandy made a circle motion above his head and the group divided into two parts. The three Liverpool lads took the right rear flank and the Welshman, the Stafford boy, the other engineer and Sandy the left rear flank. In front of them, fixed in the night was the lone helmet of a German soldier dug deep behind a machine gun camouflaged with apple blossom boughs. All had the helmet in their sights. Sandy had pulled one of his three grenades from his belt, ready to go if the gunfire couldn't take him out.

A crack of a branch cut through a moment of silence, followed by a click– then two clicks. The machine gunner whirled around. The Stafford farmer's British Enfield bolt action rifle found its mark first – directly through the machine gunner's forehead at the very moment the German soldier had pushed up his helmet to look through his night viewfinder. Was that the shot that killed him? Or was it the .38 caliber Smith and Wesson's bullets of the Liverpool boys that riddled his chest? Or was it the Welshman's Webley .455 caliber, nicknamed 'Big Ugly', which found its mark just below the gunner's throat?

He placed his grenade back into his bag as they walked over to the nest. Sandy pushed the helmet off the German gunner; a blond mass of curls and the smudged angelic face of a boy younger than any of them looked up at him. Blue eyes wide open. They all turned away from this face of an angel and up into the heavens. Paratroopers were now dropping safely into the night.

****

It was close to 5:00 a.m., and for four hours they had been moving through the dark and light. The crack, that the seven had heard in the moment before the machine gunner turned, had been made by a German sniper who had stepped on a branch as he clicked the safety off his K98 8mm bolt-action rifle with its sniper scope. The second two clicks was from an American Apache's clicker – after he had plunged his long thin hat pin like knife into the neck of the German sniper.

The Apache came to join their group from one of the plane loads of Apaches, Navahos, Blackfeet and Cherokees whose drop zone was just beyond Utah Beach. How he had gotten so far off his target, the bridge on the Douve River near Saint Sauveur, the Apache named Harry never questioned. Instead, he kept his eyes sharp and his ears fine-tuned.

On the way down he spotted a group of men circling around the gunner's nest and a sniper following them. Having avoided being blown into the burning barn, he played dead when he hit the ground. "A machine gunner won't waste bullets on a corpse," he thought.

He saw none of his fellow Indians. If they hit the ground alive, they'd be safe. He had no doubts. Survival skills were in their blood, and all had traded in their army issued thick service knives for more useful items to make their weapon of choice. Long thin like hatpins to puncture and slice were unrivaled for the practical purpose of hunting and killing men. Survive they would. The question was how many Germans would not?

Their number was again eight, as the American Apache became the new pathfinder. Although they no longer had the Eureka/Rebecca to send and receive messages, Sandy and the others felt lucky to have the Indian. He was a different kind of 'pathfinder' – one who felt at one with his surroundings and could find his way out no matter where he was placed. They still had their 'walkie-talkies', but were reluctant to use them. It was obvious the Germans could pick up and block out their transmissions.

Through the night they cut telephone and communication pole lines. The Apache would stop along the way to sever the nylon ropes from the gliders in order to silently and efficiently strangle any of the enemy. The others stood guard as the Stafford boy and the Apache took turns shinnying up the poles with wire clippers in their teeth. Even in the dark, half way up the pole, he would signal for the Stafford boy to stop or wait while he slid down and silently found a German soldier attempting to communicate. Encircling the white man from behind, he quickly and quietly strangled the German soldier with the nylon glider rope.

By morning's first light they lay exhausted near a flooded marshland. Sandy had used much of his 75 pounds of TNT to blow up two bridges and three sets of locks. When the last lock had blown, the waters rushed out in a torrent to empty the grasses which had grown high in these manmade wet lands. From Allied reconnaissance flight photos these areas appeared to be solid land – deemed safe for paratroopers to land in and soldiers to cross over from the beaches of Omaha and Utah.

Their last job before the men hit the beach was to eliminate one more of these cunning traps contrived in the recesses of the German military mind. When the explosion blew the locks, the waters which covered the bodies of the paratroopers already trapped and drown by their heavy equipment flooded out. They would stay long hidden in their watery graves.

Within the next hour the troops would hit the beaches at low tide and crawl their way inland. At that point they could lift up their helmeted heads, see the water not grass and choose another route. This particular false oasis would not lure and swallow them as it had their countrymen.

****

From sudden violence to total peacefulness was the nature of war, and such transitions could lure soldiers into reluctance – to act – to kill. However, Sidney's group of three, sharp as shards of glass, was unique. Billy, having survived the death of his best friend, came out of the reverie of his jump acutely aware that it was kill or be killed. Tony snapped out half way down. He acted from his gut. For Christian, the question never even existed. He had no nerves. Totally calm, floating as if in a sack of amniotic fluid, he knew nothing could harm him.

Sidney, as their leader, knew his mission was critical to the men who would land on Omaha and Utah within the next three hours. His second mission of getting the Russian and the Pole to Paris was critical for the rest of the world when the 'war' was won. He had to get Christian to Paris but had no idea if the Pole was dead or alive, nor could he find any of the rest of his stick. Commandeering men along the way was a decision he had already made, but securing the bridge near Chef-du-Pont over the Merderet River he must do now. Then and only then, could he proceed into Sainte-Mere-Eglise.

They stopped along a dirt road etched in the moonlight by a continuous stone wall and low hedgerows. Crouched with their backs against the hedges, Sidney indicated to Christian to look over the hedgerow. In the pale light of the moon, Sidney took out his map as Christian peered around the hedgerow. He came face to face with a shy grinning boy in a tattered faded uniform. At that brief moonlit moment, the smell of urine filled his nostrils, and Christian could hear the steady stream of water. With his hand on the drawn thin razor sharp knife, he thought, "I could end this boy's life with one quick slice to the neck," yet Christian caught himself smiling back. Something registered –

something familiar about the wide innocent face. "An act of normalcy – pissing in a bush," Christian thought. "I have to sit down. The déjà vu. The sudden sweat. It's coming. "

"This young soldier's face – the same as the prisoner's face that day in the Katyn - the face with the one eye – the tortured angelic face of the one nearest me who the older Polish soldier had tried to help. It was the one who called for his mama right before they crushed his skull." All this he thought as he looked down at the young soldier's feet. He wore no shoes, and in the moonlight Christian could see the blood-red scars of old wounds.

"Hey Sid, I think our friend is sick." Tony said in a hushed voice to Sidney who had just spread out the map in front of him.

Sidney glanced to his left. "Christian what's the matter?" He looked over the hedge to see what had so changed Christian, this young Russian seemingly made of steel. As the clouds covered the moon, Sidney saw a man half way down the dirt road who stopped and looked back.

"Was it a soldier or a shadow of a ghost? What uniform was he wearing?" The shadow soldier turned away. "Was it real or a fantasy, this shadowy ghost-like figure walking freely down the country road as he might have done in a previous life – but not in these times of 1944?" Sidney thought.

A tall dark man with long black braids was kneeling next to Christian – massaging with firm strong hands the young Russian's back in circular motions as Christian vomited in the hedges. Sidney jumped back. His nerves were raw. "Where had this man come from?" Silence filled the moment.

"Boy you look like you've seen ghost," Billy whistled through his teeth.

"I have," Christian whispered.
****

Sidney had shown Billy, Tony, Christian, and the newcomer, the Cherokee the map. All, but the Cherokee, had come from the east where Saint-Marie-du-Mont was situated. To the west was the Merderet River. By 0200 they were half a kilometer south of Chef-du-Pont. They had walked the distance in silence. Each for whatever reason felt that they had passed out of harm's way. Christian felt drained, but an even more profound aura of utter calm, and purpose cradled him. Sidney periodically glanced over at him and noticed that some of the coldness had disappeared from his blue eyes.

But Christian was immersed in his own thoughts. "The boy from the Katyn is watching over me and the ghosts of the slaughtered are still waiting to be avenged."

The Merderet River glistened ahead like pearls in the moonlight, and the five men continued on the road leading into Chef-du Pont. In the distance they could see the bridge as moon light reflected off its metal encasements. Sidney did not know how they were going to blow the bridge since their sapper with the TNT never rolled up into the stick. He had seen no other men from the 82nd or 101st except the lone Cherokee, but his mission still stood – to seal off the Cotentin from the south by destroying 'his' bridge on the Merderet. Other units needed to take care of the bridges over the Douve River, yet outside of pockets of explosions and machine gun fire, no overt activity existed.

"Get down,' the Cherokee whispered.

They immediately fell flat on the ground. The Indian nodded his head forward, and each man saw the shadow of a bicycle and its rider. They could not discern if it was a small adult or an adolescent child, but when it came within a few yards of them, Tony shoved a branch into the road.

"Merde," a woman's voice exclaimed as she swerved into the ditch on the side of the road. Jumping off the bike, she bent down to check the tires. Picking up a rock, she said in a calm voice, "Qui est ici? Qu'est-ce que vous faites ici a cette heure?"

"Vous etes francaise?" Christian asked as he stood up in front of her. The Cherokee slid silently behind her and stretched a cord between his hands.

"Naturellement, idiote. Je suis francaise. Et vous aussi, non?"

"Non," he answered. He saw the rock in her hand. He needed to know if she would use it. "Je suis anglais," he continued.

She loosened her grip on the rock, but she did not drop it. "Mais vous ne parlez pas francais avec un accent anglais."

"Parce que en realite j'etais russe." He answered.

It did not help her to know that he was Russian not English. There were too many Russians who had allied themselves with the Germans in order to fight against Stalin. She tightened her grip around the rock, and the Cherokee tightened his cord.

"Did you see the flashes in the sky?" she asked in English.

"What did you say?" he answered in perfect English.

"Flash," she retorted.

"Thunder," he said the code word.

"Good," she dropped the rock.

"Better for you," he indicated the Indian behind her who still held the cord taunt. The others slowly stood up in a circle around her.

"Get off the road," she said turning her back not only to the Indian, but to the rest of them as she pushed her bike between Tony and Sidney. She held her head high and directly looked them in the eye as though to memorize their faces for another day.

Totally fearless, she led them to an opening in the woods. They followed with the Cherokee choosing the last man position. He knew a brave warrior when he saw one – her face expressionless, her stance unmovable, her spirit courageous – and her name, Juliette.

****

Juliette and John, the American Cherokee Indian, sat cross-legged in a small clearing near the woods. She looked intently at his face with its strong sharp features and his coarse black braids hanging out from his helmet that he had tilted back on his forehead. His walkie-talkie was first on his ear and then on his mouth. Back and forth he listened and talked, but she could not understand a word of it.

The others were planting trip wires in a large circle around them. They needed to rest and eat some of their K rations. Juliette always traveled with her own rations: wine, cheese, and bread, the French staples to entice the enemy or feed her own countrymen and their allies. For these hungry exhausted men, she placed two bottles of burgundy, two loaves of crusty bread and a circle of camembert cheese in the middle. She did not seem surprised to meet them at this hour of a too cold and windy June night.

She would wait to tell them of the other one who also had been ready to kill her - the one who was waiting at this very moment at the lock house of the bridge of Chef-du-Pont. She had also convinced him not to kill her. Instead, he had told her part of his story, and she set out to look for his stick – the rest of his fighting unit whom he had described. From the accent of the Russian, she felt she had found his team, yet this tall dark Indian, unlike any man she had ever seen, he had said nothing about.

From another country, another culture, and of a strange language, this Indian from America made her feel safe. His presence and his eyes held her in a protected view. She had not felt safe since Luc had left the Dubois farmhouse. She no longer felt secure with just her father and mother. They could do nothing except get themselves killed if they tried to protect her against the Colonel, and Denis would put her life ahead of his.

For the last two nights she had been traveling from her home near Saint Honorine to Sainte-Mere-Eglise. After what Claude had told her about Renard's death, she knew she had to be with her own brother. All along the way she had used the name 'couturier', for anyone that she held suspect. The others she knew already – most of the cautious ones were still alive.

Sid, Tony, Billy, and Christian had secured the perimeter and sat down in the circle. Juliette had uncorked the wine and the bread and cheese lay on top of a dark blue cloth.

"It looks like you came prepared for us," Sidney said looking directly into her eyes, not yet certain if she was anything more than just a clever spy.

Tony too thought this was too convenient. He knew life wasn't that easy. He waited for her to taste the wine first. Knowing this, she placed the bottle to her mouth and let the deep red wine quench her nerves. She took another long swallow, this time letting the wine stay in her mouth before she let it flow in gentle gulps down her throat. She passed the bottle to the Cherokee and tore off a chunk of bread. From her sleeve, she took out a knife and dug deep into the camembert. Spreading the cheese on her bread, she noticed the Cherokee did not drink but passed the bottle to Billy.

"Thanks, I'm thirstier than a coon dog," he smiled his open grin.

"Hey Indian, who were you talking to in that lingo." Tony chided.

"No Indian. Cherokee. And John's my name."

"You can call me wop or Tony. No skin off my nose," Tony passed the loaf of bread over to him.

"There are two others from my stick. One's at the bridge, the other in the woods. We talk in Apache and Cherokee," he laughed. "No Kraut know our 'lingo'.

"Ask him if he has TNT." Sidney directed.

The others looked at the Cherokee as he spoke and nodded into his walkie-talkie.

"Not only does he have a 75 pound satchel that he took off one of ours, but he's found a guy who knows how to use it."

"Who might that be?" Christian spoke softly.

"No Indian. No ally. A Polish boy. He is inside the lock house with him and the dead German lock keeper." The Cherokee turned to listen to his walkie-talkie and answered in his tongue. "My friend says he killed the German with the same knife our stick has – a knife like this." The Cherokee took out his long thin hat pin of a knife that he had filed down.

Christian took out his knife and sliced through the cheese in one sudden movement of his wrist. He picked the cheese up with its thin pin like point and placed it on his chunk of bread. "Ask your friend for the man's name."

With eyes fixed on the same hat pin like sharp knife, John, the Cherokee, put the walkie-talkie to his mouth and spoke. He waited for the answer, "My friend says his name is..."

"Janusz," the girl filled in the answer.

"Yes, Janusz, he says," John the Cherokee clicked off his walkie-talkie and sliced himself some cheese in the same manner as Christian had.

Their eyes met one another without suspicion and the wine and bread passed from one to another. They were in business.

****

"So, this is the same guy from our stick," Billy asked.

"Yeah, number 20, the last one out. How many Polish kids can there be?" Tony answered as they crept into the gate keeper's house.

Christian entered first and hugged Janusz. It was good to see him alive and know that the boots sticking out from under the table were those of a dead German. Neither said anything; they had seen such things before. The room was dark, sparse, and dirty. A small bed where the German used to sleep sat in the corner and next to it, a chair and the small wooden square table under which the German slept permanently.

Sidney grimly looked at the body and then around the small room. "How bizarre war is," he thought, "To leave your friends, family, and country – not once, but twice."

He had formed another family in England, and now he had been plucked from it and dropped into chaos with no safety net. He had been in France for two hours, but it felt like two years. Around him – pushed into this tiny room was his new family. He nodded at the new man – shorter but muscular, and so dark he didn't even need grease paint. John the Cherokee stood next to him - two of a kind in spirit but from different tribes. Likewise, Janusz and Christian were a pair but from different countries. Billy, Tony, and he – a trio of Americans, from three different states and three different backgrounds, stood together with the same purpose. This was his unit now – his family- and Juliette was the last to enter.

"The bridge is unguarded. They must have pulled out to Sainte-Mere-Eglise."

As Juliette spoke, the nearby explosions and a night sky that turned to day made four in the group wonder about the two they need to meet at the church in Saint-Mere-Eglise. Juliette prayed that her brother and Zosia were still alive.

As though reading her mind, Sidney said, "You go into the town and take John the Cherokee with you."

"I know the way. Perhaps, I am less noticeable on my own."

"As we say in the US of A, he'll cover your back. And besides, I need him to use his walkie-talkie and scout again." Sidney told Juliette as he turned to John. "Your friend is..?"

"Thomas, an Apache." John answered.

"He'll help detonate the bridge with Tony and Janusz." Sidney finished the order.

"Janusz spoke. "I have much experience with explosives. My father and I mined every bridge on the Northwest sector of Warsaw when we fled."

Christian looked as his blood brother and smiled. Janusz smiled back. He was back in his element – fighting for the mother and country he lost.

****

By the time Juliette and John had reached the edge of Sainte-Mere-Eglise, they heard the ricochet of explosions behind them. They had braced themselves for that sound, yet what they saw in front of them was unimaginable. In the middle of the town square a huge fire, burning fiercely lit up the sky heating up the cold night. When a flame lost its lick and slid down from the sky, a steeple shot out from the flames. Juliette gasped. The church, with its cellar sanctuary meeting place for Luc and Zosia, was at the base of this inferno.

Chapter 13 - June 6, 1944 - From Dawn to Dusk

At first light they came. Sandy could hear them drop their loads. The heavier engines and loudest bombs came from the American B-17s. The Yanks called them the Flying Fortresses and Sandy now realized why. Although Caen had to be twenty-five kilometers to the East, the ground still shook from the merciless bombs that overshot the beaches and pounded the city at first daylight. The U.S. Eighth Army had taken over from the RAF Bomber Command that had started its run at midnight. Sandy and his men were barely on the ground when the RAF began clearing out Coastal Batteries and German enforcements near Caen. Now Sandy and other units that survived the night would soon be on the move again, taking out any predawn targets they could.

The lighter bombs he could hear echoing to his north, ten kilometers in that direction lay the Calvados Coast. American B-24s, the Liberators, were dropping their bombs on whatever German defenses lined France's Norman Coast. As Sandy and his men rested for the first time since they were parachuted in, he wondered what the bombs were hitting. They seemed too close.

****

Sidney, 15 kilometers to the northwest, wondered the same thing. Crouching near the square of Sainte-Mere-Eglise, he murmured, "How could anyone - anything still be left standing after those tons and tons of bombs have exploded?" The Marauders, America's B-26s, were saturating Utah Beach. "If the Ninth Air Force is doing its job right," he thought "all the anti-aircraft guns and artillery emplacements will be pounded to dust." Sidney hoped that through the heavy overcast skies the Marauder pilots could see their targets. Although daylight had broken, the visibility didn't seem a whole lot better to him than what he had come through just before midnight. "Sweet Jesus, when the troops hit Utah and Omaha, let it be a clean run - at least, have those ready-made foxholes waiting for them. That's the plan, God."

****

Sandy from the British 6th Airborne and Sidney from America's 82nd Airborne felt their job was far from over. Although they had survived the night and had linked up with Allied soldiers they were not with their original units. Cut off and surrounded, they could not sit back and wait for reinforcements. For Sandy, this was not like his other two missions. No one was coming to rescue him at a designated point - to pluck him up and into the air like some 'deus-ex-machina' machine in a Greek Tragedy.

Survival was not a guarantee. Hundreds of units like theirs were safe on their own little islands of Norman soil, but at any moment that very soil could become their graves. Most were without radios and had no idea where their fellow Englishmen or Americans were. They could not merely dig in and fight defensively. Each unit, by itself and in spite of itself, had to take the offense and attack. Their lives and the lives of the men, who were to hit the beach, depended on it. Soon the Germans would realize this was the designated day - this was D-Day, the day they had expected, prepared for, and would fight for. They would counterattack - and the fate of the world would hang in the

balance. Sandy, Sidney, and all the others knew that their individual actions would decide the outcome of the war.
****

Captain Paul 'Hank' Hudson and the men of Company C of the 2nd Ranger Battalion were to hit Utah Beach within the hour. The tide was low and would let them see the mines normally hidden during high tide. Hudson had been through this before. It would still be French soil though not that of North Africa. It was not warm like that day nor like the days of Texas he yearned for. He touched his helmet and made a mental note not to take it off. This time there would be no need to vomit. The enemy had to have been eliminated by the Flying Fortresses above and the Marauders flying low across the Channel.

"No one could survive that constant bombing." He tightened his helmet. He didn't want to lose the silk map won from an Englishman in a poker game a few nights before. Now taped inside his helmet it was his ticket to Paris. He thought about Betty-Jo. "I wrote her I'd get that Channel No 5. By the time she gets that letter, I'll be in Paris."

Captain Paul Hudson knew she would not get his letter for a long time. He hoped he would still be alive when she did. The Channel Crossing had been rough but all of Hank Hudson's men were confident that Company A had landed successfully on the right flank of Omaha Beach. They had left the transport ship Prince Charles ahead of them at a little after 0600. At 0630 they would be landing on Omaha and go up the Vierville draw to the village and clear out the area to the coastal road. Two ranger battalions would climb the cliffs of Pointe du Hoc straight up from the beach and eliminate the six 155-mm German howitzers. His men would make the same run up the cliffs of Pointe de la Percee.

Hank tried to see the beach, hidden by the morning mist and the smoke from the barrage of Navy firepower. One thing he knew from experience - the beach would not be calm. Even if there were no Germans in sight, he knew from North Africa that one burst of a machine gun could cut the crap out of any serenity. This time they would not be caught nonchalantly laughing and smoking after their easy run near the sector of the beach called 'Easy Red'. The name did not reassure him. Hank knew nothing was easy in war.

"O.K. men get ready to climb into 'Betty'." Hank yelled with as much bravado as he could muster.

Sal Marchese and Jimmy were the first ones over the netting and into the rocking metal canister of a landing boat. Sal draped his demolition charges over one shoulder and his M-1 over the other. He handed his mine detector suitcase over to Jimmy.

"Grab this Jimmy. James Earl is passing down his bazooka."

"Holy mother of God. My mama didn't birth her boy to have him die in this washtub. Sweet Jesus, let's get this show on the road or at least to the beach. I need land under my feet." James Earl bellowed as he lowered his huge frame into the landing assault vehicle.

One by one all of Hudson's men came on board. Aaron Axelrod was one of the last ones. He shored up the end of the line.

"All aboard. Let's follow the script men. Someday they'll make a movie of this to show our grandchildren." Aaron announced.

"That's right, and I say we're all going to be there to watch it."

"Amen to that brother." James Earl added

"Hell, let's just get those bastards!" a man yelled echoing the thoughts of most.

Hank kept his words to himself and stared out at the beach, lying there somewhere between hell and eternity. It seemed like hours of rocking and holding on to the sides. Many men were vomiting already.

Most of the men were low in the boat with hands over their helmets or in front of their mouths. With some waves as high as six feet, the boat rocked like a cork in the open Channel. Over the gunwales, the rough sea poured. The wind blew and the mortars exploded and artillery riddled the bows of the LCV's. The German infantry dug deeper into their trenches, the gunners inside their pillboxes steadied their sights, and the Panzer Division shut tight the lids of their tanks. The firepower continued relentlessly, stretching behind the beaches and up the cliffs, blocking all exits.

Miserable in their cramped water logged boat, they scooped out the water at their feet and tossed the contents of their vomit filled helmets into the sea - bailing out and cleaning their helmets at the same time.

"Nothing could be worse than this," Aaron Axelrod thought. He, like the other men, did not know what to concentrate on: control their seasickness, bail out the cold waters sloshing over their boots, or take comfort in the Navy's shells cutting over their heads. "At least the craters are going to be there. They'll protect us on the beach."

Aaron knew he'd remember this day for the rest of his life. "The mundane fingers of death wrapping around each of us - so effortlessly. Those who survive and see my film will recall this scene fifty years from now as though it were but yesterday." He looked over to Hank and saw Sal, slightly to his right, studying Hank.

Hank Hudson and the coxswain were the only ones looking over the LCA's gunwales and directly at Omaha Beach. Hank could feel his throat tighten up and the sweat, beginning to roll down the back of his neck despite the cold morning mist and drizzle which blanketed this 6th day of June. It was 6:45. The Navy guns had finally stopped twenty minutes ago at five minutes to H-Hour.

"Omaha is set for 0630, Utah for 0645, and then me," Hank thought. "Company A hit the beach fifteen minutes ago, but none of them is on the beach. No one's standing up joking with a butt in his mouth like in the North African assault. Maybe that's a good sign. Maybe, they're already off the beach and up the Iberville draw. Yeah, they're clearing out the pillboxes and trenches. Company C is going to have an easy go up and over our thirty meters at Pointe de la Percee.

"Jesus, are we hit?" Jimmy yelled.

"No Yanks, this is as far as we go. We've hit a sandbar" the coxswain at the rear of the LCV called out.

Then Hank did not know which came first - the German machine gun fire that ripped across the boat or the grenade that flew past him and took the head of the coxswain man in the rear.

As though in a dream, he saw his arm go up again - waving the men onward. He had done the same motion that day, but today was different. Hank Hudson was conscious of what he was doing.

"I didn't die then, and I won't die now." He thought. The fate of another group of men - this time 62 - lay in his hands. "We might die on the beach, but it's better than being a sitting duck." The LCV's front ramp splat down when the rocky boat felt the sandbar.

"Hit the beach", Hank heard himself yell as he turned to see his men vaulting over the sides and pushing past him. He felt for the heavy loop of rope slung over his left shoulder and swerved onto the slippery ramp and the freezing water of the Atlantic.

The mist smelled of salt, smoke, and blood. His ears ached from the stat-a-stat-a-ta... sound of artillery and the heavy mortar of the 8 millimeter guns and mammoth shells of the pillboxes which pounded the beach without mercy.One hundred yards to the base of the cliff. Each one of the 63 men knew how far he had to run. In slow motion, they fell.

Into the water

Into the sand

Dead,

Dying,

Living,

They fell.

Those who climbed over the sides of the L.C.V were now floating face down in the water, and those, who had pushed by Hank Hudson, had been riddled by the first spray of artillery fire. Bloodless or bloody, they bobbed like jellyfish towards the beach.

Others were fighting to keep their mouths above water. The LCV.'s ramp had swung open prematurely. Those who were not gasping for breath in the open water were trapped in the water filled coffin. Whether they swung over, stepped out or stayed in, the water was too deep. The men were drowning. Unable to stand, they tried to throw off their packs and equipment which were pulling them down like anchors.

Grabbing a body that floated in front of him, Hank used it as a shield and raft to kick himself toward the shore and the 100-yard run. He was one of the few whose feet could touch the bottom, but he had seen the waves splash into the open mouths of the men of Company C 2nd Ranger Battalion as they gasped for air in their fight forward through the foaming icy water.

Using his dead comrade, he pushed off the pebbly bottom and angled himself forward three feet with every push and bob. He kept his helmet-covered head beneath the surface as much as possible. The already dead Ranger undulated with direct hits from the crossfire on his left. The artillery sprayed the expanse of 'Easy Red', and then swung left to pick off its last corner near the base of Pointe de la Percee. The beach and water bled red.

Only the very quick and ungodly lucky were making it across those 100 yard to brush or barbwire. Those, whose luck ran out, littered the 1,000 yard stretch of beach. Those who still held a pair of aces were huddled in clusters in whatever space of security each could find at the end of their dash for survival.

The tide was low and the teller mines were visible and ominous. Their large ugly X's crisscrossed the low waters in front of the beaches. In the midst of this insanity those who succeeded in getting out of the landing boats clung to these false islands of hope. A seed of reason told them these wooden pylons in the form of X's were mined. However, too shell shocked to move, one by one they were picked off as they fought to keep themselves above the water. At other times the sharp shooters on the cliffs hit the detonating device and man and timber shot through the air. Some infantrymen self-exploded as another allied soldier - dead or alive - swept onto their no man's island.

How many of his men were still alive he couldn't tell. There was no time to count. There was no time to think. Only action gave him the license to live. This much Hank Hudson had learned from North Africa. He was not freezing into inaction-sunken in a hole, covering his head, curled up into a wartime womb, and ignoring his men and the combat they had to do. Granted, no holes existed in the water, but he wasn't hugging a teller mine in a blind panic. The deadly chaos around him appeared as flashes of kaleidoscopic color and shadows. Able to detach himself from what was happening all around him, he found himself in waist deep then knee deep water. Still, he pushed the "body' raft in front of him and made the decision when the time was right- to lift off and run those 100 yards to the base of the cliff that loom 90 feet straight up in front of his eyes.

He did not have to wait. The guns from the cliffs of Pointe de la Percee lobbed a mortar on the beach footage directly in front of him. The body absorbed the shock waves and shrapnel. As Hank's head ducked beneath the surface one more time, he felt the body rip apart. Blood, like dark oil spilled out and clouded the water like octopus ink. Surfacing and lifting out his large water soaked frame, he came up as though coming out of a Texas huddle on the end zone in the game of his life.

In that moment he glanced down at the remains of the decimated body that had sheltered him from harm. He wanted to know which of his men had given him life. The body had flipped over. Jimmy's face, eyes wide open in innocence, looked up -from the lifeless torso. A wave of nausea began and his leaden legs, like metal chains anchored into the sand, would not move.

"Never again!" he heard himself scream as he literally commanded his paralyzed frame to move. He saw himself running in slow motion as fast as he could to the base of Pointe de la Percee.

"Captain" a shout reached him like a shock wave over the deafening noise which surrounded him. "Hey Tex ... Captain, old man. You there?" Sal called out again.

"Bronx boy - that you?" a voice on the other side of Hank Hudson shouted out.

"Yeah, James Earl it's me." Sal answered. "What do you see?"

"Hollywood Aaron is to my left and that's it."

Their voices floated above his head as they had before - in another place, in another time, but in the same war. Hank Hudson forced himself to pull out of the dream. Like a man drowning, he pushed off the bottom of the ocean floor and forced the waters to separate. Fighting to the surface and to the light, his lungs were bursting, his head pounding with pressure. He surfaced out of his dream - gasping for air. Cold but alive he clung to the wet cliffs as he hyperventilated and slowly returned to the present. These were the voices of his men - now - not then.

"Jimmy's dead. Aaron, Sal and James Earl are alive. We've survived. Where are the rest of my 62 men - four out of 62 - the rest dead or dying?" he breathed through his thoughts.

He no longer hugged the cliff, but turned to sit cross-legged, back stiff, head now against the cliff, facing the sea from which he had come. Breathing deeply, he calmly surveyed the carnage in front.

"How ... why are we the only ones left? No.. push the questions away. To climb the cliff or not is the question. To become part of the dead and the dying ... or not, that is the question." Hank Hudson knew that this time.

The tide was coming in, and the only way out was up.

****

Second Lieutenant Baron and his commander, Lieutenant Wilson, were privy to rumors that the fortifications and trenches which guarded the North Atlantic wall were manned by second string soldiers - captured Russians and Poles. Only one battalion of about 800 troops would be on the defensive lines. Baron, Wilson, and so many others knew that the Allies were landing more than 400,000 men this day, yet five minutes before H-hour they each looked into binoculars at the land beyond the beach. Through the mist they could see green hills and colorful rooftops perched on the cliffs and ridges beyond the beach. An occasional church steeple pointed through the morning mist. It looked as through everything was intact. Nothing appeared leveled and blown away.

"Holy mother of God", Wilson whispered. "What has the Air Force and Navy been doing all night."

Second Lieutenant Melvin Baron lowered the binoculars and said nothing. He just turned and looked at the 30-man assault team in front of him. The lieutenant moved up front and urged the two medics to get to the rear of the LCVP. Each

commander and each infantryman was going over his briefings
or saying his prayers. They were as finely tuned as any one of the
other assault teams that would hit the beachheads. The Navy
guns had stopped and whatever allied planes were in the skies
had turned back long ago.

"Why is it so silent?" Russo said more to himself than to
O'Brien or Stone who were directly in front and behind him.
"At least we don't have to navigate no more by starlight. We can
see what's facing us." O'Brien had not lost any of his straight-
forward banter in the crossing of the Channel.

Each LCVP was bobbing more or less in a jagged line -
in unison but separate in their boats as well as their thoughts.
They knew theirs might be the toughest beach - even those
higher ups who had named it Easy Red - could not possibly
think infantrymen were all guts and no brains. Of all the invasion
beachheads, Omaha was the most naturally fortified. Cliffs at
both ends shot up perpendicularly from the golden sand, and in
front of them a 100 to 125 yard footage of firm sand at low tide
and only a few yards at high welcomed them.

"The first wave has to have already landed. Why no
firepower. Have the Krauts fallen back to sleep?" Stone
countered.

"Hey, maybe those Nazi lovers have turned tail and run -
All the way back to Berlin." O'Brien quipped.

Just then it began. More artillery, mortars, and cannon-
like booms than any of them could imagine. Over it all, the loud
constant 75 mm cannon which was firing directly down in front
of them - center stage on Easy Red.

"There's your answer," the Lieutenant shouted back.

Baron gritted his teeth at the sound and thought, "Dear
God, the first wave of Companies A through E must've got the
B-gees shot out of them. Whoever's on those cliffs and in those
trenches are killing us. That's the U.S. of A's 7,000 yard stretch
of beach - a regular wide-open killing field. Welcome to France!"

Out loud he shouted, "Hang on to that bazooka Stone.
We're going to need it"

"Shirley's all set sir, and Anderson's right next to me.
Gonna follow me right into no-man's land with the extra rockets
and carbine power?"

Anderson just nodded and slapped his heavy necklace of shells and hitched up the light rifle hung over his neck and right shoulder.

"Hey Kraut," O'Brien called Baron as he threw the slur over his shoulder. "Between Stone's big lady bazooka and my wire cutters, we'll be walking down the 'Champs a lee Zay' before you can report me"

"Yeah, the French Dames will be waiting for a Mick like ya," one of the two men on a BAR teams said as he forced his eyes away from the beach which was coming up fast.

"The Kraut and me are on the same side - right Lieutenant Baron?"

"That's right Mick. We're going to hit that beach and up to our draw. Next stop Paris." Melvin Baron retorted as he strapped his helmet strap beneath his chin. He had moved forward between his four-man mortar team, Harold, Jimmy, and the two green flame-throwers. Those six would be the last men out - not counting the two medics.

"One more thing, Second Lieutenant, Sir. You speak German?" O'Brien asked with a half grin.

"Like any good Kraut," Baron answered back. "You bet."

"If the first wave has done their job," he thought, "they'll be off the beach and in one of the five small draws - leading off the beach. If they're DOA, we're in for a bottleneck." He steadied himself against the onslaught of waves. He was amazed that most of his men took this in stride. The bouncing around like corks in a bottle didn't seem to bother them. "With luck, all the practice paid off," he thought as he put the binoculars to his eyes.

No longer could he see the rooftops, steeples, and green hills. Everything was clouded in dense smoke. He thought there had been no craters on the beach when he had looked in that five-minute window of silence while the world waited. The Allies had stopped their bombardments; the Germans had waited to return their deadly fire. Their answer had come shortly after the first waves hit the beach. When the Americans, English, and Canadians crossed into the tide mark, all hell broke loose.

Melvin Baron could see nothing - no beachhead, no flags flying, and no men - just billows of smoke blocking everything from view. Would they have a clear run for one of the five roads off the beach? If they were on course, which was highly unlikely considering their numbers and the roughness of the Channel, the Vierville Draw was their way out.

They had been told all these exits sloped gently up to small dirt or paved roads - leading off the beach. Each Company - sometimes two companies had a mission to break free of the beach and move inland through one of these five exits.

"See anything Second Lieutenant." Lieutenant Wilson demanded. "Has the first wave moved inland?"

"Can't see a damn thing." Baron answered in exasperation.

"Doesn't matter we're next. Ready or not!" Wilson stood up and shouted.

Each man in the LCVP saw a view of the front lines. Having passed through the corridor of gun smoke clouds, the inferno of hell lay before them.

"Jesus!" O'Brien murmured as he saw the bloody carnage that lay in twisted agony on the once white sand. Red was the color of the hour - H-hour. And the landing had been in process for no more than 30 minutes. Blood red the sand had become.

"Our Father who art in heaven, hallowed be thy name..." Harold had begun his prayer as soon as he had seen the men of the first wave. Dozens and dozens of men, like piles of old seaweed lay in clumps as far as the eye could see. Anderson turned to look at the men behind him and realized they no longer existed for him. Detaching himself from the horror, he began counting the ammunition clips he kept strapped across his chest.

"Anderson, I need you baby. Don't quit on me now. Bazooka Shirley is going nowhere without your extra ammo." Stone reached back and shook him.

That was the last person Baron really remembered looking at. All he could see were Anderson's glassy eyes, rounded into oval oblivion. He looked past them and beyond. Beyond Harold, Stone, Wilson, and all the others between the stern and the bow of the L.C.V.P. and into the vast wasteland in front of his face. Then he heard the scrape. The scrape sounded first, like a scratch when the metal of a heavy Buick brushes the drive-in movie post. That's what Baron thought before the explosion, white with sound, hit.

In that moment some were chosen to live by the luck of their seat placement in the L.C.V.P. All those in the middle were split open like the L.C.V.P. Body parts flew in the air like flying fish - red and luminous against the white fire of the mine they had hit. Flung onto the beach on the water line, the live fish flopped - slapped hard against the sand and into life.

Melvin Baron's chest hit flat against the pebbled beach. His face felt numb, and his vision blurred. Instinctively, a hand went to his eyes to rub out the blur. When it came back, it was red and flecked with pieces of stone and sand. Embedded in his hands, face and eyes was the beach. His vision cleared enough to see an alleyway of escape. Between two craters ran a thin alley of sand, flesh, and blood. It led 100 yards to the shrub-lined hills. Over the pieces of bodies, set like linebackers, was his run to the goal line.

His breath was short. His legs - like some erector set mechanicals, lifted him off the sand as his heart pounded, as a separate entity, fighting to escape from this Dante inferno with or without him. The pounding reverberated in his ears - beating so fast and so hard that his heart sent out needlelike pain darting in straight lines throughout his chest.

The mine that blew split his LCVP in two, destroyed not only his boat, but his carefully well-oiled team of men. He had not even heard their last screams. No sounds were registering. To Baron everything seemed underwater and shrouded in a sound proof coffin. He thought of his father - frail and bent over his sewing machine. Then he thought of Manny, coming into his father's tailoring store, from his deli next door - bringing pickle and pastrami smells with him. He saw Manny trying to comfort his father when he received the telegram of his death. With that image to defy, Baron shook his head at death and kicked off the sand. To his right his blurred vision saw the red letters, "Shirley". At the edge of the crater to his left, he grabbed the bazooka and the ammo clip that had been Anderson's - left in the middle of entrails.

With one in each hand he ran head down stumbling over life jackets - some on whole bodies, some only on torsos. His feet lifted and the bulk of his body swerved right and then left as it dodged the human debris - strewn like tires that football players had to jump through.

"My arm"

"I can't see."

"Legs - where are my legs?"

"Move - damn it. Don't die on me."

The cries, screams, and moans floated like specters closer to hell than heaven. He now could hear them all. Melvin Baron blocked out those images. He tore his way through the ghosts into the realm of the living. Not until he reached the barbed wire barrier at the back of the beach did he stop. Crouched near the hilly terrain of the back of Omaha, he looked back toward the water. As far as the eye could see, ships, boats, and men were still coming through a literal 'red' sea. They kept on coming. Every square foot of sand or sea harbored a body - dead or alive.

Too heavy and thick to move, Melvin Baron was barely aware of his arms. He looked down at each hand as though they belonged to someone else. Anderson's ammo chest band occupied his left arm and in his right was Stone's bazooka. Covering the "S" on "Shirley" was another hand stuck like a sea urchin. Stone's right hand with its index finger bearing his proud 1942 high school sapphire gold ring held tightly on to his "Shirley" his weapon of choice.

Baron gazed in horror at the sight and dropped the bazooka in the sand as though it were a burning ember. Shuffling as far back as he could go, he felt the barb wire pushing into his khaki wool jacket. He pushed his helmet off the front of his head and wiped the sweat off his face with his bloodied hand. Fixated on the hand that seemed to beckon him back to the beach - back to his dead comrades, he willed himself not to follow the call. The gold and blue of the ring, like the Holy Grail, gleamed in a ghostly hue out of the mist and smoke of this early morning of the 6th of June. He knew that no other morning would ever be the same - again.

"Hey, Kraut. Kraut, you hear me. Snap out of it, you son of a bitch." O'Brien, twenty yards to his right, shouted. "Lieutenant! Lieutenant"

Baron spun out of his haze and looked for the Lieutenant. Lieutenant Wilson would give the orders. He'd be all right if someone told him what to do.

"Yo Baron, you're the Lieutenant. Wilson's dead like all the others. It's just you and the Mick. Right. Right! God damn it answer me." O'Brien was beginning to realize he could do nothing without Baron. The tide was coming in and the Germans would come down from the trenches and push them back into the sea.

O'Brien held up his wire clippers and two mortars. "I still have these and the mortars I picked up near Harold and Jimmy on the way up. You cover my backside and I'll crawl up beneath the nose of that big 75 millimeter and clip a hole in the wire big enough for us to weasel through." He steadied his look. "Lieutenant, do you read me."

Lieutenant Baron's eyes moved to his right like sonar trying to find the warm heat of living flesh. Knowing someone depended on him, gave him a purpose. He began to think once again - analytically, cool, and with calculation. He wasn't going to be looking down on Manny reading the War Department's telegram that had dropped from his father's limp fingers.

"I read you. Loud and clear-O'Brien." Baron fingered Anderson's ammo strip and flung it over his shoulder. He slid back for Stone's bazooka. Once with his back to wire, he pulled the hand off and pocketed the ring. If he made it, he'd give it to Stone's mom.

O'Brien smiled his wide grin and his blue eyes flashed against the dark grease coving his face. "That's my Kraut. We're back in business."

Flat on his belly, he eased his compact fighter's frame across the sand parallel to the barb wire fence. He had spotted the spot where there was no fire. The waves of bullets did not seem to extend to that dip in the sand made by an eddy during high tide. The undulation of the mounds of sand provided some coverage and the sunken indentation created by the sea's eddies was just the space O'Brien needed to cut through the fence and make a fighting stance. Lifting the cutters over his head, he began to cautiously snip one wire at a time. His sense of bravado was stripped clear, and he was left with the persona of a craftsman, painstakingly creating his work of art. His finished piece had to be a hole, two feet by two feet - large enough for a man to slip through cleanly without getting caught on any sharp shards of metal or in the crossfire of German infantrymen.

"Boom". The blast was so close Melvin Baron didn't know if his last soldier made it.

"What the fuck," O'Brien shouted. He lifted his head. Ten feet in front of his face was a hole large enough for a tank to go through. "You're telling me I'm too slow!"

"No. They were telling me you were too slow." Baron pointed with Stone's bazooka at the three dead Germans waiting on the other side of the fence.

"Stone would've been proud of you Lieutenant, Sir!"

"Cut the bull, Mick. Let's get off of this beach and find some unit to join up with. I can't take just you and me." Melvin knew nothing could touch him. All his comrades in arms were gone, but he had O'Brien.

****

Chapter 14 - The Road Out

Sidney had stayed in the safety circle they had created behind the hedges near the road. Christian, Billy, and he waited as the others, Tom, the Apache, Tony, and Janusz made their way to the bridge over the Merderet River south of Saint Mere Eglise. Janusz became the designated leader of this small group of men when Tony saw how gently, yet expertly he handled the volatile sticks of dynamite. Janusz had set the small carefully wrapped bundles of TNT at the bridge's structural points until Sidney gave the orders to detonate.

Just outside of Sainte-Mere-Eglise, John the Cherokee was speaking in tongue to Thomas the Apache. Each was telling the other about any German or American traffic in the area. The idea was to keep the Germans from adding reinforcements to the area and yet allow bands of Americans to cross over and reconnoiter with their fellow soldiers in and around Saint Mere Eglise.

As he tied the bundles to each juncture, he thought of his Polish bridges. Then as now, he cushioned each parcel between the cold girders of this long bridge over which German tanks would cross down from Cherbourg and into St. Lo, Bayeux and Caen. When the Allied forces moved inward, the Germans would bring their arsenal from Cherbourg to counter the attack.

He thought of how he willingly destroyed his homeland to prevent it from becoming part of the German war machine. Perhaps, now the destruction would blow the wind the other way and loosen the black gloved grip of those German hands. In time and with God's help a hurricane of hate would blow war's fire back into Germany and blackened its own earth with the relics of war.

Tony watched Janusz carefully and handed him the bundles he had laid out on the riverbank. Each one had been tied in the same manner. Six sticks bundled by thin wire interlaced between and around the slender sticks like bundles of asparagus. Constantly, turning around, Tony made certain the enemy was not behind them. He alternately pressed the walkie-talkie to his ear and then brought it to his mouth. Thomas, perched in various trees, had a view of both the road and the riverbank. Whenever there was a wandering shadow, he ordered them to stay hidden and wait for the all clear. He would climb down from his perch and silently kill any intruder who did not respond to the click signal. A quick tightening of a cut off piece of parachute cord or a cutting slice with his thin bladed self-styled knife finished the job.

Each time Tony would whisper, "All clear". Janusz, squeezed beneath the girders of the bridge would climb down. With long skilled fingers he would begin again to play the wire as though it were a keyboard. He'd weave the wire like a scale of notes beneath the bridge, finding just the right sharp or flat to compose his piece, for he knew the notes by heart. The finale would be in the explosion.

Tony watched in amazement as Janusz finally unwound himself from the metal of the bridge. Like a cat, he had slid into crannies and crevices to place the explosives so the bridge would collapse in one momentous crescendo.

"On y va" he said to Tony.

"Yeah, let's get outta here." Tony answered the new member of his unit.

All three were on the road back when Janusz told Tony just where to lob the grenade. With the accuracy of Mickey Owen he threw the ball to second before the Germans could steal across the bridge. The trio hit the ground and covered their ears. The bridge blew in a symphony of white light.

In the safety circle Sidney, Christian, and Billy mirrored the same action. When they stood up and adjusted their helmets, they could see the smoke rise through the once held girders of steel. They moved out cautiously to meet up with the rest of their new unit. John had signaled from Sainte Mere Eglise to move in on the northwest side since paratroopers were still falling from the skies.

Thomas clicked off his walkie-talkie. "All clear. We meet the rest in the town of 'saint mother the church'."

Janusz and Tony looked at one another. They were in agreement. They liked the way this Apache spoke. Simple - direct.

****

No one was prepared for what awaited them in the town of Sainte Mere Eglise. The entire town, outlined by rooftops against a red sky, took on the appearance of a cardboard etching in an old movie viewer. The night, ablaze with fire, had turned color when tracer bullets hit a small barn next to the church. The fire made the leap to its white boards, aged dry from the sea air. Caught like kindling, it ignited. Pockets of fire jumped from thatched roof to thatched roof. A few lone houses seemed to have escaped the flames until a paratrooper or glider crashed helplessly into them. Almost on impact the dry timber exploded.

Juliette and John the Cherokee remained crouched behind a shed near the village store.

"Vite! Vite" an old man yelled.

"Plus d'eau. Le feu est impossible", another yelled.

Villagers dressed in night shirts, robes, and hastily pulled on trousers formed a bucket brigade in a futile attempt to save their church. The German garrison had come to investigate the noise and stayed. In one hand each soldier held a bucket and with the other a machine gun, which they let fire from the hip as paratroopers floated ever so slowly nearer the flames. The lucky ones were dead before the flames plucked them from the sky.

Christian and Janusz crept behind Juliette.

"Where are they?" Janusz asked.

"We know the last communication was from Colleville." As an afterthought Christian added, "Do you know what they look like?"

"I know well," she whispered.

"What else do you know?" Janusz asked.

"I know my brother is not dead yet."

Christian turned to the young woman whom he had felt he had known before. Now he knew why. It was not 'déjà vu', but simply an uncanny resemblance to Luc. Now they knew she was Luc's sister and truly one of them, and she knew they were her brother's allies and friends from his other world of England. There was no doubt in her mind that Zosia had touched Luc's heart, and that these two foreign young men who had each lost a parent to the war, were the younger brothers he never had.

"The Colleville guns could not be destroyed. We tried but failed." She knew they had that information. "What you do not know is that Paul, my brother's friend from when he was a little boy, is dead. They caught and tortured him. He never gave up what he knew." She paused before continuing. "It was his little brother Claude that set him free ... to die."

"And Zosia?" Janusz was almost afraid to ask.

Christian finished the rest, "...and Luc?"

"Over there" she gestured with her head.

All looked toward the church engulfed in flames so high that the steeple was barely visible.

"The last word I got from General Bradley before we took off was that they would be holding out out in the basement of the church at Sainte Mere Eglise." Sid confirmed. "Let's circle in threes around the perimeter of the town to the back of the church. Meet back here at 1400. John, Thomas - you stay far behind and separate to guard our flanks. Communicate in Apache. Tony, Janusz - go with Juliette. Christian, Billy - you're with me."

He wanted his new charges to be split up. "If anything happens to one of them, the other will still be alive to carry out whatever this mission is - whatever is so crucial to the free world, when… if…. this war -is over. One of the four has to get to Paris." he ran the words through his mind one more time.

If Luc and Zosia were still in the basement of the church, Sidney had already counted them as dead. Sid saw Juliette circle to the right - toward 3:00 while he took his men left toward 9:00. The church marked high noon, and each group would have to get behind this blazing sun to find the truth if the pair were still alive. They had little time to find the answer. Dead or alive they had to know quickly. The Germans were not bothering to ask questions. If you weren't a villager, or a German soldier then as the enemy, you would be shot on sight. Juliette took advantage of the confusion.

"Attendez ici. Wait here. I be back," she said as she pulled a robe from a clothesline and began buttoning it over her black sweater. She sat behind the small stone house with her back pressed against the cold. Kicking her shoes off, she slid out of her black flannel trousers. She tied them around her waist under the checkered wool robe and slid her feet back into her shoes without ever having to untie or retie the laces. She had had much practice in the nights since the Germans invaded her homeland. She tied a scarf that she had found in the robe's pocket around her head and darted into the town square. Janusz and Tony eased their way from house -to tree - to shadow - far in the background, yet with eyes fixed on Juliette. Each crept closer in their circling of the church.

"Il y a de l'espoir?" Juliette said as she passed a bucket of water down the line.

"There is always hope, my child," the cloaked man behind her said.

She stopped passing the water bucket for a split second - long enough for her to be detected. This she knew. She had given herself away, but she said nothing. Her face remained blank as though she did not understand the English.

She continued to pass up the buckets and moved forward, closer to the church to separate herself from the cloaked man. She needed to see if there were any air pockets at the base of the church where one could survive the heat and gas.

"Ca to faon libve meou" John spoke into his walkie-talkie to Thomas.

The big Apache answered, "Ya sa ta leonu"

Each had caught sight of Juliette and read the slight hesitation in her body when the cloaked man appeared at her elbow. In almost the same moment, both Indians saw clusters of paratroopers, huddled in pockets of four or five beyond the perimeter of the fire. Slowly and silently, they signed to them.

As the Apache approached one, he heard a click. The only response was a thrashing in the brush. The paratrooper from the hidden group frantically clicked again. The thrasher answered.

"Stop the god damn clicking you crazy son of a bitch. If I had my fucking clicker, don't cha think I'da clicked the shit outta it."

The hidden clicker laughed, "Well ya gotta be a regular Joe. No Jerry could string together that many swears and have it make sense.

Thomas stepped right in next to the two crouching paratroopers, "You seen any partisans?" he simply said.

"An injun - hot damn. I have to land in France to see one. I don't believe my eyes." The thrasher from the 101st Airborne exclaimed as he looked up at the mountain of a man before him.

"No - American first - Apache second. You lucky sons of bitches." Thomas grinned at the two faces, greased darker than his own skin, with their mouths open in disbelief.

"Partisans, you say," the clicker was the first to speak. "I saw three natives leave from a back window of that church."

"How do ya know?"

"I was falling fast - but not fast enough. I had too much of an Eagle's nest view - if you know what I mean?"

"Yeah, I get the picture."

Clicker continued, "The fire started before I was even out of the plane's door. The front of the church went first. The back exits were clear. Still plenty of time to exit - then I see these three berets climbing out a basement window."

Where'd they go?"

"To the cemetery behind the church."

"You better head out. There're a bunch of paratroopers 100 yards south of here. Way before the bridge crossing the Meredet. Don't plan on crossing that way unless you can swim."

The two men nodded to him and moved south - away from the heat of the square. Thomas placed his walkie-talkie to his ear and then to his mouth. He continued to talk in Apache.

"O.K I read you. I see her too - 11:00 o'clock and moving to 12:00- behind the church now. He's taking the sleeve of Juliette. He's pushing her forward. "Over and out," Thomas answered.

From the outside circle they began to move inward. Concentric circles. With the flaming church as their sun, the groups of men were traveling in different orbits, but each was moving closer to their goal.

Christian felt the cemetery before he saw it. "Dust to dust. Ashes to ashes" were too familiar a refrain to him. The white headstones flashed before his eyes. One granite cross seemed to step out from the mass of others. He blinked his eyes and the words on the cross faded; the lettering disappeared, and coldness enveloped him. He stopped to catch his breath and wipe the sweat from his brow. He was not in a hurry to find out what his vision meant. He knew Zosia and Luc would be there - one way or another.

Sidney, Billy, Tony, and Janusz had edged their way through the walking nightmare. They had gotten the Apache's message of "the birds have flown to their maker" and convoyed at the edge of the cemetery.

"Spread out. Keep in line," Sidney ordered.

The flames were behind them as they formed a line like the ones used in sea rescues. In the darkness - shot through by streaks of tracer bullets - they walked forward carefully, noting any change in the terrain – a soft clump that might be a body - a stick across a path which might be a rifle. Without speaking, they moved and stopped in unison. Through the headstones, they moved methodically to the cemetery's end, the grassy fields beyond. Once those fields were reached they would know that Zosia and Luc didn't rest among the dead - yet. If the pair could not be found, they would have to separate and make a house to house search.

As the high grass became more and more visible and the headstones became fewer and more sparsely set, Christian looked to Janusz. Still walking straight and steady Christian could not read his friend's emotions from his stance. Christian, like Janusz, knew overt feelings were only for those who never had to constantly watch over their shoulders. When Janusz slowed at the last row of stones, his head dropped to his chest. The fatigue and tension of the last forty-eight hours plus the rigorous training of the past fourteen months were heavy burdens for even his broad shoulders. At the end of the cemetery he took a deep breath, straightened his back, and executed a quick about-face to march back into the mouth of the fire and perhaps certain death in order to conduct a house to house search.

As all turned in the line to go back into Sainte Mere Eglise, they saw a larger shadow move among the other shadows in the darkness. Sidney raised his Colt 45 and steadied one hand underneath its muzzle. One lone shot among all the others would be never heard. Christian reached across to his arm and lowered the gun just as the Apache stepped forward into a blast of light. His face illuminated Sidney could see the Apache's hand cupping the walkie-talkie as he pressed it against his ear then quickly to his mouth. No one could hear his words or lip-read his mouth as he spoke in his secret tongue.

"Move 250 yards northeast," he said as he neared Sidney, pointing in the direction of the far side of the last cemetery stone to his right. Tony had his compass out.

"The guy's right on the money." Tony commented to Janusz as he hooked his compass back on his belt.

Janusz looked at Christian. Neither had a compass or had even given it a thought. Like the Apache, they knew the land as they knew their own breath. But they breathed in bursts as they closed in on the spot.

Crouched on the ground, a slim curved shape was outlined every time something or someone burst into flames. Next to the figure stood another- cloaked and hooded, this shape seemed to loom above the curved one. Christian's and Janusz's hearts skipped a beat, for they now realized the smaller shape was Juliette's. What or who was she bending over, and who was over her?

Stepping ahead of Sidney, they crossed the few yards between them and the two figures. Janusz grabbed the cloaked shape and pulled off the hood.

"Je vais avec Dieu, mon fils."

Janusz saw the cross around the man's neck before he saw his eyes. He knew one without the other meant nothing. He looked into his eyes - calm and clear, no treachery lay there.

"He does go with God, Janusz. He led me - and 'Jean' here." Juliette could not say the name in Cherokee or in English. For her it had no meaning. John - 'Jean' was simpler. She said it as the French would.

The stone slab at her feet began to lift up. The Priest grabbed one side and Janusz the other. Being pushed up from underneath, the massive granite marker slid easily to one side. All the men peered down into the hole - into the underground passageway that seemed to open up into a room. When the light from the sky illuminated their far end of the cemetery, they could see down into what appeared to be an open grave. Juliette flattened herself on the ground and stretched her body into the opening. John had been the force on the inside. His incredible strength had lifted the stone, for he had gone first into the underground tomb that the priest had led them to. Juliette and the priest stood guard after they had dragged the stone back into place. No one knew what the Cherokee would find or how long it would take.

Once the stone had cleared, John stepped back into what appeared to be a larger than normal grave. The far end dipped downward and continued into a square room. He motioned Janusz down as he indicated the supine form of woman lying in the recessed curved form of man. They fit like spoons. He was of narrow build, tall and lean. She was as tall as he. His arm cradled her head as if to protect her.

"They are not dead- just waterless but with breath." The Cherokee said. He did not know the words to describe their state of suspended life - of life that was on the brink of death, but fighting to conserve their reserve.

Janusz felt Juliette push to his side as he bent his head over Zosia's. He tilted her head toward his and cupped his hands around her mouth as he blew his breath into her nearly spend lungs. Juliette too had bent her head over her brother's and commanded her life's breathe into him. Expelling all the air from her own lungs, she blew into his mouth. Dizzy from the effort, she stretched out a hand to lie on his chest. Alternately, Janusz and Juliette expelled a breath and released a cupped hand to feel for the rise of the chest on its own. As though linked by some invisible thread, Luc and Zosia gasped for air at the same time. Their chests rose in a fight for air.

"Their spirits have reentered their bodies. They haven't given up their claim."

Janusz leaned back on his heels. His face wet with sweat and contorted with pain. How much damage could he expect? He had seen the damage of the war - of the Germans - on his mother. He did not know yet how much Zosia and Luc had seen or experienced.

"What took you so long?" Zosia weakly said as she reached up to touch Janusz's face. "You know I would not leave you. We Polish women are strong." she smiled a motherly smile - an April smile.

"Qu'est-ce qui se passe, mon frere? Tu etais ici pour combien de temps?"

"Pas de longtemps - Juliette. Nous sommes sortis de l'eglise apres le feu a commence. Ne t'en inquiete pas."

"You take the woman. I'll take the man. Air is cleaner and cooler above." John simply said.

****

From the tomb the priest had led them to his hidden home away beyond the church and its rectory. Their story unfolded as the two Indians stood watch within the recesses of the priest's stone 'mas'. This half barn, half home had one long room with a root cellar and a loft. The Cherokee and the Apache remained in the loft peering out the four tiny stone shuttered windows - barely the size for one head. Luc, Zosia, Juliette, Janusz, and Christian were reunited as Sidney stood on the outside of their circle. Tony and Billy crouched somewhere in between.

They had begun speaking in French. Juliette had started when she was bringing her brother back to life, and then when he breathed, she hugged him with all her strength. His pale face began to color. Juliette was so happy to see him alive that her defenses were down. She just talked about everything, random news from friends, family, mere, pere, and even Denis. Then she told him the bad news - those friends who had not been heard from and those who they knew were dead. Then her tone of voice changed. She spoke quietly and paused for the right words. She had saved the news concerning Renard's tragic death for last. That night at Colleville, only three days ago, seemed like 3 months.

Luc heard her words. They had not come as a surprise, for the news had traveled quickly through the chain of resistance fighters. Nonetheless, it was as though he heard it for the first time. He had built a game around losing those he loved. He pretended they had made it to free territory - Switzerland, England, Australia, America – anywhere. He never believed it, but it was his way of shelving the rawness and agonizing pain until the time when he could deal with it. He knew Renard had not escaped across the Channel. Not only had he died, but he had undergone two days of unspeakable torture before death let him escape the pain. What he had not known was that little deaf Claude killed his own brother.

Zosia felt Luc's despair. She hurt for him not only because her love could not shelter him from the truths of these times, but because she felt again the loss of her two good friends - April and Stanislaus. Zosia looked over to Janusz. He came and wrapped his arms around her. She was the link to the mother he had lost. He had left the piano key his mother had given him for his eighteenth birthday with his father in England, but Stanislaus' knife was always with him. He intended it to remain in his boot all the way to Paris.

Janusz had begun talking in English. For him, it was easier than French. He understood all that Juliette, Luc, and Zosia said and could speak French from his training in England, but for him English was his foreign language of choice. It was the language his mother had spoken as well as her native Polish, and it was for her and his beloved Poland that he fought. He also knew that the others - the Americans, did not understand the French.

Although the Americans would not think they were being excluded, Janusz knew the sharing of information could only help their cause and their chance for survival. Besides, he had come to like their sense of ease and openness, which some foolishly mistook for weakness. These Americans were strong highly trained men who had taken on a mission - a mission for the rest of the world. They had stood by when Poland was swallowed up, yet he could not blame them for not wanting to be caught up in another foreign war.

"Somehow I've come through the drop and again I've been sheltered from harm. God took my mother; perhaps that is the reason. He is not so cruel as to take me and leave papa and Helena alone again. Yet, my old friend Martin had said God would not be so cruel as to take him and leave his mother without a husband and a son. And yet, Martin died."

Janusz definitely felt mortal, but as he looked to Christian he knew his friend did not. A goodness and a power radiated from him that made him seem immortal. He had not said anything in French nor in English and remained fearless, self-contained, and totally free. His friend was the key to their mission.

It was less than a week ago in General Morganski's Office that he had heard about Christian's incredible trial. A puzzle existed within Christian that he could never understand, and now he knew why. Yet, where did his mystical ability and energy come from? Like a sponge he soaked in life - its textures and its feelings, and from that he distilled an acute awareness of the world around him.

Janusz did not know how much their General de Gaulle, had been told. Janusz knew de Gaulle had met with Luc and Zosia for a crucial mission, but was Christian's connection told to them. Had they been briefed on the whole story or did each one only carry a piece of the puzzle? His piece and Zosia's was Poland; Christian's was Russia; Luc and Juliette's was France, and Lieutenant Sidney's - the United States of America.

Each had a piece of the puzzle — in case one piece hit the floor and was found by the Nazis. All five of them knew what they would do if any of them were captured. Juliette had confirmed again what they all knew was the price for capture. Apparently, 'Renard' was grateful for the grenade his brother threw into the window of the bunker at Colleville. At least, he finally died. How much more pain could he have endured?

Janusz thought, "How much can Sidney, Tony or Billy endure? What have they been told by their Generals? Will my life at some point in this mission be in their hands – how strong are those hands. That is the question."

Janusz noticed that the commander, Sidney, kept touching his chest. A gesture of habit or something else? First, he would talk to Zosia then the rest would follow.

Chapters 15 – Letters Home – June 6 1944 17:00

Sainte Mere Eglise 6 juin, 1944

Dear Mom and Sis –

I might as well speak to you in 'American'. Yours must be AOK by now. Does Tatiana even speak Russian? I am not able to believe four years pass – for me, it seems forty.

No desire to worry you. I know what tricks play on the mind – how we exaggerate the real. Just knowing you are safe lets me deal with my life here. Few letters have been from me these past six months. In your heart, I'm certain you knowed why. As the invasion day neared, there was less information I could say. You knew that I was still alive and that is the main thing.

The money that I make in England I send to you both at that place called Hartford. There is a Hartford in England, but the name 'Connecticut' sounds so foreign to me – I laugh at that. My head spins with the languages that are now in my mind.

I pick a different American to bring you these letters with – "all is well – love forever". I bring myself each time to write it. They call these men the gun runners – but now I am glad they run the guns, for I have a Colt 45 hung in a holster strapped to my leg.

This will get to you by way of France. It's DDAY 1700 hours – five in the afternoon. They gave me a Colt 45, a parachute, and instructions for the drop from the airplane. I knowed I would make it. While those around me died, I feel at ease – calm. This American gun – although I have not fired it – is a link to the past and to whatever the future holds. Maybe this gun you made if you work in the Hartford Colt Factory. Maybe it is a gift from you to save me in some tomorrow.

I have not slept for over 24 hours. – The day – D-day or Jour-J as one says here in France has finally happened. We have landed on the beachheads, and God willing we will not be pushed back into the sea. Writing before is too painful and too dangerous. What can one say when one must wait to act. Now, the day of action is come. The secrecy is broken.

Only what I saw in our dark forest can compare to the horrid of this night – but these men – these Americans died fighting. To each and every one it was a job – a job to be done for their families at home and for the families of the world. They have broad shoulders these Americans. Comfortable, I feel with them. I feel I have known them before. You know what I mean – you and papa always knowed that I am different.

I have two Americans – no four Americans who will take me into Paris. My mission is to get proof of what I saw so long ago so that it will never happen again. I am like these Americans. I have a job to do. A job that began in another place in another time but is not yet finished.

I love you Mom – and you too Sis!

All is well – love forever, Christian.

June 6 off Omaha
                                              Beach 1944… 17:30
Dad –
    I MADE IT! If this letter gets soiled, it is because it will be full of my blood, sweat, and tears like Churchill said- that's the only thing keeping me and the other guy from my unit -alive. Maybe you'll get this letter before the one I wrote you from England – five days ago. Those five days have aged me five years,… and this day – 10 years.
    You'll know by now that this was the day - the day of reckoning. They should have called it that since the generals of this world never reckoned on how many men we would lose. The Beach as I wrote you was called – it's funny how I write about it as though it were past – it is still called 'Omaha'. Yeah, like our state of Nebraska. By now the world knows its name because it's afternoon now and the German guns are still booming away, but all the waves of men have hit the beach in one way or another.
    My sector, as I wrote before, was called 'Easy Red'. I thought that was a good sign. Instead, it was an omen – an omen of disaster. It wasn't 'easy', but it sure was 'red'.
    I came in on a LCVP with the commanding officer, Lieutenant Wilson, two medics, and 31 other men. Less than twelve hours ago they were all alive. Now, they're all dead. Only one other guy besides me made it. His name is O'Brien. O'Brien – he's from Boston along with every other Mick in the world. I am now his Lieutenant. Don't forget that name, Pop. If I don't make it, he'll be the one telling you. If neither of us survives, I pray this letter gets to you. I'm putting it in my Army issued regulation plastic pouch., guaranteed water and blood proof.
    We did our best. We did our jobs.

Love your son,
Melvin Baron, Lieutenant
        Off of Omaha Beach, Normandy -France
        To Omaha, Nebraska – United States of America –
                                              God willing.

South of Caen, Normandy
France
June 6, 1944 –18:00

Bea –

I am writing you since I have no other family other than you. You were ...
are my wife, and if I should not make it out of here, the British government
knows you are still down on my enlistment papers as my only living relative.
This letter might not even get to you. I am addressing it to Hollywood,
California since that is where your cousin, Harriet, said you left for.

You never even sent me a 'dear John' letter as the Yanks call them.
That would fit the bill since you left me for America or some American guy
although Harriet says that was not so. "You just wanted a life of
'promise'," she said to me.

Just thought you might want to know that the beginning of the end
has happened. I am writing you from France. I was dropped in over thirty-
six hours ago with my unit from the 6th Airborne. We were supposed to
parachute in behind Sword Beach or Lion-sur-Mer as the French call it.
There were eighteen of us in the stick. Our sergeant Big Al would have been
the last to jump, but the plane was hit as he stood in the door. Floating
down, I saw one of the young lads, a very religious one, get it as he was
coming down in front of me. My commander, the Lieutenant, I found dead
in the marsh after I landed.

I am sitting here on the down-wind side of one of Normandy's
fucking 'bocages'. These French pasture hedges and the marshes the
Germans made by flooding lowlands will kill more Brits and Yanks - than
mortar fire! That's my prediction.

For what it's worth to you, I am not alone. I have a group of seven
under my command. I know none of them. None of us have the same orders.
None of the terrain is familiar. We're far off our marks. Regardless, we've
fought and done a lot of damage in these brief 17 hours.

We're not moving toward Caen because we never landed behind
Sword Beach. We've determined that we're closer to Omaha Beach than
those of the British beach heads, Gold and Sword. I'm telling you the names
because it does not matter now. Secrecy and all the buildup in England is

out and on the move. Since you're in Hollywood - the Mecca of film, I know you'll see all this on the newsreels in the cinema. That was always your dream. I never knew why you married me — a British engineer.

But, I feel this engineer has made a difference so far. I do have a family now — a group of seven. Motley, we are, but nonetheless united. Three Liverpool street fighter lads, a Stafford farmer boy, a big Yorkshire man, another engineer, and a pathfinder who's as full bloodied American as you can get - an Apache Indian.

Have a fucking good life
Sandy — 6ᵗʰ British Airborne Division

Tuesday, June 6, 1944 18:30

Dear Mrs. Paul Hudson,
    My name is Sal Marchese. Your husband, Captain Paul Hudson, was my commanding officer for Company C 2nd Ranger Battalion. There were 62 of us who hit the beach on the West end of Omaha. I'm telling you this because by now you must know that he was killed in action. He never mailed the letter he had written you from England 4 days ago. When I get closer to Paris or to a Frenchman or an army Postal Station, I'll pass his letter and this letter along.
    If I don't make it, I hope these letters find their way to you. Both I am putting in the Captain's waterproof pouch to keep them safe until I can send them along. Only four of us made it off our little sea boat -your husband, James Earl from Alabama, Aaron Axelrod from Hollywood and me, Sal Marchese from the Bronx We ran to the base of the cliff. Our mission was to climb the 90 foot cliff, Pointe de la Percee. We had to take out any guns on top. We were scared. Real scared, but the Captain led us up. The tide was coming in and he said "Men we have nowhere to go but up".
    I remember his exact words, Mam, because I really thought those were the last I'd hear. Anyway, when we got to the top we could see a pill box. That's a concrete block placed deep in the ground where the enemy could fire upon the Americans who were coming ashore. I never heard what he said, but he crawled across the barren top of the cliff to approach it from the blind side – behind it. It seemed like an eternity. I was clinging to the sheer cliff – 90 feet down was the beach, but I watched him all the way.
    When he got within a dozen feet, he leaned on his side and unhooked 2 grenades. He pulled the pin on one and kept the other in his mouth. He scored a bulls-eye. It lobbed through the slit of a window and he turned and ran crouching away from us – inland. At that moment, I saw a machine gun nest. The gun turned toward the Captain at the same moment that I yelled -"HIT THE GROUND".
    Everything happened at once- The pillbox blew. I lobbed a grenade toward the machine gunner's nest, and the Captain pulled the pin with his teeth from the other grenade, twisted in midair, lobbed the grenade backwards, and hit the ground yelling "Remember the Alamo".
    He took out everything, but the machine gunner got off his round first. The Captain never felt anything. He was killed instantly. Know that

he sacrificed his life for ours. You can be proud of him. The great state of Texas can be proud of him. I am. It was a privilege to serve under him.

Sincerely,
Sal Marchese Company C 2ⁿᵈ Ranger Battalion

Sal put down his pencil and sat with his back flat against the stone wall of what was a Norman farmhouse. The roof was gone and the three remaining walls were uneven like a deck of poorly shuffled cards. He held the sealed letter of Captain Paul Hudson in his hand. The Captain's big bold scrawl was on the face of the letter. Sal read the address:

> **Mrs. Paul Hudson**
> **Great Sky Ranch**
> **Dallas, Texas**

His fingers traced the name and address before he copied the same onto his letter. The stationary was the same.

"The Captain must have gotten it at the Canteen in England. It's blue. Probably – like the view from his ranch," Sal thought as he sealed his own letter and placed both sealed envelopes in the waterproof pouch.

Sal purposely didn't tell Hudson's wife that the only thing left of her husband was the helmet that flew from his head when the explosion hit. At the moment when both men threw their grenades Sal had ducked beneath the edge of the cliff. He had hung on for his very life since the explosion rocked the earth as his fingertips and toes ached from the tension of trying not to be blown off the face of the cliff. Somewhere beneath him were Aaron and James Earl. Each hanging on – not knowing if they were closer to life or to death.

The Captain's helmet had held the pouch – forced into the inside upper portion, it stayed wedged within the metal gun metal green helmet. The camouflage netting had disintegrated along with the chinstrap. When Sal peered above the side of the Pointe de la Percee, there was no pill box, no machine gunner's nest, no Captain Paul Hudson. The acrid smell of burnt flesh filled his nostrils and the pieces of stone, metal, skin, and bone floated in the smoke. As he pulled himself over the edge of the cliff, the helmet fell from the sky two feet in front of him. He grabbed it before it rolled over the cliff.

It wasn't until the three men fought their way inland that he looked inside of it. He had simply thrown it in his backpack. Eleven hours later they stopped.

Finally, exhaustion overcame adrenaline. Two stood lookout. The third took a leak against one of the stone walls that had stood as a home for centuries until now. Each took his turn. Their adrenaline had kept them going and fear was but one step behind. Too worried to heed their bodily needs, they had pushed forward.

Sal took his turn last. It was when he lowered the weight of his backpack from his shoulders and looked inside for food that he remembered the Captain's helmet. He hadn't remembered that he had put it there. When he looked at it, he wondered why he had kept it. Was it to remember a man that was really an enigma to him – a man who had never talked about where he lived, what his family was like, and most importantly when he had fought before? He was about to toss the helmet. He did not need any extra weight and the helmet itself was useless without the chinstrap.

His body suddenly ached with fatigue. Too tired to throw it like a basketball from the top, he slowly turned it over so he could get a firm grip from the inside. It was then he saw pouch. Wiping the blood off with his dirty fingers he saw that there was something inside - A letter, a map, and French francs with American dollars wrapped in a thick rubber band. He lifted them from the pouch.

On the piece of paper the words '*Channel Number 5 for Betty Jo*' - emblazed in a big bold hand. Then Sal looked at the address on the letter. It was at that moment in the pause of war that he had decided to write the letter. "Someone in this damn war should know how we fought and how we died," Sal thought as he picked up the pencil he had never used to send any news back home to the Bronx.

When he finished, he put both letters and the money back into the pouch. He slid the silk map out and placed it in front of him. Spread out on a flat clean rock piece of marble, he studied it as he began to mix the water from his canteen with army issue dehydrated eggs. He unwrapped a slab of beef jerky and pulled off a chunk with his teeth. Washing it down with a gulp of water from the canteen, the beef tasted of metal and blood.

He wedged the pouch down into the top of his own helmet. Taking one last look at the Captain's, he tossed it high over the north side of the wall into the apple orchards beyond. As he ate, he studied the carefully made drawing of France and the enlarged section of the Norman Coast. There in blue, black, red, and gold were the beaches – lining the coast between them and England: Utah, Omaha, Gold, Juno and Sword-just names on a map until now. The towns, neatly labeled with the major routes and minor roads, provided a plan where to go.

"Paris, gay Paree" he said. He wiped his hands on his pants and traced the big bold letters with his fingertips. He had a reason to get there now.

He automatically took a spoonful of eggs as he stared at the map. He could taste the soft plump mouthfuls of salty eggs. He could hear the faint call of a mockingbird - 'who....who', and realized he was hungry.

Chapter 16 – And Night Came, June 6

The moon was bright. The fog was sliced in chunks throughout the night by the constant barrage of 'ack-acks' shooting up towards the faceless moon It slowly dissipated under the intense fire surrounding the area of Sainte Mere Eglise.

During the endless night Sidney wondered where were The reinforcements. No one came – no Americans – no Germans. Despite having blown one bridge, they could not keep the Germans on the other side of the Merderet River forever. Sidney knew they had to hold this only remaining bridge east of the railroad.

"It must be held at all costs. With one bridge blown, this other has to stay intact if the 4th Division has any hope of coming to the aid of the 82nd and 101st airborne." He could not vanquish the ghost-like apparitions of paratroopers floating into flames or igniting like Fourth of July candles.

As soon as a paratrooper landed, Sidney knew they all had the same orders: "Cut all communication in the area." All night long Sidney could see them climbing telephone poles and cutting the lines. Initially, there was silence, for these men of the 82nd and 101st had not used their guns when they first landed on French soil. Any gunfire heard, would be coming from the German occupying forces. Sidney now thought, "We're well past the element of surprise. The tigers are roused from their sleep."

At daybreak, whatever American forces were left alive

on the ground had to take up defensive positions until reinforcements came up from the beachheads. "Where are the men of the 4th division?" That was the question everyone asked. Luckily, no additional German regiments had arrived to counter the American attack, yet no American units had come up off the beaches. Sidney got a report from a Lieutenant Colonel at 1400 hours who had been giving orders on crutches since his landing. Other than that, there was no active communication from the 4th Division on the beach.

Ammunition was running low. Sidney had heard that the 'crutch' commander gave an order to collect all ammunition from men with an M1 except one 'bandolier' and all but three clips from men armed with Tommy guns. This ammo had been sent up the line to Sidney and his men to hold the last remaining bridge over the Merderet and if possible to drive the enemy back to the west side of the river. The cold overcast sky was again readying itself for night, and still the ammo hadn't come. Soon, it would be D-Day plus 1.

They told him his group was elite. Sidney prayed it was elite enough to get the job done. Beneath his shirt was the same waterproof standard issue pouch for all landing force personnel, but concealed inside were top secret orders, written on paper and treated with a special type of acid. Highly flammable, a spark could ignite them. As a non-smoker his 'Lucky Strike' cigarettes served no purpose, but the short stick matches, in a tight bundle inside an aluminum 'pinkie size' cylinder, did. A single match could set them on fire with a flick of the thumb.

The pouch also held: the GI regulation blue "French Phrase" book, the British issue Normandy and France map - written on a white silk handkerchief, two envelopes, some sheets of stationary, a set of rosary beads, and a handwritten letter in a woman's hand - personally addressed to Lieutenant Sidney Smith formerly of Hannibal, Missouri.

To the enemy, they would seem innocuous – to an American, they would seem in order. In reality, they were in cipher. Those who knew the plan could decipher the phrasing. Like an enigma - like the 'ENIGMA', it held all necessary information: Who to contact along the way, where to go, what to do, and who to see once they reached Paris.

It was time to tell his men the exact nature of their covert orders. He knew the two who joined the stick in England were part of - perhaps the key to their mission. He was left with only two Americans from his original stick; they, along with the others, had to be told.

"These men, in front of me, will have to do – and it seems they'll do nicely," Sidney thought:

Two Indians, an Apache and a Cherokee - quiet, strong, observers, men of the land.

Two young foreigners – younger than the rest but with all the characteristics of the others – stories seen and 'stuffed down' – buried beneath their calm exteriors.

His two – Tony and Billy – one brash – one naïve – made in the U.S. but honed in England to do the job.

Then there was Luc Dubois - the undisputed 'King' with the two women - independent, fierce and well trained -as his 'bishops'.

"An even ten with me," he thought. Sidney was aware of the rules of the game, and the tactics he needed to employ. He had an army of 'pawns' to protect his 'King" to insure his success and advance him forward to the purpose of the game – to secure the necessary document sequestered in Paris on direct orders of the Fuhrer himself, Adolph Hitler.

Luc and his 'bishops' had experience and personal direct knowledge of the strategy and players in this chess game called 'war'. Sidney knew his position was commander, but he was aware that his true role was that of a castle. "I have to protect my players. From the back of the chess board I will advance them, and be willing to sweep horizontally or vertically, to wipe out all obstructions in their path."

It was time for the game to begin. As Sidney walked to the middle of the large barn floor, the others moved in toward him. He saw Luc nod to the foreigners who simply and silently walked away from the room's center to post themselves at opposite doors. They did not look back. Focused on what might happen outside the barn, they would protect the others.

Luc whispered in French to the Priest who climbed the ladder into the loft in order to act as lookout from the back window which overlooked the center of town and the back road out of town through the apple orchards.

Luc crossed into the circle between Zosia and Juliette and waited for the American Lieutenant to begin. He noticed the Lieutenant's thumb and index figure feel for something beneath the point of his shirt collar. Both women had seen the same quick insignificant movement before.

"Women notice details," Luc thought before the American Lieutenant began to speak. All three knew his quick reflex - his tactile search for the cyanide capsule hidden beneath the point of his shirt collar indicated his commitment. His commanders had briefed him well – better to die instantly than be tortured to death. Take the information to one's grave rather than betray the others who would certainly die if you failed to act. Death would come to you either way. To act – not think - at first opportunity was imperative. The Gestapo didn't give second chances.

"Beneath my shirt is a pouch containing our mission." He had continued to undo the first three buttons. He pulled out the thin cord securing the pouch around his neck. The four other Americans were not surprised. Tony had noticed him touching his chest right before the jump. He, Billy, and the two Indians had similar pouches. They were regulation-issue for American landing forces.

"We are to get to Paris at all costs. If there is but one of us left, and you are the one. Take this pouch from around my neck and place it around yours. It will help you get to Paris and retrieve Russian documents. These documents were written by the Russians in command in 1940 before they switched sides." Sidney began to place the contents of his pouch on a small oak table in front of him.

"All of this," he pointed to the matches, stationary, French currency, bar of disinfectant, roll of bandages, and the rosary beads - "is standard issue. The map," he unfolded the silk square, which labeled the towns, and roads of Normandy and then gave an overview of the other major towns and routes of France, "is British issue. We, American Forces, also have a map in our phrase book."

He held up the condensed blue paperback book with the gold emblem of an eagle on the cover. The size of a large deck of cards it fit easily inside the pouch.

"What is different," he continued "is this envelope.' He placed it gingerly on the table. "It's open to seem as though it's been already read. It's addressed to me and written by a woman named Rita."

"Rita Hayward, Lieutenant? You got connections." Tony joked.

All the Americans chuckled. The rest just turned to see what could be so funny in this grave situation. Juliette, however, turned to Luc and asked him something in French. He answered in French, but she just shrugged her shoulders.

"No Private Martino." Today, Sidney lacked the patience for Tony's remarks. Outside the gunfire continued. It was difficult to hear and speak above the din. "Inside is a coded letter. If I am killed, put your issue inside my pouch – the letter, the set of rosary beads, and the matches. If you are captured, it will just seem that you took the extra beads and letter to give to my family and the extra container of matches is for you."

"But Lieutenant", Billy asked. "Won't the Krauts tell it's in code. Can't they crack it?'

"It only makes sense to the people who know what's in those documents we need to retrieve."

"And who knows that?" John, the Apache asked.

"To one degree or another - the others in this room." Sidney simply stated. All the Americans turned to take a long hard look at Zosia, Juliette, Christian, Janusz, and Luc.

"And once one of us gets to Paris?" Tony interjected with no humor this time.

"You find your way to La Place de la Concorde. Just remember 'Concordance Place'. It's at the other end of the 'Champs Elysees'. The Arc of Triumph stands here at one end", he took a stick and made a mark on the barn floor "and the 'Place de la Concorde' is there. It's a circle for traffic. Several streets merge into the Place like 'Rue' street 'Rivoli" and ….. Anyway, the 'Louvre' Museum is here – behind the Place. You can't miss it – it's a block square ancient building with a lot of statues on top."

"And once we're there?" Thomas' question shot straight to the target.

"A member of the Resistance - code name 'Moliere', will be there - everyday at high noon from D-Day plus 10 until as long as it takes. If the Allies never liberate Paris, then the mission doesn't matter for several reasons. Number one: we never got off the Beach. In that case, the communists won't control France because the Germans are. Number 2: Eisenhower won't waste the petrol and manpower trying to liberate Paris first since he knows the Germans will still not give up an inch of her without a totally entrenched battle. He'll simply swoop around her, liberate the rest of France, and go into the Rhine Land. Number 3: in that scenario, we still lose because the communists will wait for the Germans to leave and take over the city and France in the name of communist Russia – and Number 4: that is who our next war will be fought against." Sidney waited for all of this to register with his men.

The Europeans already knew this. Juliette, Zosia, and Luc had personal first-hand experience with the German master plan and Nazi ruthlessness; Christian knew the cold killing machine of Stalin's Russian, and Janusz knew of both.

"The man waiting at the Place de la Concorde will be wearing a scarf around his neck. You will ask him to show you the direction of the 'Opera'. When you thank him mention the name Moliere and offer your right hand for him to shake. On that hand you will have this bracelet." Sidney raised his right hand to show the silver medical bracelet on his wrist. "Factitious medical symbols are on it as well as a picture of a gold eagle. The eagle makes this bracelet different from all the others. Once Moliere sees this on your wrist, he will indicate for you to follow him. That is his only way of knowing you are not – I repeat – not the enemy."

He looked around. They did not ask the question that was obvious. He continued. "If I am dead or severely wounded, take the bracelet off my wrist and put it on yours. Those left alive at that moment must make the decision. It will go from one to the other, depending on who survives."

Luc looked at all their faces to see their reactions. They were trained - willing to do their jobs. Now, he was certain of this. What he did not know was who of them would survive and who was tough enough not to talk if captured and tortured. Luc realized that the Lieutenant had not given them the specifics of the Katyn. Janusz had told Zosia, and Zosia had told him. He also was privy to the fact that their contact in Paris, 'Moliere, was his boyhood friend, Simon. De Gaulle himself had given Simon this additional name for this particular mission – hopefully it would be his last before Paris, France, and the World would be free again.

Luc smiled to himself as he thought about Simon wearing a scarf like thousands of other Frenchman. That method of recognition was futile – but of course, that was the point. It would be Simon who picked out the American or the English speaking person -not the other way around. The Lieutenant of course, did not know this nor did he know that two people in this group, he and Juliette, knew Moliere on sight.. They had grown up with this first Parisian friend.

Luc, however, was the only one among the ten who could locate those documents with or without 'Moliere'. He needed the others to get him to Paris and the documents to de Gaulle before Hitler destroyed them or the Communists discovered where they were hidden. As an agent who crossed from France to England, Luc had discovered the British had broken the code of 'Egnima". After the fact, Churchill, Roosevelt, and de Gaulle received the information of Stalin's slaughter of the Poles in 1940. All realized that the next Front would be at their 'ally's' borders- wherever this war would extend them to. They could not end one war and begin another.

When the time came - if the time came, he would tell Juliette first, then Zosia, then Christian, then Janusz – In the meantime, if they were caught by the Gestapo, they could not tell what they did not know.

****

"Tu as les deux noms, mon fils." The priest said to Luc as they left the barn.

"Oui, mon pere." Luc had already committed to memory the two names of the leaders of the Priest's Resistance Cell, billeted in the largest house southwest of Sainte Mere Eglise.

While the rest of Luc's group slept in 20 minute segments, Luc eased his way into the bucket brigade lines of disheveled Frenchmen. He would confirm the names with his contact person - one of the anguished citizens of Sainte Mere Eglise. If the names were correct, his first action on the way to Paris would be to enter the house, blow the safe, and steal secret documents concerning resistance cells, collaborators or double agents. The safe at the 'manoir des Veignard' might also contain the names of small and larger groups of Germans in this sector of France.

Luc found his contact quickly, and his group of ten neatly left the still burning village of Sainte Mere Eglise. The Lieutenant, Tony, and Billy flanked Luc and the two women. Christian and Janusz covered the rear. The Apache and Cherokee were ahead of them all – cutting through the night as though it were a sunny day in June. Overhead and to their east, the first airborne reinforcements were landing.

Sidney glanced up to see the gliders that would be carrying the 325th infantry and artillery units. Members of the 4th Division had reached his bridge and he had fulfilled his military mission. Now, his civilian one would begin. He glanced sideways to Tony. At that moment they realized "Operation Overlord" was on. Ike was proceeding according to plan.

"I hope our group of ten beats the rest of our forces into Paris with time to spare." Sidney thought.

He knew they could not wait for all the infantry reinforcements to make it off Omaha and Utah. His orders were to move inland – at all costs - and to pick up any necessary men on the way. He was allotted an even dozen. Already, he was two down.

"The house is on a hill surrounded on three sides by pastures and those row hedges." John had circled back down. Sidney almost jumped. His nerves were so tense and raw, but at the last minute, he had caught the Cherokee's' shadow as he stepped out in front of the moonlight. When he turned his face toward his, Sidney was aware that he had done it on purpose –

the Indian knew the white man would always jump, for they never could hear his people as they walked the land.

"Bocage" Luc said as he came quietly alongside them both. Luc could not be caught off guard. Although his fighters were white, all had crossed this 'land of France' in one form of darkness or another.

"These 'bocage' rows are sinister as you know," Luc continued. "In which ones are the Germans hidden?"

"The center one to north. The ones on the east and west are free of the enemy."

"There's nothing on the south side?' Sidney asked.

"No. But to get there we have to circle the 'bocage'. Unseen and unheard because if only one of them escapes… John shrugged his shoulders, for all knew the answer.

"If we take them head on, it'll take up too much time. We could lose men. Is there a way to cut our losses?" Sidney turned to face Juliette and Zosia who had closed in with the others.

"Yes, I know a method." Juliette stated. "We'll lose no time, and we'll eliminate whatever Germans are in those ditches."

"Ditches?" Sidney questioned.

"'Oui' ditches – 'la terre'- These hedgerows are so old that a wall of earth has formed on both sides – especially on the north side which gets the coldest of the winds." She continued. "A natural ditch will be found at the base of any 'bocage', and that is where the Germans hide. Impossible to get them out – unless"

"Unless what?" asked Tony.

"You can send someone around the outer side of the 'bocage' and surprise the Germans who will be in a straight line shooting from the ditch."

"We'll have to engage fire first, so they take a defensive position in that ditch. I'll need two scouts to cross the field in alternate shifts until the lead man can slide through the hedgerow onto the enemy's flank." Sidney explained.

"We go". Thomas spoke for the two of them as he pointed to John and himself. If the French girl said so, it must be true.

Sidney judged the pasture to be about seventy-five yards across. He split his 'company' in half – Zosia, Luc, Janusz, and Tony on the left side, with Juliette, Christian, Billy, and himself on the right. The two Indians would be in front of them crawling flat in the pasture, the high grass making a bed for them as they inched up. It was high enough to provide cover but not so high as to make waves as each Indian moved forward. Little could be seen unless the moon came from behind the clouds.

Sidney waited until they were close enough to open fire. He did not have long to wait. As soon as Thomas and John began, the hedgerow in front instantly returned fire. They dropped down to let their team behind answer. All, including the non-regulation 'men', used the MI rifles with surprising accuracy. Boot camped trained or "Resistance' trained, they were trained well.

The entire hedgerow received spray across their front. Thomas, the lead scout, had begun the first round of fire. As soon as it stopped, John crept past him as far as possible before Thomas opened fire and sprayed the boscage again. Armed with a Tommy gun, John joined the fire, spraying a succession of bullets directly in front of him and to the right hand corner of the 'bocage'.

Ducking down, they expected the return enemy fire. At the moment when it would end, Thomas began again – this time with his Tommy gun. Spraying in front and to the left of the 'boscage' in front of him. The guns behind them continued to fire in support. All the way across the pasture, the Indians were covered until the last row of fire. It did not take long.

John was the first to reach the hedgerow. Into and through the enemy line, he slipped. Then he opened up. When the others reached him, the dozen boys in tattered German uniforms looked like marionettes whose master puppeteer had pulled their strings to make them lie in such contorted positions. Without bones, without form, without words, they lay. Just a mass of lifeless dolls, left - with manic abandon, on Death's stage

They encountered no other resistance in their approach to the great stone Norman farmhouse of Veignard. Already forgotten were the enemy slain in the earth divide of the bocage. For a moment Sidney's men thought about the other men in their stick, who never even made it - alive, to French soil. They could not bury them or even look for them. None felt remorse about not burying these German soldiers who crossed into France to kill and conquer. The scene would be repeated a thousand fold before the Allies crossed the Rhine into Germany. This land of the bocage would claim too many lives. Some who survived the beaches would not survive the readymade graves of the great hedgerows of Normandy.

The moon slid out from under the overcast but rainless night. From afar, the farmhouse seemed an ominous mass of stone and wood beams, yet it was but a skeleton. Half of the timber roof had been blown away and the walls were pocketed with holes the size of 1941 Ford tires. Sidney could detect no movement in or around the old 'manse'.

The farmhouse's far west side had no wall whatsoever. As he crept closer, he noticed everything inside remained intact. A large armoire stood next to a glass-less window frame that was precariously hanging on by only two of its corners. A huge high bed covered by several multi-colored quilts was at the opposite end of the room. A nightstand, desk, and trunk appeared in perfect condition. Even the glass oil lamps, wash pitcher and basin rested as though waiting for someone to use. The eerie scene had all the trimmings of a play. The curtain had opened. The audience could see through the fourth wall, but where were the actors?

"We'll go in pairs – an American – and an ally" it was the first time that Sidney had given the others a 'label'. Of different nationalities, they could not be called Frenchmen nor could they be called foreigners, for who in this situation was really the foreigner. Allied was the right word. For united as one was the only way they could get to Paris.

"15 minutes – that's the time when we will enter the house together. Sweep into the middle. Watch the corners – stay to the walls – check each closet, one at a time with the other 'man' as back-up." Sidney gave the orders and then they all moved out.

Luc, separated from Zosia, felt disconnected. Part of him was missing. He did not like this feeling. A discomfort level that had not existed within him before began rising to the surface. In his mind he knew she could take care of herself, but in his heart he was the one who wanted to protect her to make sure she'd stay safe. He 'stuffed it" down, as he had heard the Americans say so many times. The Lieutenant was right. They had to pair up in order to survive – the soldier's training backed up by the "ally's" innate knowledge of the land and of the language.

"On y va?" Luc said to his partner.

"Ready and willing", Billy answered.

Clearing one room at a time, they moved like clockwork. People had been living here. Cigarette butts littered the floor – some were stubbed out on burled walnut tables and cherry book shelves. Wineglasses and bottles lay on the delicate upholstered chairs and settees. Broken glass and bric-a-brac cluttered the floors. With a quick glance Luc realized what damage the bombings had done and what the occupied Germans had done. Beneath the destruction and damage the owners had tried to protect what was once theirs.

Portraits had been moved into one backroom – taken off the walls and covered with canvas and placed behind an old pie table bench. A feather duster and broom stood in the corner of what must have been the dining room. The corner hutch was stocked full of the best china as well as bric-a- brac and one statue or vase inside the other – not for use – but for protection. An old iron key lock made the door permanently shut.

An uneasy awareness enveloped Luc. His instinct took over. He motioned for Tim to stop. The oak door was shut in front of him. Slowly he pushed it open with the rifle butt. No one fired. He entered first and flattened himself against the adjacent wall. Pushing the door wide open to swing against the back of the door, Billy stepped over the threshold.

"My God" he gasped.

Eight German soldiers – officers in dress uniform were dead. Their heads were tilted downward onto their plates. Their wine glasses were half full and their bread broken in half. A clean bullet hole was in the back of each of their heads.

The smell of their last meal and of death filled the closed room. Billy put his hand over his mouth and nose, but could not turn his eyes away from this bizarre death scene. Who had executed them? Why? Where were the executioners now?"

Luc was already at one of the two exits. The first was a hall leading to the rest of the house. He could already hear the voices of the others. The other exit was to a back staircase. With his back flat against the inside, he carefully climbed. He could see the staircase circle up above and he could see no movement.

At the top of the stairs was a narrow hall. Room by tiny room he went until he neared the second to last room. Again, bric-a-brac and paintings lined whatever wall space or bureau space was available. This second room to the end opened up into an expansive bedroom, sitting room, and an atypical balcony which overlooked the back of the house - the south side of pastures and walled gardens.

The room had a small almost child size bed in the corner – hidden by walls of armoires, desks, bureaus, and tables. It was as though anything of value – sentimental or monetary – was squeezed into these rooms. Studying this personal act of preservation made him think of his mother and sister. On his last visit to them they too had taken to preserving what was special to their family. As more and more itinerant Germans passed through their doors more and more items found their way upstairs to Francoise's and Juliette's rooms.

"You are not American?"

Luc jumped around. A German Colonel dressed in full dress uniform stood directly behind him. Luc now realized he must have been behind the door when he entered.

"Cat got your tongue, as they say." The Colonel said disdainfully as he continued to point the Lugar directly at Luc's forehead. "But then again you are not American – just the rifle is." He pointed to the M1 which stood relaxed at Luc's side. "Francais – peut-etre."

"Oui, je suis francais" Luc answered to stall him. To make him think he was here on his own – to make him think he understood nothing in English.

"I was going to surrender to you – but obviously, that has changed. I need to wait for the Americans. Someone of rank – perhaps a General." He fumbled in his top pocket for cigarettes. He pulled out the empty packet, crumpled it and dropped it on the floor. "Gone. The hell with it. These damn Gallois are hideous. You – you have any American cigarettes.

Soon I'll have all that I need. I hear they feel they have to treat prisoners well. What fools!

Luc looked impassively at him. On the word 'cigarettes' he feigned a questioning expression. "Cigarettes vous desirez des cigarettes."

"Oui, tu me comprends. Les cigarettes – je les veux."
Luc made a face as if to ask permission to go for his inside pocket. The Colonel nodded 'yes'. Luc gave him his pack of blue Gallois.

"You have an American rifle but no American cigarettes?" he snarled. "I'll take them and then get rid of you." He smiled as he said this.

Luc smiled back. You "'Salaud, bastard" he thought as he waited for the right moment. As soon as the Colonel bent his head down to light the cigarette, Luc would move. Almost at the same time, each man heard a creak on the stairs. The colonel swung and shot as Luc bent his knees to jump.

"Arretez – pas si vite." Stop if you don't want to die too – Frenchman.' He pointed the Luger at Luc as he bent down to pull the M1 away from Billy who laid clutching his kneecap and writhing in pain.

The only sound that filled the house was Billy's screams of pain. The others downstairs had stopped moving at the sound of the gunshot.

"How are you doing private? It could be worse. The pain will go away soon. Get in here. I need you to kill your friend. An accident of course. I'll find a higher up to surrender to." The German looked from one to the other. "After all, my men – did not die for nothing. They died willingly for the Furher, and I willingly helped them carry out their orders."

"Whatever was in the safe has to be real important." Luc thought.

The colonel kicked Billy into the room and motioned with the Luger for Luc to move over. "Move American – or I'll kick you in your knee. So stupid are you to think everyone has rights – equality. How naïve you all are."

In his tirade Luc had time to reach and loosen the rawskin tie which held the Colt 45 to his right leg. If he could swivel the revolver up in one quick movement, he would not have to draw the gun from the holster. It was an old cowboy trick he had seen in one of Gary Cooper's black and white movies.

The German placed his gun barrel at the base of Billy's skull. "Never mind. You do not have to kill your friend. I'll just kill him for you." He tightened his grip on the gun. "I will tell them this Frenchman did it. This collaborator. Then I will kill him with your rifle. Humorous – no. He does not understand a word."

"I do." The shots ran out. The first three shots hit him directly in the groin. Bent over in agony, he looked up to see the youngest Veignard daughter. She smiled as she shot the next three – one into his kneecap, one into his abdomen, and then waited a full three minutes to place the third directly through his forehead. The colonel lay dead. His blood oozed onto the red floral carpet.

Luc's hand was still on the handle of his Colt 45.

"Ne vous en inquietez pas. Je ne vous tuez pas." She said to Luc and as she bent over Billy she said, "I'll take care of you. You'll be O.K."

Luc looked into her impassive face. A child of thirteen, but she carried herself as a woman. He did not have to ask why.

"Drag him off my carpet. I do not like his blood. Then get the bandages in the next room over. Near the bed." She did not even look surprised that he knew English. Nothing got by her. That's why she was still alive.

As the others came up the stairs, he simply nodded his head and shrugged his shoulders to indicate "don't bother to ask".

Afterwards she showed them the safe, and they blew it open; it was understood that she would get word back to the Resistance and to the American Division commanders coming up that they were on their way.

"Do not bury the others. Drag them all out of my family's.." she paused. "My house... and far enough away so I cannot smell them."

She waited in the bombed out lower bedroom where Billy had been placed. They left some morphine and GI rations with her. Soon Billy would be on his way home – with both legs, if they moved him out in time

Chapter 17 - Off the Beaches - D-Day plus 3

The first wave, either dead, pinned down, or too shell-shocked to move, had still been on Omaha when Lieutenant Wilson's LCVP and others in the second wave approached the beach. All it took was one soldier here and there to begin to do something. No one waved a flag. No one shouted a plan. No one said you do it, but some, in single acts of courage began the movement off the beaches. Melvin Baron and Patrick O'Brien were two such men. Melvin Baron had held Stone's bazooka steady and shot right through the barbed wire at the precise spot for the Vierville Draw.

Soldiers from other companies saw the hole and slid through the wires. The Germans on the hill spotted them and concentrated fire on the Vierville Draw, but it was futile. The men who fled through the hole inched up the shrub-lined hill and into the line of German trenches. As a team of two, Baron and O'Brien blasted 'Shirley' again at a pillbox emplacement. Storming the smoking debris, they grabbed two German machine guns and fired them until empty into a trench of Germans situated as the first line of defensive for those American infantrymen who had tried to get off Omaha Beach.

Men in the 5th Company Infantry never knew their names. Those who saw them passed the word to one another once they had time to breathe and reflect on what had occurred. For many that happened on D-Day plus 2 or plus 3 or 30. They just knew they were alive because of one man, or a pair or a trio of men who single handedly decided to be the first to move – to act. And to act, they did. They realized they were a handful of lucky ones who had raced across 100 yards of beach and lived. Yet, to continue to live they had to escape through one of the 5 roads out….

****

What was left of Captain Hank Hudson's unit of Rangers acted without him. Sal, Aaron, and James Earl had crossed the flooded areas between Isigny and Trevieres. Neither outside nor inside the law of military behavior and rigidity, the trio of men considered themselves militia who had stayed alive by instinct, courage under fire, and luck. Sal Marchese did not want his to run out. Always a natural leader, he was made an official one when the Captain died. James Earl was a natural follower and Aaron Axelrod, a natural survivor who just wanted to record this event for history. Too analytical and timid to lead, he knew he could continue to stay alive if he relied on Sal's gut feeling.

"Where are we now Sal," Aaron asked as he took out his pencil and small black leather notebook.

"Close to 'la Madeleine' by the looks of the Captain's map." Sal bit down hard on a strip of beef jerky and followed it by a swing of 'calvados'. The brandy, courtesy of this half-standing Norman farmhouse, heated up his insides. The weather had changed. From bad to worse to miserable.

He had thought the bailout conditions were poor. Ike had given the 'green light', but no one could account for the blackness of the night drop, the winds, the poor visibility - and the raw-to-the-bone cold of Normandy. The hitting the beach weather was not much better. He expected sitting -on -the– concrete-steps heat, coming-off-the-sidewalk type weather of June days and nights in the Bronx.

"Who could play ball in these conditions?" Sal let a thought of home pass through his mind. He stuffed it down. The only ball they were playing was with grenades. As long as his arm held out, he'd lob them where they were needed.

Gale winds had begun two days after the landing. Cold rain had pelted them unmercifully. Their hands and fingers were so cold that they could barely pull the triggers on their M1's. Soaked and freezing cold, they had found shelter in abandoned bombed out houses. All had fireplaces but they could not take the chance of making a fire. Even in this fierce rain, the sight or smell of smoke would travel.

"Jesus, why didn't the army issue us gloves?" Aaron complained as he tried to get some circulation into his fingers.

"Don't take the Lord's name in vain." James Earl admonished. "You all wouldn't give it no mind if you always wasn't writin so much."

"Someday, you'll look back and find yourself forgetting. My story will make you remember."

"Hot damn. This is really what I want to remember – being in this frigging place with you two – Mr. Hollywood and Mr. Wood."

"Hey, there ain't no mor woods in Alabama – just fields. Nice fields – hot and so skin warm." James Earl's voice began to trail off.

Aaron thought, "It wasn't good to remember too much of home. Enough to know why you're fighting, but not enough to stop you from killing. Too much civilization – too much remembrance of 'civilized' society could stop a man's instinct which kicked in along with his razor-edge training as a killing machine."

"I wasn't talking about those kinds of 'woods'. Wooden, James Earl, like in Wooden head." Sal kidded. He wanted to keep him alive.

Sal had picked up a walkie-talkie and could get in communication with men from the 1th and 29th Divisions. He knew they had gotten off 'Utah' and 'Omaha'; some had reinforced the 82nd and 101st around and at Sainte Mere Eglise. Some joined the 7th Company and were pushing up to Cherbourg. The rest were heading for St. Lo.

Sal passed the calvados around. Aaron, taking no chances with blurred ink or wet pages, put into his plastic pouch his pencil and leather book. Precise to an exactness – he chose to write in pencil. Posterity had to know. He had to remember. By recording what happened, he prevented himself from having to live it. Each man had his own method of 'getting through it'. Aaron took a swig from the brown bottle before passing it over to James Earl who was eating slabs of bread spread with camembert cheese.

Sal, spreading out the Captain's silk map under a table in the farmhouse, showed his two men their location.

"We're here at La Madeleine. We've made it from the cliffs – here – at Pointe de la Percee – east over the flooded area to this village of La Madeleine. The way I figure it – we got two choices. We ultimately join up with the 7th company and shoot for Cherbourg. See that's north to the Channel and maybe back to England or at least an occupied position in a captured contained area or we join up with the 4th Division here – just a bit southeast at Carentan."

"Any chance we'll be pushed back to the beach head." Aaron said after studying the map carefully.

"There's always that possibility, but from all reports we have them forced to take a defensive position." Sal answered.

"Reinforcements?" James Earl's one word said it all.

"I remember the Captain saying we'd build mulberries at Avranches – here." Sal pointed to the far southwest of Cherbourg in a province called Brittany. "and here at Arromanches between the beach heads. "I just hope these winds won't whip them to shreds. The Captain said tanks and supplies would begin to unload from supply ships once we've gotten a foothold. If the waves and winds don't destroy our mulberry bridges, we'll have a man-made harbor. Who knows if the worst is over? We're doing a two-prong push. The harbor at Cherbourg and the man-made harbor at Avranches will get us backup equipment, ammo, and..."

"Gasoline?" Aaron asked.

"Right. Without gas we ain't moving our tanks. No tanks, then we might as well fold up our tents and go home."

"The gas will get us to 'Paree'." James Earl said.

"That's the plan, James Earl. Either into Paris or around it to Berlin. It's Ike's call. - depends on our supply lines."

"I vote for 'Carentan'. Hook up to the 4th and hang in there all the way to Paris!" Aaron exclaimed as he pointed to Paris a long way from Carentan but considerably shorter than to Hollywood California.

"Me too. This colored boy is gonna see Miss Josephine in Gay Paree." James Earl smiled.

"Hot dog, James Earl! You can introduce me to Josephine Baker. And when we get there, maybe the newsboys will have a camera I can use. I'd like footage of her and of Paris when it's liberated." Aaron mused.

"That's what I like about you, 'Hollywood' – always thinking ahead. Let the good times roll." James Earl said.

"Carentan. The 4th Division. Paris. Not necessarily in that order." Sal said as the bottle returned to him. He took a long gulp, put in the cork, and folded up his map. They were on the move again.

****

At D-day plus 3, Melvin Baron was sitting in a café in the tiny village of le Beau Moulin situated next to the banks of the river Torlonne. He was well behind enemy lines. The British had stopped their advance of Caen, yet the Americans were moving toward Cherbourg and St. Lo. Ahead of the front, O'Brien and Baron worked as a team. Independent and clear thinking, they advanced on their own taking out German communication lines and railroad tracks. The bridges they had kept intact. They knew the Americans would need them. Ike and de Gaulle thought alike. This war, unlike the last, will be won on the treads of the tank.

"Ike will need these bridges to get our tanks into or around Paris," Baron thought as he placed the walkie-talkie to his ear. Each of them had picked up walkie-talkies from dead Americans, but Baron had two – one American and one German. By listening to both he could follow the movements of men on both sides. The American lingo and orders were easy to follow; the German more difficult, yet the basics were there.

They had put a most audacious plan into action. The village of le Beau Moulin had a bridge across one of the rivers the Germans had used to create the flood areas between Isigny and Trevieres. From the German walkie-talkie communication, Baron had learned that Le Beau Moulin was not well-fortified, stood serene and far enough away from the front to seem untouched by war, and was guarded by only a few German soldiers, whose orders were to defend the bridge. If they could not, they were ordered to blow it before the Allies came.

Baron, wearing a German Colonel's uniform, was seated in the far corner of the café de Simone next to its back door. As he gingerly sipped his cognac, Baron, blond, blue eyed, tall and superior, looked the stereotypical member of the Arian race - except for the front flap of his uniform's pocket which covered a single M1 bullet-hole. He casually patted the flap down and placed the dead colonel's hat on the table in front of him. The luger, along with his new identity papers as Wilheim von Leich, rested in the coat holster and inside pocket of the German uniform but strapped to his ankle was Baron's American issue small revolver.

The French woman – the owner of Café de Simone glanced over at him as he loosened the tight German collar of the uniform. That gesture, his minimal French, and the fact that she had never seen him before placed her on guard. Simone knew every German within fifty kilometers, and this man was not one of them. When he spoke to her in German, she pretended as usual not to understand. This had served her well for close to four years. She listened in on all her German patrons' conversations, and they were unaware that she understood every word. Every aspect of troops, movements, and fortifications she sent on to her friend and fellow resistance fighter Madame Forte, head of the maternity ward at the Hospital in Trevieres.

Madame Simone thought to herself "Is he Gestapo, this quiet stern German Colonel? Why is he here now? Does he not have some place more important to go? After all, the invasion has begun. What in my little village can possibly interest him other than retaliation or the secret button which will detonate our bridge over the Torlonne?"

She continued to sweep the floor as she thought of the detonation button. Simone, Madame Forte, and a chosen few of the Trevieres resistance cell knew where the button was located. With the final invasion underway, Simone was well aware that only she could prevent the detonation. She would allow nothing to go awry because of one single German sipping his cognac with such superiority. To kill him- with or without impunity, she must.

"Un autre?' Madame Simone asked him.

Melvin looked at her blankly trying with great difficulty to keep his face impassive.

She pointed to his nearly empty glass.

"Non merci", he wanted another to steady his nerves, but he could not afford for the edge to be taken off his keen senses.

She nodded and backed away. Something was not quite right with this German. The ones she had served rarely thanked her and although he had spoken hardly any French –what he did speak did not have a German accent. "Could he be Austrian.?" she thought as she stood behind the counter just in front of the kitchen.

It was one o'clock, and soon her regulars would start drifting in. Hers was the only kitchen in Le Beau Moulin stocked with the essentials for a tasty omelette, un pot-au- feu, and des tartes de pommes. For the last two days she had cow carcasses and lamb legs – salted and hanging in her smokehouse behind the café. Ready for when the Americans or British liberated her village. In fact she had one slow cooking and covered in the back ovens. That's how certain she was that they were coming.

"After all, the Americans boys will be hungry for an excellent French 'repas'. They will not mind that that it was the blast of their bombs which killed these animals as they grazed in between the 'bocage'." She mused.

"These Americans what will they look like?" she almost spoke out loud. She had heard they were big strapping boys. She had stopped sweeping and was drying dishes as she saw the pair of Germans enter the café. With their shift changing, it was their time to again be eating her food and paying for it with old useless German 'marks'. Worth nothing more than the paper it was written on. She had no choice but to accept it – and accept it willingly, if she wished to continue business.

One sat down, and the other marched up to demand a brandy from her 'bouteille de cent annees'.

"For our victory-going into Paris and keeping it, or continuing on to Berlin. Either way we want only the 'best' this time Madame." He said in his thickly accented French.

"Bien sur. Certainement," she smiled broadly.

"A Votre (Notre) Victoire" she added as she thought 'your' victory, never – 'our' victory for the French – yes. 'Vive la France'.

They lifted their glasses and let the hundred year old 'calvados' slide warmly and fragrantly down the back of their throats. Melvin did not lift his glass.

The other two noticed this new officer staring at them. They said something to one another before purposely lifting their glasses to him. Baron nodded and lifted his glass. He had no clue what the French woman had said or what the one German had requested of her.

She was certain he was Gestapo from the way he stared and said little. There was no attempt at civility, but then again once the Germans had occupied France their façade of gentle persuasion gave way to force and persecution. If a Frenchman didn't willingly bend to their demands and change to the 'German' way, then they were broken – crushed as though with a Tiger Tank.

Madame classified her people into three kinds of Frenchmen – those who resisted, those who collaborated, and those who sat in the middle and waited for the winds of war to destroy one side or the other. No one would have to wait anymore. As the Allies finally began their invasion, they had brought with them the winds of a century. Never before had there been such a storm to churn and upturn the Channel and coasts of Normandy and Brittany.

She, like all the rest of her countrymen, knew her history. She thought of the battle of 1066, and this time she had her money on the English. They would conquer these waves with their armada and take over French soil, not in the name of England, not in the name of Germany, but this time, in the name of France.

She smiled and raised her glass again to the two Germans by the window and to the one, alone near her back door. Two returned her smile; the other did not. She decided that when the pair returned to their post on the bridge and before the next shift arrived, she would kill this lone unsmiling, so civilized 'member of the Aryan race'.

After all the years of German occupation she wanted to see American or English soldiers cross over her bridge. She desired to set free her French, American, and English flags hidden under a floor board beneath her stove and let them fly once again in French air. She could almost taste the approaching freedom. She was not going to let it slip away for one moment longer that it took because of some transient Gestapo agent.

"Which resistance fighter had he tortured into confessing about the secret button at Le Beau Moulin? Of course, this Colonel now must know of our intention to block the detonation of all the bridges - over all rivers in Normandy and Brittany. We will not allow the German tanks and the Wermarch to retreat from our provinces, blowing the bridges behind them to slow the Allied advance through France and into Germany."

Madame looked over and the Gestapo man again, and smelled a nervous air. He was not as cool and calm as his exterior seemed to convey. His hand was steady as he reached into his top pocket. He let the cape, which covered his shoulders, fall to the chair. As he lifted the flap of his chest jacket pocket, she thought she detected a finger size hole in the gray wool fabric. He pulled a cigarette from the pack, placed it in the side of his mouth, and flipped off the head of a gold cigarette lighter. The brief flame illuminated his face and she noticed beads of sweat on his upper lip and forehead. He shut the lighter with his thumb and pulled the cigarette from his mouth with the same thumb and index finger. She had never seen any German smoke a cigarette in that manner.

The two in the corner must have seen that too, for the first seated one got up and left through the front door. The Gestapo man nonchalantly glanced out the back side window as he saw the German soldier look back over his shoulder as he made his way toward the bridge.

She walked again to his table and asked again if he wanted another drink. This time she pointed to the 100 year old 'calvados' but lowered her voice and said, 'Il y a une hirondelle…'" She waited for the coded Resistance response of "..qui chante neanmoins."

Melvin looked at her blankly. He did not understand what she had said, but his gut told him she was waiting for some sort of sign from him. He did not have much time. He didn't think the two Germans in the corner had bought his impersonation.

Baron turned and shouted over from the window to the soldier in the corner to find out from this "Frenchwoman" the best her kitchen had to offer. He was wet, tired, and hungry and he had to get some quick but excellent nourishment before meeting General Rommel.

At the sound of Rommel's name the French woman and the remaining German soldier took notice. Simone stepped back and the German began to rise. It was at that moment she caught the red letters of the word "Lucky' on the pack of cigarettes that he pushed down into his pocket. Her eyes were riveted on the hole that he quickly covered over with the flap of the pocket.

On closer look she realized the dark area around the pocket was a bloodstain and the hole was definitely made by a bullet. Her eyes met his blue steady gaze. There was a question behind that gaze so she took a chance. She knew he was not French, and his German was perfect. She knew that he thought she knew no German. If he was not French and was not really German, he had to be American or British.

She began to hum a melody and quickly sang a low lyric.. "My Country tis of thee….." it was the only English speaking words she knew, but if he was who she now thought he was, he'd know the rest. She waited and stopped singing. The German from the window table was approaching and Baron could see the other German returning from the bridge with two others.

He gambled. His dog tags were not around his neck. Those were with O'Brien where he had hidden his Jewish star in the knot of a weeping willow tree on the banks of the river. The only thing American on him was his pack of Lucky Strikes. He pulled the edge of the pack from his pocket and sang "....sweet land of Liberty of thee I sing."

She had her answer.

"Soldat", she addressed the infantry guard who was now close to the Baron's table. "Venez, Suivez -moi dans la cuisine. J'ai un gigot sale – surtout pour vous.' She indicated to both of them.

The German soldier clicked his heels and nodded to Baron still seated calmly at the back table. "This sneaky Frenchwoman had been holding out on the salted lamb, but now she seems to have a change of mind. He said in German as he passed Baron and then laughed. "They all have a change of mind. Some French have it sooner than others - that is all," he continued as they both followed Madame into the kitchen. "Let this be the last meal of this 'salaud'," she thought as she led the way.

Melvin Baron nodded graciously to the soldier and gestured him to go first. Following behind, Melvin touched his knife beneath the cloak he had tossed casually over his arm.

****

Beneath the kitchen in the hidden root cellar Baron could hear the boots of the three soldiers above him. They strode in - in confidence; then their boots abruptly stopped. Muffled dialogue all in French issued as Madame tended her gigot in the oven. The succulent smell wafted down through the floorboards. Screeching out their epitaphs, the German voices were getting more and more excited, but Madame Simone continued to peel her potatoes. Finally, Madame raised her voice in exasperation, and the three sets of boots raced out the door.

She knocked on the floor three times, their agreed upon signal. Baron wiped the knife on the dead soldier's jacket and slid open the floorboards. He jabbed the knife into the floor and lifted himself out.

"Ca va?" Madame asked as she wiped her potato knife on her soiled apron.

"Oui, ca va bien." Melvin answered.

The 'ratta – tat-tat' of a machine gun just outside the café made both of them go to opposite sides of the kitchen door. The sound of footsteps came again. Across the café floor they steadily approached the kitchen. They stopped just outside the oak door. Someone had begun to push it open. The nose of a machine gun followed by an army issue green sleeve pushed the door completely open. Concentrating on the sleeve and the gun, Melvin almost did not catch sight of the knife just coming down.

He yelled in German to Madame Simone, and gripped her wrist before her knife plunged into the arm, which held the gun. A looked of fear crossed her face as her eyes met Baron's.

"What the hell." O'Brien exclaimed. "You God damn Jewish Kraut."

Melvin laughed – he had never heard sweeter words.
****

For her first encounter with Americans she had prepared a sumptuous lunch and brought out her best bottles of wine. Together they sat and broke bread – one 'Jewish kraut', one 'catholic Mick', one 'frog', and one less bridge blown.

****

Sandy could see the high steeple of the church in Villers-Bocage. They had passed through Bayeux the day before – one day ahead of the Americans who had liberated it on D-Day plus one. With the Apache scouting ahead, Sandy and his men seemed to be slipping through the lines and advancing well ahead of any Allied troops. The German forces had come alive and were not only digging in defensively, but also counter-attacking. Rommel's 21st Panzer Division was attempting to cut between the American and British forces. Sandy figured his men would circumvent Caen and push down between it and Falaise before Rommel closed the gap.

The Liverpool boys moved through the rubble with ease. The fighting between doorways and walls suited them to a tee. The Welshman provided the heavy fire of backup and used a bazooka to blow holes in any German nests. Most of their orders were coming through the American 5th Company coming off of Omaha Beach. The Apache communicated with existing pockets of Indians who translated their locations and their orders in their native tongue. Sandy could hear through his walkie-talkie and their new Becky radio transmissions that Montgomery was beginning to take on some heavy resistance because he had not pushed forward on Day 1.

"It's best not to head for Caen," he thought. We'll travel well south of it. Since we're neither American nor British, we'll glean orders from each side's best." Their missions were what Sandy had devised – secretive, ahead of the lines – very much tailored to what he had always done: blowing up German strong holds, destroying communication links, creating havoc, and passing the information along. Alone and without an official company, they needed no more than the three-hour increments of sleep they had gotten for the last three days. With the Liverpool lads on guard, they made a makeshift camp beyond the outer 'bocage' of Villers-Bocage.

The Resistance Cells, once they knew D-Day had finally arrived, had made the paratroopers' and infantry soldiers' jobs easier by creating all out chaos. In this safe haven, the Staffordshire farm boy decided to pull off his 'Queen and Country army togs' and slip on the absent farmer's old shirt and pants in order to dig for potatoes in a deserted farmhouse field just outside the village. It did not take long for him to be spotted.

A bike rider nonchalantly called out to him in French and when the Staffordshire farm boy didn't answer but just waved, the Frenchman got off his bike and walked it out into the field. The Staffordshire man continued to dig for the half-frozen potatoes from the season before. He had made sure he had a potato in each hand when the man stopped in front of him. The Frenchman took a long hard look and knew this farmer in front of him was no Frenchman.

"It is hot in Suez," he said to him. The Staffordshire boy looked surprised.

"Well it sure in Hell isn't hot here."

That wasn't the answer the Resistance bike rider expected. At least that was not what they had said over the BBC radio airwaves the night before D-Day. "The dice are on the carpet' had been the rest of the code that told the Resistance people in the area of Bayeux that liberation was on its way. This man dressed in a farmer's attire certainly did not respond according to plan. And this lone French bike rider was well aware that if anyone was going to liberate his countrymen, it would be the 'likes' of such men as this one in front of him – who stood potatoes in hand, ready once more to fight his way out.

"Thanks for stopping by,"the Frenchman with impeccable English said.

He laughed. "You're certainly not one of Rommel's boys."

The boy shoved the potatoes into his pockets when he realized this French bike rider was Resistance. The boy believed him because he knew Rommel had left Normandy on June 5th and had returned on D-Day plus 1. That information was only privy to the Allied high command and the Resistance members in this area.

The Staffordshire boy's group had decoded the news from the Apache's translation over the walkie-talkie airwaves. The key Resistance men and women already knew it. They also knew that the Das Reich, the 2nd SS Panzer Division, had finally received orders from Rommel to move out for Normandy. His new German Tiger tanks had been loaded onto railway cars in the south of France in a little town called Montauban.

When the Staffordshire boy had brought the man back to their camp, Sandy told Harry to code up the information in Apache 'tongue' and send it along via 'Becky'. The Resistance man said it could wait after a bottle or two of wine, some camembert, and bread. He produced it all from the straw basket on the front of his bike from which only the two 'baguettes' visibly protruded.

"Weeks ago a resistance cell in the Montauban siphoned off all the axle oil of those railroad cars and replaced it with abrasive powder. Every car has seized up. Rommel's Das Reich won't be here for at least two weeks."

"I'll drink to that, Sandy laughed, and the rest of the men had their first laugh and first meal since they landed in France.

Chapter 18 D-Day plus 5

The Veignard girl's directions to the safe house had been precise. Compact and intact it stood in spite of the bombed out houses, crater like terrain, and incessant mist surrounding it. Once inside Zosia spread the maps and letters out on the solid oak kitchen table as they all crowded around. Zosia, Juliette, and Luc, the ones fluent in German, read sections of the map and the letters found in the Veignard safe. Sidney and Tony concentrated on the map's military symbols, and the two Indians looked at the size of any woodlands, streams, and rivers. Sidney, as leader of their team of ten, spoke first.

"These flooded areas, from here to Carentan, are man made by the Germans." He pointed to another section. "These two appear surrounded by water. We gotta get around or between them. A route – to the East and then South ought to get us by the worst of it. At all costs – we have to avoid St. Lo, and Caen." He looked up at his men, "From what our troops have told us, those cities have either been bombed or are being bombed; Bayeux is in British hands."

Zosia and Juliette nodded in agreement. Luc held up his letters. "These confirm the flood areas, and also tell of a small bridge crossing the flooded area which is guarded by only a handful of German soldiers." He pointed over Sidney's shoulder at the map. "so, we can cross here and continue to Carentan."

""From Carentan we can move southeast through the village of Les Oubeaux," Zosia added as she concentrated on her section of the map. Her large hands and long fingers gently grazed Luc's right hand. Juliette was aware of the electricity that seemed to pass between the two of them. Juliette glanced up from the map to see Janusz's eyes. Neither he nor Christian had missed the action. Would that compromise their mission or strength it? That was the question that seemed to rise above the table. None of the Americans caught the slight hesitation as their fingers touched.

John noticed Juliette's pause, but he thought she was just thinking. The normally quiet Cherokee added, "A forest is here. Good cover for us if we need it." Thomas nodded in approval. He and John were more comfortable in the open areas rather than in the cities which caught and confined them- somehow stripping them of their identities.

"Troop concentrations exist at Montmartin, Neuilly, and La Folie according to these letters." She held them up as she continued. "We should be able to travel east toward Caen yet south of these flooded areas." Juliette pointed to that area between Isigny and Trevieres that Sidney had mentioned.

"Any questions?" Sidney asked. All took one last look at the map and committed to memory the terrain from Sainte Mere Eglise, to Carentan, to just southeast of Trevieres where the map ended. Christian had noticed a large green area on the far end of the map, 'la Foret de Cerisy', which fell directly between Bayeux and St Lo. "That's where we'll hide if we need refuge," he thought.

"O.K." Sidney nodded one last time.

"D'accord" Luc answered.

"On y va" Tony added without thinking.

Sidney ripped the map into sections, walked over to the

large stone fireplace and dropped them piece by piece into the small teepee fire the Apache and the Cherokee had built. He was thankful that the massive chimney and roof of this resistance member's house was still intact. One by one Luc, Zosia, and Juliette dropped the German letters into the flames. They had already memorized any names they would need to know.

Janusz gazed at the trio and for a moment his mind played a trick on him. It was September of 1939, and he was still safe at home in Poland celebrating what would be his last birthday with his mother, father, sister, Zosia, and Stanislaus. The flames of the candles on that special last cake his mother had baked seemed to waiver in this fireplace's flames. Those were the beginning flames. Soon, they were consumed by another fiercer set of flames – those in the Polytech University wing when his father, Martin, and he had looked one last time at the Bridges of Warsaw. Those maps – painstaking 'blueprints' – also had been burned, but not before the 'maps' had been committed to memory. However, the flames could not be put out. The burning of Warsaw was to still to come.

Five years had passed since that day. His twenty-third birthday would mark this next 25th of September. Five years of Hitler's flames of hate had eaten their way through all of Europe. Could they finally put out them out - extinguish once and for all. The end was in sight. The question was would he be alive to see it? Would it be finally over or would Communist Russia be the next tyrant to fight? Janusz pulled his thoughts back into the present and turned away from the flames. He saw Christian do the same.*

"I need some shut eye. You take over." Sidney handed the walkie-talkie over to Tony. "Find out what reinforcements have come off Omaha, and if they're between us and Bayeux."

Cutting through the divisions, they had traveled beyond Carentan into a tiny village called 'la Fourchette' or the fork in English. With their small group they moved quickly on the side roads and avoided the German blocks on such primary routes as D544. After all, Sidney knew that was the plan - the plan to get a small group of men to Paris before the rest of the Allied Forces.

Sidney and Tony did not want to think of their original stick of men. Alive less than a week ago – yet long dead by June

11. How could five days change so much. It seemed that those men were slightly less than faint strangers – ghosts of another lifetime, and that these "foreigners' were family. He had not written to his wife since he got the orders for the mission. He told himself that he did not want to worry her, but he knew it more than that. He did not want to think about her – to see her face that might muddle up his decisions. His own death he had come to terms with. If he died doing his duty, that was how it was to be, but the pain and grief it would cause his wife and parents was something he did not want to think about.

His family at this point in time and place were these men around him. "Each one", he thought, "has kept all of us alive." He looked at each member of his team. "The Frenchman and his sister know the roads and villages like the veins in their hands. We can bypass any German strongholds. Both of them and the Polish woman speak German and can keep us in front of the enemy." He looked around at the only three Americans left, an Apache, a Cherokee, and a kid from Brooklyn. "God Bless 'em. God bless us all," he said to himself.

Lastly, Lieutenant Sidney Smith glanced over at the two foreign ex-patriots, and wondered how Christian and Janusz had such savvy. "No second guessing them. I just need a few more good men to fill out this team. An even dozen is want the Generals in England ordered," he fell asleep thinking.
****

Tony interrupted Sidney's sleep less than forty minutes later. "Hey Lieutenant, guess what I picked up – Italian with a Bronx accent."

"Give the walkie-talkie to Zosia." Sidney said as he woke up from a dead sleep.

"What's his name?"

"Salvatore."she said

'Sal', Tony answered her.

Zosia clicked the hand held unit – on and off. She was listening for any slip of and accent in either his Italian or English. Although she was not yet used to an 'American' accent, she knew neither Sal's English nor his Italian had any trance of a German one. Zosia turned to Sidney. "He wants to know if our orders are to continue on to Paris. He has no more company. All were killed."

"Ask him how." Sidney instructed Zosia. She posed the question then waited for the longwinded answer. "He says he came in with the 2nd Company Rangers and his commander and the rest of his unit were killed while climbing the cliffs at Pointe de la Percee. He's got only two men – one from Alabama and one from California."

Sidney took the large cylindrical gun metal gray 'walkie-talkie' from Zosia. "Hey Sal, what's the capital of Alabama and of California."

"Jesus, is this a god-damn history test. My test has been to stay alive and not answer ass-hole questions from some 'fuckin' lieutenant."

"Just 'Lieutenant or Sir' will do, soldier." Sidney began to question even if he even wanted such a man on his team.

"Yeah, like an initiation. O.K. California is Sacramento." Sal kept the receiver down as he shouted – "James Earl, what's Alabama's capital?" He waited for James Earl's laconic answer as he spoke into the walkie-talkie. "One of my guys is from there. He says….."

"I got a test, lieutenant. May I?" Tony reached for the walkie-talkie. So, youse from New York – like in its capital, New York City?"

"No ass-hole not Albany – I'm from New York – the Bronx."

"So how are the Dodgers doing? Has Joe Dimaggio hit his usual homers?" Tony asked.

"Listen buddy, I'm not joining up with any unit whose fuckin guys don't know a 'Yankee' from a 'Bum'. Joe's hitting nothing. He's not even playing just fighting the Krauts like the rest of us. And with my luck, pal – you're from Brooklyn." Sal stopped talking.

"He's legit." Tony handed the walkie-talkie back to the Lieutenant.

"O.K. Martino: the mound, first, second, short stop, and home. When you get there, I'll ask questions you answer with those positions. That way we'll know your coordinates, and no one else will – even if they're listening in." Sidney stated as he was drawing a map in the dirt; he motioned to Luc and Zosia to look over his shoulder. He thought to himself that he could use three more men. "That'd make thirteen - an unlucky thirteen." The baseball diamond was in the dirt. He quickly asked a series of questions to the soldier on the other end of the walkie-talkie. He had pinpointed him to be 'behind the plate' – just south of La Fourchette.

"Bring them in." he gave the order to Zosia and Luc.

"Tell Sal the 'bambino' sent you. He should answer – 'How is Ruth?'"

****

Luc and Zosia had to backtrack to an area already covered. Although they knew what obstacles lay in their path, it was hard for them to concentrate. Almost eight long days and nights ago they had been in one another's arms – spent their honeymoon night in Madame Blanche's farmhouse. To each it seemed a lifetime had passed. They dare not touch one another for fear of giving in to the yearning each one felt. By doing so they could risk the lives of not only their present new family, but their past and future ones as well. Their mission was to get to Paris at all cost, find the papers of the Katyn Massacre, show them to General de Gaulle or General Le Clerc and then bring those documents out of France. Both had seen and tasted enough of life to know what was real and what was not, and they each had that rare ability to be moved by the heart or by the head. These were not the times for the heart to lead, but for the head to take control. Luc and Zosia knew that in order to succeed and survive they had to remain objective and analytical. If they lost sight of their mission and let their own desires take over, they and the other members of the team would die. Neither was willing to take that chance.

"Zosia, we're outside of La Fourchette. There's a fork about one kilometer down that road beyond the pasture hill." Luc pointed straight ahead. "We'll meet at the exact hedgerow nearest the fork in the two roads leading into town." Each knew the password and the three American soldiers they were looking for. They nodded to one another.

Zosia had chosen to walk on the narrower of the two roads. Her dark baggy trousers, barely touching the top of her boots, the heavy gray sweater and a brown 'blouson' made her seem like a Norman. Tall, erect, and like a true Viking she walked. Occasionally she pulled her brown beret down in place to cover her hacked off hair - now shaggy and matted with dirt. In her hand with nails clumped with dirt, she carried a satchel with four frozen potatoes.

With a half a kilometer more until the fork by La Fourchette, she scanned both sides of the road and the nearby fields. "No signs of any Americans. In fact, no signs of life." She thought. A half a dozen abandoned small farmhouses dotted the countryside. She had seen the name of 'Didier' on one of them – that would be her name if anyone questioned her.

As she stopped near a large boulder to tie her bootlace, she skimmed the landscape in front of her as she emphatically double laced the knot. Her satchel of potatoes rested on the ground near her right foot. She had heard nothing – yet her eyes caught a set of high brown pull-up boots to her right. She gently put the loop of the sack over her right wrist and turned to her left. Another set of German boots appeared in her peripheral vision. As she began to stand, an arm grabbed her by the waist and another slapped over her mouth. The one behind lifted her off her feet and the weight of their bodies slammed into the large boulder behind them. As his hand slipped from her mouth, she screamed. The arm around her waist tightened and she felt the air push out of her.

"You're not going to fight us, Fraulein." The soldier to her right said. "I knew there was a woman beneath those pants."

"A nice strong French girl like you." The other one added in a drunken slur. "Parlez-vous francais?" his beer soaked breathe spat at her.

"We don't need any French – for this. Do we?" the strong one behind her added. They all laughed.

You'd think they'd pick up some German after all these years." The beer breath one said.

"These French are so superior." The dark haired one on her left added. "These frogs either collaborate with us to feed their stomachs or defy us to get themselves killed. Which are you sweetheart?" he spat out in German.

"She doesn't know what we're saying." The one behind said as he took his hand off Zosia's mouth.

"There's no one around for her to even scream to. I say we drag her behind the bocage over there."

Yeah, the ditch is soft – like a bed, non?" beer breath laughed.

"I like them stupid." Said man behind as he tightened his grip and began to drag her.

"Wait a second, I got another joke for you," he continued in German. "You know why the 'frogs' planted so many trees in Paris."

The two others stopped and looked over at their fellow soldier. Zosia thought, "I hope the punch line is a good one. Good enough for him to loosen his grip." She could feel the cold steel of Stanislaus' knife in her left boot. Janusz had slipped it in when she left. "Because we Germans like to walk in the shade."

All three roared with laughter. At that moment he loosened his grip enough for her to push him back into the boulder. He lunged for her head to get a grip on her hair. All he got was her beret and a knife in his belly. She swung around to her right and let the sack with the potatoes fly into 'beer breath's face. She tightened her muscles and dropped to the ground, for she feared a blow from the soldier to her left. She rolled to the left to knock him off his feet, but the only contact she made was with a lifeless body. Over her head a black arm lunged for 'beer breath' who had pulled out his luger. A black hand grasped the drunken soldier's wrist and twisted it. He dropped the gun and staggered forward. At that moment, Zosia heard a snap and the drunken soldier's scream. He did not cry out for long, for the next sound she heard was a splat as the black arms lifted the soldier off his feet and swung his head into the boulder.

The black hand, covered with blood, extended to her to help her off her feet. "Alabama. I presume." She said in perfect English.

He was surprised. So lady like and so lethal. "Plain – James Earl, ma'am."

"You do good work, James Earl." Zosia said matter-of-factly as he looked from one dead soldier to another. Her eyes went beyond to the hedgerow where her own life might have ended once they were through with her. From behind it stepped Luc and two others — white skinned, but in the same uniform as the American in front of her. She smiled broadly. She bent over the German soldier behind the boulder, put her foot on his groin to pull Stanislaus' knife out of his abdomen, and whipped his blood off on his own shirt. Sliding the knife back into her boot, she stepped over his body and began to cross to the bocage and to Luc.

With these three new men in the ballgame, Sidney knew the push toward Paris was again underway. He quickly analyzed them again as in terms of chess. He stuffed down the memory of how he and Marge would play chess on the white front porch. Neither one would talk; it was enough that they were together. When summer turned to fall and the October nights became too cold, they would move inside the comfortable living room and sit in front of the fireplace. He shook his head to dislodge the memory of another time, another place, and another lifetime ago.

"James Earl is definitely a pawn," Sidney was now thinking as an American officer. "He'll do what I tell him - no questions asked. Sal's the opposite. To take orders was a given, yet he seems like Tony, the kind of 'kid' who always needs to know 'why'. More street-wise and a quicker 'pawn'. One of these New York kids just might be the first one behind the German barricades in Paris and get himself 'Kinged' at the end of this game." He glanced over at Aaron Axelrod. "That one's a 'knight' or rook in the game chess. He seems unpredictable, too analytical, jumping three moves ahead in his mind. This guy wants not only to know 'why', but 'how' and perhaps 'when'. Not to do it, but to keep his own ass safe. He's not a follower - smart, but not a leader. There's something about him." Subconsciously, Lieutenant Sidney Smith was patting the pouch beneath his jacket.

Sal picked up on it. "So Lieutenant what's inside the pouch? Anything special, I gotta know about."

The others looked with much more than curiosity at this new man. Then, they looked back at the lieutenant.

"Nothing that concerns you soldier."

"No skin off my nose, Lieutenant. I just lost one commander. I gotta do a favor for him in Paris. Didn't know if I'd have to do one for you." Sal answered casually.

His direct question did not go unnoticed by them. Luc and Juliette wondered if he was a very clever agent and Zosia, Janusz, and Christian did not trust him. Would any of these three new men hold up under fire or under Gestapo torture if captured by the enemy? Janusz thought as he recalled the faces of his mother and his sister.

"You need to know something and that something is that we'll get you to Paris. Come Hell or high water." Sidney stated. "Let me add one more important piece of information. We'll get to Paris before the Allies."

Sidney did not state what they already knew. Paris would be defended at all costs. As the heart and symbol of a Free France, the Germans would not release her without a fight.

"At this point, Private - that's it. The less you know, the safer you'll be if captured by the enemy."

Aaron Axelrod looked over at his brash friend who was always like a dog with a bone. Aaron knew better than to even ask. He realized the Lieutenant was hedging his bets.

"And the last point," Sidney matter-of-factly said, "if I'm dead and you're the only one left out of the other twelve, rip this pouch off my neck and put its contents in yours. Take my dog tags and add it to the pouch and put my bracelet around your wrist..." Luc placed his hand on his shoulder, and Sidney stopped himself from saying "..and get yourself to Paris and a resistance fighter named "Moliere"

"Sounds like the makings of a script", Axelrod added.

"And in this script is written the safety and freedom for many – too many to imagine, and too many to make light of," Sidney looked through Axelrod. 'His superiority might get us all killed,' he thought.

Without any more discussion he opened his pouch and took out the silk map and pointed to the various towns that they had come through and would need to go around before the Germans started to pull the draw string on their own pouch. He did not want to be in the situation where he had only one exit –

an exit that the German Army had predicted. Sidney told them what they knew about the area between them and Caen.

Luc and Zosia did not need to hear or see the map again. Luc knew the terrain like the back of his hand and Zosia had learned nearly as much through her briefings in de Gaulle's outer offices in London. For the back roads and nuances of Normandy and the roads to Paris, she could rely on Luc or Juliette.

Both were sizing up the new additions to their team. They had seen James Earl in action and had no doubts about his ability as a soldier. To blend in – to be part of the landscape was essential as they passed through the land. James Earl would stand out – not just because of his size but because of his color. Unlike the Apache and the Cherokee, James Earl could not be used as a scout, and they doubted he had the instinct and ability to read the 'land'.

The Indians also served as communicators for all the languages they knew, Luc and Zosia could not talk over the airwaves. The Germans had just as many people who would understand what they were saying in French, in Italian, or in English. But these special native American languages they knew nothing of. Eisenhower was clever when he placed these men in special commando units to hit the beach. The Allies were equally shrewd when they made up commando units of Poles and German Jews – different nationalities and religions that had a special reason to fight and unique abilities to enable them to be effective when they landed on French soil. They had something to prove – not only to the Germans, but to the Americans and the rest of the world.

Sal, too had something to prove, but his brashness was for himself. He was one of the unique ones who seemed to actually enjoy the fight. Born with the knowledge and strength of a city kid, he would have peripheral vision whether on the streets of the new York or the streets of Paris. His antennas were always out when his feet hit the sidewalks. In that way he reminded Luc of Simon, his boyhood friend with whom he would make their last and final connection to end this game which had begun long before Paris was declared an open city and before the Germans even marched down the Champs Elysees and into their homes.

Luc looked over to Axelrod who was paying close attention to the Lieutenant's map and seemed to be calculating the odds of reaching Paris. Who among them would die before that happened seemed to be the question he was asking himself. Because of that suspicion, Luc did not trust him. Whereas Sal reminded Luc of Simon, this thin wiry American soldier reminded him of Laurent Givenchy and another Aaron - Aaron Boucheron and all the similar lot who had betrayed men and women to the Gestapo. They, in order to live comfortably during the occupation or to save their own lives, did so at the cost of their friends' or comrades-in-arms' lives.

Sal was listening to what the Lieutenant was saying, but was giving the others a long hard look and letting his 'gut' decide who the born leader was. When his eyes fell on Luc's, he had his answer.

****

Luc crossed the field in the moonless night and returned to the camp behind the hedgerow. On either end the Indians stood guard as the others slept or ate their K rations, swallowing them down hard with gulps of red wine. They had gotten used to the pattern of catching naps whenever they could, and of moving out across the undulating fields of Normandy in the middle of the night and early morning. Their ears were quickly attuned to noise whether it be a crack of a stick or the click of a gun's safety latch.

As the hours and days passed, the voices were always there - German, English, French, Polish, Russian, and yet one was never certain if this was their native language or simply an acquired one. Many retreating German soldiers tried to pass as Poles or Russians. The team could have no attachments to friends or enemies. They did what they had to do and moved on. If they captured the enemy, they turned them over to Allied troops in the area, tied them up, or turned them over to the townspeople.

From the safe house Luc had learned that Caen and St. Lo were still heavily fortified and that Falaise was getting additional German build-up. They had to get across between

Caen and Falaise in order to pick up the roads into Paris. Cutting across to the coast of Avranches and down past Mount Saint Michel might be safer but it would cost them time. They'd have to travel more kilometers and cross a good portion of France to get to Paris. Even if they caught a ride on the shirt-tails of General George Patton, it was too long and kilometers meant time.

"We have to cross the Vire River two kilometers directly to our east. Resistance forces have blown all but certain bridges to prevent the Germans from sending tanks to the Beach Landing areas. One of the 'holding' bridges is in our path. No Americans forces have relieved them. Word is out to get us over and then blow it. They can't wait any longer." Luc reported. "I'll take the three new men, plus Christian, and Juliette." He nodded to the Lieutenant who was in accord.

Sidney confirmed the choice. Luc would see how these new men followed commands and how much steel was in their backbones. He already knew he could count on Christian, and with Juliette there was no question.

"I'll cover your flank and rear. We'll always be ten minutes behind you. Once you secure the bridge, send up a green flare."

'We'll just take it day by day and see who's alive when the day ends." Sidney thought. He had begun to doubt whether the hardware store in Hannibal and his white front porch with the swing and waiting chess board. …would ever be the same for him again.

****

Luc saw the bridge and the three men in dark berets, sweaters, and trousers. There was one at each entry to the bridge and the third stood guard in the middle. Then he saw a cigarette being lit, and caught a glimpse of a fourth man in shadow, hidden behind a machine gun nose, surrounded by sacks of grain. The two with their backs to the sacks continued to walk up and down on the wooden planked bridge. The third, with a rifle slung over his shoulder, approached Luc.

Juliette hid at the far end of the bridge's bank beneath the machine gun nest; Christian sat beneath the middle portion - where the wooden pylons crossed in the maximum pressure area, and James Earl and Aaron were between the two.

Luc walked onto the bridge from the other end with Sal directly behind him. He was about to speak to the Frenchman who approached him when the bullets hit. Luc ducked as the bullets sprayed the bridge. The French guard in the middle of the bridge took them in the back as his lifeless body fell in front of Luc, Luc simply froze in the dark and waited. James Earl had not done the same.

At the moment when all the 'berets' were cut down like bowling pins, James Earl had jumped onto the bridge and was running like a tackle toward the sandbags that encased the machine gun. Aaron followed him but almost immediately stopped and crouched on the side of the bridge. Still, James Earl kept dashing to the goal line. Neither Luc nor the others made a move. Sal had begun, but Luc placed his hand on his back and pushed him to go beneath the bridge in the pandemonium that followed.

Then the guns found the huge dark shape in the night. James Earl never made the touchdown. They cut him down from three different directions. His body fell into the sandbags – one foot from the goal posts

Luc took note where the return fire had come. Christian and Juliette had done the same. The shouts began. Neither Juliette nor Luc could understand. The Americans stayed put - Aaron on the bridge and Sal beneath. They knew the attackers were not speaking German. The language was all too familiar to Christian.

The Russian voices were ordering the one on the bridge to surrender. To stand up with hands over his head and nothing would happen to him. He would be their prisoner. When Aaron did not move, the one nearest the machine gun said to his comrades that he was going to talk to this enemy soldier in German – Once he got the information he needed, he would kill him. The others answered in the affirmative.

The voice repeated his command in German. This time Aaron stood up with hands over his head. He had on a black sweater like one of the Frenchmen.

"Had he understood the command in German or had he just done the only thing he could do – surrender?" Luc thought as he stood in the shadows at the far end of the bridge.

Aaron Axelrod walked into the spotlight the soldiers shined on the bridge. Sal and the others of the unit clearly saw that Aaron had somehow gotten rid of his infantry jacket, but Sal did not gasp until he heard his friend speak German.

"Are you German because I am a French collaborator," Aaron Axelrod said in clipped perfectly accented German.
"'Danke', for killing this inferior member of the human race – this black man who would have blown up the bridge."

Two of the three soldiers stepped down from their striking zones. Their heavy nailed boots clunked onto the bridge. The soldier, who had done all the talking, walked over to James Earl's body and flipped it over with his foot.

"We'll get extra rations for this kill – maybe even some of the commandant's vodka." He said in Russian.

Christian, still frozen in place beneath the bridge, listened intently to the remarks as he tightened his grip on Juliette's shoulder. He did not want her to do anything rash. She had no intention of moving. She waited until they resumed their dialogue in German. In spite of their use of German and their German uniforms, she also knew from their accents that they were Russian, part of the forced labor core the Germans had rounded up. She was all too familiar with their kind, for they also had worked alongside her father and brother, Denis, building Hitler's Atlantic Wall. Some she knew had gotten paid – either in money, vodka, or women, and others, who had truly switched allegiance, donned the German uniform with pride. Those on the bridge were the latter. If and when the Allies were winning, they would switch sides again, and simply say that they had been forced into service by the Germans. Either way it was a win/win situation.

"Where are your papers" the second of the two Russians asked Aaron.

"They were lost with my coat when defending another bridge near Les Ouellettes. In fact, I had to take a dead American's pants. Mine were soaked in blood." Aaron answered in flawless German. Then he whispered, "Two more of them are down at that end," he nodded to where Luc and Sal were hiding. "I was following this black bastard when you shot him."

Luc could not hear what Aaron was saying. He just saw him motioning with his head since his hands were still up in the air. Why haven't they shot him? Do they understand English? Juliette, however, could understand every word of this superior skinny American. Christian sensed she was upset, but he did not know why, yet he wondered what this German speaking American was saying to prevent the two soldiers from killing him. The third soldier who had fired was still out there – somewhere.

When Aaron nodded his head toward the other end of the bridge, a wave of fear rolled over her. Was this a ruse on Aaron's part or did he intend to trade their lives for his? The larger of the two, the talker, began to frisk Aaron's sides. Out of one pocket they pulled a pack of Luckys out of the other a Hershey bar. He looked at what was in his hands.

"So you smoke and eat American", he said with a sly grin.

"I told you these pants belonged to an American." Aaron sarcastically said as though they were idiots who did not understand. "You better spray that end of the bridge or we'll all be dead soon."

The talker did not like his tone of voice. He reverted back to Russian, which made Aaron nervous.

"This guy is a little Jew. His accent is from the Jewish ghetto. I know I guarded some in Paris before pushing them into boxcars. You walk down to the end – like you're casually going to take a leak off the side; then turn and open fire at both sides and under the bridge. I'll shoot this one once you fire your first shot."

Aaron relaxed a bit as the other soldier began to walk toward Sal and Luc. The big Russian offered him a Lucky. "Americans can make one good thing. – cigarettes!" he said in German.

He did not like the way this little Jew-boy collaborator laughed. He shot Aaron Axelrod before his comrade opened fire at the other end of the bridge. The second soldier whirled around to see where and who the shot hit. The collaborator was bent over with his arms around his middle and his Russian friend had his boot against his head. The Russian quickly swung his foot like he was kicking a soccer ball and booted the collaborator into the river.

Two shots rang out – Sal took out the Russian on the bridge and Luc nailed the one directly above him. A third shot rang out and fired at the rim of the bridge behind where Aaron had being kneeling seconds before. Christian heard the moan and saw the third soldier fall into the river below him. There was no need for a fourth shot, for Juliette had vaulted into the machine gun nest and riddled it and the machine gunner with bullets.

Shoveling – one load of dirt at a time, Sal had thought his friend died heroically. He never knew Aaron spoke German- yet that in itself wasn't unusual. Not many GI's would admit to that unless they were in Intelligence. Being German and Jewish seemed an 'oxymoron' to Sal. He could not connect the two. His thoughts were random. He could not focus on the fact that these men had been his last two links with his Company and the Captain. He just kept shoveling – one load of dirt at a time – until his friends were buried.

Juliette watched over him. Would he be strong enough or would he crack at one more adversity? She would not tell him what his friend and fellow soldier said in German. Aaron Axelrod had not only been a coward, but a collaborator of the worst kind, one who would sell out his friends. James Earl was noble. A hero. He had acted nobly. The other didn't deserve to be buried next to him. She would not tell the new American, and she would wait until Christian told her what they had said in Russian. Perhaps, she was wrong – but she doubted it.

Before the others crossed over this bridge that had cost nine lives, Sal picked up Aaron's infantry jacket and took out his dog tags, his Jewish star, and the notebook he had used to record the facts for the 'film of all films' – 'fuckin better than Gone With the Wind' – as Aaron Axelrod had said so many times before. Sal had just tucked them in his inside pocket when he heard Janusz.

"Cover your ears. Hit the dirt."

The bridge lit up the night sky as the moon slide out from behind a cloud to look.

Chapter 19 – D-Day Plus 7

    While the world slept, Lieutenant Sidney Smith recounted his nine men, for the last twenty-four hours he was back again to ten, including himself. His 'unlucky thirteen' had been just that - 'unlucky'. Two were already dead - cut down at the bridge. From what he had overheard from Luc and his sister as they spoke with Christian, he felt fortunate to be rid of Axelrod. James Earl, however, was another story. It seemed Sal would take care of their belongings and pass them on when - if, he got back to the States in one piece.

    Sidney thought to himself, "I have enough 'stuff' to pass along when I get back home. Now, focus Sid. The road to Paris. We've got to continue to avoid GC5, the Grand Chemin - the 'great, big path' leading from Isigny to Bayeux. By keeping just south of it, we should slice our odds of running any German roadblocks and mines."

    Men, coming and going, fixed to a schedule and motivated by an objective, reminded Sidney of the time he had passed through Grand Central Station. Organized pandemonium was his impression, yet the absurdity of this mayhem was that these men didn't even know which train to get on. Most, like Sidney and his men, had hooked up with other companies once they got off the beach. If they had a handful of their buddies still fighting alongside of them, they considered themselves lucky.

Sidney was lucky because he and his men had a clear mission. He knew too that he had good men. With them under his command, they'd get the job done. Only the means and methods of achieving it would vary. Although he had agreed with Luc to proceed to Le Beau Moulin, where on route they'd been assured of Allied coverage and from there directly south to the Foret de Cerisy, some days he could count their advance in kilometers, others by mere yards.

Christian, Juliette, and Janusz were now into the outskirts of the village where Sidney had told them to wait and make sure the town was secure and the bridge in tact before the rest of the team moved in. In these towns across Normandy no flowers were strewn in the Allies' path - no ceremonial marches down their tiny main streets were made. The French people greeted them blandly, in shock, or in bitterness. From generation to generation, Norman farms, shops, and homes passed from father to son. Now, nothing but piles of rubble, bombed out pastures, mutilated bocages, and cow carcasses strewn in ditches would be their inheritance.

Juliette, from the hill above the town, lifted the binoculars to her tired eyes. She pushed her dirty matted hair from her face and looked over the houses of Le Beau Moulin All seemed intact except for one whose roof was left gaping open at the sky like an eye socket without an eyeball. Its walls, however, still stood above the streets, which seemed fairly clear of stone and timber debris.

Leaving them as a rear guard, she crept closer to the bridge. Below the town proper, nearer the bridge on the other side of the river, Juliette crept close to an abandoned stone house. From the front it looked like any ordinary Norman farmhouse, but as she carefully inched her way around the back, she realized there was no fourth wall. The house, like a child's dollhouse, was just a shell. With façade to the street it appeared as any other, yet no 'dolls' lived here. The only remnant of one of the inhabitants was a flowered lavender dress with a scooped neck hung daintily on a clothesline behind the fourth wall mass of stone rubble.

Juliette looked up to the north corner of the house where a rope with a pulley still hung on a massive hook from one of the stones. The line stretched out 10 meters until it met with its partner pulley attached to a large oak. Waving in the light summer breeze, the dress seemed content to wait until its owner pulled her it.

"How odd this dress is the only piece of clothing on the line. Who had intended to wear it and why? Something this delicate is not for the life of a farmer's wife who had chores from sunrise to sunset," she mused. "Did she intend to wear it when American soldiers finally liberated her village? Where was she? She left behind not only her dress but her home."

Juliette carefully pinched open the wooden clothespins, dark and weather-beaten with age. She gingerly hung the dress over her arm and tried to keep her dirty fingers from smudging it with the blood, sweat, and grease from her hands. She looked down at her hands, and could not even remember when she had last washed them. Taking off her black beret, she shoved it into the back pocket of her wet wool trousers. The trousers chaffed and itched.

Walking over to the river, which flowed under the bridge she would have to cross, she passed through the leaves and branches of a large weeping willow that touched the banks. On a low branch near the trunk of the tree she bent one of its tender offshoots and made a hanger to go through the capped sleeves of the lavender dress. Only the occasional 'whos' of the morning doves fluttered through the stillness of the morning air.

"The war must have taken a brief holiday in this hamlet," she thought as she ran her fingers through her hair. Its luxurious softness was gone and in its place were brunette snarls – oily and matted. She twisted her torso and swung her knapsack off one arm and then the other. Reaching inside one of the pockets, she pulled out a square of paper, which she meticulously opened. She brought the opened treasure to her nose and inhaled the scent of the lavender. Placing it on the ground next to her, she methodically scanned the horizon, grid by grid she searched for any sign of movement.

Satisfied, she quickly unlaced her brown boots, pulled her gray sweater over her head, and slipped out of her wool trousers. She took one last look around before she pulled off her cotton GI tee-shirt and bvd's. Picking up the soap in one hand, she glided into the cold water of the river and forced herself to let its water cover her head. She dove deep and opened her eyes and let the cold cleanse and sooth her aching eyeballs. Surfacing, she rubbed the soap between her hands. It did not lather well, but its scent was magnificent as it erased the grim from her hair and her skin. Scrubbing it into her skin, she fought to wash out the days of dirt and death. Submerging again, she let the icy waters pass over her head. She pushed off from the sandy bottom and swam eyes wide open to let the water cleanse the soap from her hair, limbs, and torso. Her hands felt the smooth stones as she breast-stroked into the shallow warmer water near the bank. She kicked like a dolphin under the water, came up and cut through the surface. Kneeling on the shallow side, she tossed her hair over her head and squeezed the water out.

Chattering from head to toe, she ran across the stones and up onto the bank beneath the willow tree. She cursed the fact that she had no towel and did not look for any in the one armoire she had seen standing in the rubble of the house. Turning her wool pants inside out she dried her body with the itchy fabric. Not totally dry, she pulled the soft tee shirt over her head and pulled up the underwear over her slender hips. The dress, hugging her firm breasts and nipping in at her small waist, slid over her body as though it was made for her. The circular skirt, which hung in folds around her hips, reminded her of her mother's work, and particularly of a sketch she had seen on her mother's desk by a young designer named Christian Dior. Such designs would have to wait until after the war. As it was, the designs of Paris' 'Haute Couture' had been practically non-existent for the last four years with minimal shows, few designs, and mainly German and French collaborator patrons.

"Whose dress was this?" These random thoughts annoyed Juliette. The dress was for the work she had to do. She knew she needed to look 'normale' in order to explore the streets of Le Beau Moulin. Regardless, she was glad to get out of her men's clothes, but the dirty warm sweater she had to pull back over her head. She had need of it. The month was June, although the cold air of Normandy told her otherwise. If there were time, she would look through the armoire to find a clean softer sweater. She shoved the pants into her knapsack and pulled the beret over her wet hair. Pushing her long hair under her beret, and pulling up her socks and boots, she performed the last touches before crossing the bridge. She had no more time to indulge.

As she turned around to go, she heard a snap. She realized it was an isolated sound, and that, for some time now, the doves had stopped their cooing. "How could I be so stupid and selfish?" She thought as a wave of fear passed over her. Fear - she knew it well; its form had cast shadows over her life for the last four years. Even her own home, she never felt truly safe.

"Qui est la?" she demanded as she stood clutching her bag to her chest. Inside the bag, she could feel the outline of the Colt 45 the Americans had given her. They had told her it was heavy, accurate, and could stop a man in his tracks. She had yet to use it. Had she left the safety off was the question, and could she get enough grasp on the trigger to fire it through her pack?

Her ears were fine-tuned, and she was certain she could hear one foot being placed gently in front of the other. Again, she asked, "Qui etes-vous?" Again, no response. She located the trigger finger. She would just have time to pull it and hope the 45's safety was off. Just then a man stepped out from an adjacent willow tree.

"How much had he seen?" she asked herself - not out of modesty, but of survival. Had he seen the army issue 'underwear'?

He was tall, blond, blue-eyed, and of course, German. He wore his uniform with a sense of irreverence. The jacket was unbuttoned; the collar rolled was under, and beneath his jacket was a dingy white tee-shirt with familiar textured ribbing. She thought it odd.

"Mademoiselle," he said as he nodded his head in greeting. He took a step forward. She backed up a step.

"Que faites-vous ici"? she asked. But he looked at her blankly and did not answer her question. 'What are you doing here?' She asked again but this time in German, and his face brightened. He said he was guarding the bridge.

Her face remained passive, but her fear mounted as she stood shivering in the cold morning air. How many more Germans were in Le Beau Moulin? She and this lone German whose rank she could not tell were within 200 meters of the bridge. If she fired the Colt, would they come running or would it be Janusz and Christian who ran – from or to death?

His German was perfect – almost too perfect. Had he been schooled in Switzerland or in France – perhaps England before the war? His expressions, animated not passive or aggressive like most Germans, also made him different. She looked hard into his eyes, for she had been told they were the windows of the soul. All she could see was a cerulean serene blue like pools where mermaids should swim. Although they lacked the cold steel of most Germans, his stereotypical Aryan birthright could not be denied. Her instinct and intellect told her he was her enemy, but somewhere inside a voice said – 'he is not what he seems'.

John had given her his 'hairpin' sharp knife. She could feel the outline of it in the instep of her boot. If she could get him off guard, she could jam in into his neck right near the aorta vein. She knew he would bleed to death – quickly and more importantly, silently.

"I haven't seen you around the village before." He said. "You have not come into the café of Simone."

She took another long hard look at him. Simone and a Madame Forte were two of the names on the letters taken from the safe at the Veignard farmhouse that the girl had guarded so well. Both were known to be of the Resistance and perhaps also known to the Gestapo who had not pulled them in yet. He seemed to drop the name Simone too casually. Was he baiting her before he killed her along with Madame Simone or was the she dead already? This was taking too long. She was thinking too much. He had on a German uniform. He was in German territory. He looked German and spoke German. She had to act now – to kill or be killed.

He turned his back on her and took something out of the knot in the tree. Bending his head down, he slipped something over his neck. He had given her enough time to act to pull the knife from her boot. When he turned around, she caught a glimpse of silver around his neck, and Lieutenant Melvin Baron caught the glitter of her knife held above her head. He grabbed her wrist and had to use both hands to knock the stiletto knife from its downward plunge. He was amazed at her strength. Staring at the dog tags around his neck, she forced her gaze up into his eyes. Her eyes locked into his – death or life they seemed to say. The question seemed to hang in the cold morning air. She shivered involuntarily.

"I am American." Melvin Baron said as he dropped her wrists and slipped off his German jacket to place around her shaking shoulders.

His broad chest and wide shoulders spoke of power. In that way he was like the other 'Americans' of her team, but the others - except for Sidney, were darker and brown eyed. The only extremely tall one was the Apache – these must be the typical 'American' not this blond – blue eyed 'underman' before her. Perhaps, he was the insidious Gestapo - perhaps not, for she was still alive. Continuing to stare into his eyes, she let his jacket fall from her shoulders and deliberately stepped back on it. She stiffened herself, for the blow she thought would come. She looked for the wrath in his eyes, but saw a glint of laughter instead.

"Ne vous en inquietez pas," he used one of his French phrases.

She thought she heard an American accent but she was not certain.

"Don't worry", he repeated. "The jacket is not mine. I am an American soldier. I made use of the jacket. You can use it too." He was deliberately talking in simple sentences and in a louder voice to make her understand.

"Come over the bridge into 'le Café de Simone'. She has plenty of 'Gigot sale' and a warm kitchen. 'La cuisine est tres chaude et vous etes tres froide, n'est-ce pas?'"

His French accent was good, - better than the others of her group, but this time he said enough so she could hear the slight intonation of American.

"Oui, j'ai froid" she answered and smiled as she corrected him.

"Yes, I know you're cold. Don't be afraid Simone will tell you 'tout va bien avec moi". I'm 'kosher'. She looked puzzled "Too much Americanism, 'non'. 'Je suis americain et juif'.

"Mon dieu! My God," Juliette repeated in English. She reached up to his dog tags and read his name and touched the Jewish star around his neck. "How goes that" she said.

"My company called me the 'Kraut' – they thought that was ironic – funny too."

"Yes 'ironique', 'drole'. Turning her back on him, Juliette knew she would not die – at least not this day - nor by his hands. She ground the jacket into the mud on the banks.

"We go to that house to get warm jackets or sweaters. Tell me all you know about that town, that bridge, and Madame Simone. We have ten minutes and that is all. My friends are waiting." She did not even turn around when she spoke to him in English, for he had passed the test and in doing so she had revealed that she knew English. He scooped up the jacket as she shook off the mud of her boots.

"Why do you have need of that?" she asked without turning.

"How do you think we got control over that bridge and earned Madame's confidence?"

Now, she turned and glanced at him over her shoulder "We"?

"The three German soldiers who were guarding that bridge are dead now. O'Brien and I took them out." He didn't think she knew that expression.

****

It was now the fifteenth day of June. Melvin and Juliette, who were crossing the bridge, and Janusz, Christian, and O'Brien, who were waiting on the other side, were well aware of that. It had been nine days since they landed and each considered themselves lucky. Sidney's nine felt they had used up some of their nine lives if, like cats, they had been granted that many. Most had come as gifts: a bazooka blast through barbwire, the blood of a fallen comrade that spurred them into action, or a bomb, which exploded onto a company, but made a crater cradle in which to hide. Like cats, these nine men and women had landed on their feet.

The sun was finally breaking through on this day in the middle of June, yet each one thought how many lives have I used up? How many more times am I going to be in the right place at the wrong time? Days and dates as a measurement of time did not exist for them - only moments were portioned out in which to live. Because of this, they had never been more alive, for they had never been so close to death – every second, every minute, every hour, and every day. To crawl across a 400 meter pasture, to dash across a four meter wide road, to inch their way from town to town, from bridge to bridge - to blow it up or not – that was always the question.

For this particular bridge at Beau Moulin the irony was not lost on Sidney nor Luc. The 'beau', the beautiful, was truly that. As Sidney gazed out Madame Simone's café to the empty streets, all was serenely quiet on this morning. He had forgotten the peace that came with the absence of noise. He could actually hear birds chirp and insects beginning to buzz. A fly droned, like a mini B-47, across the wooden beams of this small café on the other side of this tiny bridge. Panicking to get out, the huge fly would nose down toward the warm buttery croissants and hot steamy 'café au lait' Simone had placed on the small wooden tables in her place of business.

'Normale' as the French would say. It almost played out as normal. To Sidney, Madame's front door screen slammed like the one at his hardware store back home. Soon it would be evening in Hannibal and Margie would go to sleep this night – and snore just a bit as she occasionally did. Like a baby pug puppy, she would emit a little snort through her small turned up nose.

"Will I ever kiss her again and wrap her in my arms as she sleeps?" The fly buzzed him out of his reverie. It landed on the windowsill and fought frantically to escape. Luc and Sidney just looked at it. The steam rose from their coffees and the sweetness of the sugar and homemade apple 'comfiture', 'beurre', and croissants suspended them from the shackles of war.

"'Normale' - no, just a tease of normalcy - a charade played out in a mis-en-scene from a Moliere play." Luc in turn thought.

The 'petit dejeuner', the breakfast, although late in the morning, was so typically French that it felt good to be home – good to be on French soil in a French café. Yet, this was but a small pause in a play, which would not have its final curtain until they reached Paris. The climax could only come in the second act when they met their own 'Moliere' – the liaison man who knew the location of the Katyn Russian documents. Luc gazed pass Sidney, pass the fly that neither he nor the Lieutenant would swat, and thought of his dear friend and 'lycee copain', the Moliere of this drama.

Luc's past, present, and future would be tied in with the outcome of this meeting - this last mission perhaps. His eyes glanced to the back table where Zosia, Juliette, and Madame Simone chatted in French. It appeared like typical café chatter. He noticed that Zosia would occasionally glance at the two new men, Baron and O'Brien, - both tall, one he thought looked too 'Aryan'. All, however, appeared at ease, at home but far away from home: Zosia's café in London, Juliette's café spots in Paris, the Americans' roadside and corner stops for 'java', and Madame herself here in Le Beau Moulin entertaining – conducting business of sorts – in her own café. Luc marveled at her 'table' her spread of perfection. The people of Paris no longer had such commonplace delicacies. From her Normandy cows she processed fresh cream and butter, and from her apples she made the 'comfiture', the jam, they spread on the delicate flaky croissants she baked fresh with the white flour she was still able to get.

Luc thought of another scene – way above the streets of Paris. It was another June day; the sun was out, and the clouds had not yet darkened the skies of Paris. His grandfather was still alive and his mother and a few of the models, including the young and animated Colette, listened to the BBC announce the Germans advance into France. The City had not yet been declared an 'open city', and the thousands who would flee into the countryside had not yet begun their exodus. By the time the Germans had marched down the Champs Elysees and Hitler and made his first and last appearance in the City of Light over fifty percent of the population would be gone, and those who stayed would suffer the deprivation of food and fuel. The winters of 42 and 43 had been the coldest on record. He remembered how his grandfather had vowed that he would never leave his Paris. He was good to his word, for he died from the cold and lack of food that was an unconscionable and deadly burden for the old.

"Will Paris ever be 'normale' again?" he thought. "Can I go back to my old life as the real 'dressmaker' or will I always, from this point on, be trapped in the web of war. I've been wearing so many masks; I feel I am losing the real Luc Dubois." His eyes filled with love as he looked at his beautiful Zosia. "She will help me build our life after this war. How ironic that she was the daughter of a 'dressmaker', and I am the son and grandson of the same."

But Luc had lived through so many years of this war and accepted its ironies and perhaps fate. So many were thrown together in the "pas normale", abnormal conditions. Maybe that was how it was meant to be.

He gazed again upon Zosia. He appreciated that even with her chopped hair and man's clothes she carried herself with a certain 'elan'. This flair was evident even now, as her sweater worn outside her trousers, was clenched in a blouson style with the heavy wide military belt. Her beret was slanted over one side of her head. He smiled to himself at the chicness of her signature on standard army issue clothing. In contrast, Juliette looked so fragile and fresh in the lavender dress that she really had not needed to put it on, for her casual meandered through the streets to market that morning, was not necessary. No Germans were there, and hardly any French came out.

A pause or perhaps a pall seems to suspend Le Beau Moulin in time. Luc continued to look at Juliette, his baby sister, who was no longer an innocent. He thought again of the past and his mother, who had not wished to send her to Paris - who wanted Juliette to retain her youth for one or two more years. She could never have suspected that the Germans would take that innocence from her. Because of the harshness of war, Juliette had lied, connived, and killed. The war had taught her that. It had been her schooling.

"How life has changed for us all. Either we will be stronger, because of the war or we will be broken by it. We can rebuild the farm on the hills of the Normandy beachheads, rebuild the couturier house in Paris, but we can never mend the torn bloody ties with Denis."

He knew all that would have to come after – after they reached Paris, after they met with Simon, after they confiscated the safe with the condemning papers of the Forest in Katyn, after they gave them to Leclerc or de Gaulle, after the Germans fled Paris,- and only after the war ended. Only at the end, when peace finally came again, could they get on with their lives.

Perhaps, he and Simon would lunch at their 'café' near La Tour Eiffel and this time it would be flying the French flag. Perhaps, at night he would take Zosia to another 'beau moulin' the beautiful windmill of the 'Moulin Rouge'. After a night of singing and dancing, they would walk arm in arm slowly up the stairs to the top of Montmartre. At the top, they would turn and see Paris stretched out in front of them – lights glistening and sparkling like jewels with the sounds of saxophones and accordions, floating far on a hot summer night. As she leaned against a lamppost, he would kiss her and the warmth of her lips would travel down his spine. Intertwined, they would stay – safe, secure in this city of love.

Paris would become her city, for it was her destiny. Luc knew it had been her mother's dream, Tanya's dream for herself and her daughter, Zosia. The dream had died when Tanya died, but she left a legacy for her daughter. She left her indomitable spirit to Zosia who would have to fight her way out of Poland, build a life in a new country, and finally come home to France.

Looking around the café, he returned to the present and thought. "How odd that half of the people in this café have fought their way out of their own country to find freedom, and the other half have willingly left their free country to fight their way into another - in the name of liberty." These strong open-faced Americans, he wondered what sort of men they were to commit to such lunacy.

Sidney sat in front of him lost in his own thoughts – staring out a window at a small bridge in a tiny village far away from what was familiar to him. Tony and Sal were halfway between the front of the café and the back where the women were. Luc had the impression that New York must be a fine city to produce such 'joie de vivre' that these two men seemed to possess. Thomas - the Apache, John - the Cherokee, and the two new men – Baron and O'Brien sat together. They were older than the two boys from the Bronx and Brooklyn – death didn't seem to affect them as much or perhaps they were good at 'stuffing it down'.

Sal, too, was good at 'stuffing it down', barely four days earlier he had lost the last two members of his company. Only he remained to tell the story of their advance and conquest of Pointe de la Percee. He had to get to Paris for the rest of them – for Hank's wife who had been promised that Channel Number 5 perfume, for James Earl who had to see Josephine Baker, and for Aaron Axelrod who needed his film to be made. Maybe when he got to Paris, he could then let it out. He could cry for them and for all the others who never made it.

Christian and Janusz, covering the flank, sat on the other side of the café, near the windows. They were old beyond their years in spite of the fact they were practically the same ages as the two Americans from New York. Once in a while they'd even glance over at Luc and Sidney as if to protect them. Roles had switched. They were now the papas, protecting Luc and Sidney as their fathers had done for them. To these two men they had already given their allegiance; now, they would give their lives – if necessary. Christian and Janusz knew – more than any of the others – more perhaps than even Zosia – what the outcome of their mission would mean. Moreover, they knew what the failure of this mission – what the cost in lives and in freedom – would be if they did not succeed.

The two, without a country, talked quietly to one another, choosing their words and letting the other one completely finish before injecting any thought. Great pauses hung in the air that was beginning to warm; each reflected on the words the other had spoken. The pieces that connected they added to their memories; a piece that did not fit precisely, they acknowledged and put aside for when they could find an exact match. More and more the puzzle was taking shape for Christian. Would it be complete once the documents verifying the slaughter of his father and Janusz's countrymen came to light?

My dreams –my nightmares 'cauchemars' as the French say – will they end once I have served my purpose in this divine plan?" Christian thought. "Why could God not have spared my father?" He held a hard core of hatred not only toward the Russians – the Communists who mercilessly mass murdered the best of Poland in that dark forest of the Katyn - but for God, who let it happen.

The clusters of men continued to connect with one another in these pauses of respite. Each said or listened to the men across and next to them, like little islands onto themselves in an oasis of time to heal their wounds. In their imaginary oases the sun beat down and the water vibrated in shimmers on their shores where they quenched their thirst in the pools hidden among the leafy palms. Plucking dates and succulent oranges, they let the juices of life run down their throats in sweet gulps. Like beasts of burden, each man stored what he needed from one another and from the creamy café au lait and croissants piled with jam and butter. They would hoard the good with which to refresh themselves, when the bad - again, returned.

So, the team was back to twelve.

In Luc's mind this was too many – too many to get past the back roads through the Germans and into Paris – a Paris still occupied and very much defended by the Germans. He was clear about the orders that Sidney had gotten when they left England. Get to Paris at all costs. Here's a team of men. Just do it before the Germans are forced to leave Paris. Luc did not doubt Sidney's ability as a leader nor did he question the Americans' ability to fight, and he knew he needed their military might and information network about German strategy and Allied strongholds.

This was no longer a Resistance France. On the day of liberation those loyal to France had come out in full force: cutting communications, blowing up railways and pipelines of supplies, and killing the German officers who had given orders of reprisals in every little village. If they could get away with it, they did it. Chaos reigned for the Germans as well as for the 'resistance cells' since they were no longer in central units but scattered to the wind. They struck back with an unleashed fury held back during four forced years of labor and deprivation. With hardly any sleep, they did their work quickly while the iron was hot and their vengeance - certain and sweet.

The maps that Luc carried in his mind from just one month ago had changed. He could no longer be certain of who was where, so he had no choice, but to stay with this 'new' cell of new men. It might take him more time, but he had a better chance of succeeding. Because of his direct link to de Gaulle, he and Zosia knew firsthand one piece of information the others lacked, a piece that General had promised would control the French mind and effort once the battle began.

Not only were the French Communists a real threat to Paris and France, and the Free World but a second threat were the Germans garrisoned in Paris for the last four years. They would not relinquish Paris - their 'pearl' willingly. Luc had to get the documents, which condemned the Russian communists. Only the information contained in these papers would turn the majority of support from the ranks of the French communist party to allegiance to the French Free Forces of De Gaulle. In addition, Luc and others in Paris itself needed to rally together to find and defuse the areas of detonation that Hitler and put in place.

There were rumors concerning Hitler's plans for Paris. If he could not have her, it was said he would leave her in ruins when his forces marched out under her triumphal arch, and this Arc of Napoleon's, the Arc of Triumph, would be the last monument Germans would detonate as they fled the streets of Paris. What some called the greatest city in the world would be destroyed once the Allies approached her periphery. Luc was certain that Sidney did not know this, for he never mentioned it. On this calm day, Luc's thoughts were confirmed.

As Sidney gazed out the café's window, he did not comment that the Paris they would enter had tons of TNT attached and secretly buried under and in all of its famous monuments, museums, and churches.

"What else have his American generals not told him?" Luc wondered as the weight of the mission now seemed even heavier on his shoulders.

"Ecoutez, mes amis," Madame Simone boomed over the silence.

She had taken out her large radio, secretly hidden beneath the floorboards of her counter. Turning up the volume, she motioned for them to come closer. The women and Luc were smiling. To the Americans the French transmissions were muffled and unrecognizable. They heard a mixture of voices and the word 'Bayeux' that Sidney and Baron knew was the name of a nearby city that had been liberated by the British.

Christian translated what he could clearly hear from the loudest voice coming over the air waves. "We shall fight beside the Allies, with the Allies, and as an ally, and the victory we shall win will be the victory of liberty and the victory of France."

The Frenchmen in the café as well as Christian were surprised as the radio continued to transmit, the lone deep voice that had just broken into song. To the Americans it was their first introduction to the Marseillaise, sung by the most tone-deaf voice they ever hear. Tony, the Jazz aficionado, cringed. When other voices from the radio transmitter in Bayeux joined in, the vibrant marching song sounded better. The others - Sidney, Sal, O'Brien, and Baron looked on in amazement as tears rolled down the cheeks of Juliette, Zosia, and Madame Simone, who joined in song.

Luc's eyes were clear but glowed with pride at that lone voice of General Charles de Gaulle's rendition of the French National Anthem. "Now, all we have to do is beat him to Paris," he thought.

****

Sandy and his group of Englishmen were at a virtual stalemate in Viliers Bocage. Although near Sidney's team of men and women, they had no knowledge of them or their mission. Sandy concentrated on staying alive and remarkably, he had done more than that. Significantly south of Bayeux yet northwest of Falaise, his Englishmen could not move. A German column had attempted to retake Bayeux, and Sandy and his men had gone into the fray to help a core of Brits, boxed-in near a little Hamlet called Jerusalem.

The fight had been intense, and dozens of British soldiers died including some of his own. They had repelled the advance, but too many Germans blocked their path, and they were not a fighting unit.

"If we could attach to a group of Yanks, I'd get the support we'd need to move ahead with our 'engineering' mission." Sandy thought as took a drag from the Chesterfield dangling from his parched lips. What he knew best was engineering not commanding an infantry unit. Now, he had gotten some of 'his' men killed going back towards Bayeux. He had to mold them to do a job that he knew well, and so far for the first few days he had done so - until the battle of Jerusalem.

"Our 6th Airborne has done its job," he thought. "Dropped into Hell some of us have made it out, but where in this bloody mess is Montgomery. All the Apache is getting me is Yank info."

The resistance cell they had connected with treated them as family and patriots with an identical purpose – to free France. Their night raids of blowing up bridges and trestles or rebuilding them had ended with the battle at Jerusalem. This was not his kind of warfare. Tired of leading and waiting for someone else to take over, he and his men were at a standstill, yet it in this waiting period a sign would come that would change Sandy's and his men's future.

He took another puff of his Chesterfield and looked over at Harry. The tall Apache, his long braids freed from his helmet and almost touching in the grass, was crouched over his walkie-talkie. He had seen him fight like ten men at Jerusalem. If he had not, perhaps they would have lost more than the three they did.

Sandy heard music coming from the Apache's walkie-talkie. Neither he nor Harry recognized it as the 'Marseillaise', the French National Anthem.

Chapter 20 – July 1 to Independence Day - "Lucky"

"Hey Sandy, I think I got something," said Harry, the Apache, who had joined with the British 6th Airborne from day one. "Geez, it's a guy from my commando unit. The odds of finding another Apache here is like finding a hair from a buffalo."

The land seen mostly from ships on the morning of June 6 - was misty, serene, and bucolic. All that changed as soon as they hit the beach and began their slow movements into the rich dairy land of France. The picturesque bocage contorted into hellish hedgerows; the smooth first new grass 'pasturage' of spring cut open with cadaver covered craters, solid stone farmhouses pounded into 'wall-less, roof-less' ruins, and once peaceful ancient villages chewed and spit out as inhabitable rubble by the gristmill of war. As they moved inland, only islands of pasture existed between the holes and blackened earth where the grass had been, but in this chaos, chance plucked out a lucky few who would survive.

"Sandy, it's coming in from Bradley's US V11 Corps and some guys from 82nd Airborne and one guy from the 101st.

Great gods it's Thomas from my unit. He's hidden in the Foret of Cerisy. How did he get all that way from behind Utah?"

"Hell, how did you get dropped practically in British terrain off Gold?" Sandy grumbled.

"The guys he's been with were well ahead of the Front but now are at a standstill. Neither Patton nor Montgomery has moved past Caen. He says they need to move out quickly since the pocket between Caen and Falaise will close as soon as Montgomery moves in on Caen. "

"Their safe haven sounds good to me. Get the coordinates. We gotta join others. Safety in numbers and all that rubbish," Sandy muttered to Harry.

There's a chance someone else can take over the command of my motley crew,' Sandy thought as they crept through the cover of night this last night of June.

Now, a dozen 'so-called' Americans would meet up with a handful of Englishmen. Together they would form a group comprised of pairs - partnerships formed because only two had been left alive from their original stick or company. Lieutenant Sidney Smith and Tony Martino from the 82nd American Airborne, Second Lieutenant Melvin Baron and Patrick O'Brien from the US 29th Division infantry – part of the second wave that hit Omaha Beach, and not until now two weeks after D-Day – Harry and Tom from two different special commando units of the 101st American Airborne would make up the third in the trio of 'lucky pairs'.

When Luc learned that Thomas would be leading another group of soldiers in – this time British, he decided to bid his time and wait. "If Sidney decides to incorporate them into the team, then Zosia, Juliette, Christian, Janusz and I will move forward on our own. Too many men would vie for power. I've seen it before."

Even as a lyceen with Simon in Paris, he learned the rules of the street quickly. He and Simon were both leaders, yet leaders who worked as a team – each relinquishing to the other his area of expertise. He did not have that relationship with Sidney. There were language, nationality, and culture gaps that were beginning to be bridged. These bridges could be solidly built over time, but time was a luxury they did not have.

"I'll wait, but not for long." Luc said to himself.

Sidney and Luc's group had sequestered themselves for seven days and seven nights in the Forest of Cerisy. Christian had hidden them well in this dark forest, isolated from the destruction of war. Big John and Thomas had marked the lines in the earth for each time period the sun rose and set.

"This forest has neither of the breath nor depth of the Katyn – but it will do nicely." Christian thought. His old habits had not left him, and each morning he reached into his jacket pocket for the clean notebook he had brought with him into France. Daily, he marked the happenings of a particular time period, for they could not called 'days' or 'nights' because they really had none of those boundaries, just periods of time when they would move ahead or rest until the next portion of their journey. The pages collected the essence of the forest and what he felt would be necessary if they had to return that way again. As was his habit, he drew pictures that would elicit the memory of the terrain and its barriers or refuge. He found himself reverting to single Russian words – those elements of slang or colloquialisms that even those who might know Russian as their second language – would not know. It was an unnecessary precaution, but he did it nonetheless. In this foreign land where the majority spoke French and the invading minorities spoke English or Germany, he should be safe writing in Russian except if they met those few like the ones on the bridge who had killed the two Americans.

Christian had found a spot where the pines were the thickest, carpeted with an abundant profusion of needles from the seasons before onto where they could lie down. A cold deep pond below the bank of immense trees collected from a stream trickling down from higher ground. This offshoot of water was like a hidden oasis – serene, untouched by civilization or even the raids of the Vikings almost a millennium ago. Thick gnarled roots, pushed up from the ions of time, made rooms with impassable root walls on the forest floor.

"Yet, these trees have been thinned," Christian thought. "All of the wood for the farmhouses in this area had to come from this ancient forest like the trees from the Katyn made our village in Smolensk." For an instant he felt safe and reached down to pet Dame's nose as he walked. Then he remembered. He stopped as his eyes filled up with tears, and at that moment warmth issued forth from the forest's damp pines. His father's spirit enveloped and imbued his being.

Looking over at Christian who stood by the edge of the trees near the stream, Luc wondered what demons pushed this youngest man of their team and why would they release their grip in this forest.

"He seems at home here - free." Luc thought.

Christian had none of the anxiousness that Luc, himself, was feeling. Even when they had stopped and made camp, Luc could not rest, but he did allow himself to smile. When Juliette had refolded the lavender dress to put back into her sack, she told Luc the next time she would wear it would be the day Paris was liberated. He smiled, for he could see her vibrant and dancing with abandon in the streets of the city they both called home. He also smiled because Zosia and Juliette, giggling like sisters, skipped as though going to a party, down the bank to the deep icy pool fed by the ancient stream. Juliette had handed Zosia a little square package that Zosia had sniffed with delight.

During their stay John and Thomas encircled the camp and made ancient Indian traps to let them know in advance of anyone coming within a half mile of the periphery of their camp. An array of nooses hung hidden in the pine needles. The branches were pulled back to slap hard anyone who crossed at certain openings among the trees, and trenches were dug wide and deeper than a man's height to lie in wait of enemy infiltration. Gathering strength along the stream, by the deep cold pool, and in the midst of venerable pines where they looked up during the night to see the tree limbs dark and intertwined like a canopy for their bed, they waited. The bombs in distant Caen sounded like thunder, and if the ground trembled as they slept, it was like a mother rocking their cradle.

For seven days before the Englishmen came, they renewed their spirit and waited for Montgomery to provide a left flank at Caen to make their voyage toward Paris safer and successful. For seven days and nights they began to form a trust and appreciation of one another's abilities and to learn about one another as people. Inside the oasis the hunters, John and

Thomas, speared the trout, still deep in the mud of the pool and stream; Christian and Janusz, the farmers, gathered herbs and nuts, and deep at the base of a lone ancient oak tree, Christian dug for the treasures of long ago. As he lifted up with gentle hands a huge truffle, he pressed it under his nose and sighed. That he had found one here and now was so bizarre, but he never questioned the mysteries of life or his fate.

Protecting and supplying the home and hearth, the women too regressed to acts of ancient times. As a child, Juliette had accompanied her mother during many forays into the woods and meadows behind their apple orchards to gather delicate 'champignons'. Zosia too remembered when she was very young trudging behind her mother as they search in the country woods of Poland for mushrooms. As they all returned with their bounty, they saw the holes John and Thomas had dug for the trout lined on plates of large wide leaves in a straight line next to each hole. Hot coals made from beds of sticks and chunks of dried peat emitted just an occasional puff of smoke that dissipated in the evening mist. The women washed the mushrooms and placed several upon each fish as Janusz dotted them with herbs and nuts before wrapping them in the leaves. Christian washed the truffle in the cold pool and dried it carefully with a clean tee shirt. He then pulled his thin stiletto knife from his inside pocket and sliced in slivers the delicate truffle.

They ate, talked, and learned about one another. The more they lived within their common community each realized how different yet the same they all were, and that their survival depended on the skill of their differences and the spirit of their similarities. On a more intimate level, they formed a bond - a bond based on instinct derived from the character – the substance of each man and each woman.

It was at the end of the seventh day that Thomas had picked up the new transmission in Apache. Sidney had given the order to bring into the forest this Indian, this other Apache who had jumped in with Thomas' original Apache unit from the 101st. Their hiatus was over; Sidney decided they needed direct news from men who were closer to the Front.
****

An odd trio led this group of Englishmen into this forest far from the shores of Normandy. An American Indian, a French resistance fighter, and a boy walked together and ahead of the rest. The boy, in the middle, turned his head as the dialogue went from Apache, to English, to French. Walking and communicating, alongside one another, they pushed step by step – deeper and deeper into the Forest. At the periphery of the Foret de Cerisy Thomas waited strong and silent. Although Sandy never heard him, Harry was not surprised at the sudden appearance of the dark face framed by two black plaited braids hanging out of the camouflaged green GI helmet.

Greeting Thomas in Apache, Harry placed his hands on his friend's wide shoulders and brought him to his chest in a strong embrace. In their clear deep Apache words, they spoke to one another of the deadly hazards he and John had made. Harry had seen the traps as he approached but listened carefully to the Apache words and motioned the boy and Frenchman to follow. They obeyed and just followed his steps in silence. From the onset the boy needed no translations; he had found it natural to move alongside his new friend of few words. They communicated by hand signals. Harry had begun to learn the special signing of the boy.

As they entered the camp in the evening mist, some thought they saw a ghost from the past. The boy flew into the arms of Juliette and Luc, the other Apache made a sign to John the Cherokee, and one of the Englishmen who followed the trio boomed in a Welsh accent, "Hey mates where did you come from."

The Americans had yet another taste of culture shock. Tony and Sal looked at one another and laughed. Baron and O'Brien just shrugged as if to say 'here we go again'. Sidney had proof again that Luc was a natural leader, and now he realized much of his power was based on compassion. The genuine love and allegiance this small boy had to Luc and also to the two women was obvious.

"Claude mon petit frere." Luc exuberantly yelled as the boy jumped into his outstretched arms."

"Tout va bien, maintenant, cheri," Juliette cooed as she kissed his face.

The women, Luc, and the boy held one another tightly, and when they separated, they still reached out to touch the boy's hair, face, and fingers as Claude began his rapid nonstop signing that only his mother, his brother, Juliette, and Luc could understand.

Sidney and the others watched from the outside of this tight knit circle He still could not put his finger on the connection between the Frenchman, Luc, and the Polish woman, Zosia. When he saw them together he missed his wife, his Marjorie, yet this pair had not shown outright affection to one another, but even in this scenario an intimacy existed. They seemed totally at ease, dependent, yet independent of one another. Of one thing he was certain, they were all equals.

****

It was Luc- not the women, who spoke to Claude about Paul. Paul 'Renard' Fortin was his friend, and this boy, who had lost so much over the years, was his brother as much as Paul had been. At times Luc felt he would not have had the strength of spirit and mind that Claude demonstrated time and time again. 'Normale' – was but a memory for the boy. Too many years had passed for him to remember what it was like to be with speech and sound. After that, the deprivation - he lived under the threat of war and then under the reality of it.

Paul, much more than a brother, had been the only 'father' he had even known. The teacher, friend, brother, and father all- in-one was now dead. Paul Fortin's love, showered on his young weaker brother, was like a deep clear well that sprung from the deepest core of the earth or like a baptismal font – soothing and protecting him from the harshness of life. As Claude grew, the waters changed. For the last year the well poured out arctic cold – like a glacial spring – hardening and shocking the boy into action against those elements and people who would hurt or ridicule him.

Now his source of strength and mentoring love was brutally buried under the cold concrete slabs from the bunker at Colleville. Claude could not cry nor mourn the loss of Paul. Instinctively, he knew he would not be able to stop if he gave in to his emotions. With his brother gone he had to be even stronger, for his mother was but a shell of herself, walking and going through the motions of life like a ghost within a ghost. Claude comforted her - held her tight and rocked her to sleep as she sobbed. The more she cried the less he felt grief. An anger – fiery and dangerous – had grown inside of him day by day during the occupation of his town, of his country. With Paul's death it had become a volcano. The only way he could survive was to thrust himself utterly into the chasm created by his brother's death.

He left his mother in the care of his aunt. Wondering if she even knew he was leaving, he vowed never to return until every German soldier, every French collaborator was driven out of his country. With this resolve he had put himself to use – day and night – in the 'Maquis', the formidable iron resistance underground. Although he was just twelve, he had stopped being a child so many years ago that he could not even remember.

He had thrown the grenades that had killed the broken body of his brother just thirty days before, but during the past thirty days and nights the faceless face of Paul floated before his eyes. No guilt gnawed through his bones for having pulled the pin and dropped the grenade into the shaft of that dark deep room in the concrete bunker. What was strapped to the chair was no longer his brother. It was an animal – brutally terrorized again and again, until its bones were raw and its mind was lost. The only question that seemed to float around what had been his brother was "when will the unbearable inexplicable pain end?"

"Luc, it seemed that Paul was happy that I was going to kill him." Claude whispered in an odd cadence of speech that had only begun after his brother's death.

Luc took his face in his hands.

"You did not kill him. They did."

"Do you think he knew?" Claude asked so that his brother's best friend would answer - would answer the question that haunted him - the question, that in his heart and in his mind, he already knew the answer to.

Since that day, he had told to no one although most in the Maquis instinctively knew the action he had been called upon to take. He had to tell his mother that Paul was dead. His version to her and to his aunt was that he had died in the blast when they tried to blow the pillbox at Colleville. He told them Paul had died instantly. Madame Fortin was in such shock and pain that she did not realize that Claude had spoken and not signed to her.

"You gave him back his life because you gave him 'choice' and 'freedom'. He knew death was better, and Claude, he thanked you." Luc confirmed what Claude already knew.

"Yes, I know". He said so softly. "His eyes shone with joy when he saw the grenades." He spoke to Luc, for he knew that Luc loved his brother as much as he.

"My brother nodded 'yes'." For the first time Claude's eyes filled with tears.

"Claude, you gave him a gift – a gift of ultimate love." Luc pulled the boy to his chest and let his eyes be pressed against his soft jacket.

Fixed like statues in a garden, they kneeled, pressed together like hands in prayer. Both held back the stream of tears which rose to the surface. Each gave strength to the other and prevented the uncontrollable dam from flooding over the dike. Juliette and Zosia, like ephemeral angels with wings for arms, stood above and encircled the two figures that knelt on the floor of the forest in the mist of this hot July day.

Juliette now spoke. "What of our brother?" she said in disdain. "Can it be that he is still alive? Someone as righteous as Paul is sacrificed so that the likes of Denis may live. "Quelle absurdite'!"

Claude continued, "I have word that he had fled two days after the invasion."

"And the Colonel?' she hoped he was not dead for she wished to have that pleasure herself.

"Both fled – together – for Paris." Claude paused before he continued. He looked from Juliette's face to Luc's. "Your father was beaten before they fled because he raised his hand to strike the Colonel down. That was enough – for him to be left for dead."

"And our mother", Luc was almost afraid to ask.

"She was not touched. Both were found by a member the 'Maquis' in the wine cellar of your home. Much is destroyed, but much is left. 'Votre mere' had dragged him down to the cellar and nursed him away from death, they say."

Luc's jaw stiffed. "How much alive is my father and how dead is my mother?" he said to himself. He knew he could not have any answers until after – if, they returned from Paris.

July 3, 1944

Somewhere far from the beaches

My love Marjorie –

There's so much I want to tell you, but I have to keep it brief.

I am here with a fine group of men. They are not my original stick, but that is O.K. Each one is an expert on what he does, and although we are from different states and different parts of the world, there is no division among us.

We have been in France for almost one month. Tomorrow will be our Independence. I know all will go well. So, when you are sitting in Biney Park down the hill from Riverside Elementary School look at those red, white, and blue spiral blasts of fireworks and think of me. Know that a day – and hour – does not go by that I don't think of you. Your beautiful face is always in my mind's eye.

We've had some time to rest, and now we can move out.-where to, I cannot say. The names of those who are with me must also stay with me. The Frenchmen who have brought others into our group will be getting this letter back to the companies behind us and then over the Channel and then stateside - to America.

The name has a special ring to me now. It really sends shivers down my spine. I am so proud and thankful to be an American. The world was waiting for us. It waits no longer.

Let the screen door slam shut when you return home tonight. Smile and let it remind you of me. I'll fix it again when I come home. Walk up the stairs and take me in your arms. Perhaps, we will meet in our dreams tonight.

Love forever and ever, your Sidney, Lieutenant – 82nd Airborne

p.s. I can tell you two names those new additions to my team – A British engineer named Sandy and another Apache Indian named Harry. They'll get us through this next crucial gap.

another forest- early morning, 4 of July

Mom and Sis –
Today this morning is the 4th of July. My 'mates' in England never mentioned this day, but the Americans whose unit we've joined say it's a big holiday in America. My new American 'pals' say the English still don't like to admit they lost the American Revolution. Sometimes, the English call America – the colonies.

I wrote you when we landed safely. Now, I am writing again. It's been one month. I hope by now you've gotten my letter from the landing. Hopefully, by the time you will get this I'll be in Paris.

We have stopped to rest and regroup in a little Forest in France. I am comfortable in this Forest for it reminds me of Papa – in a good sense. I sleeped well for the first time since we arrived. The forest it is quiet. Hardly can the blasts of bombs and the barrage of artillery be heard. The pine needles make soft cushiony beds.

We picked herbs and nuts from the forest. My friend from England is here with me. I told you about him and his father and sister. He's is much like me.

We are moving out this day. When I reach Paris, I will bring you home gifts. I hear the war has been especially difficult on the Parisians. They have hardly had any food or fuel for their stoves. Maybe still, there is some pretty thing; I can get for you and Tatiana.

I guess sis, you're too old for dolls now. I miss you both. Will you even recognize me? I am no longer a boy - perhaps, I look like Papa though.

Love …and kisses, xoxoxoxoxoxox –

For now – good-by….Christian

Mama and Pop –   July 4 … 04:00
        Bet you've eaten big fat tomatoes by now Pop. Mom – I can taste your great olive oil and seasons drenching those slices of juicy tomatoes! We certainly don't get them fresh vegetables here. We had a great meal the other night though. Our two 'injuns' - (We meet up with two real 'American' Indians) - went hunting in this forest I'm now in. Hunting with spears for fish.
        We don't do that in Brooklyn! When we want fish, we go to the nice iced stand of Alphonso on Stuyvesant Street around the corner from our apartment – right Mama?
        Anyways, these guys bring back the fish. And the two foreign boys get a bunch of plants. The French "babes' got the mushrooms. Dug em outta the earth. They better not get a looksee at this letter. First of all they'd kill me if I called them 'babe' and secondly, they know more languages than you can shake a stick at. So, they'd know what I'm writing. Yeah, Pop the tall girl even knows Italian. Those are the first 'broads' I've ever met that think and act like men. If they do find this letter, ya know, that's a compliment, coming from me. Oh, I forgot to mention they joined us along the way too.
        Anyways, they baked these fish – trout wrapped in some leaves- in holes in this forest where we've been staying this past week. Don't get me wrong mama, but it was the best meal I ever had! That tells you what our rations have been like. We've been eating them all month.
        I'm O.K. I survived the landing along with my Lieutenant. The rest of our 'American' stick was killed.
        We trained, but no one could have prepared us for what we saw. Other men are with us now. We've met em along the way. Believe it or not one guy is from the Bronx. Jesus, I was happy to hear his accent over the walkie- talkie.
        We're moving out now at four fifteen in the morning of the 4th of July. We're heading straight for Paris. Four is my lucky number so everything will be oaky doky.
        It must be hot in the good old U.S.A. tonight. I can see Pop and Uncle Guido in their undershirts sitting on the roof with the rest of the block. I bet the fireworks will be beautiful. Know I'm over here for the whole GD block!
Love from 'your Bambino' – Tony -82nd American Airborne

<u>Fourth of July</u>

"Geez Mel, why are you putting that on? At least you could wait until after the Fourth of July." said Tony.

"So, I look the part." Baron said as he turned around in the 'new' German Colonel gun metal gray dress uniform he had ripped off a dead officer in the town just after Le Beau Moulin.

"Yeah "Kraut'. No blood on this one." O'Brien said.

"Betcha bottom dollar, 'Mick'."

Tony was betting nothing. The last time was when he took a 500 franc bill out of his winning pot and had all the guys he could get from the 82nd and 101st sign their 'John Hancock's'. Those days of waiting in the damp dark 'snakes' off the coast of England seemed so long ago. "How many of them were still alive?" he wondered.

Sal looked up at this blond blue-eyed specimen of Aryan perfection and felt a shiver go up his spine. If he never opened his mouth, Sal would have taken him for any other German. It was too close for comfort. He wouldn't bet any of his money against him. He had gotten a bird's eye view of 'Kraut' action at the bridge over the Torlonne. He thought of Aaron, who had also tried to impersonate a German. It bothered Sal that he never knew what Aaron had said in German.

"Did what he say or how he said it got him killed?" Sal thought. He looked back up at Baron. "This guy holds all the aces. Hot Damn he looks like a Kraut."

"Let's hear you speak, 'mate'." Sandy ordered.

"I can smile and kill you without blinking an eye, and still use my free hand to light an American cigarette." Baron said in German. The smile never left his face.

"For a Yank he sounds good to me, but then again I don't "sprechen sie Deutsch'. I'm the last mate aboard, so you tell me." He turned to Sidney who was now higher than he in rank. He was glad to hand over the authority to someone else - even if he was a Yank.

"Nor do I. What do you say?" Sidney turned to Luc.

Luc nodded his approval, and little Claude slid behind the two women and Luc. His wide eyes said it all, and Juliette's and Zosia's stiffening of shoulders and facial muscles reinforced Sidney's gut instinct. Baron could get them to Paris.

****

They had covered more area in half a day than in the first two weeks. Fear still sharpened their instincts and actions, but it did not overpower them as it had. Perhaps, they were getting used to this as a way of life or perhaps, they were just well fed and rested. For a group of fourteen, they cut quickly through enemy territory. Sidney had more than his 'dozen' but he had selected those whose abilities would complement the others. He kept Sandy and the rest of the Englishmen joined up with the British 2nd Army's 8th Company. Sidney had taken along Sandy, the other Apache, and the boy. He had no choice with the boy, for it was the boy who decided he would stay with them.

An invisible steel wire intertwined three of the foreigners - the Frenchman, the French girl, and this boy named Claude. The fact that all three knew German was a plus, and he had held additional aces with Janusz whose first language was Polish and Christian whose was Russian. Zosia, his ace in the hole, was fluent in all but Russian. As they moved out of the forest, it was she and Janusz who contacted a commando unit made up of German American Jews and Free Poles near the Orne River. That would be their crossing point.

****

The devised plan would have Luc and the boy crossing a small footpath of a bridge after Baron had already crossed and lit up a cigarette as a signal.

Luc and the others watched as Baron adjusted his cap, pulled up his leather boots, and checked the luger at his side. He slid his hand into his pocket to make sure the German cigarettes were there. He had handed over his 'Luckys' to Juliette. He wasn't going to find another Madame Simone at this bridge began his leisurely walk across this bridge at high noon. He paused to look up at the sun and unbuttoned the first button on the high collar German uniform. He took off his hat and ran his fingers through his thick blond hair before putting the hat back on. Anyone watching his actions would think he was an officer enjoying a country walk in a pocket of secured territory in this area far from the Beach heads.

Sidney had divided his team into two flanks – at least one woman, one Indian, one foreigner, one American were on either side of the bridge. When Baron paused, all they could do was wait. It seemed too quiet – too easy.

Then they came. A trio of efficient German soldiers.

Baron did not even turn his head towards them. He casually hit his right hand against his side and front pocket. As the trio's thick- soled boots hit the wooden planks of this old bridge, German Colonel Baron fixed a cool steady gaze at them. Luc had no doubts about this American's 'sangfroid'.

Juliette had told him what Madame Simone recounted about the American's actions in her café. Simone like the rest of the French in Normandy had expected the British to be their saviors – not the Americans. No one in Normandy had had any experience with Americans. It was the British who had been fighting undercover within France for the last three years. The BBC provided French citizens with news; De Gaulle had made sure of that, yet Madame had deemed this America worthy of the best in her Resistance cell. If all the American invaders were like him, the war should end soon.

"Das... what is that?" Baron shouted in German to the lead man in the trio as he pointed at the German soldier's boots. He continued berating him in German, "You call yourself a member of the Wehrmacht... the Fuhrer's great army?"

The other two raised their arms to 'heil Hitler' as the lead soldier bent down to tie his laces tighter and brush off the dust on his leather boots.

Luc, waiting behind the bushes, had his arm around Claude's shoulders. If all was fine, Baron would signal soon. They waited as they heard Baron's harsh words upbraiding the soldiers. Then Luc saw what he needed to see. Baron had taken out the pack of cigarettes and offered one to each man. He appeared to be casually asking them about the surrounding area. His hands went to his pockets again. The lead soldier clicked his heels together and offered a light to Baron.

"On y va", Luc whispered to Claude as he took his hand. They slowly and subserviently stepped onto the bridge. The

Germans continued to chatter and smoke – barely acknowledging the presence of the French man and boy. They had gotten use to the quiet defiance or outright collaboration of the French. As long as they obeyed, the Germans didn't ask why.

They didn't see the piece of wire Luc had taken out of his pocket and wrapped around each hand nor the piece of pipe Claude had slipped out of his right pants leg through the hole in his pocket. As Luc turned, he hooked the wire around one soldier's neck and Claude swung the pipe across the back of the other soldier's knees. The lead soldier in front of Baron turned and reached for his luger. He never saw the blow from Baron which broke his neck. Two lay dead as Claude hit his soldier with a second blow - this time to the head.

"This one's still alive. We can kill him now or hand him over to the Resistance." Luc stated.

"Geneva Convention, give him to the Resistance."

"That's as good as dead," added Luc.

"Maybe – but I'd like to get out of this war with some degree of moral integrity," Baron continued.

"Not all of us had that luxury." Luc curtly answered.

Baron just looked at this pretty boy Frenchmen. He knew then and there that he would not want to cross him – ever. "This guy doesn't give out second chances." Baron thought.

With a Gaelic shrug, Luc showed he really did not care one way or the other. He just nodded for the rest of the team to cross the bridge. No one, except Sandy even glanced down at the bodies of the two Germans floating face down in the Orne River.

"Whatever their reason for getting to Paris first, they are expedient soldiers at best, merciless killers at worst." Sandy thought.

****

They did not have to drag the unconscious soldier far, since a Resistance group ready to secure the bridge stood just beyond it. Although not large enough for any tanks, the bridge would suit any soldier who'd rather walk than swim across the Orne.

Barely past noon, the July sun made the sweat poured down their necks. The next stage would be more difficult. If they could get through Rommel's panzer troops – through the noose that his soldiers wanted to pull tight around the Allies' neck, they could hook up with any Divisions coming up from Ecouche and Falaise.

Sidney and Sal took out their silk maps as Luc translated what the Resistance men had told him about the area between the Orne and across the imaginary line which connected Falaise to Caen. Juliette, Zosia, Janusz, and Christian critically read the map and listened to the Resistance as they spoke slowly in the hopes that the Americans would understand some of it.

Sal, Tony, the Indians, O'Brien, and Sandy along with Sidney waited for the translations to understand the difficulty or ease of the task in front of them. Baron, by catching Juliette's eye, could follow most of the conversation. Mentally, he checked the distance they had traveled so far in comparison to the distance to Paris. They were less than half way there.

"Would we even get there in another month?" Baron thought. "One month gone – one to go. With no guarantees." He thought about Sidney's brief of the mission and that perhaps Juliette would fill in the rest.

"They tell me our best route is from here to here." Luc pointed to the spot on the Orne where they now were and to a pinprick northeast to a tiny dot called 'La Jalousie'.

"How long?" Sidney asked.

"By tonight. They say the Germans are concentrating their power in Falaise and Caen. That gives us the territory in the center to squeeze through and exit out of."

"And us?" Baron added.

"There's still time to pass through before the Germans are forced to flee. When they do, the Allies will probably set up an executioner's scaffold at the mouth of this pocket near the Dives River where any German tanks and armored corps will have to cross. Luc pointed to two towns on the map... Morisssy and Saint Lambert

"Alright then men - let's move out." Sidney commanded as he thought about what Luc said and thought, "The man has inbred military genius, a God given gift. He's aloof - but that goes with being French." Sidney laughed to himself. "I'm beginning to sound like Tony. But even Tony would agree. The man's a player. He knows the rules of war."

Out loud he ordered, "Sandy, you scout ahead with John. Harry and Thomas, you fork out the other way and scout in that direction. Leave a quarter mile between the two of you for us to pass between. We'll close the gap as we reach La Jalousie." Sidney ordered.

******* ***

A total silence hung in the air as they entered the outskirts of La Jalousie. Eerie and complete, it enveloped the town in a shroud. The heat at a quarter of six was beginning to rise, yet a yellowish green mist lay low and still on the ground. Luc knew this picturesque and peaceful tiny village held a reputation for rebellion and was always a seat of insurrection throughout the Occupation. Deep in its innards slept a tiny mustard seed - a core of hope, and from it had come the leaders of the regional cells. Always considering themselves lucky, the villagers played the game. Audacious plans would germinate from the core of this mustard seed and eventually break through the ground surface, flower in a burst of light, then submerge, and lie dormant until the next spring. The village of La Jalousie always survived. There had never been any reprisals.

Nearing the village, an uneasy sensation began to grow in the pit of Luc's stomach. Christian, too, felt the dizziness and nausea that came in his dreams or in his 'deja-vu's' during the day. None had the same intensity as that day in the Katyn, but now he could feel the waves of head pain building and the stiffness inching its way up the back of his neck. Like fingers, a dull throbbing pain reached up the side of his neck until it tighten and pressed against his skull like a vice. It was when the fingers turned into nails and jabbed behind his eyeballs that he wished for a knife to gouge out his eyes and kill the pain behind them.

It had begun again. What horrible truth did this village of La Jalousie hold? The mist was getting thicker.

The steeple of the church pointed upwards through the mist. It was the time of day that lights in houses should have appeared like beacons in the sea of mist.

There were none.

No dogs barked. No children's voices prattled.

But a rattle began to shake, hissing quietly at first - from the bowels of the earth. When the rattle shook louder and began to moan, only Christian and the Indians heard it. They tilted and violently moved their heads to rid the rattle's incessant hissing and moaning, but nothing could calm the rattle of death.

All moved toward their objective, the center of the town. They kept the steeple in sight and put one foot in front of the other. Scanning the horizon and looking left to right, no sign of the enemy appeared. But, as the team edged closer to town, no townspeople appeared either.

Into the town entered the fifteen. Each came from a different point, but all were converging toward the center – toward the steeple that they now could see only if they tilted their head up high. Sliding in and out of corners, each man and woman flattened their backs against the cold stone of houses and stores. Each one peeked into the windows – bobbed their heads into doors left open, yet they saw no one.

A black cat slid across Luc's leg and his nerves were so raw that he instinctively swung his rifle down and its barrel lifted the cat in the air. The shrieking meow cut through the silence of the mist.

It was then that the stench slapped him in the face. The church, a silent witness, jumped out from the mist, and in the parting of the mist the mounds of bodies gyrated in the center of the square. Mother upon child - father upon son - husband and wife arms clasped together - All dead. All cut down.

Luc steadied his hand against the cold stone of a building. His fingers felt the holes in the stone and the even colder metal of the machine gun bullets imbedded in the stone.

Christian's excruciating pain continued. The waves of nausea could not be stopped. He bent down, doubled over in pain and vomited again and again in the gutter of a little street called 'Rue du Pere'. His head vibrated from the vomiting – each time the knives cut even deeper behind his eyeballs. Each time he could see the faceless faces of the blond blue-eyed Poles in their death march. He was sick – so sick of shameless deaths – of evil so persuasive that it claimed the lives of the innocents.

Churning from the dry heaves, he steadied himself on a stack of the dead. When he pushed himself up, he was looking into the open eyes of a child no more than five. His mother's arm was around his shoulder, but that did not prevent the bullet holes from penetrating through her arm, into his back and straight to his heart. One lone bullet pierced her temple. Had she died first? Had she thought she saved him? Or did he die first, and she felt the pain of his death before hers?

Beneath the cords of bodies he felt movement. Was it a dream or reality? The mist had cleared. The church bells rang, marking the hour of six. A small hand pushed out from the mound of corpses. Head pulsating, he pushed the dead off the living, and pulled the hand and arm out to find face of delicate boy. A black beret covered the boy's head, and his once white shirt was splattered with blood. Pulling the boy out from the pile of the dead, he touched his chest to see where he was wounded. The boy was lifeless; he did not move at Christian's touch; except for the terror in his eyes, he seemed but a lifeless doll.

Quick clear shots of sniper shots echoed through the soundless square. Christian looked across and saw O'Brien and Baron hit the ground. In the street next to them John had thrown himself in front of Juliette knocking her to the ground. He looked up and saw the German on the steeple of the church. It must have been him who rang the bells for the dead to come to mass. Swinging his rifle up, Luc made a clean shot right through the soldier's head. The body fell in what seemed to be slow motion into the square and thudded onto the bodies below. Looking across again, he saw only Baron and Juliette move toward the church.
****

Within moments the barrage broke the silence. Voices in German – shouts of commands – machine gun fire – bursts of grenades – combined in cascades of sound cutting sharp like razorblades. Luc, inside the church, looked around for Zosia and Juliette. He caught their eyes looking for him and then for Janusz, Christian, and Claude. Would they all be silenced here? For now, the five were intact, and another added. Next to Christian was a small boy- stiff, wooden, and expressionless.

"Count up men. Who are we missing?" Sidney's voice boomed through the empty church.

The slamming of doors and the shutting of shutters reverberated in the cool calmness of the sanctuary.

"O'Brien's dead," Baron choked on the words.

"So is John," Juliette softly said. She and Christian knew he had traded his life for hers.

"Everyone else accounted for?"

"Oui" Luc was thinking in French, and his mind was racing ahead. What were their options? How could they escape this death trap?

"There are dozens of them. Coming out into the square." Sandy said as he lobbed one grenade after another out of the window high up in the balcony of the church. As they exploded one after another, the Germans fell behind the human sandbags.

"You got one machine gunner's nest, but they're setting up bazookas on two of the streets facing us." Sal shouted down from the other side of the balcony.

"How are our flanks?"

"They got them covered. An entire company. The scum mustta been hiding in wait to ambush us like the rest of those poor sons of bitches." Tony shouted out over the noise of gunfire.

"Our rear?"

"Looks clear" Zosia answered the Lieutenant.

"Like the Alamo, Chief." Thomas added.

"Well, Alamo or not. Looks like we've got one exit free", Harry countered.

Then a tiny voice sounded out in the cool church. Like an angel, it spoke. Trance-like, without trembling, this male Joan of Arc stood before them and spoke with words shot out like machine gunfire.

"They told us we were being evacuated because of the invasion by enemy forces. My brother who is … was a resistance fighter told me to run since it was a reprisal action not an evacuation. I tried, but they shot us. Laughing… they were. I fell before the first shots sprayed the square. I lay there forever – alive – with the dead - waiting for them to leave."

They listened, mesmerized by the boy's story. He stopped as abruptly as he had started. They saw him pull off his beret. A cascade of rich brown hair fell to her shoulders. An eight-year-old girl stood before them and with a deep breath, continued, "I know a tunnel that connects the church to the woods. I too helped my brother in the Resistance."

All followed her to the altar of the church. With all her strength she pulled on the iron cross and turned it like a heavy fortress key. The altar swung aside. Down into the dirt passageway a dozen of them went. Luc, the last of the twelve, was followed by the thirteenth man, Sidney. Luc had gone down before him and felt Sidney tap him on the shoulder.

"Take this." He said as he removed the pouch from his shirt and put the cord that connected it over Luc's neck. "I'll create a diversion and keep them from entering the church. Move as fast as you can for five minutes; that should get you to the woods; then I'll follow. Don't wait for me; just keep moving." He paused without adding the words he wanted to say. Unclasping the eagle bracelet from his wrist, he fastened in onto Luc's. Looking him straight in the eye, Luc nodded his head. "Merci, mon ami".

When all had cleared the tunnel, Luc heard what he knew was coming – the deafening, ground-shaking explosions.

Sidney had called in his coordinates and asked for Allied support – whatever they had. The order had been to hit the village with everything - to take out the site - to pulverize it into oblivion.

Just before he had entered the tunnel, Sidney spoke into his walkie-talkie. He told them the village had been massacred - all resistance fighters - all villagers - men, women, and children. 'Jalousie' was a German stronghold now.

"Count down from five minutes then hit me with everything you've got. Do not forget this village - 'Jalousie' - You read me 'Jealousy'?

The last words Luc heard as he ran from the tunnel were: "Bury them - NOW!"

Lieutenant Sidney Smith called fire upon himself knowing it would bury them all – the Germans, the townspeople, and himself on this fourth day of July, 1944.

\

Chapter 21 – the Fourth of August

<u>Chaulour</u>

"When we cross the Seine tomorrow, you will have done your part. Without your sacrifice we would not be here."

Zosia, Juliette, Janusz and Christian nodded in agreement toward Luc.

"To the 82nd Airborne."

"To the 6th Airborne." Sandy smiled at Tony. He couldn't let the Yank paratroopers get all the credit, but he wouldn't want anyone but this 'Yank' covering his 'backside' as the Americans would say. "And..to American Lieutenant Sidney Smith who gave up his life for ours.

"To Captain Hank Hudson, James Earl, and Aaron Axelrod and the rest of the damned good men of Company 2." Sal slowly wiped his eyes with his sleeve.

"To the dead left on Omaha, to the living who escaped only by chance, to my Company C, and to O'Brien – one Mick I'll never forget." Baron toasted.

"And the commando units of my people – our people, and the 101st, and to John, a proud member of the Cherokee nation".

"You're really drinking the 'firewater' Chief?" Tony teased.

"This is Champagne. My first. Where better to drink it…"

" .. than in France and right outside Paris." Sal finished the sentence for Thomas.

"May your second glass be in Paris when she is liberated my friend." Luc raised his glass high.

"To Paris…to our brothers and sisters in blood." Motioning to the five foreigners and to 'petit' Claude, the Resistance fighters, and the rest of the team in the mill by the Seine, Harry finished the toast.

'In the sous sol' or basement floor, covered with sawdust and flour, of this ancient mill were all of Sidney's remaining men and a half a dozen resistance fighters. Three round wooden 'spools' of thick heavy rope served as tables for their last supper together. Luc and the others each had their own thoughts about how far they had come and how far they had yet to go. Who at the end would still be alive? For Luc, the mill was similar to the apple pressing barns of Normandy.

Wide three-hundred-year old planks and a high stone ceiling surrounded a stone thresher which still grinded, as it had for three centuries, kernels of wheat into flour. For the surrounding farms, it had busily carried out its duties at the end of each dusty summer. At the end of this long summer of 1944 it would grind again, but after four long years the fruit of its labor would be in the hands of the French not the bellies of the Germans.

He was certain many tales could be told from these walls. Tales of love won and lost, of fortunes gained and spent, and of wars and their dead and those left to live on. He shut his eyes. "What stories will I be able to tell? There are so many I want to forget."

This supper tonight would be one of the happy memorable moments. All the delicious delicacies on the table had cost a price. Quail eggs in thick béarnaise sauce, omelets fluffy and stuffed with mushrooms and 'chevre' goat cheese, pheasant roasted and covered with small perfectly shaped onions and red potatoes, and 'canard a l'orange' duck with oranges, and trout and bass pressed with 'citron' or lemon, and the French famous 'haricot verts' and 'pommes frites' and 'salade mixte' - all were spread on the wheel hub tables.

It was a victors' gourmet repas - grown, hunted, stolen, and bought on the black market. Each ingredient for the meal was procured with pride and love as a thank you for what this team of men had begun in blood and would end in blood. This meal was a celebration – a graduation of sorts. For here they would separate and walk on different paths.

All knew it was just a matter of time before all the armies would be moving across one of Paris many 'ponts'. One had to cross a Parisian bridge, which stretched over the Seine, in order to move from one side of Paris to the other. Each man and woman in this dark bottom floor of an ancient mill was now privy to Hitler's orders that "Paris must not fall to the enemy – if it did, the enemy must find it reduced to rubble."

"Gentlemen the tide has turned. I've received word that the British have taken Caen and that the massive American bombing 'Cobra" operation has succeeded in letting General Patton take over Avranches." Luc held his glass high. "When the Americans broke out at Avranches four days ago, every German soldier, every French citizen, and every Resistance fighter in Europe had the same news. It is only a matter of time before Germany is defeated."

"Yeah"

"Here, Here."

"Naturellement"

"Bravo"

"Thank God"

"Merci le bon dieu"

The tide had turned with the real tides at Omaha, Utah, Juno, Sword, and Gold, but just when the other shoe dropped for the Third Reich, no man or woman here could define. Only history and time could assess that moment or moments. Perhaps, it was late in June when a sergeant in the American 2nd Armored Division put large saw teeth on the front of American

Sherman tanks. He listened to the frustration of Sherman crews and had improvised teeth from the scrap of German beach obstacles. At that moment they were no longer pinioned or blinded by the hedges and sitting ducks for the German Panzers. Instead, the Sherman tanks could literally chew through the 'bocage'. Or perhaps the war turned on June 28 when Parisian Resistance fighters assassinated the propaganda mouthpiece of Nazi Germany, collaborationist Philippe Henriot? Or did the tide turn on the twentieth of July when members of Hitler's own staff and Wehrmacht attempted to assassinate Hitler?

History would make its case, but for now Luc looked over this group of men he had come to rely on. As the war for France seemed to be coming to an end, he was allowing his emotions in. He mourned the death of Sidney, and on this night of August 4 Luc took off the pouch from around his neck and placed in near his plate. He touched it and could almost feel Sidney's presence. He could not open it when Sidney placed it around his neck on their last day together in the church of 'La Jalousie' one month ago on the fourth of July nor would he open it now.

The irony was not lost on Luc. These men – these Americans who had come to France's aid were from the very same nation that had sparked France's fight for independence from her Kings. He knew much of French pride and arrogance, but now he could see not only as a Frenchman but as a soldier in a team made up of French, English, Polish, Russian, American, and the first Americans, the Indian. To think France alone could have freed herself from Hitler's yoke was absurd.

He had been in the Allies camp ever since the 6th of June. Up to that point he acted solely as a Frenchman. Luc knew he was in part the 'typical' French freedom fighter – all for France. The propaganda Hitler had churned out for the English and the Americans had fed on the stereotype of the average Frenchman's sense of superiority. The French themselves believed it and collaborated for their own advantage, denied it and resisted German intervention at the cost of their own lives, or ignored it and continued to live their lives in the 'French' manner of shrugging their shoulders as if there was nothing they could do about it.

The propaganda for the typical American was that he was lazy and self-centered. Luc never believed it. In the last two months he saw first-hand their courage, integrity, and ingenuity. Nothing could stop these strong strapping young men – they had the bodies of the German war machine, but the heart and mind of a people grounded in freedom and fairness. He smiled as he looked out at their newly washed faces and hands. The war could not prevent them from trying to put on their 'Sunday best'.

"They're so self-effacing," he thought. "That would be unique for a Frenchman. A quality most Frenchmen would never have. I really consider them my friends. Mel, Sal, Tony so totally different - yet totally the same: American."

He did not remember which one or ones had told them about their generals. They seemed to speak of them as 'one of the guys' not as a savior - a God-like de Gaulle. He had learned about one of two of their Generals besides Eisenhower. Bradley was said to be a soldier's soldier, a real man of compassion, yet it was George Patton, Bradley's friend as well as his choice as a leader for the 3rd Army, who was the analytical, calculating soldier. Perhaps, he embodied the French mind, for like de Gaulle he learned from history. He would have been happy in Caesar's time or sparring against the tactics of Napoleon. Unlike Bradley, Patton liked war, and his keen sense of history and military command, led him to sweep into Avranches and move out at breakneck speed towards Argentan.

Regardless, Luc was thankful, yet these brave brash Americans would not be guaranteed the right to liberate Paris. Because of de Gaulle's insistence and Eisenhower's understanding of French morale, that plum would be given to the French. For that reason General Leclerc was attached to Patton's push to Paris. All the French backed Leclerc and the majority revered de Gaulle; Luc was no exception. He felt, however, that the Americans should be the first into Paris. They had paid the price.

The pouch rested under his hand. He would open it after the celebration and before their parting. At that moment all needed to know the cost Sidney and the others had paid for them, and to know what still had to be done before peace came again.

<u>Montmartre, Paris</u>

They had left Chaulour and had carefully picked their way to the bohemian haunt of Montmartre. They had entered through the "Porte de Clichy' rather than across to St. Denis and down towards the Basilica of Sacre Coeur. Perhaps, Luc was superstitious, but this close to the end he did not need his head served up on a platter by the Germans. He wanted to complete this mission alive and not be a modern day saint. According to legend, the hill 'la butte' of the martyr, Montmartre, had Saint Denis who carried his head on a platter to the top of the hill. Martyrdom and carrying one's head on a platter up the 'Butte' of Montmartre was not for him, but the Butte's wild lifestyle was - for it would allow them to blend in.

From its pallet, dusk had painted Montmartre a dusty gray. Through the muslin mist, he and Zosia traveled hand in hand as they walked up the steps to the Chateau des Brouillards.

Occasionally, he would tilt her head up and kiss her full lips. It was not an uncommon scene in Paris, and by this time the Germans had long gotten used to the French demonstrations of love, and for these two it was not a pretense.

Janusz and Juliette mimicked their actions in a charade of their own. Following quite far behind, they did not have to hurry, for she knew where her brother and Zosia were going. Janusz put his arm around Juliette's waist and occasionally would whisper a question or French phrase in her ear. To anyone else on the street it would appear to be little endearments between two lovers. They turned right to follow Luc and Zosia, and could hear the footsteps of Christian not far behind. Into the shaded path skirting the Chateau they sauntered. Passing through the grounds, they walked to the end of Rue Simon-Dereure where the statue of St Dennis stood and where it was said that he washed his decapitated head.

It was an appropriate place for his old 'lyceenne', his school friend Laure, to have hidden a note for him. If he survived, it had been agreed that he would return to this spot when Paris was on the threshold of liberation Here she would leave word. Through her cell she knew of his trips in and out of England, and now her oldest contact had told her that the 'couturier' was heading for Paris.

Luc, in turn, had a prolific memory. All the intricacies in the lives of his friends, relatives, and cell contacts could be called up instantly from the black lined file cabinets of his mind. Laure and he had had worked together; initially, as part of the team that he and Simon had drawn up more than four years ago, – and later on, independently.

Now back in Paris he would see her face to face once again. He took his time at the statue and fountain of Saint Denis and enjoyed his city with Zosia. She took off her shoes and soaked her feet in the basin of the statue. Bending down, Luc kissed the back of her neck where her short moist strays of hair curled up. His hand caressed her shoulder and slid down her side and hip to linger on her calf. Like a cat, she stretched her leg out and his fingers followed to her anklebone and to the bottom of her foot. He gently cupped his hand and cleansed her feet in the cool waters of Saint Denis. With the other hand, he supported himself at the heel of the statue. Casually, he pulled loose a stone from the back of the statue's foot and pulled out a folded piece of paper that he expertly palmed into his sleeve.

They rose. She leaned on him as she slid on her sandals and then turned to wrap her arms around his neck. Passionately, she kissed him. They appeared in no hurry - just two lovers in Paris with all the time in the world. They reluctantly pulled themselves apart, and she rested her head on his shoulder as they continued on down the Avenue Junot. He stopped at a 'pissoir' and in the darkness of the urinal he read the note, lit a cigarette, and with the match burned the note and let his urine flush it down the drain.

Past old artists' studios and the windmills of another century, they strolled. "I cannot believe I am finally here in your beloved city and the city of my mother's dreams." Zosia whispered to Luc. "I feel somehow my mother is watching over me."

"Certainement mon amour." Luc kissed her freckled nose. Her mother's stories about such artists as Degas, Renoir, Monet, and Toulouse-Lautrec flooded her mind as she turned her head to look at an ancient café and almost heard the music of this former dance hall and the swish of fabric from dresses brushing the floor. All pulsated in the mist of Montmartre. In her mind's eye she could see the batting of long lashes beneath full-rimmed feathered hats - the kind her mother loved to replicate. Zosia's fingertips tingled from the imaginary touch of velvet and silk, the fabrics her mother had sewn for ladies of another era, in another city- that her mother had never known.

Luc pulled her out of her reverie as they walked quickly down the steeply winding Rue Lepic, the old quarry road. She wondered why he had quickened the pace. Janusz and Juliette, still wrapped in each other's arms, leisurely and effortlessly danced over the cobblestones. Christian, further back and out of view of all of them, stopped to stare at a man who had jumped frantically upon the cigarette butt he had just flicked into the street.

London had hardships, but nothing could have prepared them for the gaunt figures of the old men and the skeleton frames of the old women. Although life went on, it went on tiptoes – never knowing when it would slip away in a frigid room with an empty cupboard.

Montmartre was different from the rest of Paris. Only the adventurous and independent of spirit lived here. Below the hill was Pigalle – infamous for its nightlife. Its cabarets and 'boites de nuits'- night clubs rivaled their counterparts in Berlin. Despite the severe deprivation in Paris the night club performers and singers in the nightclubs managed extravagant costumes. Feathers and pearls, strategically placed to enhance a dancer's lithe, sleek body were the fashion.

No thanks to the German occupancy, the women of Paris were leaner and more muscular. One meal a day and the absence of petrol did that. Bikes replaced cars and Parisian women rode their bikes with skirts hitched up. Luc and Zosia did not even have the luxury of a bike, and he knew they had to get to the cemetery of Montmartre before the sky turned from gray to black.

"Laure or 'Lavande" says for me to go to the cemetery. She addressed the note to 'Dumas Pere'." Luc whispered to Zosia as he took her elbow to steer her more rapidly through the narrow streets.

'Lavande', the singer he had heard of must be Laure for the note behind the hollow heel of St. Denis was written to 'Dumas pere', Luc's other pseudonym, and signed from L. The Cemetery of Montmartre held the tomb of the novelist Alexandre Dumas, author of the <u>Count of Monte Cristo</u> and the <u>Man in the Iron Mask</u>. Luc had worn so many masks since this war began that his face was permanently frozen – made of iron and expressionless, and the 'Monte' could refer to Monte Cassino – the push that had come from the boot of Italy in May. Soon, those from the Beaches of Anzio in Italy and from the beaches of Normandy would meet to battle against and in Germany.

Luc took Zosia's hand as they walked into the cemetery built on the hilly terrain of the Mont. He thought of himself as the young boy who used to accompany Grand-pere Michel on his walks. Despite his keen business sense and strict tailoring discipline, his grandfather hid a radically bohemian creative side. Often they would even stroll among the flamboyant at the bottom of the 'butte' before it was known as Pigalle and among the artists at the top of the 'mont'.

Montmartre, Michel Morneau's playground, where some of his best ideas came from, colored his mother's memory. She, too, as a child she would walk there with her father. Often they'd go and pay their respects to Edgar Degas, one of the dead buried in the Cemetery of Montmartre. An original Degas charcoal sketch hung on the wall of his office. Many a time, Luc remembered how his grandfather would inspect the lines on the tulle skirt of the ballet dancer.

However, this time, as he entered the cemetery, Luc carried other memories about his grandfather. "How he'd adore the many cats that would come and rub against his loose pleated trousers. Mon dieu, grand-pere would reach down and pick up the dirty strays and place them on his cleaned pressed immaculate trousers. He did not mind that their fur was left in the crease of each pant leg. He just preferred their purring and pleasure at his touch," Luc remembered. The fur of each cat would tickle Luc's bare legs for he, like all French boys, did not wear trousers until he reached the age of thirteen.

The graveyard was so different now. Paris was so different. Both seemed as though they never blossomed from the cold barren constraints of winter. It was during an 'occupied' winter that Michel Morneau died, and it was winter that killed many Parisians. The unkempt cemetery reflected the spirit of the Parisians. They had to be more concerned with the living than the dead. The old women who always tended the graves, plucking out the weeds that grew between the stone paths and planting flowers to border the headstones, had not done their work. Too tired and too malnourished, they came only to pluck up a cat or two for dinner. All this Luc knew from his grandfather before he died.

The last walk he took with Michel Morneau was in August of the first anniversary year of German Occupation. At that time he was not teaching Luc about the names of the masters who were buried in this Cemetery, but was absorbing and gathering strength from those who lay before him. They walked the streets and paths of La 'Butte', and now the roles were reversed. It was Luc who would wait for his grandfather to rest and pause half way up each steep graded street. It was Luc who would talk about each house and person who had walked these streets before them. When his grandfather would catch his breath again, they would continue on.

Luc wanted to assume the role as teacher for Zosia, but for now they walked in silence. Janusz and Juliette had stopped in a small cabaret owned by the brother of Henri Gallet. Throughout the long four years of occupation, the Germans kept an eye on Auguste Gallet, even though he had collaborated when the scum of the German army began to frequent Pigalle. To the Germans the brother of Henri Gallet could be bought. Henri Gallet, himself, could not. He remained aloof and noncommittal even when he was forced to serve up his best wine to the officers of the Third Reich as they sat like tourists viewing the Eiffel Tower from his café on the Rue des Freres Perrier.

It was not until half way through the Occupation on one sunny spring day in 1942 that they dragged Henri Gallet out from his cafe and shot him in the street. A member of his resistance cell, unable to withstand the Gestapo's hideous torture had talked before he died. He named names.

They never dragged Auguste Gallet into the streets of Pigalle, for they assumed the brothers had parted ways. From the day his brother was murdered Auguste Gallet, always kept an American Derringer hidden in a side pocket of his apron. If they ever came for him, he "would shoot the swine". Never a collaborator - always a poser, he had fed information to Henri on the affluent side of Paris and waited for when the tide would turn.

Juliette and Janusz had a glass of what appeared to be the house 'table' wine and received the obligatory half-filled basket of stale bread. From the moment they wandered into his cabaret, Auguste Gallet controlled his impulse to run up to Juliette and smother her in his once large muscular arms as he used to when her grandfather would bring her up to Montmartre. His arms were thin now, and he no longer had his full belly. He signaled the woman at the door to replace the 'Vin de maison' with a bottle of his best wine from the vines that grew behind the cemetery of Saint Vincent. He, himself, brought a fresh baguette and a tray of goat cheese and camembert. Inside was a note – 'bienvenue ma petite. Va a l'arret de Metro des Abbesses'.

Christian was sampling his own choice of cheeses in the little shop four doors down from the cabaret of Auguste Gallet. The Resistance men and women of Montmartre and Pigalle were keeping track of any 'new' faces in their territory. They did not get a knife in their sides because the leader, Lavande', knew well the face of 'le couturier' and his 'petite soeur', Juliette. They had grown up together – Luc, Laure, and her brothers and he would play 'le football' daily in the stone courtyard of their lycee. They'd hurry through their two-hour lunch at their homes to run back to the lycee for a match of soccer before classes began again in the afternoon. Christian was in good hands. He, too, was slipped the note of 'Les Abbesses'.

Luc and Zosia had also stopped for a mini 'repas'. The note beneath the rock at the "Dumas' tomb said two words 'Lapin Agile'. Facing the large white dome of Sacre Coeur, they had chosen to sit outside the café Lapin. They were not alone. The tables of La Place du Tertre were occupied by residents who were getting a bit of sustenance before the night's work began. Many of the girls of Pigalle had just woken up. They were served omelettes or perhaps an occasional 'quiche lorraine' or braised 'lapin', a rabbit side with thick gravy, onions and small potatoes. The regulars came – some on the arm of a German soldier whose hand would run up the girl's leg as they sat down at a red checkered clothed table.

Laure came alone. She walked inside the Café Lapin Agile and sat at her usual table on the second floor. There she commanded a view of La Place, the courtyard, and its surrounding little shops. Her eyes scanned the narrow streets which led into La Place du Tertre, and on occasion she would allow herself to scan upwards to the dome of Sacre Coeur. At those times she wondered when God would return to Montmartre, to Paris, and to France. She had only two brothers left – her oldest Jean-Paul and her youngest, Gustave. Robert and Pierre, the middle two, had been caught during the student demonstration on November 11, 1940. She sat and gazed out into her beloved quartier and thought how the 4th year anniversary of their death would coincide with the falling of the leaves as Paris began another winter of cold and misery.

"How brave and foolish Robert and Pierre were to demonstrate at the Tomb of the Unknown Soldier right under the Arche de Triomphe - under the noses of the German forces. Our summer honeymoon was over with them. Mon dieu, how their iron fist came down." She took a sip of red burgundy and looked again at the church of the sacred heart. "My Elizabet and Lucie too were sacred - my lovely twin sisters should have been so lucky to be killed by one burst of machine gun fire."

She turned away from the white dome of 'Sacre Coeur' and did not want to think of them. "Having been caught and tortured separately, did each in her agony reveal the name of the other?" At times Laure thought that was what actually killed them. She learned afterwards they had been taken to different 'houses', one on the elegant Avenue Foch and the other on the Avenue Victor Hugo. Each 'house' had a cellar equipped with the necessary tools of torture. She knew they were first raped by the Gestapo's male guards – a common practice to teach them their bodies were no longer theirs. Then they were turned over to the special forces of the Gestapo: the lesbian collaborators. They endured one act of repulsion and pain after another.

"Was it with a clear cold calculating mind that led each to reveal the other's name or was each one's name whispered weakly from a weary and broken spirit?" Laure kept wondering. "Had they simply been playing for time so that others could escape? Did each one reveal the other twin's name with the last ounce of strength because each, in her heart, knew that the other was already captured? They knew what their captors were doing – they knew each step of their plan to make them surrender their mind and spirit as they had surrendered their bodies into the expert hands of the Gestapo."

She always tried to stop these thoughts that kept entering her mind like insidious intruders. Friends, lovers, family - so many gone, the deadly game had continued for years. Was it the irony of fate that her bothers were killed at the beginning of the Occupation and that her sisters were killed at the end when it seemed the long years of deprivation, fear, and humiliation were coming to a close? She had decided she would not tell Luc. He had been sent back into the fire for a reason, and he did not need excess emotions clouding his mind. If Luc did not ask her, she would not tell him what had happened to Elizabet and Lucie.

Luc was finally returning to Paris in the last act of the Germans' five act play, a tragedy of their making, whose climax had come with the invasion on June 6, and now two months later all of Paris – all of France was waiting for the end - to close the final curtain on a play that had a captive yet participating audience for all of its scenes. The 'denouement' was inevitable – the 'where' was Paris, but the 'when' was the question.

No one could contain the Resistance cells. German soldiers, who had sauntered down the avenues and boulevards, now ceased to walk alone. During the night or the day, they went out only when necessary and only in groups. Their force seemed quite invisible except for retaliatory acts that they continued to do in force against any act of resistance.

Laure, again, gazed out the window over the Paris that she loved so desperately. Why its beauty could still ensnare her after the deaths of her beloved brothers and now her sisters amazed her. Four years they had been gone, yet to her it was just a heartbeat away. Her sisters and she loved to sit in 'La Mere Catherine' or at the 'Lapin Agile' and mingle with the real people of Paris. How could she go on without them? How had she continued after the deaths of her brothers? Her heart was raw with a raging fury and with a wound that never healed. Years, months, weeks, days – it did not matter.

"C'est clair, I am never accepting of their deaths. C'est toujours that I am always going to expect them to enter this café from la rue - the street Casse Cou. We were to meet across at the Place du Tertre..," she studied each leaf on the chestnut trees that surrounded the square as she sat alone sipping her wine. "Helas,' she sighed with almost a cry. "We were to meet here once Paris was liberated and hold our glasses high as the sun shined again over the Basilica."

This now could never be. All she could do was to continue to glean information from the common German soldier who came into her club to drink and to take home one of the girls for the evening. Less and less frequently, the soldiers came, for Montmartre was an area of Paris too remote and enclosed too many corners where a Parisian bent on revenge could hide in the shadows.

On this evening in August the white of Sacre Coeur's dome and the purity of the prospect of their newfound freedom pulsated in the night air. The sun was not shining; darkness had flung its cloak over Paris, yet she lifted her glass to Sacre Coeur and the memories of Robert, Pierre, Elizabet, and Lucie. Then, as though by fate, he appeared. Tall and dark, his physique even leaner and more muscular than she remembered, Luc's face stood still in the light of the lone gas street lamp. He casually looked at the windows of the closed stores. No one turned the corner after him and no face cracked open a door or peered from behind lace curtained windows.

Laure held her breath. Her regular table commanded an eagle eye's view of Luc, 'La Place du Tertre", and a rear view of the open staircase leading from the floor below where no one could come up without her seeing them first. From this solid oak square of wood she could see the streets below. She ran her fingers across the table's gnarled and marked surface, worn smooth by the tides of time like a huge rock on the beach.

'How many tales could this table tell?' she thought as her eyes looked around the room and panned the street below. No one was following Luc. The girl who was with him she did not know. She did know about 'Renard' who had been like a brother to him. "At least his sister, Juliette, is still alive and so is his real brother, Denis. How could that one still be alive – and mine dead?" She had asked herself too many questions like that. She forced her mind back to the present.

Luc had come full circle – back to his early Paris days when they were all just 'lyceens". He had returned to his city to connect with one special 'student' – the 'lyceen', Simon. Her notes had led him and his group this far and now she would tell him in person where to find Simon.

****

Juliette, Janusz, and Christian had made their way around or through 'La Place du Tertre' to the Metro stop, ' Les

Abbesses' on the far side of the hill of Montmartre. Down the dozens of steps, they edged themselves against the smooth cold curved wall of rock. In the semi darkness the mold was even more noticeable. Soon there would be no light.

As they dropped deeper into the innards of the ancient city of 'Paris', the natural light dimmed and no 'electric' light would show them the way. The Germans had instituted blackout periods in order to conserve electricity. As the war year turned into years, these periods became more and more frequent. Paris was literally being thrown back into the dark ages – without food and fuel- everything came to a standstill. During this last winter Parisians huddled -listening to the rumblings of their empty stomachs in the freezing darkness of overcrowded apartments that still had some coal left.

The metro stop, 'Les Abbesses', had been in darkness since the Occupation began. The Germans preferred to use another metro stop at 'Pigalle' where the true 'red light' district of Paris operated. Healthy and well fed, they could easily walk the many steps to the top of the hill – but why bother when most of the girls lived next to or above the cabarets they worked in. If they chose to follow one of their favorites to the top of the hill, the long walk up the stairs was in full view. The Parisians would not snipe at them out in the open – but in the curved dark stairs of 'les Abbesses', they could. Either way the reprisals came, but the Germans did not want to close down Pigalle. They wanted to be serviced.

Now was different. Few came to Montmartre for its street people would kill for a crust of bread or simply for vengeance. It did not matter why a German soldier was murdered, but just that he was. No German – Gestapo or otherwise would dare to come down into the darkness of the hell at Abbesses. Juliette was French and not afraid. She led the two men into her Forest of Katyn - her streets of Warsaw. She was comfortable here.

****

When they reached the last set of stairs before the metro platform and tracks, a hand reached out with a lit torch. It cast an eerie light upon their faces.

"Suivez-moi," the torch man said.

They followed him through a passage that led to a metro- stop control room. A wire panel, dotted with mushroom like protruding bulbs, covered one wall. On the left, a cot pressed against the wall, and a wash stand with soap and a pitcher of water sat. On the right cold clammy wall of this tiny room, they groped. They followed the torch man until he pressed against a large stone that pushed inward. He slid his hand into the crevice and felt for the latch, releasing part of the stone wall. Inward, they went. The wall of stone was slid back and pushed closed from the inside.

The dampness and smell of mold did not bother Christian, but the hard muffled breath of men in darkness flung him back to the Forest of Katyn where he had lain so long ago with his face pressed into the forest's floor of pine needles, leaves and dirt. All he could do then and all he could do now was listen to their difficult breathing in the dead silence of the tight closed air. Perhaps, when they retrieved the lists of the dead that the Forest of Katyn had claimed, he would find peace. Until then, he moved out of his body and let his spirit follow Juliette.

As they passed deeper and deeper into the darkness, they became accustomed to it. What their eyes could not see, their ears and fingers could. The constant flutter sound as they passed down each set of stairs reverberated in their ears. Its constant low rhythm could drive a man crazy in time. Still, they kept descending. The sound of a chirping joined the chorus of the 'hums' and a ticking sensation whipped across their ankles. The walls felt slimy, wet, and cold.

"Where are we going?" Christian thought.

"Who is leading us?" Janusz wondered.

However, both trusted Luc and in turn his sister, Juliette. The answers would come soon enough. On level ground now, they followed. An outline of a door glowed in the darkness.

"Nous venons." the torch man shouted ahead.

At the sound of 'we're coming' the door opened a crack. As its light slid out, the flurry of sound and the chirping chorus became louder as though it were building to a crescendo.

"Depechez-vous," a voice behind the door cried out.

The trio did as they were told and hurried through the door as the fury of sound tried to follow them in. Christian and Janusz realized they had descended well below the railroad tracks, but they had lost their bearings when the descent got steeper.

Because Paris was her city, Juliette knew what was in the tunnels under the metro system of Paris. She had let them enter before her, and as they did, she turned and looked back. The light from within the room flooded the corridor through which they had passed. She swallowed hard, and she saw what she knew would be there. Skulls lined the walls and rested in piles on either side. Amid the piles, rats scurried looking for fresh flesh among the bones, the majority of which had rotten out and were picked cleaned hundreds of years before. Above the skulls in the crevices of the tunnel, bats strung themselves like shirts hung out to dry on clotheslines over the rooftops of Paris. Layered one upon the other, these live shirts fluttered in the light of the artificial sun as it streamed down the corridor of bones.

"Bienvenue aux catacombs, mes amis. Shut the door - 'vite' quickly."

The door shut. The light was within. The bats, the skulls, and the rats — all the inhabitants of the catacombs were outside. The resisters- the still-living with the forever-dead - would spend the night in this island hole of sanctuary. Juliette had always heard stories of the catacombs. Whenever someone disappeared from sight, it was said that the catacombs had swallowed them up. Before the war the catacombs were hide-a-ways for thugs - now saviors called them home. How ironic that this inferno would hold such angels.

Far above them in Laure's cabaret, 'La Nuit Eternelle, a few Germans lingered for their last nights in Paris, and a typical French couple sat in a corner of the smoke filled room — fingers and eyes locked into one another. The girls on the stage sang off key and swayed to the music of the accordion. The waiters served diluted beer and wine but charged full price to the German tables, and brought the best in the house to the couple in the corner. Between warm kisses Luc and Zosia looked over one another's shoulders and listened to the voices around them. They did not need to speak to one another. However, the wine had not dulled their senses. Still surrounded by danger, they were listening to any too casual comments by the clients of 'La Nuit Eternelle'.

Luc and Zosia would be the last to leave, waiting until the Germans wobbled down the rail-less steps to the streets below in Pigalle. Too fearful of taking the dark steps of 'Les Abbesses' and knowing if they missed the last metro, these Germans would have to walk arm in arm with a fellow soldier. They looked around to see if any girls were still left in the cabaret. If they were lucky, one of the French girls of mademoiselle Laure would escort them out the cabaret door.

Many - even under such escort had run out of luck when they tripped on the steep steps of Casse Cou. In the morning light they would be found with cracked skulls bleeding on the pavement - sixty steps below. The street cleaners would sweep the blood into the gutter; a café owner would wash the pavement down with the icy water from the pan beneath his ice box, and two men with dirt smudged faces would drag the bodies down into the catacombs where they would pile them atop the bones from the revolution of 1789, until the flesh would begin to rot and to be dined upon by the vermin of Paris. Death knew no nationality and leveled all to equal status.

Luc and Zosia passed by the steps as the girls nodded to them. They climbed higher into the early morning clouds of Montmartre to the 'Hotel des Anges'. In this hotel 'of angels' Laure had selected a large airy flowered room with a distant but clear view of the Arc de Triompe and La Tour Eiffel. As they gazed out the window, Luc thought of his life on the Avenue Georges V, one of the twelve spokes jutting out from 'L'Etoile' that circled the Arc de Triomphe. Soon he would see Simon and learn who was still alive. Soon he would see once again his home, his grandfather's house less than a kilometer from the Triumphal Arch, where Michel Morneau had died. Triumph had not reigned in his beloved city, but Luc knew that it would soon again.

Luc gazed from Paris to his one other love - Zosia. He looked deeply into her eyes that were always changing like the sea - from blue to green to gray. In this light they were green. Mysterious, mischievous, honest, and always filled with love. Luc wondered how he could be so lucky. He pushed down the fear that his luck might run out.

They turned from the open window and left its open shutters wide to the hot August night. Like on the cliffs of Normandy, they felt alive again - their first night together in Paris.

La Place de la Concorde - Paris – august 14

"L'opera est ou?" Christian asked the man on the far end of the Louvre. He stood in front of the Obelisk, the pointed high Egyptian monument which had, since Napoleon's time, shot its tip like a finger into Parisian skies. It marked the end of the Champs Elysees, the most noted Avenue in Paris and perhaps in the world. Black and white newsreels had documented Hitler's first and last visit to Paris in June of 1940. Arrogant and cock-sure, he rubbed the French and the world's noses into the dirt of Paris.

Christian looked for the first time down this long straight tree-lined wide avenue to the Arc of Triumph at the far end. Soon, he hoped the stain of Hitler's presence at the Napoleon's Triumphal Arc and the German leader's footsteps on this most famous avenue would be washed clean and forgotten in time. God willing, it would be replaced by the image of de Gaulle or Eisenhower, leading the Allied Forces under its arc, down the Champs Elysees, and into Triumph.

Christian's eyes were so fixed on the Arc of Triumph that he, for a moment, forgot why he was there. The man in the black beret and black sweater looked at him in surprise. Then in an instant his emotion registered as indifference. He simply shrugged his shoulders.

Christian did not know if this shrug was because of the question he had asked concerning the Opera or because of his apparent lack of interest about the answer. Christian thought this was the man – the man named Moliere. He wore the scarf loosely tied around his neck and in that moment after he heard the question there was a spark of recognition before all went blank.

"Cinquante centimes pour vos journaux", the man shouted weakly from his corner. His hands shook as he held his stack of newspapers under one arm and waved a single paper over his head.

Luc and Christian had come to this corner several times each in the last ten days. The man had not appeared until day seven. Luc had looked at Simon from afar, and could not tell if it was he. The man he had known for more than ten years was not as thin as this stick of a man selling newspapers from this city island at the foot of the Obelisk. Standing on the Rue de Rivoli, Luc looked across and had seen Christian approach the man and then part ways.

If not Simon – then who? Who was the man who had appeared these last three days? Time was running out. General Leclerc had finally gotten out of the woods south of Argentan and had met up with the American 4th Division. They were on their way to Paris, and the city glowed in anticipation. Every Parisian wanted the yoke of oppression off his neck and those of political conviction wanted either the rule of Rol Tanguy and his communist forces or that of Charles de Gaulle and his Free French Forces whose plans had formulated in England four long years ago.

The word was out that those who had abandoned the city in June of 44 were coming back to reestablish themselves, retrieve their property, and celebrate in the liberation of 'their' Paris. If Luc and his team could not get the incriminating documents concerning Russia's Katyn massacre of Poles into the hands of Leclerc or de Gaulle himself, the communist commune of the city would cause such an uprising that the revolution of 1789 would receive but a footnote in France's future history books.

This slight man selling newspapers might be the final piece of Luc's puzzle. Was he the one who could fit through the gates of the Pere La Chaise Cemetery? Did he possess the key to the tomb of Moliere or was he the key himself?

Christian again approached the man and this time he bought a newspaper which he opened. Glancing at the headlines, he shook his head slightly side to side as though in exasperation of what he read. He folded the newspaper and placed it under his arm as he stepped toward the curb.

Luc had only two choices. He could go to Pere Lachaise, taking only Christian and Janusz since each, in his own way, could verify the authenticity of these documents written in Russian about the Polish high intelligentsia and military of that time in 1939. But, if it were a trap, all three would die. His other choice was to cross the street now and find out from Simon himself if a trap waited for them at Pere Lachaise. However, if the man, who held himself so crookedly and appeared shorter and older than Simon, was not Simon but instead a Nazi collaborator, then Luc, himself, would be trapped. As soon as Luc set foot on that island of land, which began the Jardin des Tuilleries and the former palace of the kings, the Louvre, there would be no escape. He needed to cross the Place de la Concorde. His life or the lives of all three?

There really was no choice. He stepped off the curb on the Rue de Rivoli and angled across the wide strip of pavement. Normally, in the Paris before the War, that would have been an impossibility. A taxi or Parisian Citroen would have careened into him. In this Paris, however, few cars drove down her avenues, and to anyone who might notice, Luc appeared to be just another Parisian crossing the street to buy a paper from a vendor, bundled up against a nonexistent cold on this hot Monday of August 14, 1944.

The sun was not yet directly overhead. As Luc walked toward the newspaperman, the man moved slightly into the sun. Closer and closer Luc walked, but still the man's face was unclear. The beret, cocked off kilter on the far side of his head, the scarf high on his neck practically muffling his chin, and his face constantly turning into the glare, making it impossible to see the features of the man. An uneasiness crept over Luc with each step that he took. His natural instinct that had kept him alive so long kicked in. He was fighting the impulse to turn and run from this strange figure of a man. He felt for the piece of fabric loosely woven under his right lapel. The outline of the cyanide capsule felt somehow comforting. One quick gulp and his fear of betraying his sister, Zosia, Christian, and Janusz would vanish like his life.

One foot in front of the other, he had crossed the street and stepped onto the sidewalk in front of the metro- stop, Concorde.

"Allez! Allez! Allez!" the newspaperman yelled as pulled off his beret and swirled the scarf from his neck.

Luc instinctively jumped backwards, away from this demented man who violently reacted to one lone pigeon that was landing to pick up a crust of bread in the street.

"Hey mec, c'est mon diner, pas le votre!" the man continued to yell.

Luc had no intention of stealing the pigeon for his own dinner. In the passing seconds, Luc did not remove his fingers from his lapel nor get distracted by the bird in flight. He had known 'tricks' that were far better rehearsed than this one. He focused on the man instead.

To himself Luc said, "Stop. Walk by him. Head for the Metro. Choose one – but look at the man, and know one way or the other my fate – and that of my friends."

He did not know what registered first – the pale gaunt gray face with the grin he knew so well, the rope burns that scarred his neck or the way he turned his head to hear from the only ear he had left.

Simon noticed Luc's eyes fill with tears and his hand drop away from his lapel.

"Journal, Monsieur" Simon shouted.

Luc found his voice. "Ouais". He pressed a franc into Simon's hand and fought the impulse to pull him toward him and hug him as he has seen so many Americans. Instead, he felt the cold glancing brush of his friend's fingertips. He looked toward and saw Simon had no nails – just bluish black lesions where his nails had been.

"Voila, votre journal jeune homme." Simon stated as he handed Luc the newspaper.

Luc took the newspaper and pretended to glance at the front page as he looked at his old friend's crushed fingers. His eyes moved quickly to his face and the bloody bandage that covered what was once his left ear.

"'Yes', Luc thought. "I am still a young man, but you 'mon vieil ami'" have aged a decade for each year of this hideous war."

Simon read his thoughts.

In a whisper – in English he said. "I am O.K. Go to metro Denfert-Rochereau.

"Merci", Luc said to the newspaper seller and walked by him to the nearest metro stop. He casually walked down the steps into the stop 'Concorde' and read the front page of his newspaper.

Not one word registered. He could not even see the words. He stood on the 'quai' waiting for the train to come down the tracks. All he could see were Simon's sad eyes and beaten body. He squeezed his eyes tight to stop the tears from coming. He slid the paper under his arm and stepped into the subway car of the metro line toward 'Chateau de Vincennes'. He would have to change lines twice before Denfert-Rochereau. It would give him enough time to 'stuff it down' as the Americans would say.

It would take a Herculean effort to suppress all the emotions coursing through his veins. His mind and body were hot with rage and a sorrow so deep that his heart physically ached. He had not been prepared for that old crippled figure of a man to be Simon. All the 'when's' and 'why's' and 'how's' had to be pushed beneath his heart and out of his mind. He had to go by his gut – and his gut alone, if they all were to complete this mission, and still live.

Chapter 22 – Countdown to Freedom

<u>Sunday, August 20, 1944 - Denfert-Rochereau</u>

"It's been a long day, an even longer night, and an intolerably long, painful four years - 'plein d'agoisse'." Simon looked around this small damp annex, deep beneath the Paris streets, and knew of the 'angoisse', the agonies each resistance fighter, who was still alive and who surrounded him on one of these last intolerably hot days of August, had experienced. Simon felt their pain through his own skin, beneath his bones, and deep within his core.

"We're days or even hours away from freedom, but still we are walking a tightrope. This room we've 'borrowed' from Colonel Rol-Tanguy."

Simon gestured to its slimy cold walls. A young man laughed with a little too much abandon, yet all knew it was one of the many rooms in the catacomb command post of the only organized French military in France, the Communist forces of Colonel Henri Rol-Tanguy's.

"He and his men have constantly fought against the occupying forces of Germany and have never bowed down to German tyranny - Not because, France must be France, BUT France had to be their France - under communist rule. The 'salaud' has always wanted to trade one yoke of tyranny for another. However, yesterday, it was we who began the ultimate and... pray - 'merci au bon dieu'- for the 'successful' uprising of Paris!"

Shivers went down Luc's spine as he listened to Simon speak. They were one – once again – commanding and leading their lycee yard boys. Simon's words electrified his group working within arm's reach of Col Rol's extensive army of communist followers.

"To the barricades!" the scruffy young boy who looked like a ghost from another insurrection of so long ago. The battles of 1830', 48', and 71' were in the collective memory of all Parisians, for it was in the previous century, in the 1800's, when other generations of Parisians barricaded the streets with walls of wood, furniture, and carriages in order to reclaim their Paris. Now, these men and women had come again. Resurrected by the death of their city - their country, they walked like mist out of the minds and hearts of all true Frenchmen. Like the dead, rising from the Seine, pushing back the tombstones of every Parisian cemetery, and climbing up from the catacombs' piles of skulls and bones, they began to once again block the enemy in their streets.

"To the Cross of Lorraine!" another child cried out. Whether a boy or a girl, it did not matter. The hat, with its yellow cross, marked another hero of the Republic, Joan of Arc.

"To Justice." A man joined in

"To Simon," another man added.

"To Simon," all cried out in chorus.

Luc noticed that Simon had taken off his beret once down in his headquarters of Denfert-Rochereau. The musty dank smell of death and the feeling of being buried alive permeated the air. Simon had escaped death, and because he had, he removed his beret in a gesture of defiance and freedom. His wounds were healing. Where his ear had been, a hard series of scabs, free of infection, had formed. Where the noose around his neck had hung, the ugly purple lacerations were turning to red blistering scars. Where his nails had been, hard purple tips and the faint whispers of a new pink nails were edging their way out from his cuticles.

In the six days he had been with Simon, Luc never asked what the Gestapo had done, nor did Simon speak of it. It was enough that he was alive. They had not broken him, and perhaps in time, his sleep would not be racked by his own screams in the middle of the night.

"The Barricades must wait. The Colonel is not aware that he has helped our cause, - the cause of the Free French and de Gaulle. Colonel Rol-Tanguy's posters on the walls of our city and his destruction of the telephone exchanges and the German wiretapping equipment along with it, makes our job easier. His groups have attacked small groups of German soldiers and seized their weapons, but it is a leader of our Gaullist resistance, Alexandre Parodi, who organized a polan to take over the Prefecture of Police. At his moment, Parodi controls the hub of the Police. He has taken his stance at the Prefecture." He paused and waited for their cheers to ebb.

'They deserved to let it out,' he said to himself 'to feel release and hope for all their years of suffering.' He waited and spoke again.

"Nothing, comes without reprisals, non? This uprising cannot get out of control. Succeed, we cannot - not without the Americans and the British. We must wait and pray that they get here in time."

Simon looked around at the dozens of faces that were so familiar to him. When one of them did not return, Simon knew he was dead or as good as dead - if the Gestapo had him ... or her. They would wait until all was clear, and then a new face would appear in their midst to take the missing man's place. The new person was always accompanied by a familiar member of the cell: joining and disappearing in a sea of faces – all different- all the same. And now Luc, once more, appeared in the final storm of this war; Simon knew in his gut that Luc would be with him at the end. And he too - brought new faces with him, Janusz and the other, Christian, who stood by him on this early morning of August 20.

"'Rien marche pas' - nothing works in Paris anymore - the trains and Metro," Simon gestured around him. "The Post Office, the Press, the Undertakers, the Police," he paused for all knew that the Police, in spite of their corruption, had begun yesterday's uprising. Throughout the Occupation, some had willingly carried out their duties as henchmen for the Gestapo. However, in this eleventh hour – with prodding from Alexandre Parodi - they had begun to fight. For the first time in history the Police and the people of Paris were fighting on the same side of the 'barricade'.

"We are so close to our goal – but we must – MUST be prudent. The Prefecture of Police is our only stronghold. It stands near its square as a symbol of civil authority, and on the other side of the square rests Notre Dame, a symbol which shows Paris, France, and the world that God is on our side."

"Vive la France."

"Vive la liberte."

"Allons aux barricades."

"Non, pas maintenant. Not now." Simon shouted over their fervent cries of freedom. "That very square has been sealed shut with German tanks. Our men – our Police cannot be buried in a tomb of stone."

"Cannot we join them in their fight?" One in the room questioned.

"Only if we want to die as martyrs – and for what? If we so do, we give our enemy a reason to retaliate and slaughter all of Paris." Simon paused and then he whispered. "Colonel Rol would prefer that. 'Paris is worth 200,000 dead', he says."

Luc listened to Simon's reasoning. He was in complete accord. Paris and her citizens must remain as a whole. She could not fight and win against the stronghold of Germans still guarding and ready to detonate her bridges and monuments. Luc remembered what Janusz, Thomas, Zosia and Helene had told him about Warsaw: the total destruction of their city, their university, and their people by the Germans and … the Russians. Nor could he could forget the story Janusz had told him about Christian. He could almost see his face as he told his memories of the massacre of those remaining Poles - now long dead and buried by their own hands in the mass graves deep in the Forest of the Katyn.

"As of last night we are under a cease-fire."

A few murmurings of discord resonated through the

damp humid cell of the catacombs, ancient and irreverent. A hush then followed.

"Our hope lies with our Allies –especially the Americans. It is they who have the military power to break the iron chains of Germany that have bound us like prisoners in our own country. De Gaulle has been working to persuade General Eisenhower to come to our rescue. He has four days to do it." Simon paused to let the men calculate the time left to wait for freedom or for destruction.

"We – they – have until midnight – Thursday, August 24th"

All eyes focused on the calendar fastened to the wall of the catacombs. The days of this New Year have been counted down and meticulously crossed off. Four days more in the middle of 1944. Nothing yet everything. Four years of hell spent. Four days of eternity left to spend.

They looked around at each other. Each knew it would be the longest four days they would ever have. Who would be alive at the end of the four days? That was the question in each of their eyes. Christian turned to Janusz whose eyes were fixated on the calendar and the x's.

"You were alive Mama. Alive before my birthday of eighteen years. It was so hot that August as Helena x'ed off the 31st and turned the page to September." Janusz thought. His eyes welled up with tears. "You made my favorite lemon pie and a fine last supper for us all on that day before the 25th. How I pouted - even the piano key you had wedged out of my precious piano meant little to me. All I could focus on was what would not be for me. What I would give to relive that day." He wiped the tears away with the back of his hand.

Each one's respective burden of the last five years would end one way or the other in this short period of days. Simon's eyes met Luc's. They were together again. And in this cease-fire, they knew what they had to do.

<u>Monday, August 21, 1944 – Pere- Lachaise Cemetery</u>

The truce was dying before it had barely begun. Communist insurgents attacked every German squad or convoy caught guileless in the narrow 'no-exit' streets of Paris. Nonetheless, within this window of fragile time, ministers of de Gaulle had circumvented both the Communists and the Germans in order to establish themselves in key government buildings. One Gaullist cabinet, now in place, had for its headquarters - the Hotel de Matignon, yet time and ammunition were running out, and the communists refused to wait. If the Gaullists did not join in an outright battle with the Communist occupiers, Colonel Rol Tanguy would plaster Paris with posters declaring de Gaulle a traitor to the people of Paris.

Buying for time, Simon, Luc, Christian and Janusz, crossed back over the Seine to head northeast through the streets of Paris. This mission, for all four, had not begun with Operation Overlord on D-Day, but more than four years earlier. Only Simon had been waiting in occupied France. Now those three, plus Simon, could move swiftly to free France and push the tide which had lapped onto the beachheads of Normandy to wash over the land of occupied Europe. They intended to get the incriminating documents into the hands of the American Generals.

Although Generals de Gaulle and Leclerc wanted Paris' liberation, it was the Americans who commanded the arena. The entire invasion operation had been and still was under the direct orders of General Dwight D. Eisenhower. It was he, and he alone, who made the ultimate decisions for all Allied Forces. Rumors of Leclerc's 2nd French Armored Division as the liberator were just that – rumors. It was true that French tanks had been mobilized and were pressing in from the west, but without American support they'd die dead on the roads and fields of France, along with the hopes and lives of thousands of Parisians.

Amid the chaos, Parisians continued their life 'comme normale'. Luc marveled at the spirit of his native Parisians. Never had he felt more at home. As the four trekked through his streets - the 'rues de Paris', he saw men fishing in the Seine, women shaking rugs out their apartment windows, children playing 'cache-cache' - hide and seek- in the barricades piled high in the streets, and resistance fighters fighting and dying alongside of these very children for whose freedom they fought.

The Gaullists tried to contain the spontaneous violent acts against the Germans, for they did not want to give the German general, who controlled the city, reason to bring his whip down upon Parisian heads. Just a few weeks before in this same month of August, the German Police crushed an uprising in Warsaw. The Red Army, who waved its communist flag- the flag that so many in Paris revered, stopped just short of the city proper and let the Germans slaughter the Poles. When they were finished, the Red Army didn't free Warsaw; they just left her bleeding and too dazed by death to put up another fight against her future masters - the Communist Soviets of Russia.

The communists of Paris, the Leftists, said they- not the Russians- were in control of their fate. Warsaw was not, nor ever could be Paris. So, they ignored the cease-fire, and the noise of shellfire to the west encouraged them to rebel. The Germans began to burn incriminating documents and continued to mine the monuments of Paris. On this drizzling morning of the 21st, SS engineers were inspecting the Eiffel Tower's four great arch supports in order to determine the best spot for dynamite charges. Sappers were busy, and all Luc could do was pray that engineers like Sandy would get to Paris in time.

Moments before, Luc and Simon had heard that the Germans had just finished mining the cellars of Les Invalides. Whether the 400-year-old barracks along with the tomb of Napoleon Bonaparte and the French Army Museum, or the 55 year old Eiffel Tower, which symbolized Paris herself, blew to pieces could not be Luc's concern. Getting the documents about the Katyn was.

He pushed from his mind the last supper he and Simon had in Monsieur Henri's café overlooking the Eiffel Tower. He remembered how the spring sun had glistened gold over the Tower's copper frame and how their wine seemed especially fine that late afternoon. He did not know that their freedom would be snatched from them in a matter of days nor that the German flag would be raised upon that very copper-laced structure - that symbol of Paris. Now, Monsieur Henri lay dead; Simon was disfigured for life, and the German flag still flew from the Tower.

"Perhaps," Luc mused, "along the way, we can save one historic monument." He turned around and paced his hand on Janusz's chest to stop him from turning the corner of another narrow street. "Let's make certain one four truck convoy packed with high explosives never reaches its destination." he whispered to Janusz.

Janusz nodded. He crouched down and moved slowly to the back of the parked lead truck. The soldiers had climbed out to dismantle a barricade in its path. Sliding under its chassis, Janusz placed the TNT with precision, just as he had done with the bridges of Warsaw and the bridges of Normandy.

"Waste not -.want not." Janusz thought of his mother's favorite maxim. "Mama would be proud of her boy child now." He mused. "I guess her steel does runs through my veins." April's face appeared clearly to him at the moment he rolled out from beneath the truck. The trucks blew before the barricade was even cleared.

Luc and his trio of men did not stop again until they reached the border of the green plots of Pere-Lachaise. Although de Gaulle had stepped foot on French soil that past Sunday, Luc knew he could not enter a city caught in the clutches of the Communists. They had already attempted to assassinate Andre Parodi for his role as peacemaker. De Gaulle, despite all his French pride, would not let Paris- on his account - erupt into a raging fire.

For the leaders of each Gaullist Resistance cell it was getting harder to put out the brush fires that sprang up spontaneously in their 'quartiers'. With less than thirty-six hours to maintain peace, they must not fail. If they did, Paris's shroud of brown, worn for four years, would simply be exchanged for a red one. The salvation of Paris and of France lay interred in the bones of the Pere-Lachaise Cemetery.

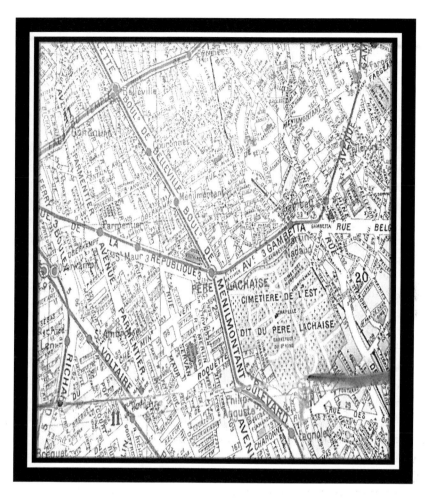

****

On the far east side of Paris a vast green corner of land was an island onto itself. Spring rains and four years of neglect made it appear more like a jungle than the ancient renowned cemetery of Paris. Once the site of a monastery for the Jesuits and Father (Pere) Lachaise in 1682, it was converted to a cemetery in 1800 as a burial site for the famous sons of France. Moliere, Hugo, Delacroix, Balzac and La Fontaine were only some who rested there. For almost two hundred and fifty years family and friends have passed through the 'Portes' or gates named 'des Amandiers', 'de la Reunion', and 'du Repos'. In the northeastern corner of Pere Lachaise stood the Federalists' Wall,

'Le Mur des Federes', where the last revolutionaries of the Paris Commune of 1871 fought their last and most bloody battle among the graves and died between the tombstones. At dawn of that clear day in May, the survivors stood against the wall on this far northeast corner and were shot.

Seven decades later just two pairs of resistance fighters were fighting within this holy ground. Two of them were pressed against another wall, the interior one of Moliere's tomb just inside the opening of the cemetery from Avenue du Boulevard and Avenue Principale. The smell was the same as that of the catacombs, but there was a taste of iron and a scent of copper to the dank dark air of the tomb. Luc and Janusz each held a tall tapered prayer candle, taken at the entrance of Pere-Lachaise. Except for candlelight, the mausoleum's tiny sliver of a window provided a vent for air and nothing more.

"Slide your hands along the walls. Nothing is laid on the coffin itself."

Janusz did as Luc commanded. Sliding Stanislaus' knife across the inlaid stone, he held one hand flat and used the knife as a backup for whatever the fingers missed. They worked in silence, as Christian and Simon stood guard behind the tombs of France's famous men. In the silence of the morning mist the voices of the dead seemed to cry out in despair at this new and violent world.

"Chopin is buried here, yes?" Janusz said as he meticulously worked. "You're right," Luc answered. It no longer surprised him that men thought and spoke so randomly. The mind, he knew, was a delicate mechanism that bolted from one idea, one thought to the next - sometimes with no connecting link.

"Oui, he was one of your people. His body is buried here, but his heart is buried in Warsaw."

"Yes. My mother had told me that story." Janusz paused. "I thought she had made it up to keep me playing at the Piano. Chopin's Nocturne in F#, Op. 15 No. 2, was her favorite composition."

Luc could hear him swallow hard and the tremor in his voice was almost palpable. Neither spoke. They each continued their slow work. No sounds were coming from the outside, yet the two foot thick walls of the tomb and the heavy iron door pulled shut behind them could obscure most violent sounds.

Janusz had begun to hum the chords of Chopin's Nocturne, which permeated the cloistered walls of the mausoleum. The ghost of Chopin, of April Puratski or of both were speaking to the gentle boy, who had been asleep too long in Janusz's body. His change from boyhood to manhood was not a transition but a caustic leap, forced on him in the short pause of but a few hot September days. The shock had buried the gentleness, the dreams, and the hopes of a boy deep in the body of this man who would turn twenty-three if he could live through the next 31 days until his birthday on September 25th.

He stopped his humming. "I found it – here". He held the candle close to the stone. His long fingers traced the new mortar that surrounded the chunk of stone. His knife edged through the fresh cement on each side of the stone rectangle. As it fell to the ground, he slid his knife between the stones and shimmed it until the stone began to protrude from the wall of stones.

"Voila" Janusz passed his lit taper to Luc and pulled the stone out of the wall and onto the ground.

Luc positioned the candles on either side of the hole so Janusz could look inside before he placed his hand in. He paused and pointed his knife inside the hole. When he gently taped the walls and interior of the whole, he heard a metal ping.

"Hand me a candle."

Janusz shone it directly in the hole.

"A grenade - with wires on either side connecting to the pin.

"Can you sever them?"

"Yes."

If he was wrong, they both knew they'd join Moliere and the rest of the dead in Pere-Lachaise. He placed his left hand on the grenade and his left thumb directly over the pin. With his right, he slowly scraped the knife through the wire connecting the pin to the inside of the adjacent stone.

"The right side is done. Now I just have to pull the wire through the pin."

Luc held the candles steady and Janusz held his breath.

"Done." He slid the wire out of the hole with his right hand, and pulled the grenade out with his left. He traded the grenade for one of Luc's candles. Luc checked the grenade's pin, and once convinced it was secure, he put the grenade in his pocket.

With the candle Janusz peered into the hole once more.

"This is it" he murmured and pulled out a thick roll of papers tied together with a blood-stained handkerchief.

The scraping of another knife was heard outside of the tomb.

"Gestapo coming ... with a Russia," Christian shouted through the vent in a hoarse whisper.

Luc lifted the stone and placed it back in the hole.

Janusz shuffled his foot over the chunks of mortar on the floor and blended them in the dirt of Moliere's tomb.

Each blew out his candle. Luc kicked the lock from the floor into the nearest corner. Shutting the heavy door behind them, they breathed the fresh air of this humid August morning and ran quietly away from the voices coming out of the mist.

By the time Luc and Janusz hid behind the outside tombs with Christian and Simon, the voices materialized from the mist of Pere-Lachaise. The tall one wore the uniform of the Gestapo and the short one - civilian clothes. Obviously agitated, both talked in fast short choppy German phrases.

"The little one is Russian." Christian said. "A Russian spy – sent ahead by secret espionage unit of the Red Army. He says he's under strict orders from Joseph Stalin himself to retrieve and destroy papers buried in one of these tombs."

Christian thought how history would record again the mass killings by the Russians. All four knew that just a few weeks previously, the Red Army had waited outside Warsaw, as the Germans - this time, massacred the Jews of the Warsaw Ghetto. The Russians again provided the opportunity for this calculated slaughter as they had done four years ago when the Russians were Germany's ally. At that time they provided the 'clean-up' for the Germans after the Blitz on Warsaw in September of 1939. They, along with their German allies, rounded up those Christian Poles who were not killed and forced them on a death march deep into the Forest of the Katyn.

There, as all four knew, the Russians slaughtered the remaining Polish military and intellectual leaders, but not before they had forced them to dig their own mass graves.

Christian listened carefully to the short one who had apparently made a deal with this Gestapo agent. Most of the Gestapo had fled Paris two days ago. This one had remained on for some extra cream. Only two kinds remained: the looters, who continued to rape Paris one way or the other, and the true sadists who simply enjoyed torturing those still in their captivity.

Janusz had unrolled the documents onto the flat surface of a tombstone and was reading the Polish names one after the other. Each name was meticulously written along with rank, job, serial number, and age. – With some there were even addresses. Christian read over his shoulder – translating out loud the instructions and remarks the Russian officers in charge had made. He shivered from a cold not caused by the damp cemetery, but one so deep that it seemed to permeate his very soul.

"One other name," he murmured. He knew they would have identified him. His fingers touched the name. "Perr Harr, - father," he whispered. "I knew I would find you again." His fingers crossed over to the one word next to his father's name. With Russian accuracy they had included what they believed to be the name of his boxer, 'Chris'. "You died trying to save him. Rest in peace 'ma Dame'." Christian said, convoluting his English, Russian, and French. He did not realize he had even spoken in Russian. The suppression of his maternal tongue had been deliberate. He knew the reasons why. Russian words would open the dyke - the flood of memories would crash and splash throughout his mind. He had to forget all- to survive.

The shouts from the tomb came swiftly. Nodding to Luc as to their authenticity, Janusz rolled up the papers, and wrapped the blood stained handkerchief back around the roll. When the tall man and short man stormed out of Moliere's Mausoleum, the two other pair of men followed. Just as the cemetery opened onto Rue de Bagnolet and lead into Rue de Alexandre Dumas, Luc quickened his pace, pulled the grenade's pin, and tossed it between the 'users' of mankind. Then he watched as they exploded into the morning mist.

Tuesday, August 22, 1944 – Ville de Grandchamp

  Hot and humid, the night and the tension in Paris sat on its haunches as palpable as the air enveloping it. When they crossed back over the Seine, the mist from the river met the night air and no one could tell where the night sky ended and the river began.

  Through the night they had inched their way out towards Paris's northwest periphery and into the charred countryside. Luc still had Sidney's pouch around his neck, and around his wrist, his medical bracelet with the raised eagle. The Allied soldiers he met along the way took one look at it and directed him to the General they called 'Ike". Luc wished he had Sidney, or the talker, Tony - the sharp kid from Brooklyn - or just one convincing American from his American team to verify the story.

  He turned to Christian. He was thankful that the Russian, at least, was with him. "As an eye witness to the Katyn massacre, Christian can tell his story to Ike when the time comes. That along with my assessment of the communist strongholds in Paris should convince the General not to go around but to enter Paris." Luc thought.

  Exhausted, dirty, and with a massive headache, Luc followed Christian fourteen miles to get to the village of Grandchamp. Through the night they stumbled, and it became even more impossible after midnight. Through German pockets of strength, through resistance fighting, through British and American units of artillery bursts, they inched their way into and out of the humid mist. All the while Luc looked for the familiar faces of Melvin, Tony, Sal, or an American Indian. He knew it was like looking for one lone skiff in a sea of bobbing boats.

  He needed that all-American push, a dash of savvy and a top layer of no 'bullshit' to make it happen – to get him through to the 'chief'. However, when words would not convince, he showed the higher-ups Sidney's bracelet. Like Sidney's voice from the grave, it spoke to them. They took one look at it and then a closer longer look at the pretty boy Frenchman. In that second glance, they saw the steel in his eyes and the rigidity of his jaw. Then – and only then – did they break orders and pass him through the lines to the next commander.

As Luc's stamina and patience ebbed, Christian's increased. His serenity and conviction about their mission fed his energy. When they had to stop because of obstacles, Christian waited and then moved out at exactly the right time and in exactly the right direction. It was uncanny how Death continued to miss them. A dozen times they dodged disaster because he paused, moved, or made the right choice out of two possible ones. If his odds were statistically only 50/50, how did he keep stacking the deck and giving them no odds – just a 100 per cent guarantee?

At 6:00 a.m. Luc did not care anymore. Whatever luck or destiny Christian embodied, Luc knew that he himself was along for the ride. After their first two hours of flight, Luc did not attempt to second-guess him. His head, throbbing in pain, caused Luc to constantly run his sweaty hands through his black hair and push his fingers into his temples. This time he shifted his neck from side to side, straightened his back to follow the Brigadier General, who ushered him into the rooms of the Supreme Commander of the Allied Forces in the tiny village of Grandchamp.

General Dwight D. Eisenhower stood behind the huge cherry planked kitchen table in the salon of this 'maison de maitre'. No ancestral portraits hung. Instead, maps decorated every available inch of the floral clothed walls. The five-star-general's 'desk' held masses of paper stacked in neat piles, three black phones, several white enamel coffee cups, and the pouch that Luc had just given the Brigadier General intelligence officer. Luc thought the general suited the 'master's house'. Shorter and older than he had anticipated, this obvious 'master' of the free world had a comfortable 'grand-pere' countenance about him.

In order to meet him Luc had to cross the entire room to the General and his 'desk' set up in front of the large glass doors leading out to an enclosed garden. In that long minute of crossing to this five-star general, known as Ike, Luc amended his assessment. This was no one's grandfather. The General's body was slight but sinewy with the muscles of a swift large cat lying just beneath the surface of his clean starched pressed uniform. His blue eyes cut through Luc with an edge, sharper than any knife. His forehead was smooth. It rose up quickly and into his bald head, his only 'grand-pere' characteristic.

As Luc reached across the makeshift desk to shake Eisenhower's hand, the General stepped in front of it and its highly classified piles of papers. Luc noted the American five-star General moved like a twenty-year old and possessed a directness inherent only in the very young or very driven.

He shook Luc's hand with vigor. "Tell me about this," he had slid his other hand over the bracelet with the eagle on Luc's wrist that he still had in his strong grasp ... "and that." The general pointed to the pouch that lay open on the makeshift desk.

Luc had to choose his words carefully. This general had no time to waste. Luc did not hear Christian enter the room, but he saw the General's eyes shift before they again riveted on him.

"The bracelet and pouch they were given to me by Lieutenant Sidney Smith of the 82nd Airborne. He, in turn, had received both from General Omar Bradley in London just before the Lieutenant and his company parachuted into France. He was one of the first. The night was June 5 and the drop site was Sainte Mere Eglise. To get to Paris at all costs were his orders, and in the event of his death, the bracelet and the pouch would be attached to the next officer in command. Thus, the bracelet and the pouch would pass from man to man until the outskirts of Paris. At that moment in time, the soldier left standing had to place the pouch in the hands of the highest American commanding officer. That would be you 'Mon General'," Luc said as he saluted this American who had been weighing the fate of his own country, France, and the world.

Eisenhower returned the salute - deliberate and crisp.

"At ease, my son. You've been through enough for more than a dozen men."

Luc was taken aback. Perhaps, that is just an American expression he thought before he continued. "Lieutenant Sidney Smith did not die on June 5. He met me and my fighters, who had similar objectives. His orders were to protect us and get us to Paris so that we could secure secret documents hidden there for the last four years. The coded letter in the Lieutenant's pouch was the key in getting you the documents and delivering them to you. They record a specific massacre - by the Russians, in April of 1940."

"The Katyn".

Luc looked at Ike. He did not know why he should feel surprised that the General knew - after all, it was he, the Supreme Allied Commander, who had to have given the orders for the dozen men that Bradley hand-picked. However, when had he known? Before or after Stalin's Russia became an American ally?

"The Lieutenant did die. He called down fire on himself in the town of 'La Jalousie" on the 4th July. The Germans had massacred the entire town by driving them into the town square and then machine gunning them down. We took one survivor with us a child – a girl of eight." He waited for the news to register.

Luc noticed a slight stiffening of the General's jaw as Eisenhower turned to look out the morning mist, which covered the gardens in this house he had secured.

"And this contact in Paris – 'Moliere" did you find him?"

"I knew him from before the war. We had set up a strong Resistance cell when German occupation seemed inevitable. It was he and Christian". He nodded his head toward Christian who was now by his side. "and Janusz, a Pole, who were part of our mission as directed by London."

"And Paris? How does she stand?" Eisenhower asked.

"Paris cannot hold out much longer. We have a cease-fire as you know, but it runs out in less than 3 days. There is little ammunition left and the communists will not adhere to the peace agreement. Orders from Germany - from Hitler himself - have been given to destroy Paris's industries and all its bridges by today. However, the German General in charge of Paris had agreed to the cease-fire and is stalling Hitler's commanders in their orders to burn Paris." He paused before he continued.

"Unless the Allies come to liberate us there will be a slaughter just like the Katyn…just like Warsaw… and also the complete leveling of Paris. It will be reduced to rubble."

The General turned away again. He seemed to be looking through the distance beyond the pastures into the future.

"And you?" the General turned to Christian.

"I was in the Katyn that day. I am the only living witness. I will remember, until the day I die, the face of the man who killed my father. The Russians, like the Germans, have no mercy. If Paris is not given to de Gaulle's forces, the Communist Colonel Roy-Tanguy, will claim France in the name of communism and by default, Stalin."

"You know it will cost more American and Allied lives than all the deaths in Warsaw, in the Katyn, and in Paris herself. By stopping to save Paris, we delay the end of this war." Eisenhower spoke more to himself than to the men in front of him.

Then he looked directly at both men. "There is a man you know – Andre Parodi. He came in last night with the same concern regarding the communists. Tell him about the Katyn and my people will make copies of these documents to be circulated by him to those communists who are on the line – those who see the similarities between the brown coats and the red. As for you two, get some food, clean clothes and a few hours' sleep, we'll get you back by jeep as far as we can."

The Supreme General of the Allied Forces brought himself up to his full height and with a sense of finality, saluted both men.

<u>Wednesday, August 23,1944:</u>
<u>Rue de Victor Hugo, Gestapo Quarters</u>

Zosia could barely think anymore. The light was beginning to come through the torn curtains in the atelier. Her sense of time was gone. She tried to think logically. Time … what was that? How long was 'time'? How long is 'time'? She glanced towards the window. The sun is rising. At most I've lost just half a 'day', she thought.

But she knew she had lost much more than 'time'.

The strength and beauty of her young womanhood had been ripped and sucked from the very marrow of her bone. Crushed and bleeding, her body hung on a hook, like a slab of meat in a butcher's shop window.

Their interrogation of her had begun the night before. Just when she realized the two men in the cafe were traitors, she did not remember. She was not certain of anything anymore. The only way to move beyond the agonizing pain was to will herself out. She was floating above her body, dangling from a large rusty grappling hook by handcuffs which pinned her arms together over her matted bloody hair. A thick stream of clotted blood crossed her forehead and down one eye over her cheek. Had she being hoisted up by the pulley through the entire ordeal? She did not know, and would not force herself to remember. It was dark then. It is light now. Suspended in front of a small square attic window, she had a room with a view.

"How thoughtful of the Gestapo to allow me to see Sacre Coeur. Salvation so close ... but so far. How Christian of them – to allow me to die so Christ-like," Zosia bemused out loud as her 'spirit' self-floated above her physical body.

Walking the line between sanity and insanity was getting more difficult. Her arms were of no use, dislocated at best...crippled for life at worse. Would she ever hold Luc again so tenderly in her arms – with these useless dead weights, which were now no part of her.

"How long had it been since they spent the night here in Montmartre in the lovely room Laure had selected for them in the 'Hotel des Anges'? And Juliette? " She did not know if she was speaking out loud. "Juliette, yes, she is still alive. But when was the last time I heard her cry out?"

She tried to count the days back. She began to count in French, then in English, then in Polish.. but never in German. Her mind was blocking out, short circuiting simple operations such as counting. Deep in its recesses, it refused to acknowledge anything German. It tired her to process numbers -names, in chronological order. As she dangled she thought, "Yes, almost ten days ago we entered Paris. Luc was by my side that first night. Or has it been 10 times 10, 100 days ago? I do not know anymore. God, help me!"

Out loud she began, "Though I walk through the valley of death, I fear no evil, for though art with me...." She continued, but her spirit pleaded, "Take me to your angels before I reveal any names, I pray."

****

Three rooms away down a narrow corridor to the far corner back room lay Juliette cold and shivering strapped by leather ties to the iron hooks in the wall. A woman across the room was tied face down on a narrow wooden plank – wrists and ankles bound separately with each rope knotted together beneath the board. Juliette had thought at first it was Laure, but she did not think her screeches of pain and bellows of agony were hers, nor did she recognize any of the smashed features of what was once her face. She was quiet now – the quietness of the dead. Juliette was sure. Now, they could concentrate all of their games on her.

They seemed to prefer the whip for her and the rubber truncheon on the poor woman who had revealed nothing to her persecutors. The two huge lesbian torturers enjoyed raping her and would keep her bones intact for that. The other woman cried out too much ... and they had to quiet her with the truncheon. When a bone broke, her cries turned to moans, and the lesbians found that more pleasurable.

Juliette could not lean against the tiny room's walls for the slashes on her back were too deep and too painful from the salt they had poured on her wounds. Beneath each nail of each finger and toe they pierced her flesh one at a time with sharp-pointed matches. The larger horse-face woman spat in her face as her partner wrapped Juliette's wrists and ankles with rolls of wadding. Inside each wad 'horse-face' stuck sharp-pointed matches. Throughout the night they took turns lighting one match at a time. When all her fingers and toes were blackened by the phosphorous burns, they started lighting on fire her wrists and ankles.

They would not break her. She would never reveal her brother's name or the names of the others. She wondered had they been watching her at La Nuit Eternelle. She had hardly been there. Why had she been selected? Had someone else revealed her name? And why now, when all the higher echelon,

SS and Gestapo had fled Paris, would they torture her? What was to be gained?

She had her answer when Horse-face's lover came back into the room.

"Vous etes prete ma petite chou? Oui, je peux dire – 'Tu' es prete. After all, we are on intimate, friends now, yes. And, don't pretend that you are unable to understand me. You are ready. You – little 'anglaise' French whore of the English. We French must unite together."

She approached her with a lascivious grin on her dark jowled face. As she was about to touch Juliette's naked breasts, the door swung open. Horse-face's frame blocked most of the open door, but in that instant, Juliette looked between the legs of the 'bowled' lesbian and saw part of a profile and shoulder of a man. Even with her eyes almost swollen shut, she could squint and see. She was certain she knew the man.

"Have you started without me, Gertrude", Horse-face snarled.

"Of course not, Magalie. I was just seeing if our guest was still with us."

"Well that one is not," Horse-face pointed her whip at the inert nude body on the plank. "Nor do I think this one's friend is. Drag that bitch out. She's good for nothing now. Throw her down the stairs with the others. This disgusting heat is making the corpses rot more quickly and more pungently. We can't stay much longer."

"Just a little while more Magalie. We've had such fun."

"Perhaps my dear', Horse-face whispered as she caressed her lover's face with the handle of her black whip. Gertrude smiled an almost girlish grin.

"Close the door when you leave my dear and check on our friend's friend down in the last room. She too is dead." Gertrude swung the corpse over her shoulder and exited the room closing the door gently behind her.

Juliette had nowhere to look as the giant of a woman approached her. If she were lucky, perhaps she'd die this time. At least Zosia and the frail woman who had occupied the other room had made their final escape from the pain.

****

Two days before, Janusz had returned to join Zosia and Juliette in Montmartre. He had helped Luc and Christian leave Paris to bring the crucial documents to General Eisenhower. It was decided that he would stay behind in Montmartre. The night before he had seen the two men, dressed in civilian clothes, enter 'La Nuit Eternelle'. They appeared as any other clientele looking for a night of reprieve from their day of toil and hardship. Although Janusz had not seen them before, that was nothing unusual. Men could always find the money or the time to come in for a few hours of relaxation and forgetfulness in these hard times.

The taller of the two interested Janusz, for he was like a large dark shadow, more ominous than the other. The later seemed to have an acquired grace and breeding; the former bore a brutish and uncouth manner. They had taken an unusual interest in Zosia who was sitting by herself in the back of the cabaret. Dressed in a red and yellow flowered dress, her short auburn curls shone in the light of the candles. The dress caressed her long legs – from the length of her hip to the tip of her open-toed high heels.

Janusz noted their reaction, but Zosia was a beautiful woman that all men noticed no matter what their nationality. It was however, when Juliette crossed the back of the room to Zosia's table that an instant look of surprise registered on each man's face. Her lavender dress slid uniquely and perfectly over her lithe figure. But it was neither her face nor figure that caused them to react that way, for their surprise quickly turned to concern and contempt.

When the women left for their room that night, the two men got up to follow. Janusz made a decision he would later regret. He went to tell Laure before following the men in the narrow passages of Montmartre. When he stepped out of 'La Nuit Eternelle', they were gone.

****

In 'Les Abbesses' Simon questioned Laure and Janusz about the two men, for no one had seen the women return to their rooms the night before. Although the Gestapo had fled like rats from a sinking ship, Simon knew pockets of the most sinister and sick still kept up their tactics of abasement and degradation on any men or women they rounded up. Demented, they still believed that the Nazis would control the world, and they, as loyalists to Hitler's cause, would get a piece of the proverbial pie.

Simon looked out the second story window of the Montmartre night cabaret and café. The sun streamed through the tall curtain-laced windows as a huge orange tabby rested in his spot on the wide windowsill. Below, the people of Montmartre were promenading in the narrow streets and cobblestone sidewalks. The waiters of the cafes were wiping the dew from the tables and tossing their white napkins over their shoulders as they went from table to table to clean the remains of the night before. The stubbed-out 'Gaulois' or even 'Players' cigarette butts they brushed into the metal dustpan that they held in one hand. When no one was looking they picked out the 'Players' stubs and carelessly put them in their apron pockets. Laure watched this ritual as she had for many months, but now more and more butts were being shifted from dustpan to pocket.

The 'anglais' cigarettes indicated an increase in the infiltration of 'downed' pilots who roamed the streets and cafes of Montmartre at night. It was these pilots or resistance fighters, rewarded with English cigarettes, who put out their prized 'jigs' in the ashtrays and sidewalks of Paris. All the 'garcons' of Paris knew these men had to be protected, and so they continued the ritual, the habit, they had taken up four years ago when the Germans began their 'Occupation' of Paris - of France.

Laure turned to Simon to listen, for she had told him all she knew about Juliette and Zosia.

"Luc and Christian got through the lines." Simon quickly changed from questioner to informer. "The documents they secured are being used to turn the tide of the communists occupying Paris. They talked to Eisenhower, himself. The news, directly from the Allied General, is that they will liberate us. The clock is ticking. Eisenhower has given the orders for de Gaulle's tanks and those of Leclerc to enter Paris first. The Americans and British will allow us to liberate our city; then the Americans will come. A little more than 24 hours remain in the cease-fire. Pray to God we are liberated before the time runs out." Simon paused before he began again.

"Let us drink to that.' They lifted their noontime glasses of red wine, each glass twisting and reflecting in the glint of the glistening rays of sun. The cat stretched and opened his eyes as the glasses clinked. "And to the rescue and release of Juliette, the sister of my boyhood friend, and Zosia, our Polish Patriot. They have been snatched from this hill of martyrs. Let us pray they do not become one." He fixed his gaze outside over the rooftops of Montmartre. "The Gestapo has them somewhere on this hill."

Each sipped from his glass and gazed out the window in silence. No one wanted to speak about what had and was still being done to the two women who were now in the hands of God. Simon, Janusz and Laure each said a silent prayer to God to release them - soon - into their hands; and if God, himself, could not do so within the day, to carry them to heaven where they could slip beyond the bonds of flesh and … pain.

<u>Thursday, August 24, 1944 - Montmartre</u>

As midnight rolled the 23rd into the 24th, the last day of the cease-fire began. The German General in command of the remaining German forces had just aborted a direct order from Hitler who wanted the Luftwaffe to raze the city of Paris. The general reasoned that it would kill as many Germans as it would Parisians, and his sources had informed him that Leclerc's 2nd French Armored Division and the U.S. 4th Infantry Division were ready to enter the city that he and his forces had occupied for more than four years.

He looked out his from an old Hotel to gaze once more at the Eiffel Tower in the moonlight. The German General had grown fond of Paris as though she were a former lover .No longer jealous, he was willing to return her beauty and light to the world. He did not want to go down in history as the man who allowed Paris to be burned to the ground. Yet, in order to save face and his own life, he could not let her go without a fight. After midnight tonight he could give Hitler no more excuses. He had no choice - no other options than an all-out battle to crush any citizen of Paris who would rise up to fight against the remaining well armored, well ordered German Wehrmacht.

As the German General looked over Paris for perhaps the last time, another General, an American, was lost in his own thoughts on this particular Thursday, the 24 of August 1944. General Bradley of the 4th Division wondered when he got to Paris what would remain of her?. He too had received orders. His were to 'slam it on'. He nodded as he read and reread the words delivered by an infantry soldier covered with blood and mud.

Bradley turned from the words to the face of the strong young man in front of him. "What a boy, a child playing at war," he thought. The soldier's face was covered with grime and his eyes were tired, yet he stood at attention and saluted the General in front of him. Bradley took a longer look. The salute said it all: To hell and back - until it was over. Bradley looked deep into his eyes and saw the grit of metal, forged in fire that had carried this soldier and all the others to this point in time.

"God willing, it will carry him through and back to the soil of America," Bradley thought as he brought himself up to his full height, and with the formality and respect that he would salute his supreme commander, the President of the United States, he returned the infantry soldier's salute.

Bradley had also received word on a thin piece of folded paper from Eisenhower on the success of 'Operation K'. He opened the hand written note that had no date and no signature. He recognized Ike's hand writing and after he read the paper he folded it up.

"Only one man survived." He thought. "All the others from the original stick we sent out that first night are dead or missing in action. That young Italian from Brooklyn - that 'lucky bum', is alive. I remember Sidney telling me about him –' how he had to watch over the kid.'

Bradley, left alone, eased himself down into the only chair in the bare room. "How long ago was that June night? The night the world had waited so long for. A lifetime in eleven weeks. Lieutenant Sidney Smith and all the others from his original stick were gone - except for Anthony Martino. How many others died that night and in the nights and days which followed? How many more before it's over. Somehow with a lot of courage and luck the kid made it. Jesus he's gotta have the luck of the Irish with him." Bradley grinned.

His smile quickly faded as he reached over to a large box of gray stationary with the formal emblem of the United States of America blazoned in blue. He had written too many letters - to too many mothers and wives telling them their sons - their husbands would not be coming home. In addition to Tony, the two young foreigners added to the Lieutenant's stick at the 11th hour and their two compatriots inside France also had 'lady luck' on their side. These four had guided the American men for as long as their luck held. For more than two months - with the aid of GI's along the way and 'foreign' resistance fighter guides- they had inched their way from the beaches of Normandy into the heart of Paris. They had done their share – more than their share.

Bradley knew Leclerc had been given the go ahead to enter Paris and had even commandeered the 4th Division's assigned route. Many American higher-ups in uniform and many head French resistance fighters in no uniform blanched. The Americans knew the price they had to pay to free the City, and although the French wanted to free her themselves, these other soldiers of France felt it should be done shoulder to shoulder with the Americans who had laid down their lives for her. Despite all, however, Eisenhower handed over the robe of savior to the General de Gaulle, and the sword to General Leclerc. Leclerc's underhanded, unmilitary tactics to get himself to Paris put him in the right place at the right time in these last days of August 1944. Ironically, his lack of luck or as some would say 'just rewards' had him bogged down a few miles short and southwest of Paris at Rambouillet.

"I can't tolerate that pompous Frenchman." Bradley muttered under his breath as he began to write the letters to both Mrs. Smiths. "Leclerc gets the glory and all the Smiths of the U.S. of A, the coffins."

****

Another commander, Major General Leonard Garrow of the V Corps, with another band of soldiers - the 4th Division, gave an order to a team of men that he had found resting in an old mill just outside of Paris. The Major General hid the remaining members of Lieutenant Sidney Smith's team under mounds of potatoes, 'haricots-verts', and other vegetables in an old red truck belonging to a French farmer. He had found them with guns and knives already drawn and ordered them to climb among the vegetables and settle into pockets of air. Two drivers in dirty caps and overalls sat in the front seat of the red truck as it lumbered over the dirt roads toward Paris. Beneath the large leather front seat the team's cache of Camel cigarettes, Hershey bars, and Colt 45's nestled in place as the two resistance fighters rolled their cargo along in typical casual French fashion. It was this very feigned casualness and their 'Gaelic shrugs' that got them across the periphery of Paris and up to Sacre Coeur. The red truck bounced along the ancient route of the martyr onto the 'Butt', Montmartre. The truck made two stops – one just down the street from 'La Nuit Eternelle' and the other past the 'Lapin Agile' across 'La Place du Tertre' to the metro stop - "Les Abesses'.

****

The Kraut entered in his Colonel's uniform through the front door of 'La Nuit Eternelle', Sal through the side, and Harry, the Apache, through the back. Moments later the other half of their team Tony, Sandy, and Thomas, the other Apache, laughed roguishly as they reeled like drunks down the steep steps of 'Les Abesses'.

A flash of disbelief crossed Laure's face as she saw the German Colonel enter the cabaret. No German officers had dared to enter since the cease-fire.

"Why are they here?" She could no longer think straight. "They've killed my brothers, sisters, and now more than likely Luc's own sister and his sweetheart. Mon dieu. How much more?"

"Don't worry," a soft voice whispered in her ear. Janusz had seen Melvin Baron enter. Despite all, Janusz was grinning - ear to ear.

"He's one of us. He saved us once. He'll save us again."

"Une biere", Melvin commanded in a thick German accent.

He stood next to Janusz at the bar. Janusz turned to his right and saw Sal, dressed as a farmer, near the table at the side door.

"Let the Colonel have the best beer in the house." Laure ordered her bartender in French. Then she approached the Colonel and said in German, "I am Laure, the owner of this cabaret."

"Enchante", Melvin answered in his guttural French as he clicked his heels together and bowed.

"I have not seen you before." She continued in German.

"I have not been here before." He tersely answered in German as he smiled falsely through pure white teeth.

In the mirror behind the bar he caught the eyes of Janusz and the imperceptible nod toward the front door behind him. Melvin Baron swept the room with his arm holding the glass of beer. He got a clear view of the two men who had just walked through the door. One was as tall as he but heavier from good food and drink, and the other shorter – slim and well turned out.

"You have a fine place here. But where are your girls?"

"We are between shows. They can come down now for a chat, but would you like a private visit later?"

"Ja " Baron laughed heartily.

The two men, who had entered, sat in the back. They drank and continued to drink as they watched the Colonel enjoy the parade of scantily clad girls. The girls were experts. They knew this was no German. His eyes, although a light clear blue, and none of the emptiness and disdain they had come to know. To the two men in the back, however, the German Colonel seemed not only to have money but power. Who else would be new to "La Nuit" at this late date? He must have come from Berlin with others, sent by Hitler to see if the grip on Paris was still tight enough.

They whispered to one another that he must have spent the night before on the lower streets of Pigalle. His uniform was a bit too disheveled - the typical spit and polish was missing. Smirking, they could just imagine where in Pigalle the Colonel had his uniform soiled. The taller of the two men in the back smiled to himself.

****

After the last show at two in the morning when they figured the Colonel had sufficiently drunk enough, they sauntered up to his table. The shorter one bent down, and with liquor-laced breath, said something quietly to him. The Colonel looked into the man's glazed eyes. Melvin Baron had what he wanted to know. Abruptly, he shoved the girls off his lap, clicked his heels, and said 'bonne nuit' to Laure.

As the three men walked down the street with heads bent together, Janusz could hear their laughter. He would not lose them this night. And besides, he had backup. He turned to see Sal come out the side door and a large figure closing in behind him. In the lamplight Janusz saw the sharp strong features of Harry.

****

"Velcome to our little home," said a short little dapper man with a trim even mustache. His gray uniform and black riding breeches fit him tightly and matched his unsavory habit of hitting his tall black boots with the riding crop he kept in his right hand.

'Who could this clownish imitation of Adolf Hitler be? Certainly not an equestrian. Horse stables disappeared at the turn of the century when artists and bohemians had taken root in the once rich farming community.' Baron thought as he fought not to twist his neck in the tight collar of his German Colonel uniform.

"We have here an array of stables you might like to view."

The two men – one obviously German and the other French – who brought him here grinned slyly at this statement.

Nodding his approval, Baron once again clicked his heels in typical Gestapo fashion and indicated that they should lead the way. His most excruciating nightmares did not prepare him for what he was about to see.

In the middle of the room was a huge white porcelain bathtub that held the naked body of a young woman. Two huge sweaty women with rolled up sleeves were pushing simultaneously on her head to keep her under water. As she fought for air, they grinned and forced her down more.

"Enough my beauties", the dapper little Gestapo man murmured.

Her head bobbed up as she gasped for air. The women laughed and Baron held his breath. His stomach turned over, and he fought to keep from vomiting. Her face was black and blue, her eyes swollen shut – but it was Juliette.

"And what is this" Baron swallowed hard and forced his voice to be blasé.

"We are doing our duty for the Fuhrer. The Resistance has to be forced into total submission."

"I see. And these two women?" Baron pointed to the horse-face one and her companion.

"Frenchwomen. Loyal to our cause."

Baron could see where their loyalties lie – to their bestial desires – psychopaths. He wondered about the two men who had led him here. Obviously not Gestapo, what however was their purpose in this scene from the Marquis de Sade?

"And what information has she given you for our cause?"

Horse-face proudly spoke, "She mumbled about a brother"

"His name…the cell's name… location?" Baron spit out like a machine gun.

The large woman blushed. It might have been coy in other circumstances had she not been so obscene – in stature, and in deed. Pleasure not espionage was obviously her forte.

"How long have you had her?" He shouted at the miniature Hitler.

"Twenty-four hours." The small man nervously hit his riding crop against his right boot.

"Who picked her up? Are there any others? What information can we use?" Baron shouted out in rapid fire German. He looked at their four blank faces.

"Time is running out 'meins camarades', he added in heavily accented French. "'Les Americains' will be crossing Paris' bridges tonight."

The large haphazardly dressed man who lacked any refinement for which the French were noted, answered, "We ... the Colonel," he indicated the well-dressed German civilian at his side. "and I grabbed her and her friend outside 'La Nuit Eternelle' because..."

"Because..."the well-dressed good looking German said. "They had a suspicion air about them."

"And that is it? A suspicious air? You wasted valuable time and effort on a whim? This second one" Baron indicated the mass of humanity on the tiny cot, "what did you get from him or is it a her?"

"A 'her' ... 'mein' colonel the little man said flagellating his croup again. "She was whimpering for her lover. I guess she did not like our two." He mockingly pointed his croup at the lesbians who by this time had pulled Juliette out of the tub and dropped her near the hook dangling from the ceiling.

"Her lover's name?"

"She never said."

"So you tortured her to death and got nothing."

"We know..." the big man began but was cut off by his German companion.

"...that the other woman is Polish." The German Colonel finished the Frenchman's sentence again.

Baron walked out of the room in disgust. He pulled out his walkie-talkie and gave a command in German to bring the car to the front of the building. As he slid it back into his inside jacket pocket, he saw Sal at one end of the hall and Harry at the other.

It was the middle of the night and the air still hung hot and humid. A stench of rotting flesh permeated the hall. It would not be considered unusual to follow the foul odor. He walked down the hall and turned to the left. The back stairwell, just barely lit to avoid tumbling down, was piled with decomposing bodies. Most were missing hands, arms, or legs, but the maggots and flies had no preference.

In horror and anger he clicked his heels and marched back down the hall to the room. "Get out of here. Destroy any records you have. If you've been as sloppy with your interviews as you've been with your interviewees, they'll kill you on the spot. Fools! The Allies are down our throats, and you're still playing your little games."

The torturers were agitated. How little abuse they themselves could take was not lost on Melvin Baron. The other two were more calm. The German in civilian clothes was cool; despite the interest Baron felt he had in Juliette. Baron also knew Juliette did not have time for him to find out.

"That one." He pointed at the naked form that was Juliette. "Is she drowned or still alive?"

The large Frenchman went over to the body.

"Alive. She just doesn't have the sense to die." He spat.

"Wrap her up in that sheet", Baron pointed to a filthy piece of muslin. "I don't want blood in my car. She'll go to the Quarters at the 'Carnavalet'. If the weapons of torture were good enough for the French aristocracy during the Revolution, there'll be good enough to get whatever truth she knows out of her. If not, we'll toss her carcass in the Seine, so the 'Americains' will have a scenic view when they cross the bridges of Paris."

The large Frenchman hoisted her up on his shoulder like a sack of flour and was the first one out the door. Baron made the mistake of going second. The civilian colonel followed him.

"I will take her my friend." The civilian colonel spoke. Baron turned to see a German luger pointed at his head. "First, you will get a bullet and then her."

The Frenchman carrying Juliette in front of him stopped. At that same instant Baron felt a hand go beneath the inside armhole of his jacket where his Colt 45 rested strapped in its holster. As he raised his arms over his head, he felt the Colt slip out of his holster and heard slight click of the safety release before the gun fired.

Neither of them heard the first sweet sound of vengeance. By the time they heard the second sound it was too late. The Frenchman whirled around and saw the German – his

Colonel with a bullet hole right through his forehead. He was dead before he hit the ground. It was then that the Frenchman felt the hot muzzle of the Colt 45 press against his neck and saw two men step out from the rooms at the ends of the hall to open fire on the Gestapo man with the croup and the two lesbians. However, unlike the German Colonel, they would not die quietly; all three had been hit in the gut.

The large Frenchman, with Juliette still wrapped in muslin over his shoulder, said pointing to Baron, "He's the 'Boche'"

"Yeah, he's the 'kraut'." Sal said. "Give him the girl".

Juliette let Baron's Colt 45 drop to the floor.

The Frenchman smiled, handed his bundle over, and let his hands fall to his side as though happy to be rescued.

Once in Baron's arms Juliette whispered, "let me introduce my other brother, Denis – the traitor." Then she passed out.

Baron realized this was not the brother she would have died for. Baron calmly bent down and picked up the gun. Denis looked in amazement at the two Americans still at opposite ends of the hall.

"He German – the enemy," he shouted in the little English he knew. He grabbed for the gun in Baron's free hand.

Baron held on to Juliette and kept his gun hand steady. "Yeah, that's me – the 'kraut'," Baron responded in perfect English. "Your sister and I say welcome to the good old U.S, of A." Baron said as he pulled the trigger.

He looked down the hall to see Harry passing through the doorway of the corner back room. He returned - carrying out Zosia, and by his side was Janusz, stroking her bloodied matted hair and singing softly the Polish song of the nightingale. She opened her eyes, and for the moment, she was still alive.

They stepped out into the night and into a cool clean breeze blowing up and through the ages. Through the years of the Gauls, the fishermen and boatmen of the Parisii tribe who discovered the largest island in the Seine and named her Lutetia, and the warring tribes that finally christened her 'Paris' in the 4th century. Through the attack of Attila the Hun in 451 and the saving of Paris by a maid called Genevieve – and through the cries, shouts, groans and pleas of the people of Paris as she rolled from century to century until the Revolution of 1789, the second Revolution of 1830, and the Revolt of the Paris Commune in 1870. Then came the war to end all wars and after it WW11, and still Paris and her people survived. The people of Paris were hard.

The winds of war had always blown through her narrow streets, over her many crowed bridges and into the souls of her people. Baron could feel all this as he stepped out of this one last door - into the open cobbled stoned streets, hundreds of years old. The wind was sweet and fresh and clean on this ancient hill of martyrs. The violent wind hushed into a whispering wind. "Enough is enough", it said.

With Janusz by his side he crossed over the curb into the narrow street as two American jeeps pulled up. Tony, Sandy, and Thomas were in one. Simon drove up alone in the second. Janusz hopped over the side into the back. First Baron handed up Juliette then Harry, Zosia. Janusz cradled both their bodies and covered them with olive green army issue wool blankets.

Harry climbed into the back with Thomas and handed the map to Sandy. The English engineer would have one more minefield to get them through. With map in hand he would guide them through the back streets of Paris to the 'Hotel de Ville', the residence of the German Commander in Paris. Across from Notre Dame and the 'Prefecture de Police' the 'Hotel de Ville' was the command post. This age-old building for the Mayor of Paris was where the French under Leclerc's command or under Col Rol Tanguy's would get the signed surrender of Paris from the German General who had agreed to the cease-fire.

"Go south toward the Seine, and when you can smell the river, get onto Rue Rivoli and look for a right onto Rue de Renard, a side street off the Rue Rivoli," Simon shouted to Tony and smiled. "And bonne chance mes amis." He added over his shoulder as he put the jeep into gear.

They wondered why he seemed to smile to himself when he said the name of the street. Simon still smiling thought, "Renard.. Renard mon vieux - old friend of Luc. You will have your justice. Luc has gotten it for you - we all have."

Simon pushed the gears from second to third as he took the curve past Sacre Coeur and down the steep road toward Pigalle. "Renard died fighting for what the world wanted - and had waited for," he thought. "The two in the back are on the brink of death, but Death will have to wait this time. We paid enough for freedom."

"We're heading for the periphery." Simon said to Baron, who was bending to pick up the machine gun on the floor of the jeep. He slung the strap over his shoulder. He was ready to be point guard. "When we're just about parallel to the Tour Eiffel, I'll veer left – up the side streets to Avenue Georges V. Welcome to Paris mon Americain!" He took off his red beret that had covered his mutilated ears and flung it high into the morning sky as Sacre Coeur's bells began to ring.

Simon turned and steadied his driving. He knew Luc and Christian would be waiting in the house on Avenue George V. He had to get his precious cargo to them as quickly and gently as he could. The rooms Luc's grandfather had held so dear were being prepared as hospital quarters for the severely wounded. Simon could hear the moans from Juliette and Zosia. For their sake and for Luc's sanity he had to get them there in time. Luc would have already opened the flag Michel Morneau had gingerly wrapped up when his city had let the German flag loose on the monuments of Paris. Simon, in his mind's eye, could see Luc fling the flag of Michel Morneau out over the balcony. It would be waving to them, fluttering in the breeze of this 24th of August, 1944.

Baron turned to this old friend of Luc's and decided this was not the time to tell him he had killed Denis, Luc's brother.

λ

Chapter 23- Friday, August 25 – French Flags Fly

Just before midnight, when the cease-fire would have ended, a small force of Leclerc's 2nd Armored Division cut over Paris's periphery, through her wider less familiar streets and crept over one of its bridges, 'Pont d'Asterlitz'. Having crossed the Seine, Leclerc followed the river's right bank as it curved like a cat, awakening for its nighttime prowl. Throughout the centuries, the sensuous catlike Seine had flowed through Paris - seeing and understanding her many battles, living beyond the lives of every king, and stomaching death on her banks and waters, running red with blood. This year of 1944 was no different.

Leclerc reached the 'Hotel de Ville' and entered as the bells of Notre Dame, began to ring. Across the bridge of Notre Dame on the 'Ile de la Cite' stood the church of Notre Dame herself on the original island that begot the city of Paris. Sanctified for than 2000 years, the church's official construction had not begun until 1263. Now, almost seven hundred years later, this church, that had viewed so much of history from her tall spires, sounded her bells again - with the call of freedom and hope. As Notre Dame came to life, General Leclerc stopped his tanks to listen to the knell of its heavy perfect tones. He remembered his lycee text of Victor Hugo and imagined Quasimodo swinging in ecstasy from bell to bell.

Soon the other churches of Paris echoed their chorus of bells. Sacre Coeur's sounded the deepest as the music of bells flooded the entire City. Flags, deeply hidden in cupboards and chests, were flung with abandon from balconies and windows throughout the ancient city of Paris. Chords of 'La Marseillaise', clear and concise like crystal, cut through the hot August early morning mist. Soon the anthem spread like a sunrise, pushing its way through windows and over thresholds. Greeting the anthem and the bells were the Parisian sounds of life and joy being born again - sparkling anew on this 25th day of August 1944.

Few Parisians had gone to sleep the night before. Luc and Simon had sat in his grandfather's rooms, untouched since the winter of his death in 42'. - the first freezing December without food and fuel. As boys they had always come here, and grand-pere Michel and grand-mere Genevieve always had trays of cheeses, fruit and bread for them as part of their leisurely two-hour lunch which followed their vigorous lycee mornings. It was always a grand meal that had to hold them through the late afternoon schooling.

After four years of Occupation, life had changed. An older rail-thin Francoise, looking more like mother than sister now, prepared the meal with help from an ancient Gabrielle, and a hardened Colette, who had left her youth and innocence behind. Digging into the cupboards for the delicacies they had saved for when this day would come, they worked in familiar motions. Champagne had been uncorked, yet for each the act of rejoicing was bittersweet, and for Luc, it was most difficult, if not impossible. He had given so much - and lost so much - that he was numb.

Luc lifted an early morning toast to Simon, his oldest friend, and to Paul 'Renard', his Norman friend whose spirit he still felt and whose loss he would forever mourn, and Melvin Baron, his new American friend in whose debt he would always be. They all took a sip of the Moet Chandon. Luc and Simon gazed out the tall open windows of Michel Morneau's grand apartment on the Boulevard Georges V and looked over a Paris that would never be the same - again. Baron, who had shed his

German Colonel's jacket, appeared in a white tee-shirt and army issue pants. Tall, blond, and very much American, he stood behind the two Frenchmen.

He could see over their heads. From every window and balcony, French flags waved, free in the tumult of voices that rose from the streets and bounced in abandon between the age old stone buildings. 'This moment I will remember for the rest of my life', he thought. 'The past two and a half months have been a lifetime. How strange that I had to cross half the U.S., an ocean, and the English Channel to feel that I belong. For the first time in my life I feel a part of something. This city is a door to my future,' he let his eyes rest on the two men in front of him. 'not a window to the past as it must be for Luc and Simon.'

When they had entered the grandfather's home early that morning, Melvin had known that Simon needed to carry Juliette, as Janusz needed to carry Zosia, into this childhood home of Luc Dubois. Baron stepped aside; he did not enter the room where these older friends of Luc had placed the bodies of the two women. Luc kneeled alone by each bed. Distraught beyond words, he let four years of tears flow and did not leave until they were all spent. Baron and the others heard his sobs and when he came out from the room, he said nothing except to ask Baron exactly how Denis had died.

Baron chose his words carefully. With clinical preciseness he repeated Juliette's exact words. "Juliette had slipped my Colt 45 from my shoulder-holster, shot the Colonel through the head, and whispered in my ear 'Let me introduce my 'other brother' the traitor', and then she passed out. Her shot brought Sal, Thomas and Harry into the room. Your brother shouted - denied any connection with the dead Colonel and told the Americans that I was a German who was going to kill them. At that moment your brother went for the 45', and I made a decision. With the same Colt 45 Juliette had just fired, I killed your brother."

Luc knew the confrontation all too well. Feeling like a cord of electricity — so wired that he would burn if any more voltage were added, he just asked Baron one more question.

"Did Juliette really kill Denis?" He looked deep into Baron's icy blue eyes. Baron met his gaze directly and shook his head no. Luc rested both hands on Baron's wide shoulders and nodded his head downward.

"Merci, mon camarade," Luc murmured. He was
thankful that she did not have to pull the trigger. She would have enough to live with - if she lived.

Old Gabrielle came up and kissed Luc on the forehead,
"They will live, mon petit. It will be difficult, but they are strong women – your sister and your woman."

Francoise gazed with a vacant stare around the room that had always held such happiness.

"All of Montmartre was looking for them. Why could we not have found them earlier?" Simon stared out the window as the morning light glowed on the glistening black iron of the balconies across the way.

"Simon, do not punish yourself. Why did they not find you earlier, mon vieux."

Simon still could not speak of the horrors he had endured. Luc doubted he would ever speak of them. That is how the strong survived. They separated their minds and spirits from their flesh. One had to force the mind to immediately forget the inflicted pain.

Simon spoke what Luc was thinking. He knew him so well. "If God is with them, Juliette and Zosia will not remember."

Colette entered from the old Morneaus' bedroom through the vaulting hallway arch that connected it to the salon. Both women had been placed beneath beautiful, cool, clean soft white eyelet sheets, and their heads rested on down pillows in the two large mahogany beds. Francoise had gently covered each women with the hand crocheted flowered duvet made by her mother, Genevieve Morneau, sixty-two years ago when she had become the young bride of Michel Morneau.

Colette spoke directly. "Both are lucky. They will be able to have children." She said this with such conviction Luc did not ask her anything. There was a knowledge and hardness in her sad eyes that seemed to say she was not so fortunate.

Gabrielle shook her head and wiped tears away from her eyes. She walked over to Colette and placed her ample arm around the young woman's slender waist.

"Who is that solemn young man who has not left the other woman's side?" Gabrielle asked.

Christian, who had been standing by the window, answered. "Janusz. He lost his mother and nearly his sister in September of 39'. Zosia has been with him since his childhood and she was there with him for all the rest of it."

"We will take care of them. They know where they are. They know they are safe together and that you are here." Colette added.

"Go, do what you must do," Francoise said as she crossed over and turned on the radio that still rested on the same dark mahogany table.

Luc remembered when they were all last together in this room. His mother, his grandfather, Gabrielle, Colette and the other mannequins had listened to the surrender of Paris and saw the German planes beginning to darken their skies. Luc heard his grandfather's voice again.

"I will not live through another war."

'How right you were 'grandpere'.' Luc thought. 'C'est dommage' that you did not live long enough to see the 'melange' of men that it would take to lift off the yoke of German oppression forever.' Luc looked around at these bizarre patriots.

Simon and Juliette– the Frenchmen, Baron – the American, Janusz – the Pole, Christian – the Russian, and Zosia, his own dear love, - English and Polish in upbringing – but French at heart.

This glorious day barely registered with Luc. Two – out of the three most important women in his life – might never totally recover from their tortures. They might live in their prison of memories forever and never have total command of their bodies' capabilities again. When they were healed, when they could walk, he would take them to their Norman home.

Francoise knew the war was not over. Luc, Simon, and the others still had work to do, and her job would be to stay with her daughter and future daughter-in-law, god willing. She thought of the young fragile looking Juliette and how she had not wanted to send her to the lycees of Paris. How she had wanted her to stay young and innocent for a while more. But the war came and her innocence and fragility was taken from her, and in its place, day by day, a steel strength solidified. She played the German Colonel and flaunted her power into Denis' weak submissive face. Her actions were discrete. She never acted rashly or gave the Colonel any reason to doubt her feigned obsession with him. However, Francoise knew the Germans never really needed a reason for punishment.

Francoise, nonetheless, had treated with icy civility the German Colonel who had taken over her country, her home, and Juliette, but boiling beneath the surface molten lava flowed. She was waiting for the right moment to let it erupt - to kill the Colonel and avenge her daughter's violation. Long ago she had come to terms with the fact that if her other son was killed in the process so be it. Juliette had saved her the trouble. Baron had told Francoise that there was no doubt in his mind that her daughter would have killed Denis too if she had had the strength. It would take more of that strength to mend.

Luc knew neither woman would forgive ... but could they forget. 'Why am I thinking ahead? They are neither here nor there, but instead are still are locked in the past. I must bring them back into reality and pray they have the stamina to face it. Juliette and my dear Zosia must live- must sit together in the sea air of Normandy, for which they have fought so dearly.'

He glanced over at Francoise and saw her staring at him. He nodded to her and smiled a half smile. In that familiar facial expression, she saw a glimpse of the boy whose hand she so often took down the steep slopes to the pebbly Norman Coast beach of Saint Honorine, down the 'casse cou' break-neck stairs of Montmartre, and across the cobbled stoned streets of most of Paris. Then she saw the man he had become - fearless, proud, kind, and infinitely committed.

It was her turn to acknowledge in herself that same unbending strength. She had endured much; she would not break at this point but forge ahead to nurse the bodies, minds, and spirits of her two daughters. She would see them through the nightmares that would most assuredly follow.

Luc let the warm of the sun caress his face as he turned once again to the open balcony. He looked down at the street where pandemonium let loose. Sal and Thomas sat in one jeep as a dozen French women, half in and out of the jeep, tried to embrace each American soldier.

"Hey ladies, how about over here," he heard Tony say. More women turned the corner of Avenue Georges V and laughed in delight at spotting two American jeeps.

"Hey Brooklyn you always gotta get in the act, " Sal yelled as he tried to unwrap the many arms around him.

"Bonjour Mesmoiselles'." Luc shouted down from the balcony. "Laissez-les tranquils. Il faut qu'ils partent. Les allemands sont encore ici!" To the Americans he translated. "They have to leave you alone because you have to leave. The Germans are still here."

"I need some action. We got time. We got all the time in the world now. Sal can't get it all for New York. Hot damn - remember he's from the Bronx and that ain't the real New York." Tony chided as the girls planted red lipstick kisses all over his smiling face.

"Hey Luc where does a guy get Channel No.5? I still gotta a mission to do." He felt for the watertight pouch that contained Captain Hank Hudson's dog tags and the letter to his wife in Texas. Sal looked up towards the balcony.

Sal thought, 'Christ, O'Brien never made it off the beach. Big beautiful black James Earl, God I wish he coulda seen this. All he wanted was to see 'Paree' and his Joseph Baker. Aaron Axelrod, Mr. Hollywood who was going to film our entrance into Paris, ain't here either.' Baron, the Kraut, looked down and smiled at his fellow Americans. He tossed his German uniform into the street below. "Vive la France," he yelled.

"Vivez les Americains," the girls answered.

Gabrielle and Colette had found for him a pilot's brown leather bombardier jacket and trousers that were a perfect fit. They even supplied him with new dog tags Samuel Stein, a man they could not save and had to bury the cellar of this grand building on Avenue Georges V.

Baron slipped the dog tags over his neck. He remembered how he had taken his own off to go into Le Beau Moulin and placed them in the hollow the tree before he crossed over the bridge into Madame Simone's café. That was where, less than two months ago, he had first met Juliette. Now he had two sets. It seemed more like twenty years to him, - a lifetime in which he made friends and lost them. Now he looked down on a few friends that he still had left and turned his head back inside.

"Where was this Samuel Stein from?" He asked Luc's mother.

"7th Avenue New York City." Francoise answered.

"A prestigious spot for a Jew garment maker." Baron retorted.

Francoise nodded. She knew how to tailor, and she knew where the best came from - even in New York.

Baron clinked his tags together. "Well if I get killed on these streets of Paris at least Sam's parents will be notified, and he got a Jewish burial. If I live, then I'll tell Sam's parents myself."

He walked out down the ancient apartment buildings steps, through the enclosed courtyard into the midmorning light, and passed the heavy metal door to the Avenue Georges V. He looked up at the balcony of Michel Morneau's ancient house in Paris on this Avenue of Georges V. He would remember, but now he had to find his own kind – an American unit.

****

In their quarters on the Rue Renard the Americans and Sandy had not slept much. There had been no bridges to blow or any to build to span the Seine and to move troops in. Those bridges that had crossed the Seine for centuries still existed. Sandy had spent the hours of the 24th removing TNT traps and complex detonation traps on Pont Neuf, the oldest bridge in Paris. By the early morning hours of the 25th, they had finished and tried to catch an hour or two of sleep before dawn. Instead, they had heard the coming and going of a barrage of boots, shoes, and feet padding across the floor above them. It wasn't until all the church bells in Paris masked the noise that they fell asleep for 30 minutes.

As the morning sun burned through the mist, they realized they had chosen the floor beneath a brothel. The noise had been the German officers saying their last "good-byes' to the 'ladies' of Paris.

Sandy looked up as he walked out. French flags flew in abandon and mixed in were American, English, and Canadian flags. A few Polish flags flew, for some knew the price the Poles had paid. Sandy noticed French soldiers walking in and out of the Hotel de Ville, and realized de Gaulle's faction was insuring its control. The documents Christian, Janusz and Luc secured provided one more element of proof to the French vying for control that communism was not the wave of the future. The Germans were being swept out, why sweep in more debris? The welcome mat had been officially withdrawn for the Communist party - backed by the new Soviet Union.

Sandy saw no Germans, except for the dead and dying on the streets this morning. The Gestapo had fled and in their place were French citizens, men and women, dragging other French women into the streets. The scene was repeated in every arrondissement in Paris. Pulled out of their houses, these women were lined up as though waiting for their 'coiffeuse'.

In the middle of the narrow streets of Paris a person would place a chair. Near the Hotel de Ville Sandy noticed the chair was red. Into it the 'citoyens' of Paris pushed the first woman waiting in line. One man pulled her hair back and the other shaved her head. 'The scene's from Charles Dickens <u>A Tale of Two Cities</u>,' Sandy thought. 'The French Revolution all over again.'

****

In another Paris arrondissement far from the maddening crowd sat Luc Dubois and his old friend Simon de la Croix. With a view of the Seine and the Eiffel Tower they gazed in silence at the view before them. The seats in the small café on the Rue des Freres Perrier were empty. It would take a while for the Parisians to be comfortable taking up old habits. But old habits die hard, and time would pass quickly. The next generation would have no direct memories from these hard days and nights. They would look up at the Eiffel Tower and never remember the German flag that had flown from the copper network of metal.

A bottle of red Bordeaux sat on the green table and its contents filled the glasses of Luc and Simon. Monsieur Henri Gallet had not lived to serve his two young friends, for he had been dragged out into his beloved street and shot dead by two Gestapo officers. Each man thought of how long ago that was. Time was reverberating and reflecting like a prism in their minds - two years already? Four years since they last sat together here - making their plans for when the Germans would occupy Paris.

They had survived, but so many had not. They were too raw to count up - to reminisce about who died, when and where. Perhaps, fifty years from now when they were old men, they could relive these days of pain without it touching them so sharply, but for now they lifted their half- full glasses into the noon light.

The sun, like spun gold, reflected off the Seine and danced through the iron works of La Tour Eiffel. Each man - not young at heart any more, lifted his glass to the other and to Paris. The sun shot through the glasses and they sipped from the liquid fire as time stopped. From the mast on the Eiffel Tower, the black spider on the red flag was descending and the Tricolor ascending in the breeze blowing in from the west.

Simon spoke first, "De Gaulle entre Paris demain, le 26 aout."

"Oui, mon vieux –when he enters tomorrow, let us hope de Gaulle brings us peace as well as freedom, for the world has waited long enough - To tomorrow."

"Oui, A demain - to tomorrow."

Le Fin

25512934R00245

Made in the USA
San Bernardino, CA
01 November 2015